THE CAROUSEL

*Also by Belva Plain
and available from Coronet Books*

Evergreen
Random Winds
Blessings
Harvest
Treasures
Whispers
Daybreak

About the Author

Belva Plain is one of the world's best-loved writers.
Her first novel, *Evergreen*, was published in 1978
and she has since entranced an international audi-
ence with ten further bestsellers, including most
recently *Blessings*, *Harvest*, *Treasures*, *Whispers* and
Daybreak.

The Carousel

Belva Plain

CORONET BOOKS
Hodder and Stoughton

First published in Great Britain in 1995
by Hodder and Stoughton
First published in paperback in 1996 by Hodder and Stoughton
A division of Hodder Headline PLC
A Coronet paperback

10 9 8 7 6 5 4 3 2 1

British Library CIP

Plain, Belva
The Carousel
I. Title
813.54 [F]

ISBN 0 340 62311 X

Typeset by Hewer Text Composition Services, Edinburgh
Printed and bound in Great Britain by
Cox & Wyman Ltd, Reading, Berkshire

Hodder and Stoughton
A division of Hodder Headline PLC
338 Euston Road
London NW1 3BH

On a table in the center of the upstairs sitting room stood the carousel. High as a wedding cake, and of purest silver, it drew to itself every ray of the lamplight, returning each, magnified and glittering, to the dimmest corners of the room. It was a paragon of the silversmith's art. The horses pranced; the children riding wore ribboned hats; pennants above the rooftop balustrade appeared to fly as though a wind were moving through; all was fretwork, filigree, and rococo.

Absurd, extravagant toy. Yet it had linked the momentous events of a life. The birth of love. Grief. And now, murder . . .

CHAPTER
—— 1 ——

She was not ready to go home, and not ready to face anybody, neither the five-year-old nor the infant, not prepared to answer the telephone or speak a civil word, after what had just happened during this past hour. Never had Sally Grey felt so wretched, so small, as if she had physically shrunk, as she sat huddled behind the wheel of the car and fled the city.

On the first plateau in the chain of mountains that stretched toward Canada, a scenic overlook had been set aside, very likely for the benefit of tourists. On this waning, windy afternoon it was deserted, and here she stopped the car. Below lay Scythia, an old city, its small factories ringed by tracts of new-built bungalows and highways; beyond them to the east, west, and south came farms. In the north, the dark mountains.

Lights winked on in scattered spots, but to Sally's left, where lay the headquarters of Grey's Foods, light was a solid yellow oblong, marking the place to which one quarter of the city's population was in some way connected, either employed by the company or related to someone who was. As to that, the other three quarters of Scythia had been touched in some way by the Grey family's generosity: the library, the hospital, the neighborhood swimming pools, all were gifts from the Greys.

'You're thinking such things don't happen in families like yours. I understand,' that woman, that doctor, had said.

No, Sally had thought, you don't understand. You thought

1

I was feeling some sort of superiority, above the flaws of the common people, that I was feeling some sort of nasty, idiotic snobbishness. But I was thinking only of how happy we have been, of how *pure* our life has been. *Pure.* Such a Victorian word! But all the same, it fitted. There had been nothing dirty in their lives until now.

Somewhere within that compact mass of light, at this very moment Dan was working at his desk, not knowing. Tonight he would have to know. And if it should be true – no, of course it cannot be true, of course not – it would devastate him. His baby! His darling Tina.

No, there's no doubt in my mind. Your Tina has been molested. Sexually abused.

Dr. Lisle had already explained herself at length, but still Sally had simply stared at her. She had a homely, square face and a cool manner, this woman who, although no older than Sally, was dressed in authority, buttressed by professional knowledge.

Scolding me, that's how she sounds, as if I were a schoolgirl instead of a woman who has had her own experiences, has traveled all over the world in peace and war with her cameras, having her photographs published all over the world. Well, I guess the truth is we simply don't like each other. What kind of a crazy thing is this to tell me?

And as if looking for help, she stared about the spare, plain office. Its inexpensive desk and chairs were new. Its diplomas and certificates were recent. The view led over the back of a run-down three-story commercial building in the run-down heart of town. It was an uncomfortable, dispiriting place with no help in it. But the doctor had been so well recommended!

'This is incredible,' Sally said abruptly.

'No, it's credible.'

'I can't believe you. I won't believe you. How can you even think of such a thing?'

'It's natural for you to resist. What parent would want to believe it?'

2

'It's incredible.'

'It's credible, Mrs. Grey.'

'I live with Tina! I bathe her, and I've never seen a sign of – '

'There doesn't have to be penetration. There are other ways, as you know.'

Revolting images flared. She had almost felt them burning, pressing inside her skull.

'Yes, I know. I read. But how can you be so sure? Has Tina told you anything?'

'Not directly, in so many words. Children rarely do. They're too afraid.'

'Well, then, I ask you, how *do* you know?'

'There are many ways. For example, they play with dolls. Mine here are anatomically correct. I watch the child, I talk to her, and I listen while she talks to herself.'

'Tell me what Tina says. Exactly what you remember.'

The doctor put on her reading glasses. How long it took for her to fumble in the case and adjust them on her nose! It was a torture to watch.

And now, in the car, remembering, reliving, Sally's head began to pound.

'Here. Friday the tenth, the visit before last. I quote: "You take your panties off, then you put that thing –"'

'Oh, no!'

'"And you put your mouth –"'

'Oh, no!'

'"Then she took the doll and threw it across the room, and she cried." Are you feeling all right, Mrs. Grey? I can stop if you wish.'

'All right, stop. I have the picture.'

It was then that there had come the onset of terror, a quick, slashing pain in the chest and wet hands, twisting themselves together until the ring dug into the flesh. It was then, too, that she had straightened her back and sat up. For if you panic, Sally, you drown.

3

She said positively, 'Tina is never left with strangers. She's very well supervised, by me when I'm home and by a marvelous nanny, a sweet, grandmotherly lady who helps take care of Susannah, the baby, and takes charge of everything when I go away on business. I'm a photographer, you remember. But I never stay away for more than a few days at a time. No, it can't be, Doctor. It's – it's bizarre. Your diagnosis has to be mistaken.'

'Tell me, then, how for example you explain Tina's talk to the doll?'

'Well, children of that age are just starting to discover things, aren't they? And I'm sure there are children in school who have older siblings who've told them about sex. God knows there's enough of it on television. We don't let Tina watch much television, but many other people do, and it filters down to the rest of the kids.'

The doctor waited. She had been trained to observe, to listen for what people did not say. Sally knew that, and she sat up even higher in the chair.

'How have things gone this past week?' the doctor asked.

Yes, Sally thought, let's get back to reality, let me give you some plain facts and then you tell me how to deal with them, if you can. Fact, not fantasies.

And she said honestly, 'The same. On and off. Sometimes the average five-year-old and sometimes not.'

'Tell me about the "sometimes not".'

'Well, at school, I'm told, she's still doing some hitting and biting. At home, we've had some temper tantrums. And her bed is still wet every night. She still asks me when we're going to take Susannah back to the hospital. No matter how carefully I explain, she keeps asking. To my mind, Doctor, that's the source of the whole trouble.'

'As easy as that? What I've told you makes no impression on you?'

'I'm with Tina all the time, I'm her mother! She plays with dolls at home, so wouldn't I have observed something strange

4

too? Surely, she would have told me if someone had – done anything to her.'

'I've explained to you, not necessarily. In fact, most probably she would not. A child can, in a vague way, feel guilt. She knows that something is wrong, although she can't explain it. And she may be afraid to betray the person who abused her. She may even in some way, in some fashion, have liked the person. It's not all that simple, Mrs. Grey.'

Sally was silent. And the doctor, with a sudden surprising change of manner, said gently, 'You should really, very seriously, consider what I've told you. I can read you much more from my record if you need to be convinced.'

Sally put up her hand. 'No. Please, no.'

'You're afraid, Mrs. Grey.'

'Dr. Lisle, please believe me, I respect your knowledge, but mistakes – even you, excuse me, even you, anyone can make one – and in this particular case, you're wrong. The way we live, this is impossible.'

'People always think it is unless they see something with their own eyes.'

'Everything was fine before the baby came. We had no problems at home, none at all. Maybe you think I'm exaggerating when I say that Dan and I have had a charmed life. I suppose some people say things like that to cover up the truth. But that would be foolish. Why should I come here for help and then lie to you? We have a good home, believe me. I wish every child in the world could have a home like ours, and a father like Dan. Sundays we cook together, Dan's proud of my work, we love each other. It's been such a happy house, and surely Tina must have felt the happiness. Everyone said she was such a sunny child – '

She had prattled. Now, alone in the car recollecting, she was certain she must have seemed foolish. But she had almost gone out of control. That resolute, stiff posture of hers had been a sham.

A solemn gaze had been turned to her while she prattled.

It had been uncomfortable to confront that gaze, but to avoid it had been awkward, too, so she had alternated between the gaze and the dingy warehouse across the street. Her voice had petered out and still no comment had come. I have to get out of here, she had thought. Tomorrow we'll find another doctor. This woman, well recommended or not, was like a surgeon, an alarmist who gives you only a month to live unless you undergo an immediate operation. It was outrageous.

'What I decided,' she had resumed, 'what's clear to me now is that I have to refuse any new commissions for a while. Or until Tina is back to normal. Yes, that's what I'll do. Basically, Tina is fine, I'm sure.'

'With all those symptoms you say she's "fine"? The hitting and biting and all the things you've told me before, that she won't allow you to hug her, that she's afraid to let you leave the house – '

'I meant – well, she's certainly not fine, of course not. That's why we brought her here. I feel that she needs more of my attention until she gets over the baby, and I definitely intend to – '

'You're making a big mistake, Mrs. Grey.'

Sounding doom. And all of this doom was based on slim evidence, supposition, textbook theory. So Sally had stood up and put on her coat.

'Tell me, then,' she said concisely, 'what you advise me to do.'

'I advise that you keep Tina here in treatment, or, if you're not comfortable with me, with somebody else. And I certainly advise that you start looking very carefully into the circumstances of her life. The child has been abused, Mrs. Grey.'

It was cold in the car with the motor shut off, and she drew her scarf tightly around her neck, crossing her arms.

Abused. How horrible.

But could it be true? Then who could have done such a thing? Some father in a house where Tina went to play? She

6

went over the list, the possible contacts. That retarded man on the country road near her parents' house a few months ago? Of course not. The grandmother was fanatically careful. No. It wasn't true. It wasn't possible.

That doctor had been so positive. Could a doctor make such an egregious mistake? Of course she could. You read the papers. Still, it's not a thing that happens every day.

She must pull herself together and go home. Thousands of lights, electric polka dots in the looming night, had come on in the city below. It was late. She turned the key in the ignition and headed the car uphill.

On either side the road was sheltered between old stands of spruce and hemlock. Gaps in these natural walls revealed stone gateposts, long driveways, and, rarely, the glimpse of a handsome house. At a bend of the road on the left stood the imposing gates of Hawthorne, the Greys' huge, formal family seat. Here Dan, aged seven, had gone to live with his relatives after the air crash in which his parents had died. Behind the house, hidden a quarter of a mile away from sight, there began the wilderness, the eight thousand acres, pristine and precious, that belonged to the Greys but, by their willing consent, was open to all, provided that they would do it no harm, would cut down no tree or wound no animal. So it had been, for how many generations Sally did not remember, but so it was still. An extraordinary family, the Greys.

In a grassy clearing some few miles farther on, a square white house with green shutters and the austere simplicity of New England was home to Sally. She always thought, and thought now as she drove into the garage, that it could hardly be more different from Hawthorne or any other Grey family home. But she was a child of Maine, and Dan was not a typical Grey, so this was what they had both wanted. The dog, a lumbering Newfoundland, was sitting on the front step. His presence there made the scene almost hackneyed: the picturebook house and the family dog, she thought ironically, lacked only a child to sit beside him with her arm around him.

Actually, Tina sometimes did just that. The dog was the only 'person' she would hug. The enchanting little girl with the ruffles and ribbon braids was hardly ever pleasant or affectionate anymore. Outings that they all used to look forward to were now undertaken with trepidation since they were never sure how she would behave. At night, when at last she was asleep, they could quietly read and could quietly talk to each other . . . although not in peace. For what had happened to the picturebook family? What was wrong with the once enchanting little girl?

Is it possible that I don't want to believe that doctor because we didn't take to each other, because 'the chemistry wasn't right'? A stupid reason, if so. I don't know . . .

Tina was finishing her supper in the kitchen with Mrs. Dugan, known by all as 'Nanny'.

'Hello, darling. My, that pudding looks delicious.'

Tina frowned. 'It isn't. You eat it.'

'I wish I could. But Daddy and I are going out to dinner. It's Uncle Oliver's birthday.'

'You're always going out.'

'No, honey. We haven't been out all week,' Sally said, putting her arm around Tina and kissing the top of her head.

'Don't do that. I don't want you to hug me.'

Nanny's puzzled gaze met Sally's distressed one.

'But why? Mommies like to hug their little girls.'

'I don't care. When are you going to take Susannah back to the hospital?' Never a day passed without at least one such petulant demand.

'I told you, we don't take babies back,' Sally whispered gently. 'We didn't take you back. We love our babies.'

'I don't love her. She's not my baby. I want you to take her back tomorrow.'

'Here's Mr. Grey now,' said Nanny, who had been standing near the window.

'Good heavens, and I'm not dressed yet. I've got to run up and change my dress, Tina.'

'Take her back tomorrow,' Tina wailed, 'with her crib and her blanket and all her toys.'

You weren't supposed to lie or evade, and Sally rarely did, but this day was different. Her energy was spent, and she fled upstairs, leaving Nanny to cope with Tina. That's what the trouble is, she told herself yet again. That's all it is, simply jealousy, plain as can be. What more proof could you want? It's just exaggerated in Tina because she's a sensitive child. In time, with help, it will die away.

Yet that stern-eyed woman had been so sure.

CHAPTER
—— 2 ——

'Yes, yes,' said Oliver Grey from his armchair at the head of the table. 'I remember very well when my father had that bow window built on. I was about five years old, so it must have been in 1932. Or thereabouts,' he added precisely. 'My grandfather thought it was a sacrilege. He would have kept everything unchanged from the time his own father lived here. He would have kept the horse cars in town, too, and the gaslights, if he could have. He was what they call a "character".'

Erect and thin, with graying hair that would, like his forebears', become a thick white plumage. He did not look sixty-three.

The little group assembled in the dining room listened respectfully to these familiar reminiscences. Ian and Clive, his sons, Dan his nephew, along with the wives of Dan and Ian, all turned their faces toward the patriarch.

'Yes, he loved this home, this "Hawthorne". Every year he'd plant another hawthorn. The oldest must be over eighty by now, and as you see, they still come to bloom every summer. I hope you will plant more of them when I'm gone.'

He was feeling a birthday's emotion. The champagne also helped, for he was not a frequent drinker, yet they all knew it was really the genuineness of his love that was speaking to them. And they followed his glance to the wall where, above the mantelpiece, hung a portrait of his wife, Lucille, made

11

shortly before she was killed when her car overturned. Her smile befitted her regal pose in evening dress; yet someone had remarked – quite foolishly, it was said by those who had overheard – that she looked sorrowful, as if she might have been foreseeing the manner of her death.

Indeed, Oliver had had a fair share of sorrow. Perhaps that was some part of the reason for his very personal philanthropies, which extended far beyond the mere writing of large checks that he could well afford, beyond the mountain camp he had established for city boys, or beyond the wheelchairs in the lovely garden of his old-age home.

With a determined smile, he looked back at his fine young people, and then down the length of the room toward the diamond-paned bow window hung with heavy crimson silk. Clearly, the scene pleased him: the lavender roses clustered on the table, the tapers in vermeil candle-sticks, even the pair of chocolate-colored German pointers lying obediently on the old rug in the corner. No object in the splendid room was excessive, no person without dignity.

'Yes, yes,' he resumed, 'long before a place like this could have been dreamed of, the Greys were hardscrabble farmers from the Scottish lowlands. Whatever possessed them to settle in New York State, I don't know unless they thought it would be like home. But I have an idea they don't have winters like ours in Scotland. Anyway, let's drink to them, to their courage and their honest labor.'

Dan thought, as they all raised glasses, that it never fails; people who certainly wouldn't boast of their own rise from poverty take such pride in their ancestors' 'hardscrabble'! It was amusing, a harmless quirk of Oliver's like his old-fashioned courtliness, which certainly had its charm.

How much he owed to Oliver, this uncle, this second kindest father! When their parents had been killed in the crash of a sight-seeing helicopter, he, aged seven, with his sister Amanda, aged twelve, had been brought to

Hawthorne to live, and Hawthorne had been his home until he married Sally.

The sight of her hand lying on the table made him smile to himself. The ring, the only jewel she ever wore besides the small diamond studs in her ears, had been Oliver's idea.

'Her engagement ring must be as important as Happy's,' he had insisted. 'It will not be right any other way.'

And so Dan had bowed, not unwillingly, to Oliver's sense of order and equality. Sally certainly would not have minded one way or the other, nor, he suspected, would Elizabeth, known as Happy.

Under the candlelight the 'important' ring threw off sparks. Whispering, 'You're very quiet,' Dan stroked his wife's hand.

'Not really. I've just quietly been eating.'

'You look so beautiful in that dress. You match the red curtains.'

'Yes, isn't she beautiful?' asked Happy, who had overheard.

Happy Grey was a large-boned blonde, pink, generous, and good-hearted. Too intelligent to live an idle country club life, and having to her deep disappointment no children, she had started a nursery school and worked hard to make it the most sought-after school in the area.

'You must be tired from all your travel these past weeks, Dan.' Oliver's quick eyes missed nothing. 'I have an idea you want to get home early. So just leave when you're ready.'

'Thanks, but I'm fine. I sleep on planes, you know.'

'Everything went well, I take it, or you wouldn't be looking so cheerful.'

'Yes, yes.' Dan had acquired the mannerism from Oliver. 'Yes, yes. The new manager in Brussels is the best we've had. He's young and smart and willing to take suggestions. You can't want more than that.'

Oliver nodded. 'I'm lucky to have three young, smart,

willing men of my own. Now that the business is all yours, I can sit back and be lazy.'

'Hardly lazy, Father,' Ian remonstrated, 'with the Grey Foundation and how many charity boards? Eleven, by my last count.'

His wide-spaced eyes were as quick as Oliver's, and he was equally attractive; but he was powerful, while his father was supple, and vigorous rather than restrained. He had in his early youth been a problem, having been expelled from two preparatory schools for shooting crap. Eventually he had straightened himself out, making Phi Beta Kappa at Yale – where Oliver had studied and sent both Clive and Dan, too – married, and lived now a conventional life, except that he spent money, Oliver tolerantly said, 'like a rajah.' Also, he liked to bet on almost anything between Monte Carlo and Las Vegas.

No two brothers could have been more unlike. Clive stood barely an inch over five feet. His round face was already, owing to a fondness for sweets, sagging into a fold of fat under his chin. He consumed cigarettes. He suffered. It was said of him that he should really be teaching graduate mathematics in some university. Instead, he was lovingly called the 'living computer' for Grey's Foods, who double-checked the work of outside actuaries, watched over the company's foreign investments, understood insurance equities and currency fluctuations.

In his cozy office, in spare time and for recreation he worked over abstruse equations, inhabiting the world of numbers. Numbers, being impersonal, could be mastered even by someone who mastered very little else – except horses. He was an expert rider. A man can look tall on horseback.

After having been silent all through the dinner, he now spoke up. 'I have Tina's birthday present ready. It's a pony, a gentle, very small Shetland, and I'll teach her to ride it. You said it would be all right,' he reminded Sally and Dan.

'You'll be a good teacher,' Oliver said affectionately. 'If

I didn't know otherwise, I'd say you must have been born on the back of a horse. Incidentally, I've missed Tina. You should have brought her tonight.'

'You forget she's only five,' Dan replied. 'She's safely asleep by now.'

'Then you must take some of my birthday cake home for her. Ah, here it is.'

Two pairs of hands were needed to support the huge white edifice blazing with candles that covered the cake in a sheet of flickering flame. Inside, as everyone knew, were layers of dark chocolate interlaced with crushed strawberries and whipped cream. It was the traditional Grey family favorite; no birthday, no celebration was properly observed without it, or properly observed without somebody's lament about calories, or some gentle joke about Clive's ability to eat two portions, to which Clive would respond with a somewhat childish giggle.

'Hold it, Father!' said Sally, reaching for her Leica, which was under her chair. 'Look up at me and then blow out the candles. Don't worry about moving. This camera is fast, fast.'

All this was ritual, as was Oliver's benign, concluding remark about peace and harmony.

'This is what life is all about, a family gathered together in peace and harmony.' He pushed his chair back. 'Shall we go inside?' 'Inside' meant of course the library, where liqueurs would be served in spite of the fact that in 1990, hardly anyone drank liqueurs anymore, and where the gifts would be opened. Like all rooms in the Big House, the library was large, and like most of them, it had a fireplace. In this one tonight, a hearty fire burned. Chairs and two sofas made a semicircle in front of it, where a silver coffee service had been set on a low table. Propped against the curve of the piano at the far end of the room was the family's joint gift.

Happy said, 'Sally, you open it for Father. It was your idea and you arranged it, so you deserve the honor.'

Sally shook her head. 'I don't deserve any more than anybody else. You do it, Happy.'

Two vertical anxiety lines formed between Dan's eyes when he looked at Sally, but he said nothing. Happy cut the string, and the paper fell away from a painting of a large, rambling log house, a palatial Adirondack 'camp'.

'Red Hill at my favorite time of year! All those oaks and sumacs – it's beautiful!' Oliver exclaimed.

'We thought,' Ian said, 'you might like to be reminded of it when you're not there, since you've got a picture of Hawthorne when you're at Red Hill.'

'Perfect. A beautiful present, and I thank you all. I'm going to hang it in my upstairs den.'

The fire crackled. Outdoors the March wind roared, making the room, in contrast, even warmer and brighter. On the floor-to-ceiling shelves crowded books made a mosaic of soft colors. More books lay on well-waxed tables. Both shelves and tables, as well as cabinets, displayed collections and curios, Roman coins, enamel miniatures of eighteenth-century courtiers, gem-studded thimbles, a black silk Japanese fan, an old parchment-colored globe, a silver carousel.

Clive, who adored their child, said to Sally and Dan, 'Your Tina is crazy about the carousel.'

And Dan, still with that faint look of concern, put his hand on his wife's shoulder. 'Think, if it hadn't been for the twin of this thing, we wouldn't be here together.'

'Your lucky day, Dan,' said Ian, coming alongside.

His eyes always seemed to roll downward, not so overtly as to insult his cousin's wife, but enough to make her aware that he was judging her, reckoning her as a sexual object. And then, raising his head to the level of hers, his eyes would widen ever so slightly with a kind of conspiratorial sparkle.

'My lucky day, too,' Sally retorted, a trifle too sharply.

At parties, discreetly, Ian flirted, even with a young waitress passing hors d'oeuvres. Sally was almost sure she had seen him a few years ago picking up a woman at a salad bar while Happy

was at the table. And Happy adored him so! Was it possible
that she didn't see? More likely, she did not want to see. And
an old saying came to mind – French, was it? – about there
always being one who loves and one who is loved. She had
repeated it once to Dan, and he had replied that it was not
always so, that it was surely not true of themselves.

A sudden pity for Happy rose in Sally, and she walked
deliberately to sit beside her, saying, 'Tina loved the yellow
dress. You're so sweet to think of her all the time.'

'I never can resist buying things in the children's department. I could just see her in that yellow with those black
braids of hers. Besides, since the baby came, she needs an
unexpected present, a little extra attention.'

'Yes,' said Sally.

'Not that you and Dan don't give it to her.' Happy was
pouring coffee. 'Sit here, Clive, and have some cookies.
I know you want some, and it's nobody's business but
yours,' she said firmly, adding to the rest of the group, 'so
no comments.'

An object of compassion, Clive was thinking as he bit into
an almond macaroon, that's what it's come down to. Or what
it's always been. Of course, Happy's admonition was directed
at Ian. Once Oliver, not aware that Clive was within hearing,
had talked to Ian about 'being kinder to your brother.'

And Ian replied, 'I am kind to him. It's just that he always
thinks he's being slighted.' Whereupon Oliver, my father who
loves me and is loved by me, only sighed and sighed again, 'I
know.'

I suppose, Clive thought now, taking another macaroon,
I probably do think I'm being slighted even when it's not
so; one gets in the habit. Everyone is, after all, so polite,
so generous with compliments. For am I not the genius with
figures? 'Genius'! What do they know about the marvel of
numbers, their tricks that are so honest and so clean; there's
nothing devious about numbers; they tell no lies, give no
flattery. Those so very respectful employees do not know

17

that I know what they call me: the half-pint, whereas Ian is the gallon.

Why do I have these waves of – yes, admit it – hatred of Ian? And none at all for Dan, who also has everything I don't have? Ian sits there talking low-voiced to our father, with his long legs crossed, at ease; at the same time he is probably savoring the memory of his latest woman. Not that I can ever prove anything, and yet I know. I know. For me, a purchased woman now and then, hating myself for the purchase, while his women will be beautiful, as why should they not be? Look at him! Tell me, to what accursed ancestor do I owe this body of mine? And I am getting bald, too.

Clive turned, then, to observation. Had it not become his role in a social situation, removed as he was from the active center, to analyze and observe? Very little escaped him. Tonight, he saw, Sally was withdrawn from them all, staring across the room at nothing. It was not like her. She was a striking young woman, with her very white skin and very black hair, vivacious and ready with clever anecdotes about the people and places that she and her camera had seen. He wondered what was wrong tonight, what she was seeing in the empty air.

She was looking not into empty air, but at the silver carousel. After the shock of this day, a kind of nostalgic melancholy had come over her . . .

The woman in the antique shop said, 'It's solid silver, you know, a nineteenth-century piece made by a court jeweler in Vienna. A rare treasure.'

'And a rare price, too,' the young man retorted. 'No, I'm only looking because we have its twin at home. My uncle bought his in Vienna years ago.'

'This one plays "Voices of Spring".'

'Ours plays "The Blue Danube" waltz.'

It was just then that their eyes met. She was used to being looked at and knew how to turn away. That time she did not turn away, and they went out together.

They were in Paris. The afternoon light was turning a clouded sky from blue to an opalescent green. He asked her name. She hesitated. He was proper-looking in his dark blue business suit, striped tie, and polished shoes. He was tall and muscular, with sandy hair and a good-humored sunburnt face. Still, she was wary.

'Stupid question. Why should you tell me your name? You shouldn't. I'll tell you mine, though. Here's my card.'

'Daniel R. Grey,' she read, and under that, 'Grey's Foods, International Division. That's you? The coffee, the pizza and the preserves?'

He nodded. 'I'm here in France to buy a chocolate company. Wonderful chocolate stuffed with marrons and liqueurs and other good things.'

Of course, anybody could pick up a business card. And yet, there was something about the man that said 'Believe me.'

'I'm Sally Morrow. I'm a photographer. I do celebrities and authors for book jackets, stuff like that. I've just given myself a week's vacation in Paris.'

'Will you give yourself an hour to have coffee with me? I have a favorite place on the Ile de la Cité. We can sit in the sun and watch the people.'

A pickup, she thought, that's all this is. And yet, what harm can come from sitting outdoors in a public square?

No harm at all. Six months later, they were married . . .

Dan got up and crossed the room toward her. 'What is it? You look far away. You look sad.'

She wanted to stand and put her arms around him, wanted to say I love you, I'm so grateful for you, I'm so terribly scared, and I don't want to dump all my fear on you.

But she said only, 'I was just reminiscing, seeing the carousel on the shelf.'

'And that made you sad?'

'But I'm not sad. Really. Truly.' She smiled brightly, willing her face to sparkle.

'I said,' Ian called, 'I said, Dan – '

Dan blinked. 'Sorry. I wasn't paying attention.'

'I had another call from that Swedish consortium today.'

Instantly alert, Dan said, 'I thought that proposition was dead.'

'It did seem so, but there's been a revival. Some powerful money, British and Dutch, is eager to participate. They want to start talking again.'

Dan shook his head. 'I don't want to talk, Ian. I haven't changed my mind.'

'But you haven't heard what they're offering. Twenty-eight million.' Waiting for a reaction and getting none, Ian added, 'That's if we sell it all off, and I see no reason why we shouldn't.'

Dan said then, 'I gave you plenty of reasons when this came up a year and a half ago.'

'We didn't have an offer like this one then.'

'If it were twice the size now, I would still say no.'

Ian's posture changed from ease to tension, and leaning toward Dan, he demanded, 'Still worried about the trees and the birds?'

A good-natured jibe, Ian would call it if he were challenged. Ordinarily, it would not have bothered Sally; they were all used to Ian's manner, always blunt and sometimes even rough. But today, with her nerves on edge, she resented it.

'I definitely am. We're killing them both, right and left. And a lot more besides.'

'Frankly, I'm concerned about people, Dan.'

'I'm thinking about them too, Ian. About people hiking or just sitting and feeling the natural world around them.'

'You're a sentimentalist.'

'I don't think so. I think I'm highly practical. You build your "new city", you put thirty thousand people up there – isn't that what you said last year? – and you'll destroy the water supply God knows how far away. I'm no engineer, I can't give exact figures, I only know, and you do too, that forests are natural cover for a water

20

supply. But what's the use of going over the whole thing again?'

'You admit you're not an engineer, so why not leave water and all the rest of it to the engineers? Listen, Dan, listen – you'd like to stop progress, but it can't be done. Set your mind on the twenty-first century.'

Gloom settled on Dan's face. 'My mind's already on it.'

'Well if it is, you're aware of how the population's growing. People are going to need roofs over their heads. This group I'm talking about has a brilliant concept, a handsome planned community, no helter-skelter growth – '

Dan interrupted. 'A roof over their heads! Before you pollute the mountains, installing people miles away from their work, incidentally, why not tear down the old ramshackle factories and warehouses in the heart of town? Rebuild the town with the same kind of handsome houses but that people can afford.'

'Okay, do that too. I'm for it. But the one has nothing to do with the other. You don't want to cut down trees, but they're doing it all over the world, anyway. These few more won't make a damn bit of difference. Why should we be so holy? I'm telling you if we don't accept this proposal, we ought to have our heads examined. Ask any man on the street whether he'd turn this offer down, and he'd laugh at you for even asking the question. "Why, take the money and run," he'd say. And he'd be right.'

'That's your opinion, not mine.'

'Listen to me. The way we work, you flying all over the globe to keep this business running . . . the more I think of it, the more I'm tempted to enjoy life while I'm young, get rid of this land, liquidate the business, and find something easier to do with our lives. Give me one good reason.'

'I can give you plenty. You shock me.' Dan's voice trembled. 'Because the land has been in this family for – how many generations, Oliver?'

Suddenly Oliver looked old. His voice was tired. 'First,

in the eighteenth century, there was the farm in the valley, running up into the foothills. Then later when money came into the family, they bought mountain land for a couple of pennies an acre, I suppose.' He gave a short laugh, tired too, and continued. 'During the First World War my grandfather rounded out the whole, just because he loved wild places, I guess. We've kept it ever since.'

'Loved it,' Dan repeated with a bitter emphasis. 'Yes, yes. An inheritance, a trust. Now we sit here talking, after two centuries, two centuries, mind you, of ruining it all, throwing it away for a bellyful of thousand-dollar bills.'

'Make that million-dollar bills,' Ian said.

'No matter!' Dan's voice rose, so that one of the dogs, feeling the reverberation of it, got up and laid a head on Oliver's knee. 'No, let me finish. You asked for reasons. Liquidate this business, you said. Grey's Foods. Four generations of labor. Grapes in the west, apples in the east. Farms, salesmen, packers, canners, bakers, truckers, bottlers – why, one of every four families in three counties has or has had a member who works for Grey's. Talk to any of them and you'll find out how they feel. They want their jobs, and they want their familiar environment. We're an institution, Ian, another trust. I don't know what the hell you can be thinking of.'

Ian laughed. 'Money.'

Dan fell silent. No one moved. Happy stared into the ebbing fire, Sally looked anxiously toward her husband, Clive examined his nicotine-stained fingers, and Oliver stroked the dog's head.

Presently, Dan asked, 'Don't you want to say anything, Oliver?'

'This is very hard on me, Dan. I guess I don't need to tell you my feelings about the business and the land. But they're all yours now, you young people, yours to decide among yourselves. I made that very clear to you when I turned the company over to you. I resigned. I told you I would take part in no decisions from then on and I meant it.'

There was another silence. Then Dan said thoughtfully, 'Funny, I wouldn't have any hesitation in parting with some of the land, as much as they'd take, if a conservation group would keep it forever wild. That might actually be a way of protecting it against some future generation's fancy building project.'

Ian raised his eyebrows, exclaiming, 'Oh? I daresay you would let them have it for peanuts. Why not just give it away while you're at it?'

'Tell me, Ian, why the devil you want more money. Haven't you got enough? It seems to me you live pretty well.'

'Show me anyone who ever thinks he has enough. Nobody has. It's against human nature.' And again, Ian laughed, showing his healthy teeth. 'What do you think, Clive?'

Clive looked up from the contemplation of his fingers. 'You're asking me? Why me? I'm not supposed to think. I'm only supposed to compute. I'm programmed.'

At that, a wretched cough strangled him, and turning purple, he bent over, head to knees. No one came to his aid, for there was no aid, nor anything to be done except to watch him cough, speed from the room, and return still purple-faced, but calmed. At the very least, this was a daily occurrence.

'Well,' Ian remarked, 'you're doing better and better, aren't you? Just keep on smoking, Clive, keep it up. The emphysema special.'

Dan said quickly, 'I'm sure Clive's tried hard to break the habit, but it's an addiction. Like gambling.'

Ian, having recently been in Monte Carlo, had no immediate retort, but Happy spoke up for him.

'Ian's a workaholic. He needs to break loose now and then.'

'Spoken like a loyal wife,' said Oliver. 'Never mind. I know my son's a high-stepper and I forgive him. Right, Ian?'

'"High-stepper." Define it for me, Father, I don't know what you mean,' said Ian, rejecting the pleasantry.

'Just another one of my archaic expressions. In my grand-father's time it referred to carriage horses, the lively trotters, and lively men, high livers, were called high-steppers, too.'

'Sinners. You make me feel like a criminal.'

'I don't understand what's happening here,' Oliver complained. 'We were all in good spirits at table, and suddenly we're quarrelling. I don't like that in this house.' He was still smoothing the dog's head. 'Even Napoleon's upset. He's not used to it. Are you, Nappy?'

'My fault, Father. I'm the one who began it. I should have known that Dan and I would lock horns over the subject. I did know it. The fact is – might as well come out with everything, now that we've gone this far – I've had a rough couple of days. I had a call from Amanda while you were away, Dan, and let me tell you, your sister in ten minutes can rob a man of a year's life. Two nights' sleep at any rate.'

'My sister? Why didn't you tell me? I've been home for two days.'

'Because I didn't want to bring up troubles before Father's birthday. Now I've gone and done it anyway. I'm sorry.'

'What made her phone you?'

'She asked for you, not knowing you were away. So they connected her with me.'

'What did she want?'

'First, the usual list of complaints. She has no seat on the board because she's a woman. I told her, as she's been told often enough before, that being a woman has nothing to do with it. But you can't deal with these strident feminist types. No wonder she's had two divorces.'

Dan corrected him. 'Only one.'

'Well, anyhow, she doesn't know a thing about this business and never will as long as she lives three thousand miles away. She's getting a hefty income from her quarter share of the stock, so what more does she want? Oh, she says it's not fair that we three men make so much more than she does. Salary, I said. For heaven's sake, a child can see that. We work eight days out of seven, don't we? Well, then she wants us to buy her out so she can have a lump sum for investment.'

'Buy her out?' Dan was incredulous.

'Yes, yes. And listen to this. If we don't, she'll sell her shares to the highest bidder. She's already talked to investment bankers about doing an evaluation of her shares.' Ian spoke rapidly, with mounting excitement. 'I'm sorry to say it. I've said all along and to deaf ears, but it's the truth, we should have had, our lawyers told us to have, an agreement to keep this a family-held company, to prevent a loose cannon like Amanda from doing just what she wants to do now, sell out. A take-over, with God-knows-who coming in here and holding the balance of votes. Yes, we should have had it, but Amanda didn't want it, and we all caved in. I can't help saying it again, Father, that woman's nothing but trouble, good for nothing except to collect her money and put us under a third degree every time to make sure we haven't cheated her out of a nickel. And now she wants a fortune for some damn-fool project, to boot.'

'For homeless girls,' Dan said. 'I remember her saying something about that a while ago.'

'She wanted to talk my head off about it, but I wouldn't let her. To tell the truth, I'm starting to think she's crazy.'

'No.' Dan made quiet correction. 'I'll admit she can be difficult, complicated, and confusing. But she isn't crazy. I don't believe in using that word lightly. And a project on behalf of desperate girls is hardly – '

'Desperate? We'll be the desperate ones if she carries out her threat to sue.'

'She's threatened?'

'Yes, if we don't buy her shares,' Ian said, impatient now. 'What company has enough cash flow to come up with twenty-five percent of its worth, I ask you. Yet if we don't do it, she'll try to put her shares on the market, and when we try to block her, there'll be a court fight with legal fees enough to choke us. To say nothing of the chance that we

25

might lose. Probably would lose. And all because you people wouldn't make her sign the buyout agreement years ago. She was younger and not as feisty then. If you had insisted, Father, she would have had to do it.'

Wanting to rescue Oliver from attack, Dan said firmly, 'That's past. There's no use looking back. It's water over the dam.'

Ian got up and strolled to the windows while everyone watched him. A dead stillness lay heavily upon the room, until he returned to stand with his back to the fire.

'You can all see that Amanda is another reason why the European consortium is a good thing,' he said. 'With money like that, we could afford to buy her out and get rid of her.'

'You only want to sell that land,' Dan responded. 'That's the long and short of it, Ian. You wanted to do it more than a year ago. Amanda's demand came two days ago.'

'Okay, okay, I don't deny it. I'm only saying there's more reason now. It's all intertwined.'

Facing each other, the two young men were obviously uncomfortable with such overt anger. Neither was used to it. It wasn't 'civilized'. Yet now it was palpably there. And Sally, watching the blood suffuse Dan's face, felt double dread over the far worse blow that he would have to receive tonight.

Then Dan stood gripping the back of a chair and, controlling himself, said reasonably, 'I'll talk to Amanda. I'll straighten this out.'

'Good luck,' Ian said. 'I'll take a bet that it won't do any good. There's no reasoning with her. You don't know her.'

'I don't know her? That's a strange thing to say. She's my sister.'

'Dan, you don't know her. None of us does. A girl who went off to boarding school in California at thirteen and has never come back?' And again Ian appealed to Oliver. 'Why don't you talk to her, Father? You're always a peacemaker, a mediator.'

'I told you, I'm not part of this anymore. You're asking me

to decide between my brother's children and my own, and I won't do it. You must settle among yourselves, I said. Take a vote.'

Ian said promptly, 'Fine. I'm for the sale. Dan isn't. Amanda will be for it because it will be a sure way for her to get what she wants. So that leaves Clive to determine the outcome. Either reach a majority or deadlock. How about it, Clive?'

There was a short delay while Clive underwent a minor bout of coughing. When it was over, he said testily, 'I never answer off the top of my head. Anyway, this talk is premature. It'll be closer to a year before those people can get their plans and their financing together. I suggest you table the whole thing for now. That's what I suggest.'

'Oh, fine.' Ian's laugh was sarcastic. 'By all means, let's table Amanda for a year.'

Abruptly, Oliver became decisive. His rising was a signal that the evening was over. 'Clive makes sense. He always does,' he said with an encouraging smile at Clive. 'As to threats – people often make threats that they have no intention of carrying out. My advice to you all is don't do anything hasty. And a second advice is go to church tomorrow. I seldom miss a Sunday, no matter where I am. Pray for peace, inner peace. Yes, yes, inner peace.'

They were all standing as he concluded, 'Even with these disagreements, it's been a wonderful birthday, and I thank you. And I love you all. Get home safely.'

They had not far to go. The two cars filed down the long driveway and out at the iron-lace gates, Dan's Buick after the Maserati, until the latter turned in at another graveled drive not as long as Hawthorne's, on either side of which a double row of lighted lanterns revealed a low, elegant French manor.

Anxiously, Dan repeated, 'You were so quiet. Tell me what's wrong.'

Her heart subsided as if it had literally sunk into cold fear and died somewhere. But she answered simply, 'It was an awful evening. I felt so sorry for Oliver. There was no reason for Ian to spoil his birthday party. He could have waited until tomorrow.'

To the right of the car there appeared through the trees a sudden glimpse of the city below. Dan slowed down.

'Look there. Scythia, home of Grey's Foods. I could wring Ian's neck. Ten to one, Happy could, too, if she dared say so. Maybe she does dare, for all we know. I can't figure out what gets into him. He and I have scarcely had an hour's worth of disagreement all these years. I thought I knew him inside out. I know he loves money, but even so – ' Dan broke off, then continued, 'If he pushes this thing through, sells the land and quits the business, how are Clive and I supposed to run it without him? Clive's only good in the office. I can't do my job and Ian's, too.'

'I'm sorry, darling. You don't deserve this.'

'My sister's another story. She's been a puzzle from the year one. What's gotten into her? A quarter interest in the business, for Pete's sake!'

'You always said she was difficult.'

'"Difficult!" What does that mean? What do I know? To my sorrow, I can't really *know* her. How can you know a person with whom you've never spent more than a few weeks at a time, an annual visit in California while I was growing up and now, during these last busy years, sometimes only a few hours? When I'm going west I make a stop in San Francisco or if she happens to come east, we'll meet in New York. She never comes here, you know that. It's ridiculous, it's sad, and I don't know what to do about it.'

She had an acute sense of Dan's pain. She had always, in a way, been a loner, not given to the intense relationships that people found in college and afterward, so she was still amazed at what had happened to her. Now at twenty-nine, after six years of marriage and with no loss of her own proud identity, she could feel sometimes that Dan and she were almost grafted to each other. And right now, knowing that he did not want to talk any more about Amanda, she was silent.

Then in spite of the darkness, she became aware of his turned head and troubled scrutiny.

'Sally, it's Tina, isn't it? You've had a bad day and you don't want to tell me.'

'Oh, it was simply more of the same. Thank goodness we have Nanny. Nothing fazes her.'

That was it. Keep the tone light. Wait till we get home, see what's happening there, then quiet down and tell him . . .

Nanny was reading the paper when Sally went in, asking at once, 'Everything all right?'

'Everything's all right, don't worry. We had a little set-to over her bath. She didn't want me to undress her. But we got straightened out and she's sleeping now. Susannah's a dream, that baby. Had her bottle and there hasn't been a peep out of her since you left.'

Something in Sally's expression must have touched the older woman because she added kindly, 'You young mothers worry too much. I raised four, and they're all different. Some's easy, some's hard, but they all come out right in the end.'

While Dan was taking his shower, Sally looked in on her children. The baby, smelling sweetly of powder, lay sleeping in her pink crib. At Tina's door she removed her shoes, not making even the whisper of a sound, for the child had been sleeping so lightly. The pale shine of the lamp in the hall made a stripe across the floor, and in its glow, she could just discern the small mound on the youth bed.

She made fists. She clenched her teeth. 'If anyone has harmed this child, I'll kill him,' she muttered.

While she was taking her turn at the shower, Dan came to the door. She had been there ten minutes at least, postponing what she knew she would have to tell him.

'Come on,' he said, 'are you going to stay there in the shower

29

all night? Get out, I'll rub you dry. And now are you ready to tell me what really is the matter with you?'

'Yes,' she said, 'I'm ready.'

When she had finished the story, they were in the bedroom sitting on the little sofa at the foot of the bed. He had his arm around her, for with the reliving of that afternoon's bad hour, she had started to tremble again.

She had expected to shock him, had dreaded the sight of his pain, had thought that he would perhaps get up and walk about the room in agitation. She ought to have known better. He was a clear-sighted man, and his first reaction was 'What can we do about this?'

'That's what I want to know. What can we do? What should we do?'

'We should first and foremost get another doctor. To tell you the truth, I was not impressed with that woman. She's very young and inexperienced.'

'She was so certain, Dan.'

'She'd have to be, making a statement like that. She wouldn't inspire much confidence otherwise, would she?'

'But so many of the things she said about Tina, the way she won't let us hug her and doesn't want us to go out, are accurate. Remember how Tina carried on when we went overnight to Washington two weeks ago?'

'Sally,' he said patiently, 'I had a dog once who climbed into my suitcase. Little fox terrier mutt, he was, smart enough to know that I was going away. If a dog can do that, what do you expect of a child?'

'I don't know . . .'

'Well, I know. Listen, let's analyze this. Where does Tina go? No place much except nursery school. And I'll tell you what I think. I think some little guy in nursery school is a bit "precocious", shall we say? Kids all play panty games. Hell, I remember doing it myself, don't you?'

'Yes, but – but this is different.'

At the doctor's office she had been defiant in her disbelief.

Now she was almost upholding the doctor, playing devil's advocate, wanting Dan to keep arguing her down. 'Happy recommended her highly, you remember.'

'I know Happy recommended her, so she's undoubtedly got good qualifications. But I'd be more at ease with someone else. Tomorrow we'll both ask around for names, compare notes and get Tina started somewhere else before this behavior of hers becomes a habit. That's what it is, Sally, a bad habit. She's jealous, she wants attention, and we need to be taught how to handle her. That's all it is and nothing more, I'm convinced.'

'You're truly not scared that she might possibly be right?'

'No, I'm not. I don't see any signs of what she's talking about. It's not possible, the way we live, the way the child is cared for and watched. Listen. A lot of these accusations of pedophilia are exaggerated. Sure, it's high time that these atrocities be brought into the open. I'm all for that. But still, you can't let good intentions run away with you. You know what I mean. People misinterpret totally innocent actions. They tell me that some schoolteachers are even afraid to hug a child these days.'

'I know what you mean,' Sally murmured. 'I just hope you're right.'

'Well, when we get another opinion, we'll know whether I'm right or not. But I'm so sure I'm right that I'm not going to lose any sleep over it. I'll tell you something, if I do lose any sleep, it'll be over all that business that we heard tonight.'

'Ian and your sister?'

'Yes, and I'm afraid it'll be a whole lot worse before it gets better. Come on, honey, let's go to bed.'

In the warm and quiet darkness they lay together. It flashed through Sally's mind that sex was not only rapture, but comfort. The union was healing. It gave strength, so that fear faded. When she opened her eyes toward the black window and the black night, the world seemed less hostile than it had all day. In a kind of miraculous turnabout, it seemed to her that she, that Dan, that they together could weather any trouble, whether Tina's, or Ian's, or Amanda's. As for Tina, Dan was right; that doctor had terrified her for nothing. And with her lips upon the back of Dan's neck, she fell asleep.

CHAPTER

——— 3 ———

April 1990

In the Sonoma Valley the bare earth lay in dull gold stripes between vine rows that stretched away as evenly as ruled lines on drafting paper. Up toward Napa the soaring hills were drenched in green, blue green, pine green, lettuce green, and then as the light veered among enormous cumulus clouds, they were drowned in black. On a pond beneath the rise where Amanda stood, a flight of ducks had settled, their wakes marking the water as if drawn by a silver-tipped pencil. It had been raining, and a brilliant, unfamiliar leaf, flat as a plate, that she had torn from a shrub was still glistening in her hand.

'It looks fantastic, like something you'd see in a painting of the South Seas,' she remarked.

Todd was looking at her, rather than at the leaf or the splendid view. She had not known him for very long, only a few months, but she had come to expect this look, this slight, thoughtful smile that reminded her vaguely of her brother, although they did not look alike. He was darker than Dan, and not as tall. Still, there was that same calm quality about him, as well as a delicate touch of humor about the eyes. Todd's were blue; even framed by wire glasses, they were a striking blue. He had a resonant, low voice. Possibly it was this voice, heard through a jumble of dissonant chatter at a cocktail party, one of those horrible, uncivilized mass meetings that, so it turned out, he abhorred as much as she did, that had first attracted her.

'You have the voice of an actor,' she had told him.

'Sorry to disillusion you. I'm a lawyer,' he had replied in mock dismay.

But she had not been disillusioned . . .

'Well, what do you think of it?' she inquired now, waving the hand with the leaf toward the spread of land below.

'Of its beauty? Paradise, of course.'

Like a lawyer, he measured his words, and she was quick to detect hesitation.

'What's wrong with it, then?'

'Nothing except the price, Amanda.'

'My real estate friends tell me it's not at all unreasonable.'

'That's true if you want a commercial property, a vineyard, for instance. You'd get your investment back. This is vineyard country, after all. But for what you want to do, it's sheer extravagance.'

'My investment isn't grapes, it's human beings. If you could see the girls I've worked with, fourteen-year-old prostitutes – '

'You're a wonderful woman, and your plan is wonderful. But this isn't the place for it.'

Frowning and with a petulant gesture, she threw the leaf away.

'I'm disappointed,' she said.

'You asked me to come see it and tell you what I thought. And I think you should start smaller, much smaller, with a good-sized house on a few acres in one of the outer suburbs.'

'That's not what I want.'

The words came out as if she were annoyed and aggrieved, as if he had somehow failed her. Since that had not been her intention, she felt awkward. Whenever that happened, the awkwardness, the pause that often followed, made her more angry at herself.

And Todd admonished gently, 'You look angry.'

'I'm not. I'm disappointed, I said.'

34

When he went to the car to use the telephone, she stayed where she was. Looking out over the land, she understood how a piece of earth can possess you, how every standing tree seems to speak. A fresh rush of wind flattened the cotton shirt against her breasts and billowed it out between her shoulder blades. Damp and cool on her face and her bare arms, it came from the northwest; from the ocean or down from Alaska? she wondered. And she gazed out again over this coveted land, drawing a mental picture: Here on the rise the main building would stand, to the left in an arc would lie the cottages, like nineteenth-century village houses, each with its front porch where a girl might sit and study or simply do nothing for a quiet while. And inwardly she cried, Oh, I need to build here and work here; I need this!

She wanted so much, wanted to give of herself, to – to be *alive*! She looked back toward the car where Todd was standing with the phone at his ear. Catching her glance, he waved. If only she could be sure of not losing him! But the likelihood was that, like so many others, she would lose him, too. She could never depend on men. They were attracted to her brains, her thick fair hair, and the good figure that she owed to tennis. They stayed awhile, slept with her, then as they began to slide away, made excuses, came less often, and finally did not come at all.

'You're cold,' Harold had told her after they had been married almost three years.

She had loved him, but he had been too hard to please. On his way up in an investment banking firm, he had high, perfectionist standards for everything: friends, entertaining, house decoration, table service, and clothes.

She who had been doing volunteer work with new immigrants and starting a course in Mandarin Chinese was suddenly presented with a list of duties: a daytime life with important wives at important charity luncheons and a nighttime life with 'contacts' at dinners, the opera, and the clubs. These people were all polished, smooth and glib, sure of themselves and sure of where they were going. They were decent enough people, friendly toward Amanda, perhaps especially eager to be friendly because Harold had let them know that she was of the Grey's Foods family. Being of that family, she was carefully, curiously watched.

She hated it, hated the empty hours buying clothes, consulting decorators, and dusting the growing collections of French porcelains and English silver that were too precious to be entrusted to a cleaning service. The collections reminded her of Hawthorne: walls full of fussy, costly objects, the gilt-edged leather books that no one read, the black silk Japanese fan, the silver carousel.

They quarreled often. The time span between quarrels grew shorter and the time span between their sexual unions grew longer. Sex was perfunctory and joyless. Rising from their bed one night, Harold stood looking down at her.

'You don't really care whether we do this or not, do you?' he asked.

She did not answer at once because to admit the truth would be so final. Disappointing as the marriage might be, she did not want to end it.

He continued, 'I don't think it's only that we have differing tastes. People adjust to those and they compromise. I think there's something missing in you. I don't say this to be unkind, Amanda.'

No, he was not unkind. He was just so large, so commanding. His ways, his voice, his body, all so commanding. Perhaps if they had a child, she began to think, she would feel different about him; he would be its father and everything would change. Yes, she wanted a child, wanted one badly, so very badly!

But when she told him, he refused. 'We're not ready to have one, you and I. People don't make babies to patch up their problems for them.'

Not long afterward he found another woman. The marriage was over.

Like running water life slips between your hands. And she was thirty-four . . . She smiled toward Todd.

'We've had a lovely ride, anyway. Would you like to have lobster salad for supper? I made it this morning,' she said.

'That was good,' he told her. 'Best feed in town.'

'I like to cook. Even when I'm alone, I eat well.'

She had made hot biscuits, new potatoes, fresh peas, and a lemon snow served with a light French wine. A handful of rosebuds nestled in damp fern mingled with the fragrance of food and sweetened the air. The table at the window end of the living room overlooked Nob Hill and the Golden Gate Bridge beyond.

'A postcard view,' she said, waving toward it.

She was pleased with the apartment, which she had decorated herself, so that unlike any other in the city, it was purely Amanda's, from the blue walls and ceiling, colored like summer sky, to the pale simple Swedish furniture, to the dark red oriental rugs.

'This place looks like you,' Todd said. 'If I were brought in here without knowing beforehand to whom it belonged, I would say it's yours.'

'Really?' And pleased, she pressed for more. 'Why?'

'I guess I'll have to fall back on that old word "indefinable". It's the same as trying to explain an immediate attraction. Like explaining love.' He smiled. 'Still, I'll try. This room has your spirit. It feels free as outdoors. Simple and easy. No clutter. And yet it is filled with very civilized, very elegant objects. It's all a subtle contradiction, like you.'

'Contradiction? That sounds awful.'

'Oh no, it's tantalizing. It's a puzzle, an intricate jigsaw puzzle that you know will be a great painting when it's finished.'

'So, you're telling me I'm not finished!' Teasing, she was aware that her light tone, prolonging the subject, was a mask over an intensely human wish to hear more about herself.

'No, it's I who am not finished solving the puzzle,' he said, suddenly sober. 'As long as we've started, do you mind if I go all the way?'

Fear, light fingers, ran up and down her spine. At the same time, she needed to hear the rest.

'It's a subtle quality in you,' he said. 'Maybe I'm crazy, but I often feel that for all your competence and all your elegance, you don't like yourself.'

'What on earth makes you think that?' she cried, still feigning ease.

'You hold back. There's something in you that you won't – that doesn't want to give way.'

Over the blue and white porcelain coffee service their eyes met for just an instant, an odd fraction of time through which each of them fled.

'Forget it. I don't know what I'm talking about,' he said.

The little fingers on Amanda's back subsided. She served the dessert and filled Todd's cup again, exactly as if nothing had interrupted the gracious little dinner.

After a while, Todd said, 'That photograph of your brother. I never noticed it before.'

'I moved it from the top of the bookcase.'

'You look alike. Are you alike?'

'I don't know him very well, so I can't say. Probably not.'

'Then what makes you say "probably not"?'

'He's very "settled",' she replied. 'In his niche.'

Todd nodded. 'Nothing wrong with that, especially for a man with a wife and two children.'

The phrase 'wife and two children' disturbed her. It carried an echo: *He has responsibilities, and it is heartless to burden him.* So without replying, since no reply was necessary, she got up to clear the table.

Todd helped. When the few dishes had been removed to the kitchen, he walked around the living room.

'You've got a miniature museum here. This Bonnard's a

38

treasure, the meadow and the hedgerows, and this little still life, the green grapes – beautiful stuff, Amanda.'

'Unsolicited gifts.'

'The Grey Foundation made a very generous gift to the museum here a few years ago, six exceptional American primitives.'

'The best of everything, always,' she said wryly.

'What is it about your family, Amanda? I keep getting these hints, but nothing more.'

'Oh, I don't know,' she said, wishing he would stop his discomfiting questions. She gave a little shrug. 'Anyway, I do have a family, my mother's people, the cousins down in San Jose. Where you picked me up last Thanksgiving weekend. Phyllis and Dick were really like a mother and father, keeping track of me at school, taking me home over vacations, doing the dentist and clothes business and all the rest. They were wonderful and sweet to Dan, too, when he visited in the summers. Sweet people.'

'But the other side? You never visit them, do you? Not even your brother?'

'He comes here. Years ago when I first came West, I missed him terribly. But when people are three thousand miles apart, they lose touch. Things can' – she hesitated – 'even grow cold, even a trifle sour sometimes. Sad but true.'

The blue eyes shone kindly within the gold-wire circles. 'Yes, it is sad when things go sour and cold in a family. The world's a cold place. You need each other. As you grow older, even more.'

Her words, in spite of her, came out with a wry, sharp twist. 'I've been managing rather well all on my own, I think.'

'Oh, "managing", of course. What I'm talking about is closeness. Take my brother, for instance. We're as different as can be; we argue like hell over politics and things, but all the same, we're close as two fingers on the same hand. And when my kid sister got a grant to study sculpture in Rome, it was a personal triumph for me, silly as that may sound. But it was.'

39

He was lecturing her, and she didn't like it. Of course he meant well, but today was a wrong day, and had been altogether wrong from the beginning. And he kept on.

'The Greys seem to do a lot of good. My brother went to a medical meeting in New York and told me about the Grey Cancer Research – '

She blurted, 'Let them hand *me* some of their philanthropy for a change so I can do something with my own philanthropy! You know what I do. That time you went down to the settlement house, when I brought that poor little thing in off the street, you saw her, weighed ninety pounds soaking wet, rouged like a clown, impertinent and bold and scared to death, fresh from the boondocks out of some "dysfunctional" family, as they call it. Just plain horror – ' She stopped.

'Yes, I saw,' Todd said gravely. 'She wasn't any older than my niece in junior high. Tragedy.'

'Exactly. "There but for the grace of God," et cetera. What's needed is people who care enough to come to the rescue and undo the damage. And money's needed, naturally. Always money. I've learned so much ever since I took that one course, Todd. You don't need to be a trained social worker. I can hire them for the hands-on work while I run the thing and pay for it. There are seven girls living now with two staff in that house I rented downtown. And you should see how they've – what can I say? – flowered? Five are back in school, one has a job, and we lost one back to the streets.'

'Pretty good record, I'd say.'

'I took two on vacation before I knew you, did I ever tell you? Took them camping in Yosemite, in the high meadows. They were like a dog who's been tied up. When it's suddenly unchained, it can't stop running and looking and sniffing. I think the grandeur overwhelmed them, only they didn't have the vocabulary to express it. At night when I was alone, I cried. That's why I want that land we saw today.'

'I understand, Amanda, I really do. But I still say you'll have to compromise.'

'I don't want to compromise! Why should I? Dammit, the money's there! You should see that place, that Hawthorne. Talk of the British aristocracy, the landed gentry! *I* don't live that way.'

'I have the impression you don't want to, anyhow.'

'I don't, but that's no reason why I shouldn't have the means to do it *if* I should want to. As it is, I want the money for a better purpose.'

'You'd need millions before you were through. To buy the land, to build and to maintain. Millions.'

'All right, let them buy me out. I own a quarter of Grey's Foods, from orange groves to potato chips.'

'Have you discussed it with them?'

'Last month, with my cousin. My brother wasn't there, not that it would have made any difference. They hang together. The answer was, naturally, no. The explanation? They haven't got the cash to buy me out.'

'That makes sense,' Todd said. 'They'd have to be twenty-five-percent liquid, and nobody is.'

'That's their problem. Let them get liquid. Otherwise, I'll sell my shares to the highest bidder. I told Ian, and he almost had a fit. Over the telephone, I could actually feel his face reddening.'

'I don't blame him. The spectre of strangers taking a quarter interest in a family-held firm would be enough to turn a man's face red.' Todd looked thoughtful. 'But I'm surprised they don't have a buyout agreement to keep any member from doing just that.'

'Hah! They wanted one when my generation took over, but I'm the person who held out. They could have outvoted me, but they didn't. The old man made them back off. I can be fierce when my rights are threatened. I will not be pushed around, Todd, I will not!' Indignation boiled. 'As it is, the three men, the cousins and Dan – the men – get huge salaries. And I, the woman, what do I get?'

'Equal dividends,' Todd said promptly.

'I want my principal!'

'You're not being reasonable, Amanda.'

She hardly heard him as she looked at her watch. 'It's seven back east. I'm going to call my brother right now. You can listen on the other extension.'

He declined. 'No, I'll go inside and turn on the television.'

Across the continent, the telephone rang. She imagined a room she had never seen. It probably had a view of the Adirondacks – those houses were practically *in* the Adirondacks – which now in April would scarcely be turning green. When the receiver was lifted, she heard a child's angry scream, Dan's voice saying, 'Take her, Sally,' and then, 'Hello.'

She plunged right in. 'You can guess why I'm calling, can't you?'

'I think I can.'

'Well, I went to see that property again today. And I want it, Dan. I really do. It's magnificent.'

'I see it is. I read the prospectus that you sent with the photograph.'

'I thought I'd hear from you before this. I left two messages at your office.'

'It's been about two weeks, I know, but I've had – some problems here. I'm sorry,' he apologized.

Dan's even temper only increased her exasperation. 'My project is important, Dan. I'm trying to bring life where there was death. Ian didn't want to understand it. I'm hoping you will.'

'It's a tremendous idea. But unfortunately, costs get in the way, as they do with most things. You – and we – simply can't afford it.'

'Well, I could afford it if you paid me properly.'

'You get the same dividends we get, Amanda.'

'What about those lovely salaries you all have?'

'We work hard for them.'

'Because you're *male*.' The instant she said it, she knew that it sounded peevish. But having begun, she had to continue. 'Don't you think I, a woman, am capable of working as hard and earning the same as all of you?'

'Of course you are. Just come do it and show us.'

'I don't want to. I have a different goal. Buy me out and you'll be rid of me.'

Dan's sigh carried over the wire, yet he still spoke patiently. 'No one wants to get rid of you. But your demands are unrealistic. We simply can't afford to buy you out, and that's the whole truth.'

'Then somebody else will do it. I've been inquiring around, and I've already gotten some rough figures from investment bankers.'

'Amanda, listen. Must I plead with you? Would you really want to bring in strangers and wreck this old firm that has, after all, done so well by you?'

'I don't want to wreck it, Dan, but if that's the only way I can accomplish my aim, then that's how it will have to be.'

'Amanda, we'd have to sell off most of our plant to give you what you want. We'd be a wagon with three wheels. It's impossible.'

'You could borrow the money.'

'And load ourselves with debt? I feel as if I'm being hit on both sides of my head at once. And it's all greed that's doing it.'

'Greed! I live here in three rooms, nice ones, yes, but I buy almost nothing for myself, everything else goes into my project, and you call me "greedy"?'

'Maybe you're greedy for admiration. Why must your project be so grandiose?'

'"Grandiose"! Nice talk from a brother. I had thought you'd stand up for me, not against me.'

'Don't be foolish. I am not against you.' Dan sighed again; his patience was going. 'God almighty!' he exclaimed. 'Between you who want to buy a piece of California that you

43

can't afford, and Ian who wants to sell a piece of New York State that's been in the family for the last two centuries, I'm about to lose my marbles.'

'Ian wants to sell?'

'Oh, he's gotten involved with some foreign group that wants a few thousand acres of Grey's Woods to build a new city. It's wanton destruction, all to fill their pockets with money they don't need.'

'Who are you to tell people what they need or don't need? Personally, I don't think it's such a bad idea, assuming there'd be enough to take care of *my* needs.'

'Oh, yes.' Dan sounded bitter. 'More than enough, I'd say.'

'Well, then I hope it goes through.'

'Streets and houses in a historic forest. Trees gone, habitat gone. Land that should go untouched to the state, to the public. I expected better of you, Amanda.'

'You may be concerned with deer and foxes or with trees, but I'm concerned about people.'

'You may have a different aim from Ian's, but just now you sound like him, though it hurts me to say it.'

'So Ian and I have something in common! It looks as if, for different reasons, we're on the same side, he and I.'

'With Clive and me holding the truncated tail of a great enterprise.'

'And a trunkful of cash, you're forgetting.'

'That we don't want, you're forgetting. No,' Dan repeated, 'I never expected this from you. Never.'

'It's nothing I'd choose, believe me, but I have to look out for myself. If you don't look out for your wants in this world, it's a sure thing nobody else will, Dan.'

'I don't agree with that at all.'

'Let me tell you – '

'Let's talk another time, Amanda, may we?'

'Okay, I'm not pressing. The property I want is part of an estate, and it'll be months before it's settled. I've got an option on it till then. So I can wait for whatever happens on your end. As long as I get what I want, I don't care how it's done.'

'You'll really have to excuse me, Amanda. Good night,' Dan said.

When she hung up, Todd came back to the room.

'Did you listen?' she asked.

'I told you I wasn't going to. Do you really think I would do that without his knowing?'

'Sorry, I didn't think. Sometimes I don't think. Dan's probably furious with me. I truly didn't want to quarrel with my brother, and the child was carrying on – '

'For a person who didn't want to quarrel, you did a thorough job. I couldn't help but hear your end of the conversation, and it was pretty sharp.'

Rebuked, she felt the sting of two immediate tears on either side of her nose. Seeing them, Todd put his arms around her.

'I hate to see you this way. You've let that thing take hold of you and almost strangle you. It's not worth it,' he said gently, smoothing the back of her head. 'And if you destroy that business, you'll really be strangled, especially if – I heard you say something about "Ian", and I don't know who he is – you take sides in whatever's going on there back east. You're not making sense, Amanda. You have cut yourself off from those people of yours, and you may end up losing your income, too.'

'You don't know anything about it,' she mumbled.

'I know that you, for no matter how noble a reason, want something you can't afford. Be sensible. Don't be the odd man out. That's sad.'

'Odd woman out, you mean,' she sniffed, raising her head. 'Funny that it's always the woman who's asked to give in. Always.'

'Not always. Too often, maybe, but not this time, in my opinion.'

'Right now my opinion is the one that counts, though.'

'Ah, how you love to argue. You should have been the lawyer,' he said, laughing a little, pulling her close.

She knew he meant to calm and comfort her and she wanted his comfort, that masculine heat of which there is nothing more reassuring to a woman who loves. Over the past months she had come to rely on his presence in her life; often during the day she would feel, at thought of him, the tiny twitch of her own smile, or the sudden harsh jolt at his approach on the street, or at what she had mistaken for his approach; the mistake would only serve to remind her that in a few hours he would be with her again. And she knew as one *knows*, as every nerve and every speeding rational thought proclaims, that he was different from any who had gone before him, that he was the real, the real and final one.

And yet there were days and nights like this, when he was too positive and, no matter how gentle, too sure of himself, of his very power over her, robbing her of independence.

He raised her head to find her lips, which were closed; his, soft and persistent, were pressing hers to open. She was braced between the door and his body, demanding, swelling. His breath came faster.

'Come inside,' he murmured. 'Come on, Amanda. Darling.'

She didn't want to. Not now. It was humiliating, when her mind was so agitated and every nerve jumping. She wasn't a pleasure machine, an engine to be turned on. Her hands pushed against his chest. Her face twisted away toward her shoulder.

'I can't. No, Todd. Please. Not now. No!'

He let her go at once and stepped back, frowning.

'Not now? When, then? Christmas? Or is that too soon for you?'

'Don't be ridiculous, Todd.'

'It's not so ridiculous. You haven't been exactly loving lately.'

Of course. The male ego was hurt. God knows she hadn't

intended to hurt him, but she just wasn't in the mood. Couldn't he see that? Still, he considered himself rejected, so she must try to soothe him, to explain the turmoil that was in her.

'Please, Todd. I've had all this stuff on my mind. You said yourself that when a man is worried, he doesn't feel passionate. Well, the same goes for a woman, doesn't it?'

A cool silence crept into the room. For a few moments neither broke it. Then Todd walked away to stand at the window.

Help me, she thought. Todd, help me. I get this way. It comes on all of a sudden. Please, Todd, I love you. Help me.

There was a sadness in his posture, although he stood straight. Perhaps it was his stillness that was so sad. Impulsively she went to touch him, saying, 'Todd, I'm sorry. It was only a mood. You do understand, don't you? Another time. You know I always – '

She stopped, and he turned about, looking down at her with a troubled, soft expression.

'I know you always try, but you don't feel anything. I know that, too.'

'That's not true, not true!'

He shook his head, denying her denial. 'You're too angry inside, Amanda. You have to learn, or be taught,' he faltered. 'I care about you so much, and that's why I'm saying this.'

Again, he was lecturing, being the wiser, the mature advisor, and, however smoothly, dominating. Always, always, things were spoiled that way. Unless, for once, he – somebody – would give in.

'You really love me?'

'You know I do.'

'Then will you help me?'

'If I can, I will.'

'Take this case for me.'

'What case?'

'The inevitable lawsuit.'

47

'Surely you aren't going to sue your *brother*?'

'The firm. All of them, if I don't get some sort of satisfaction before this property goes on the market for somebody else to grab.'

His astonishment chastised her. Then he said, 'I'm seeing something in you that isn't pretty. It's hard, and not worthy of you.'

'"Hard"! I'm hard? That's a queer thing to say about me, of all people.'

'No. You're doing wrong, Amanda. And in the long run, you'll destroy yourself.'

'Not if my lawyer proves capable.'

'I'm talking about morals. It's morally wrong, and if you don't see it now, you will see it someday. You have been fairly treated, I have to tell you so. You have no grounds for a lawsuit, none at all.'

'Then you won't take the case?'

His expression was very stern now, too stern. 'No, I won't take the case.'

'That's what you call "helping" me?'

'It really is helping you if you think about it.'

'I am thinking about it. You could take it even without agreeing with me, couldn't you? Lawyers make their living that way, don't they? I'm sure you've argued on behalf of people who you know are guilty. And I'm not guilty of anything.'

'That's a silly argument. I'm only advising you not to do something you'll regret. You can be very stubborn, Amanda.'

'Because I don't want to take your advice, I'm stubborn. Because I'm a woman.'

'When you get this "woman" chip on your shoulder, it's ridiculous. This lawsuit that you want to file has nothing to do with what sex you are.'

He had an expression, a tightening of the lips and a lowering of the eyelids, that was quite unfamiliar. She thought at once, he doesn't *like* me. Everything had gone bad. The symptoms had been there all day. They had been sliding downhill, the two of them, and while seeing the inevitable wreck at the bottom, had been unable to stop. And in some crazy way unwilling to stop?

Now it was necessary to be totally honest, to know where they were.

'No,' she said, 'I think, I think it has very much to do with sex in the literal sense.'

'You're far too intelligent to believe that's all it is. It's far, far deeper and I am terribly, terribly confused.'

There was such a pain in her chest, a real pain that was almost taking her breath.

'I think it's because I didn't feel like making love just now. That's why you're angry, Todd.'

He looked away at the Bonnard on the wall, at the uncomplicated countryside under the empty sky.

'Yes, I suppose you could say it was symbolic. It has been rather difficult for us lately, hasn't it? Because you have to admit that, haven't you?'

They were almost there now, at the wreck at the bottom of the hill. Yet, she would not, could not admit it before him. And she said bitterly, 'I guess there's nothing more for us to talk about, is there?'

'If you would only unlock the lovely woman who's locked up inside you, there would be. Can't you try, Amanda?'

His hand was on his briefcase, which lay on the chest by the door. Yes, she thought, he is waiting for some 'feminine' response, for some sweet submission, for a request to leave or a plea to stay. If only she were able to put her arms out, to cry *Please, please, don't leave me, I love you*. But that would be loss of autonomy and loss of all pride. It was what men expected of you . . .

And besides, very probably after all this, he did not really want to stay. No use, she thought; when it's over, it's over. There's no sense in prolonging the agony.

And he answered her silence. 'Thank you for dinner.'

'You're welcome.'

At the door, he turned back, and with an expression that was half reproving and half pleading, said very gently, 'Take care of yourself, Amanda. Don't waste yourself.' The door closed quietly.

The first thing I ever asked of him, she thought, and the answer was *no*. He wanted to control her. As soon as he saw that she wouldn't be controlled, he bowed out.

When the first wave of wrenching sobs was past, it was already dark. She had no idea of the time, just sat quite still by the window.

She had lost him. It was as sure as sure can be that he would not come back. For, as it now appeared, he had been having his doubts anyway. Oh, why had she embroiled him in an affair that was really not his concern? After all, she could find a dozen lawyers when the time came who would be eager to take a case against Grey's Foods. It had been stupid of her. Stupid.

But he had hurt her, humiliated her with the revelation: *You try, but you don't feel it.* So he had known all along! How could he have known? She always tried so hard to respond as one was supposed to . . .

All men thought of, when you came down to it, was sex. They didn't want to know *you*, the human being that was you.

She thought back over her conversation with Dan. She hadn't meant to hurt him tonight. He was the last person in the world she'd want to hurt. There was such a sweetness in him! Even though anyone could see at once how quick and smart he was, there was still that sweetness, a trust and honesty that seemed to her almost boyish. Her baby brother, only a handful of years and also light-years younger than she! Lucky the girl who had married him. And her mind went back to that day when everything was white: the clapboard country church, the bride on Dan's arm with her swooping skirt and the veil strung out in the white, blossom-filled wind. Let everything always be good for them both, she had prayed.

But he had said tonight that he had problems. He'd sounded stressed, with voices in the background, the child's voice screaming. Domestic troubles . . . Divorce? Oh, please not. All the business about the forest? Grey's Woods, they called it in the town.

Grey's Woods. Black miles and the lonely wind blowing at the window all night, all night . . . Abruptly, she stood up, sliding Sheba to the floor. Far below across the city, the glitter was dimming as thousands got ready for night. And among the thousands, there was no one.

'Little brother or not,' she said aloud. 'I will fight for myself. That's how it has to be. Good night, Sheba.' And suddenly she found she was crying again.

CHAPTER
—— 4 ——

May 1990

Dr. Vanderwater looked like a doctor. When, leaving his office after their first visit, Sally had made that comment, Dan had been amused.

'What does a doctor look like?'

'It's something indefinable. Probably just a manner. But I liked him, didn't you?'

He agreed. 'I was sure we would. The man has an established reputation without being old, and he's solid. He's a commonsense guy, no alarmist. Sally, we're going to get at the bottom of this, and Tina's going to be okay.'

Now, with a vast mahogany desk between them as she sat opposite Dr. Vanderwater, she remembered that. On the desk stood a leather-framed photograph of his four cheerful boys, whose identical heads of curly dark hair copied his own. He was a father. It meant practical understanding to add to the dozen certificates and diplomas that hung on the wall. All of this was reassuring, as was the man's easy bearing.

'How's Tina this week?'

'It was a pretty good week.'

'Fine, fine. She's a nice little girl. My wife and I often wonder how it would be to have a little girl in the house,' he said, looking fondly toward the photograph. 'So then, you feel she's making some progress?'

The very word 'progress' had a bright ring to it. Still, needing to be accurate, Sally added, 'There was one dreadful scene last Sunday when some friends came to see Susannah.

53

I was holding her, and naturally everybody crowded around, talking to her the way people talk to a baby. Then when somebody very thoughtfully remembered Tina and said something to praise her, she wouldn't answer, started to cry, screamed when this nice old gentleman patted her head, and kicked his ankle.' Sally made a rueful face. 'It was embarrassing. Yet not, I suppose, too unusual?'

The doctor nodded. 'Not too unusual. It's obvious that Tina's an excitable child, her reactions are somewhat extreme, either very positive or very negative. But then, when we look at the adult population, we see the same thing in many of us. We see every possible variation in temperament, don't we?'

'You're saying that what we are looking at now is Tina grown up?'

'In a sense, yes, but she's certainly not going to remain at a five-year-old level, is she? Essentially, inwardly, I would doubt that she will ever be exactly a phlegmatic person, but there's nothing wrong with that. Right now she's in a temporary phase of great anxiety because she's being challenged. In her mind, the baby has moved in and usurped her place in the family. Therefore, we have to teach her how to find her way toward acceptance, toward reality and understanding, that her place has not been usurped, that there is room enough for her and for the baby. This understanding will take time.'

'Very long?'

'Mrs. Grey, I have no crystal ball. Psychotherapy isn't orthopedic surgery, where you can either walk after the operation or you cannot. But I'm sure you've done enough reading about sibling rivalry, anyway, so you don't need much more explaining on my part.'

Now Sally was able to smile a little. 'Then my husband was right. I have to tell you he didn't think much of the first diagnosis. My husband is a believer in common sense.'

Dr. Vanderwater returned the smile with a slight reproof. 'Common sense, unfortunately, is often more common than sensible. In Tina's case, though, I do agree with your husband. I have, of course, no idea who made the first diagnosis, and I don't want to know. But after having had twelve sessions with Tina, I can find no basis at all for it. Frankly, Mrs. Grey, it troubles me to encounter faddism in my profession. Now that we have come so far in uncovering so many of the evils that used to be hidden and denied, we sometimes tilt in the opposite direction. We speak, we anticipate child molestation, for example, where there is none, uncovering a "memory" of something that happened thirty years before – something that did not happen. It's the misuse of a very useful concept.'

Sally wanted to laugh. Bubbles, impetuous and airy, filled her throat and turned into a trickle of tears that she blinked away.

'I feel,' she said, 'I feel a relief that I can't begin to describe. You've given me a mountain of gold dust, a hundred years of life – ' She had to wipe her eyes. 'All this spring, it felt like carrying a ton of lead on your shoulders. I couldn't understand how this horror was possible. Tina knows very well where you mustn't let anyone touch you. No. I couldn't understand.'

The doctor said kindly, 'So now take the load off your husband's shoulders too. Go home and live hopefully and normally.'

'Do you still want to see Tina, Doctor?'

'Oh, yes. Bring her here once a week.'

'And my traveling? I've been asked to go to Mexico for an article on migrant workers. Do you think I should still keep it on hold?'

'Yes, do for a while. Stay home and keep on with what you're doing. You're a good mother, Mrs. Grey.'

Departing, Sally thought what a difference this was from the day she had left that other office. Dr. Vanderwater's confidence was contagious. He was what Dan called a 'can do' person. Having always been such a person herself, Sally liked the feeling. It was healthy. It was strong. Driving home, she turned on the radio and sang along with it, all the way.

* * *

'Well, Tina, here she is!' cried Clive. A diminutive pony, marked in cocoa brown and creamy white, was led out of the stable. 'Came all the way from Pennsylvania yesterday, a long trip and none the worse for it. Isn't she beautiful? What do you say, Tina? What do you think of her?' He could barely contain his excitement, his pleasure, in the bestowal of so superb a gift.

The child's eyes were stretched almost round, and almost, thought Sally, as large as the pony's.

'Maybe you thought I forgot my promise,' said Clive, urging a response. 'Did you? Did you think so?'

Still holding Dan's hand, Tina shook her head.

'No, of course you didn't. You knew I wouldn't forget. But I had to find just the right pony for you. Come, I've some sugar and a bit of apple for you to feed her. That way she'll get to know she belongs to you. Come, Tina.'

'Go on. You've had pony rides lots of times before. See how gentle she is! Here, take the apple and hold it to her mouth,' Dan instructed, taking Tina's hesitant hand. 'Watch me. Feel how soft her nose is.'

'It's wet.'

'That's all right. It's supposed to be.'

The small hand ventured and drew away. 'Her tongue feels funny.'

'Yes, rough. It's the way her tongue's made.'

The pony, reaching for Tina's withdrawing hand, prodded it, and suddenly seized the apple; as suddenly, then as unexpectedly, Tina gave a shriek of delight.

'Look what she's doing! She likes me. She wants me to feed her.'

For an instant, Sally felt a small leap of the heart. The familiar, original Tina had flashed back – the changeling gone – with her distinctive, quick enthusiasm, her own vivid, bold expression. And she knew that Dan, meeting her look, had seen it too.

'Of course she likes you! She's going to love you. Shall

56

I lift you onto her back? She's saddled and ready,' he said.

Clive's satisfaction swelled. 'I bought a hat for Tina, a safe hard hat. I would have bought a whole outfit, breeches and jacket, but I don't know anything about sizes, so I'll leave that to you, Sally. How about a little ride now? A mile or two down the trail and back?'

'I want to go, I want to go!' Tina cried.

Dan assented. 'Okay. We'll wait for you.'

Sally sat down with him on a bench near the stable's wall until Clive appeared, mounted on a splendid black mare. Out of earshot, she murmured, 'His one luxury. He paid fifteen thousand for that quarter horse.'

Nervous, in spite of good resolutions not to be, Sally and Dan watched the horse and the pony walking their riders very slowly away. Clive was straight-backed and at ease in his impeccable boots and habit, while Tina, equally straight-backed, was proud in purple sweater and new velvet hat. When they had disappeared around a curve in the trail, Dan reassured Sally.

'Don't worry, he'll make a rider out of her. She was really thrilled, wasn't she? This may be just the thing. Did you think she'd take to the pony like that? Frankly, I was afraid it would take a lot of patience to convince her. But I guess she's a plucky gal at heart. Like her mother,' he said, putting his arm around Sally.

The May day was a late reminder of March, the sun having abruptly gone in behind gray-white clouds that, colored and curled like a sheep's back, lay low in the sky. The riding academy was deserted this Saturday afternoon, the paddock vacant. Horses and people were all indoors.

'Gray or not, it's too nice outside to be stuck in under a roof,' Dan said. 'Quick, Sally, look up. Red-tailed hawks. They fly two hundred miles a day.'

Following the line of his raised arm, she saw a swift parade in the sky. Rising and dipping, it was moving northward.

'You will see them from now on up into October. They're on the way to nest.' He stood up, the better to follow the circling, erratic flight. 'Watch how they follow the wind, the updrafts. What a sight!' Then, swinging around to face the greening forest, he exclaimed, 'Chilly as it is, I can still make myself smell summer. Grass and heat. It's in the air. Oh, Sally, can you imagine cutting all this down to run roads through here? It sickens me to think about streets and shopping centers here.'

It had been some weeks since Dan had talked about the project, so she knew how deep his distress must lie. His most troubled moods were always kept to himself. She knew that well. And, like a very amateur psychologist, knew, too, that in doing so, he was denying the existence of the trouble.

'Has Ian said anything since Oliver's birthday?' she asked.

'No, nor have I. We care about each other too much, you know that, to want to become enemies, so we're both avoiding the subject. We're putting it off as long as we can. But when the interminable paperwork is finished and the time arrives when we sign on the dotted line, or we refuse to sign there, then we'll have to talk. And it won't be pleasant,' he concluded grimly. 'I don't look forward to it at all, Sally.'

Yes, it was an ugly conflict that loomed before them all. For even if the foreign investors were to withdraw their offer, there would still be Amanda Grey. Where was the money to come from that would pacify her? A strange woman, contradictory and eccentric . . .

On the day of their wedding, she had been waiting on the steps of the country church for the bride and groom to come out. They had not expected her; she had sent them a wonderful set of English dinnerware, along with an excuse for not attending.

'Bless you both,' she had said. 'I suddenly decided to come after all. I'm glad you've married my brother, Sally. I looked up your work when Dan wrote to me, and I can tell by your photographs what you are. You have compassion.'

'But where are you running to, Amanda? Aren't you coming to the reception?'

'No, no, I have to catch a plane. I'm going straight home. I only wanted to see you.'

How very odd . . .

'If it's not one problem, it's another,' she said now, bitter that Dan should be so afflicted.

He stood over her, raising her face up by the chin. 'No it's not, Sally. You solve one thing and go on to the next. That's what life's all about. We're almost over the worry about Tina, aren't we? Think about it. Why, when I told Clive that she – '

'You what? You told Clive about Tina?'

'Just that we've been having some problems with her – '

In one second, compassion turned to anger. 'You discussed our child with Clive? I don't believe it.'

'Hey, wait a minute. I only – '

'You spilled out our most private business. I thought we agreed it wasn't going past our four walls.' She was furious.

'Hell, Sally, Happy sees the kid in school. She's been reporting to you. And everybody else has seen Tina acting up now and then. Where's the secret? It's all in the family, anyway.'

'Family or not. I think the world of Happy, yet even to her I haven't confided the whole thing. But Clive – my God, you didn't tell him what that first doctor, the woman, said, did you?'

'Well, not exactly, but – '

'What does that mean, "exactly"? Yes, you did, didn't you? I can tell you did.'

'I didn't, but if I had, it wouldn't matter. He'd never repeat anything told in confidence. Clive's an honorable man.'

'He's sad. He's a strange, pathetic misfit.'

It was Dan's turn to be angry. 'That's an exaggeration, and it's grossly unfair. I never knew you disliked Clive.'

'I don't dislike him. But that doesn't mean I want to make

a confidant of him.' She paused, seeking words to define a vaporous, vague feeling, perhaps impossible to define, that had not even begun to take shape until a moment ago. 'He's odd, he's lonely, he's got problems – '

Dan interrupted. 'I hope you don't think you're making any sense, because you're not. You're talking like an idiot. "He's odd, he's lonely, he's got problems,"' he mocked. 'So we shun him. We only like tall, good-looking, happy people. Right?'

'That's not what I meant and you know it perfectly well, Dan Grey. I'm just terribly upset that you told him about Tina. He knows nothing about children, he – '

'Seems to be getting on very well with this child, anyway,' Dan said sharply. 'Here they come.'

The horse and the pony emerged from the woods at a brisk walk, on the verge of a trot. Tina's braids were bouncing, and her round face was reddened by the wind. She was laughing.

'Let's do more,' she said immediately when the two animals came to a stop.

Dan lifted her down. 'So you liked it. You liked having your own pony.'

'Yes, and we gave her a name. Do you know what it is?'

'No. Tell us.'

'You have to guess.'

Sally said promptly, 'Princess.'

Dan said, 'Brownie.'

'Whitey.'

'Speedy.'

'Wrong. All wrong,' Tina shouted. 'Susannah. Her name's Susannah.'

The parents looked at each other in a kind of dismay. Dan was the first to object.

'No. That's your sister's name, not a name for a pony.'

Sally followed him. 'We can't have two Susannahs. Nobody would know which one we were talking about.'

'We won't have two,' Tina retorted, 'because you're going to take the other one back.'

'Now, that's enough of that,' Dan said firmly. 'We're not taking our Susannah anywhere. She's ours, you've been told that a hundred times, and you'll have to think of some other name for the pony or you won't keep the pony.'

'Take it easy,' murmured Sally, putting her hand on Dan's arm. 'Tina, I'll help you think of a much nicer name for the pony.'

'Uncle Clive said I can call her anything I want because she's mine.' Saying so, Tina screwed up her face in preparation for defiant tears.

'I didn't mean your sister's name,' Clive said hastily. 'Come on, don't cry. Here, give over the reins' – for a man had come out to lead the animals into the stable – 'and we'll go back to the Big House for hot chocolate with marshmallows. Plenty of marshmallows. How's that?'

Undeniably, he had diverted Tina and squashed the argument, but bribery was not the way. No matter how well meant, interference was unwelcome and made more complications in the end. Somewhat resentfully, then, Sally went along to the Big House.

In a moment, the tea wagon would appear at the door to the library. You could hear it being trundled down the hall, could hear the clink of china cups. It seemed as if the kitchen must be a mile away. Two large families could fit easily into this house, Sally thought. It must be dreary for Clive here in these echoing spaces, especially when Oliver was away, as he often was, and was right now.

'Father phoned from Washington this morning,' Clive said. 'They've put him on another museum board. And there's some sort of project, going to bring art to inner-city schools. Of course, that's the kind of thing he feels is so important. He sounded pretty pleased about it.'

Clive was sitting on a cushioned, low chair that might well

61

have been specially ordered for him so that his feet might rest on the floor. Known as a 'slipper chair', it was a kind that was usually placed in bedrooms. The jaunty, erect appearance he had presented when on horseback had gone; he looked not merely frail as usual but ill, Sally thought. Here now he was drawn and wasted, as if he had suddenly lost weight.

Taking a cigarette from his pocket, he asked politely, although surely he knew what the answer would be, 'Do you mind, Sally?' And when the reply was as always a shake of the head, he struck a match, tilted his head back in a movement almost luxurious, and let the smoke drift from his nostrils.

'Your cough,' Dan chided gently. 'Your lungs. When are you going to stop?'

Clive grinned. 'Probably never. Or until it kills me.'

'A man with your brains! Maybe you should go teach graduate mathematics at Harvard or someplace. Then you'd have to wear corduroy jackets with elbow patches and smoke a pipe. At least a pipe would do you less harm than what you're doing to yourself with cigarettes.'

'Trying to get rid of me, are you? No, I'm satisfied the way things are. More or less.'

Clive was positively jovial today. He was rarely so, especially when Ian was present, when his spirit seemed to retract into a shell.

His laconic speech was often curt. Sometimes, it seemed to Sally now, you catch him looking at you and feel he's having strange thoughts; you can't tell whether he likes you or not.

There was no doubt about his liking Tina. Helping herself again from a plate of marshmallows, she had just dipped one into an overfilled cup of chocolate, then dropped the wet marshmallow onto the rug.

'Oh dear, look what you've done. It'll stain,' said Sally.

'That's okay,' Clive said. 'It was an accident. Somebody'll clean it.'

Sally was not sure it was an accident. Tina had her own ways of getting attention, and spilling things was one of them.

However, this was neither the time nor the place to make an issue of it.

'I've been thinking,' Clive said, 'have I mentioned it to you? – that I'm going to build a cottage for myself up at Red Hill. It'll be only a quarter of a mile from the main house, but still, it'll give me privacy. I've been feeling a need for something of my own, where I can get up at five in the morning without disturbing Father or his guests and go out riding. I might even stay there part time in the winter and commute to work.'

'That's a long commute,' Dan observed doubtfully.

'Sixty miles are nothing on the open road, especially early in the morning. It'll be worth the price to be able to ride alone out through the woods in the winter. Down here at the riding academy there are always too many people. I love the winter silence up there, not a sound, not even birds and on a still day, not even the wind.'

Dan nodded. 'I see you know, then, how I feel about the woods. Not that I'm as solitary as you, but I can empathize with you. That's more than your brother does, with his plans for Grey's Woods.'

Clive's response was surprising. 'He'd leave part of it. After all, it wouldn't be the entire tract.'

'Part of it!' exclaimed Dan. 'You're satisfied with that?'

Clive shrugged. 'Whatever Father wants.'

'But he won't commit himself. You heard him say so quite definitely. It was on his birthday here in this room. He's leaving it all to the three of us.'

Tina had been wandering about, touching things while Sally kept watching to prevent damage to any treasures. Now she sprang up to rescue the silver carousel.

'I want to hear it. Play it,' Tina commanded. And when Sally refused, telling her that it was not a toy, she kicked her mother on the ankle.

This time Dan sprang up. 'See here, we will not have this, Tina. You may be tired, you may be upset about something,

63

but you may not hurt people. Go sit in that chair and be quiet until we're ready to go home.'

'Tina's a good girl. Come sit here on my lap,' Clive coaxed. 'Someday, if you're a really good girl, maybe you can have the carousel to keep.'

Sally's and Dan's exasperated glances met, and Dan began, 'No, she has to learn – '

But Tina was already on Clive's lap, where she sat triumphantly scattering cookie crumbs over him and onto the floor.

Offended and uneasy, Sally sat on the edge of the chair, wanting to leave. But Dan was tenacious and wanted, she understood, to get back to the subject that troubled him.

'"Whatever Oliver thinks," you said, but since he hasn't told us – at least I haven't heard anything – where are we?'

'Oh, somewhere in the middle,' Clive replied. He was stroking one of Tina's long braids.

Dan persisted. 'In the middle of Grey's Woods, do you mean? I'm surprised that you can even consider Ian's idea. Especially since you so often don't agree with him.'

'It's not what I consider. It's Father. He told me last week that maybe, after all, it might be a good thing to take the money and give Amanda what she wants. Cheaper than costly litigation.'

'That's been said before, and I don't agree.'

'It was just a thought. Father isn't sure.'

'I don't think we should fold up under threats, no matter whose.'

'Perhaps not.' And Clive gave the customary shrug that said he was bored with the subject.

The discussion was getting nowhere, so Sally intervened. 'You've plenty of time to make up your minds, all of you. Months. Tina's had no nap, it's been a long day, and I'm tired.'

She was cross, and she knew it. It bothered her to see Tina sitting on Clive's lap . . .

As they rose to depart, Clive said, 'When my house, my log house, is ready next fall, I'll invite Tina to stay and go riding with me. You'll bring the pony along, Tina, but only if you'll give the pony a name that your Daddy and Mommy will approve of. I had a mare once named Rosalie. How does that sound to you?'

'Okay,' said Tina with a yawn.

'That's settled, then. Rosalie and you will visit me at Red Hill.'

'Just Tina and yourself?' There was an edge to Sally's voice. 'Really, Clive! Who would take care of her?'

'The caretaker's wife is a very responsible woman. You'd have no cause to worry, Sally.'

'We'll see. The fall is a long way off.'

Except for the new pony, it had not been a very satisfying afternoon for anyone. There were too many and various undercurrents . . .

'I don't want Tina ever to stay with Clive at that cottage,' Sally said, whispering, although the child already lay asleep on the far rear seat of the station wagon.

'A couple of days' adventure like that visit at your parents' house would be good for her.'

'Clive isn't my mother. There's no comparison.'

'What harm would there be? The Merzes have been at Red Hill for years, and they even have a granddaughter there who could play with Tina.'

Sally's own thoughts disturbed her. They were sordid and dark. It occurred to her that maybe she was not even being rational. Yet she spoke out.

'I don't like the way Clive behaves with Tina.'

'Oh, you're right,' Dan agreed. 'He does interfere too much, and it did annoy me. But you can see how he loves her. Having no one of his own, I can understand and make allowances.'

'Why has he no one of his own? The way he lives . . . He's just strange, Dan, strange. I never saw it before as clearly as I did today.'

'I didn't see anything different about him today. What are you talking about?'

'Did you like seeing Tina on his lap?'

'For God's sake, Sally, what are you driving at?'

'I'm driving at something, I'm not sure what. You never see him with anyone, male or female. Where does he go? What does he do?'

'Do? Go? What the devil do I know? He goes out. I don't ask him where.'

'Maybe you should.'

'I still don't know what you're getting at, but obviously you're hinting at something dirty, aren't you?'

She was silent. The words wouldn't form themselves in her mouth. Yet, having gone this far, she had to answer him.

'Maybe. Probably. I don't know.'

'Really, Sally, it's dirty of you to talk this way about a decent man, or even to think it. Clive's all right. He's got his odd ways, but he's okay. I grew up with him, and I ought to know.'

'You were a little boy, and he was – what? – eighteen when you were brought here?'

'Clive's all right, I said.'

Dan was angry and hurt. He was intensely loyal, and she was offending his loyalty, which surely she did not want to do. Yet what was on her mind would not stay there, and words did finally form themselves.

'Do you suppose – oh, hear me out and don't be so angry with me – that the first doctor, that Dr. Lisle could possibly have been right about Tina?'

Dan jumped on the seat. 'For God's sake, you almost drove me off the road! Clive? Clive? Is that what you mean? You must be going crazy, Sally.'

The reaction startled her. Perhaps he was right. It was a dreadful thing that she had just said.

'I'm sorry. Sorry to have the thought. It just came to me this afternoon, I swear. It's a hateful thought. I wish I didn't have it. But people can't stop their thoughts.'

'Hateful is right, to accuse a decent person, even in your mind. Listen, you had your answer from the top, from Dr. Vanderwater. Forget that woman and her damn theories. Forget the whole business. Gee, poor Clive, of all people!'

She thought, then said, 'It was a moment's aberration. Forget I said it, will you?'

'Of course, of course I will.'

'Truce?'

'Come on, Sally. I've forgotten it already. We're all okay.'

An aberration, yes. Crazy thoughts. She was even beginning to feel hot shame at having had them. She had nothing really tangible to go by. Not really. So she would say no more.

Nevertheless, quietly and secretly, she would contrive to prevent Tina from any such stay at Red Hill. This she resolved. It might be completely absurd and probably was; nevertheless, it was her resolve. She was the mother and had to take a stand. Sometimes a woman had to be devious with her husband, even with one as wise and good, as beloved, as Dan.

CHAPTER
—— 5 ——

May 1990

Some fifty-five miles from Scythia down the state highway, then left and north onto a two-lane blacktop road, on the edge of a bleak wooden town, stood a dingy compound of brown structures: a sandwich shack, a gas station, and the Happy Hours Motel. A floodlight in the parking lot protected the two cars that stood there and filtered through the shades onto the bed where Ian Grey lay sleeping.

The first buzz from his wristwatch alarm woke him at ten o'clock. He had actually not been sleeping very soundly, although ordinarily, after making love, he slept like a rock. But that depended on the location. In Las Vegas last year with Roxanne, or on that weekend at the Waldorf in New York, there had been no need to worry about getting home at a plausible hour before midnight.

He had better wake her, although it seemed a pity to disturb such lovely peace. One cheek and one hand were buried in the chestnut hair that spread across the pillow. How he loved to bury his own face in that hair! Against the blanket lay her other arm, on which, in the ribbon of glare from the window, there glittered a pair of gold-and-diamond bracelets, last year's and this year's gifts, one for each year since they had met. Her new mink coat was draped over a chair. She would wear it, he supposed, as long as chilly nights could provide the slightest excuse. And he chuckled soundlessly. Greedy little gold digger! Yet she loved him. She really loved him.

He knew her inside out. He knew the whole pathetic story

69

about her mother's death, her father's prompt remarriage to a woman only six years older than Roxanne, the two new babies and the senile grandfather, brought to live in the miserably overcrowded house. He knew how she guarded her younger sister, who was still in high school. Out of curiosity he had driven past her house. With a broken-down porch and in need of paint, it was not far from the plant, where she worked in the shipping department. Her family had worked at Grey's Foods for three generations.

So you might ask, he thought, how I met Roxanne. The executive offices and the shipping warehouse were hardly side by side, after all. They had met in a restaurant where a group of friends had taken her to celebrate her birthday. They had met at the circular salad bar in the center of the room. Looking across from the shrimp bowl, he had seen directly into the most startling eyes he had ever beheld, pure black, deep as a northern lake, and with such lashes! Thick and curly and long! He had just stared.

'Well,' she said, 'well, well. And how are you?'

'Pleased,' he said. 'Very pleased.' And he had let her see his own eyes traveling downward over white cleavage, shapely bare shoulders, and swelling hips.

Her lovely mouth smiled. 'That's nice.'

'What's your name?'

'Roxanne Mélisande.'

He was amused. 'Say it again? "May" what?'

'Not "May"; it's "Me" with a little mark over it. French, you know?'

'Come on, don't kid me. You're not French.' And he gave her the wide-eyed look suggestive of passion, that never – or almost never – failed to bring response in kind.

She laughed. 'You're not French either. What's your name?'

'Ian.'

'That's a queer name too. How do you spell it?'

'I-a-n. It's Scottish.'

Since they were monopolizing the shrimp bowl, he had to act quickly and move on. 'When we go to the dessert table later, I'll get in line behind you. Slip your phone number to me, okay?'

'Okay. I saw you before at your table. Is the blonde one your girlfriend or your wife?'

'Girlfriend.'

'Like hell. She's your wife. I can tell. She's pretty.'

'Never mind. Are you going to leave your number?'

'What do you think?'

Of course she would leave it. She had later even taken care to watch him drive away with Happy, had probably marked down his license number, too, to find out who he was. In her place, he would have done the same. It was a game, as exciting as roulette at Monte Carlo and a lot more fun.

The room was cold now, and it would be good to fall back under the covers, but it was already ten after ten, and time to get up. Five more minutes, he thought. Then I'll wake her. The women always hated to get up. It was different for them; they did not have to hurry home.

Sometimes they passed in review before his mind's eye, and he wondered what had become of them, the dark, hot Armenian – or Gypsy, was she? – or the cold blonde, almost six feet tall, with the scornful gaze that said *You don't dare touch me*, until he had touched her.

Yet in the end, when the affairs were over, they had all meant very little. Most likely, he reflected with a kind of wistfulness, it would be the same with Roxanne. But that time was not nearly close yet. She had lasted longer than any of the others, and at this moment the very idea that she might leave him, the very concept of her lying in some other man's arms, were enough to send him into a frenzy of jealous rage. He knew himself.

He also knew that Happy was a permanent part of his life. They had been married when he was twenty-one, just out of college. It was true that his father, having been impressed by the young girl's refinement and charm, and impressed also by her family of old colonial stock, had pushed the marriage. But he himself had fallen in love with Happy and loved her still. That sort of love had nothing to do with sex. And in a man's life, the two could exist simultaneously with no trouble at all. Women, especially wives, never understood that. For that matter, his father would not understand it either. Suppose – an impossible supposition – he should suggest that he might leave Happy. The old man's words would fly like bullets. Family. Loyalty. Decency. Love. Why, he would tear the house down! And Ian thought of his mother, his lovely, gentle mother, so much like Happy . . .

The five minutes were not up, but wide-awake now, he rose noiselessly to dress and comb his hair in the bathroom. His hair was all mussed because Roxy liked to run her fingers through it. She liked to run her hands all over him. Remembering, he smiled at himself in the mirror.

'Yes, you're gorgeous, and I'm mad about you,' Roxanne said. Coming up behind him, she pressed her naked body against his back and, on tiptoes, placed her cheek against his to make a dual image in the mirror. 'Don't we make a stunning pair?'

'Not bad at all.' He swung around and held her at arm's length. 'I love your outfit. The bracelets are just the right touch.'

'If you love it, show me.'

'Honey, I can't. I've got to get home. I'm supposed to be at a business meeting, and they don't last all night.'

'It won't take more than ten minutes.'

'Hey, get away from me. Get some clothes on before I –'

'All right, all right.'

'I'd rather watch you undress, but this is nice, too,' he said, sitting on the bed while she put on her black lace underwear. 'You really love those clothes, don't you?'

'Why not? You're a darling to give them to me.'

'Do me a favor, then. Get rid of that thing you're putting on, will you?'

'What, this?' she said as her neck emerged from the collar of a blood-red satin blouse. 'I love it.'

'Well, I don't. It's cheap.'

'Cheap! It cost enough.'

'I don't mean that kind of cheap.'

'Oh, I suppose it's not your wife's taste.'

Ignoring the jibe, Ian said calmly, 'Don't be insulted. I mean it for your good. I want you to learn something about clothes, like not wearing junk jewelry with real. You're too beautiful not to do yourself justice.'

Appeased, she said, 'Okay, I'll listen. You do so much for me, Ian, and for Michelle. Indirectly I mean. I bought her some decent clothes last week.'

'She has no idea about us, I hope?'

'Oh, honey, I don't tell her everything. Of course I don't. But she's my sister, and I trust her. She'd never harm me, so that insures you, too.' Roxanne picked up the coat. 'Okay, I'm ready.'

'How have you managed at home to explain the mink?'

'I said it was cheap, just mink tails. They don't know the difference. I got it on sale out of my Christmas club money, a present to myself after I'd taken care of everyone else. I said I worked overtime this year.' The fur around her face made a dark frame on a pastel picture. 'All my life I've dreamed of having something like this. It makes you feel like a queen.'

A sudden thought of Happy made Ian smile again; devoted as she was to animals' rights, she wouldn't be seen in fur of any kind, ever. The contrast between Happy's horror and Roxanne's delight was almost comical.

Roxanne jumped and squealed. 'Oh my God, a mouse! Look! Look!'

'No, where?'

'It ran into the closet. Shut the door, for God's sake, Ian, before it gets out again. Shut it! Jesus, let's get out of here!'

'Wait, let me tie my shoes, will you?'

'Oh, I hate this damn dirty place, all these ugly places. Look at it. The wallpaper's peeling, the curtain's torn – the only good thing is there are no bedbugs. Why do we always have to come to places like this?' she wailed.

'Well, for one thing, the Waldorf's too far away. And this place is safe, too, that's why.'

'It wouldn't have to be the Waldorf. But this is awful.'

'I know. And I'll tell you what I've been thinking lately. I've been thinking about a little place for you out of town. A nice little apartment in some place like Titustown? What do you think? Wouldn't that be great?'

She did not answer.

'Wouldn't it?'

'Titustown is seventy-five miles from Scythia, Ian. What am I supposed to do, quit my job?'

'Sure, quit it.'

'And what about my sister? Just walk out and leave Michelle in that hellhole with our bitchy stepmother, a crazy old man who has to be told to zip his trousers, and our father, who doesn't give a damn about anybody?'

'Put your sister in a first-rate boarding school. It would do her good.'

'So then I'd be stuck out there alone seventy-five miles away in the sticks, seventy-five miles away from my friends. Everybody I know lives in Scythia.'

'Seventy-five miles on these highways are nothing. It's not much more than an hour's drive.'

'Yeah, in that tin can on wheels. All I need is to get stuck out there in three feet of snow.'

'I'll buy a good car for you. You should have one, anyway, and I should have thought of it before. We can run over to New Hampshire or Boston or any place where I – we – aren't known, and I'll get you whatever you want. Cadillac, Lincoln, Mercedes. You name it.'

Roxanne pouted. Her full lips pursed and her eyes narrowed. 'That's fine, but I'd still be all alone out there. I'd go crazy shut away by myself. You can't talk to four walls, no matter how expensive they are, and you can't talk to a Mercedes, either.'

Ian, not liking the pout, grew impatient. 'Well, what do you want? You're sick of dumps like this, and I don't blame you. I'm offering you an apartment as close to home as I dare make it. I can't put you any nearer, and you know it. So what do you want?'

He knew in the instant he had put the question that he should not have done it. He had practically asked for another battle.

'You know what I want, Ian. You know perfectly well.'

She stood in the center of the room with the mink coat wrapped around her, sashed at her waist. Her pose was provocative, but what he heard in her voice and saw on her face was a plea. *The* plea.

He answered mildly, 'I can't do it. I told you at the very beginning that I will not leave my wife. I told you.'

'Why not? She's wrong for you, or you wouldn't be here with me.'

'That's not so. The one has nothing to do with the other.'

'With her nose in a book all the time – and it's not as if you had children. She hasn't even given you children, after fourteen years.'

Again, she had said the forbidden thing. And although he replied still quietly, there was a sharp edge to his voice. 'Leave my wife out, please. We don't talk about her, Roxy.'

'How often do I have to tell you that my name is "Roxanne"? I hate being called "Roxy", and I hate being told what I can and can't talk about.'

Up to two or three months before, she had been blissfully contented with things as they were. And then marriage had all of a sudden become Topic A. He was tired now, ready for sleep, concerned about getting home and in no mood for Topic A. Not that he ever was in the mood for it.

'Listen,' he said, 'you've answered to "Rosemarie" a hell of a lot longer in your life than to this Roxanne business, and you can talk about any damn thing you want except one thing, Roxy.'

'Don't you say anything about my life! If you cared about it, you'd care about my future. What's going to happen to me? We're starting our third year, I'm getting older, and – '

'God damn it, you're twenty-two and you're worrying about getting older! Take each day as it comes. Enjoy it the way I do.'

'It's easy for you to talk. You've got security. You're going home to your own house tonight, your own mansion.'

'It's no mansion. It's a house.'

'A damn nice one. I saw it, I passed by. You've probably got marble bathrooms and velvet toilet seat covers.'

Angry as he was, he had to laugh.

'Oh, is that really so funny?'

'No, but you can be so superbly common, darling. That's what's funny.'

'Common? Damn it, if I had something here to throw at you, I would.'

'Ah, come on. Let's not keep this going. We had a great time tonight, and there's always more to come. How about Tuesday? No, that's too soon. I can't cook up so many evening meetings that close together. How about Friday?'

He knew he was thwarting her, but what else could he do? She ought to understand and be satisfied. Never in her life had she had it so good.

'No, not Friday. Not any day that you pick out just because it's convenient for *her*, because she's your wife, whom you don't love.'

'I never said – ' he began.

'Well, then you don't love me. A man can't love two women.'

'I love you, Roxanne. What does a man have to do to prove that he loves a woman?'

'Marry her. If we were married, you'd be home with me tonight.'

Round and round. He was growing more tired, more frustrated by the minute.

'I'm not good enough for your family, that's it. You're afraid of your father. Big-shot philanthropist's son marries Rosemarie Finelli – there, I've said it – daughter of Vin Finelli of Dugan Street. Big laugh, huh? You wouldn't dare. You're afraid of your stuffed-shirt father.'

'You've got some nerve, little girl. What the hell do you know about my father? You've never laid eyes on him, and you don't know one human being who knows him.'

'Except you. And you've dropped enough hints, whether you know it or not, for me to get the picture.'

The little devil! She was smart. Send her to one of the Seven Sisters and she'd graduate with honors. The little devil!

Ian was stung. She might say what she would about him, but not about his father. No one was allowed to taunt the Greys . . .

'Well, if this sort of thing makes you feel better, Roxanne my dear, keep it up. As for me, I've had enough for tonight.' He put on his jacket and turned the doorknob. 'You'll get the last word, though. It's a woman's privilege. Will Friday suit you?'

'If you'll give me an answer now. I don't want to pin you down. I'm not asking for a definite time like next month or anything, but I want a *yes* or *no* answer now. I'm tired of being in the middle of nowhere. Are you ever going to divorce your wife or aren't you?'

A blazing, furious beauty, standing erect and tall with her hands linked behind her back, she faced him boldly with her demand. He was not intimidated. He never was. In a few days, angry or not, she would be back in bed with him because she

was as crazy about him, regardless of cars and bracelets, as
he was about her.

'No,' he said precisely. 'As I long ago made clear, I am not
going to divorce my wife. And I don't want to hear any more
about it. I'm sick of the subject.'

'Then go to hell. And don't call me. Ever!'

She pushed past him, rushed out, and had almost started
her car before he had reached his. He stood for a moment,
watching while her car whined, coughed, rattled, and sped
away. Then he headed for home.

The highway was a clear, lighted streak in the moonless
night, with almost no other cars on the road. The loneliness
seeped over Ian like a fog. What a nasty way to end the
evening! It had begun so merrily, too, with a basket of fine
snacks and a bottle of Veuve Clicquot.

Damn her temper! She knows I'm not going to marry her,
so why all the fuss? Oh, she'll come around in two weeks!
No, she's stubborn. I'll give her a month.

He began to feel more cheerful. But on the final stretch,
past Scythia's main street, past the dark bulk that was the
headquarters of Grey's Foods, as he was climbing the long
hill above the city and almost home, there came a nervous
fluttering in his chest.

Did Happy still trust him? Once a long time ago, a long time
before Roxanne, he had been careless. She had found out and
had been devastated. And truly sorry to see her pain, begging
forgiveness for what he had called a 'meaningless escapade',
he had promised that it would never happen again. For a time,
it had not happened. Still, life being short and the world so
filled with beautiful women in such tempting variety, he had
had to break his promise.

He had been very, very careful that there be no slipups. Yet
perhaps it wasn't as easy to 'pull the wool over Happy's eyes' as
he liked to think? Possibly she, suspecting all his excuses, had
simply decided to pretend ignorance and accept him as he was.
She loved him, after all, and their life was good together.

It was good except for the want of a child. Or children. Happy had announced at the very start that she wanted a large family. He imagined that he would have liked it if it had happened, especially if he could have had a boy, a fine son. But since Happy was already thirty-five and it still had not happened, he did not allow himself to grieve as she, in her heart, in her silence, did grieve.

Definitely, he did not want to adopt. He knew many childless people who, rightly or wrongly, agreed with him. Why look for trouble where ancestry was unknown? You could have trouble enough with your own flesh and blood.

He was uneasy about meeting Happy's eyes when he walked in. It wasn't always this way, only occasionally after he had been with Roxanne. Tonight he was hoping that she would be asleep.

As soon as he rounded the driveway circle in front of the house, he knew she was not, for the bedroom was dark and the ground floor lit. He garaged the car and went in.

Happy called, 'That you, darling?' She came out of the living room with a book in hand. 'That meeting took forever. I was starting to worry.'

'Some guy was in love with the sound of his own voice. Took an hour to say what could have been said in ten minutes.' He kissed her. 'That's nice perfume. A new brand?'

She laughed. 'I've been using it for the last two years at least. Are you hungry? I'll bet you skipped dinner.'

'No, I ate.' Pâté and champagne.

'Well, have a little dessert with me. I got tired of reading, so I baked a batch of chocolate brownies. Let's have some, they're still warm.'

He had a sweet tooth that, because he was in fine shape, he could afford to indulge.

'Sounds good. Does ice cream go with it?'

'Of course. What flavor?'

'Coffee, please. Can I help you?'

'No, you sit. You've had a long hard day. I'll bring it in here.'

He sat down. A wave of the most peculiar feeling passed over him. It was not guilt exactly, for he had years ago worked that out: As long as you harm no one, you cannot be guilty. And he had not harmed his wife. What he was feeling now, he thought as he analyzed himself, was *embarrassment*. He was embarrassed, here in his own living room, leaning against the needlepoint pillows that Happy had made, facing himself silver-framed in his dark morning coat with his girlish bride enveloped in white satin, white orchids, and innocence.

But he had never harmed her, he repeated. And the name still fitted her: Happy.

She set the tray on the table between their chairs.

'You've done something different to the brownies,' he said. 'I like whatever it is.'

'It's an experiment. I added some coffee.'

'Good idea.'

He looked over at her. Her pink silk housecoat was ruffled. A single strand of pearls lay on her deep chest. Her fair hair fell softly, as naturally as a child's. She was wholesome.

'What are you looking at?'

'At you. You're a lovely woman, Elizabeth Grey.'

You wouldn't turn and gasp at the sight of her, he thought, but you wouldn't tire of seeing her, either, any more than you would tire of seeing a vase of roses in your room.

'I'm glad,' she said, smiling.

'How did things go in school today?'

'The accountants were there. We're way in the black, and we've had to close registration for next year. Filled up.'

He heard the pride of accomplishment in her voice. She was entitled to pride. A domestic, gentle woman had learned a profession, taken on a business, and made it succeed under no one's direction but her own.

And he said, 'I'm proud of you. Very proud.'

For a while, until they had finished the ice cream, they sat and discussed the school. After that, Happy had a couple of neighborhood anecdotes to relate and laugh about. Presently she remarked that it was late and they should go to bed.

It occurred to Ian that it had been more than a week since he had made love to her, about two weeks to be exact. Something in her manner as she said 'bed' suggested that she might be having the same thought. She was a healthy, vigorous woman.

'Come on up,' she repeated.

After tonight, he could hardly be feeling the clamor of heated blood. Still, if she began it, he would have to accede. A long, long shower would have to come first, though. He was soiled; within himself, he was soiled. And he was very tired. The conflict and the deception had taken his strength tonight.

Yet why should he permit them to? In sudden defiance, he sat up and walked with his arm about her to the stairs. They belonged together. He had obligations, and he wanted to have them.

But there was also Roxanne, a delight that he could not, absolutely could not and would not do without. Why should he feel conflicted or feel anything but pleasure in different ways with these two different women? The one had nothing to do with the other. Nothing at all.

Later that week, Ian received a telephone call at the office from his father.

'Stop in on your way home. I need to talk to you. It won't take more than a few minutes.'

When Oliver used a certain clipped manner of speech, one knew that he was not making a request, but was issuing a summons. He was finishing his solitary dinner when Ian went in. The scene was a setting for a comedy of manners, he thought; the white-haired gentleman at the head of the long table, dining by candlelight beneath the portrait of his wife in her white satin evening gown.

'Sit down. Coffee?'

'No, thanks. I haven't had dinner yet.'

'Ah yes, of course.'

Ian faced the portrait. As strongly as his mother always drew him toward her face, she also troubled him in some vague way that he had never understood. What he remembered of her was her gentleness, a bright spirit that was still spoken of by everyone who had known her. And yet, there was something else there . . . what? The sadness? He shook his head and looked away. No doubt he was only seeing the artist's lack of skill.

'I've heard some things about you that I haven't liked to hear,' said Oliver.

'About me? I don't understand.'

'You don't? There's nothing you've done that you're ashamed of?'

Ian, feeling heat rise into his neck, said, 'Well, naturally, everybody has done things he shouldn't have done. But I still have no idea what you're talking about.'

Oliver poured cream into his cup, stirred it, lifted the cup, and looked over it at his son.

'Let this be a lesson to you,' he said. 'You run into people when and where you least expect to. You were seen in New York a while back dancing at the Waldorf-Astoria with a young woman. Of course, I'm not going to name the person who told me. I'm not saying he meant any harm with his report, either. It may well have been entirely innocent. On the other hand, he might have meant to give you, and me, an oblique warning. Apparently you seem to be on, shall we say, intimate terms with her?'

Ian's flush had mounted to his forehead. Good God, some damn snooping old fogy might even have been in the elevator when he and Roxanne were going up to their room.

'Father,' he said quickly, 'this is nonsense. I was in the city to meet our southwestern distributors. Happy was at her family's place in Rhode Island, otherwise I would have been dancing with her. The woman he saw me with was – was the wife of a guy in my class at Yale. We ran into each other in the lobby and – '

Oliver raised his hand. 'Stop, stop, I wasn't born yesterday, Ian, and this wasn't the first report I've had about you, either.'

'What is this? The FBI out following me?'

'No, but as I told you just now, it's a smaller world than you think. You've been seen at roadhouses out on the highway, way out where people go to hide. Just casual mention, you know, "Oh, we saw your son" – that sort of thing. Casual. Or not so casual. Do you get my drift?'

'I get it, but it's all wrong. I never – '

Again, the hand went up. 'Enough, Ian. I was your age once and there's nothing new that you can tell me about being young. The difference between us is that I cut out all that stuff when I married your mother.' Now Oliver swung around in his chair to face the portrait. 'I was totally faithful to her and never regretted it for one moment. You have a beautiful wife in Happy. Why are you looking for trouble? Shape up, Ian. I mean it.'

This humiliation was unbearable. You couldn't argue with anything his father had said, nevertheless it was pretty nasty at the age of thirty-five to be reprimanded by one's father as if one were a schoolboy.

He stood up. 'Well,' he said, 'I've heard you and I'll keep what you say in mind. Is that all?'

'Yes, that's all. I haven't enjoyed putting you in this position, but as you must realize, it's for your own good. So no hard feelings, I trust?'

'None. Good night, Father.'

Yes, he thought, on the ride home, undeniably Father was young once, but he wasn't me and I'm not him. He doesn't understand nor can he forgive because he hasn't got the same zest for life. Probably he never did have, any more than Clive has, poor guy, whose only women are the ones he buys. Or any more than Dan has. Dan has different zests; you can't imagine him in that motel. He's in love with Sally and with trees. Yet he would never condemn me the way Father does; it's not Dan's way to condemn people. A good sort. A prince.

Now how to handle this. I don't want to be on bad terms with Father, and yet I'm not going to break with Roxanne. No way. An apartment, that's the answer, where we can meet in privacy and comfort. She'll love it, no matter what she says now. I'll have it fixed up like a little palace. She'll love it.

At the thought, Ian began to whistle, and he whistled all the way home.

CHAPTER
—— 6 ——

Coming home after a periodic visit without Tina to Dr. Vanderwater's office, Sally was comforted. Or, she asked herself, feeling at the same time guilty of being ever so slightly doubtful – ever so slightly – was it a case of needing to be comforted?

'Feel at ease with your child,' the doctor had reiterated. 'Your tension can be communicated, so if the child wants to tell you something, it holds her back. For the child to be at ease, you have to be. The household has to be.'

Well, of course. It was elementary. And goodness knew their household was cheerful. It was the home of games and songs, of Dr. Seuss and Winnie-the-Pooh, a veritable kindergarten-at-home. And how Dan did it with everything that was on his mind, all the mess at the office, she did not know.

'Don't you feel the improvement?' the doctor had asked.

It had been difficult to sit there and deny improvement when actually she was uncertain about it. Last week at a birthday party Tina had been a model guest, quite charming, so that one of the mothers had remarked to Sally upon Tina's 'sunny disposition'. So maybe there really was improvement.

'She's playing upstairs,' said Nanny when Sally went in. 'The yard's still soaking wet after last night's rain.'

From the big sitting room, where Dan had a desk and Sally had another at which to conduct her recently neglected business, came the tinkle of a waltz. Upon a table in the center of the room stood the source of the music: the heirloom, the treasured silver carousel.

'What on earth? What's that doing here?'

'It's for me!' cried Tina, exulting. 'For me!'

'Honey, it can't be. This isn't a child's toy.'

Indeed, it was not. For a long while Sally had not observed it up close and had forgotten how exquisitely it was made. No two of the horses that rose up and down as they circled were alike. They pranced or they trotted, heads were held high or bent low, and one even seemed to be looking over his shoulder. The tiny couple on the seats, he so neatly suited and she in the bonnet and wide skirt of the Second Empire, could have been worked by Cellini. Only an expert could estimate the value of such a piece.

'Who brought it here?' she asked.

'I don't know.'

Nanny knew only that the chauffeur from Hawthorne had brought it. There at the main house, the people thought only that Mr. Clive had ordered it to be delivered.

Clive was terse on the telephone. Probably she should not have disturbed him at the office.

'It's a present from the house, that's all I know, Sally.'

'Where's Uncle Oliver?'

'Father left last night for a weekend in Boston.'

'I don't understand,' said Sally. 'What are we supposed to do with it? Tina thinks it's for her.'

'It's a present. What's the fuss? Time we got rid of stuff from the Big House, anyway. The place is cluttered up like a museum. I have to go, Sally. Sorry. I've got calls waiting.'

For the rest of the short afternoon, Tina fussed with the carousel, creaking out 'The Blue Danube', and could not be lured away. *River so blue, da da, da da –*

It was unbearable, and Sally retreated to the bedroom. The light on the answering machine was blinking red as frantically as if it could know the urgency of the message. Sally knew. It would be Dora Heller again. Dora was the editor-in-chief of a major magazine, and this would be her third call in a week with perhaps the most exciting offer Sally had ever received. They were planning an issue to be almost entirely devoted to the life of a great author, a man nearing ninety, who had been born in the Appalachian outback and was known all over the world. Would Sally do a series of photographs for the magazine, Dora wanted to know.

And Sally's heart had risen. She had thought quickly, a session in New York, rising early and taking the latest possible plane, would involve one night at the most away from home. It could be done, and she would love to.

But no, the author was not prepared to travel. He was to be photographed at home, near Atlanta. And then Sally was to travel, to follow the path of his life, with car and driver provided, naturally, to his mountain birthplace, then to the school near the Florida line where he had briefly taught. In short, they would need a week of her time. And her heart had sunk.

She picked up the phone and dialed the number. Dora's voice on the other end of the line was almost incoherent.

'Sally! I've been waiting for an answer, to tell me that you've changed your mind. I can't believe that I've been hearing you right. This is a plum of plums. I fought for you. There were other names, you know that, but I dragged out every sample of your work that I could find and convinced them that you have the style and feeling that we want. You absolutely must say yes, Sally.'

'I can't, I have some problems here, and I can't leave. It's too far and will take too long. I'm sorry.'

'You're not sick, I hope.'

'No, not sick.' Then she knew that she sounded weak and was being too mysterious. And putting strength into her voice, she added, 'Nobody's sick, we're not getting a divorce or anything. It's our little girl who's having some problems, and so –'

'Not too bad, I hope?'

'Oh no, but I can't. I really can't, Dora. Please don't beg me.'

'I'm sorry, darling. Really sorry. Well, another time.'

River so blue, da da, da da –

'What's going on?' demanded Dan, coming in with his tie loosened and flung across his shoulder, so that she saw at once that he was in one of his rare bad moods. 'What's that thing doing here?'

'The carousel, you mean?'

'What else can I mean? So they make a dump out of this house,' he said, when Sally repeated Clive's remark about clutter.

'That doesn't sound like you. I'm sure it was well meant.'

'Well, okay, but the thing's worth a fortune, and Tina will only break it.'

'I don't think she will, but I'll admit that "The Blue Danube" is driving me a little crazy.' And seeing that Dan had flung his jacket on the bed and had sat down with a groan, she said mildly, 'She'll get tired of it, and then we'll hide it someplace or try politely to return it. It's not worth getting yourself upset over.'

'That waltz will drive me crazy too. The damn thing's too loud.' He got up, and opening the door, called, 'Tina, turn that thing off, please.'

'No, I like it.'

'Yes, but we don't. Turn it off,' Dan said firmly.

'No, I said.'

'Tina, you will do what I tell you to do.'

When he strode out across the hall, Sally followed. 'Dan, take it easy. You're awfully tired and troubled. I can see, but –'

'But what? What do you think I'm going to do to her?'

'I only meant she's had a pretty good day today, and –'

'And that's a reason why she mustn't be made to obey a simple command?'

The Carousel

'Of course not. But I do think we're making progress, and Dr. Vanderwater said today – '

'Dr. Vanderwater doesn't live here. We do. Maybe we ought to stop following all these books and theories. Maybe we should just use our own heads.'

The child was leaning on her elbows at the table as if the carousel had hypnotized her. Dan strode over and switched off the music. Tina let out a howl, a roar, as if he had struck her, and kicked him sharply on the ankle.

Dan picked her up under the arms and held her.

'Now listen here, Tina. You are not allowed to kick or hit. You're five years old, and you understand perfectly – '

She kicked his knee. 'Don't touch me! Put me down. I hate you! Put me down!' And howling still, she ran from the room.

The parents stood and stared at each other. Dan looked stricken.

'Danny, she doesn't hate you.'

He frowned. 'Don't you think I know that? But did I do wrong? Do we let her get away with murder? She runs this house and runs our lives, don't you see?'

Oh, she saw it all right. A week's work away from home should not be an impossibility.

'We tiptoe around her moods, we're afraid of her. What's it going to be like when she's fifteen? Tell me that. I'm going downstairs now and have a little talk. Don't look so scared. I'm not about to lose my temper with a child.'

'Please. This isn't the time. Leave her to Nanny. She'll calm her. Come back to our room and tell me what went wrong today.'

She sat down on the arm of his chair and laid her cheek on top of his head. 'What is it? The same thing again?'

'It was a bad day. Ian's impossible. Can a man get a new personality overnight? The last couple of weeks he's been a different person. Here's what happened this afternoon. You remember the coffee drink I told you about that some fellow

89

in Michigan thought up? It should be a bonanza if we can make the right deal with the right Colombian party. So I got an appointment set up, the Colombian flew in, the Michigan man drove – why, I don't know except maybe he likes to look at scenery.' Dan was breathless. 'Anyhow, he was an hour and a half late, which is a bother, but not a calamity. And Ian went wild, bawled him out and generally humiliated him. The fellow's very young and eager to make the deal, but he was so offended that he walked out. Took his briefcase and walked out! I had to run after him, apologizing. Finally, when I got him to come back in, Ian apologized, and I'm keeping my fingers crossed that we can make the deal. But it used up every ounce of my energy. That's why I came home early. They're all still at the office, but I had to get out.'

'What did Clive think of it?'

'He's at the other end of the hall, and I don't think he heard it. Anyway, if he did hear it, he would only shrug his shoulders and go back to his numbers, poor guy.'

The telephone rang. 'Answer it. I'm not home,' Dan said. 'Whoever it is, I'll call back.'

With her hand over the mouthpiece, Sally whispered, 'It's Ian with Amanda. A three-way call.'

Sighing, Dan took the phone. 'Here I am.'

Sitting on the edge of the bed, uncomfortably slumped, he listened. What an awful day, Sally thought, watching him. She was used to seeing him in charge of affairs, reckoning, confident, and cheerful, and it hurt too keenly to see him like this.

'I know, Amanda. I understand your position. You've made it clear. We've had this discussion before, haven't we?'

From across the room, Sally heard faintly a voluble female voice. Amanda evidently had a lengthy story to tell.

'I know,' Dan repeated. 'I know why you want the money, and I agree it's for a good cause. The problem is that we don't have it. Our bankers have been clear about that. We can't do it without destroying our business.'

There was more talk. Dan's right leg, crossed over the other one, began to swing, while his left foot tapped the carpet.

'If we sell off the woods, we could give Amanda her share. But I don't want to sell off the woods, that's the whole point. And I don't know how many times you want me to say so, Ian.'

Ian will never be moved, Sally thought with rising indignation. And she recalled his jibes about how Dan 'hugged trees'. In his eyes, ever since this proposal had been under discussion, Dan was 'sentimental', not 'practical'. How absurd! Running a business as he did, Dan wasn't practical? Could a practical man not be gentle and have ideals, too?

'Clive and I can't run this operation by ourselves. It's far too big. I've told you that before, too. And if this firm collapses, have you any idea, leaving ourselves out of the picture, what it will do to the community we live in?'

Pause. 'Yes, I'm well aware that you give plenty to charity.' Dan spoke sarcastically. 'And I'm not asking you to sacrifice anything you have. I'm asking you not to go grabbing for more when doing so will hurt so many people.'

Pause. 'How? Well, I'll tell you how. I stopped at a gas station yesterday, and the owner, who knows me well, came over to ask about that item in last week's paper, the rumor about the foreign investors. He was mighty upset, for the same reasons I am. And even our nanny told Sally and me that people in town, relatives of hers, are worried about talk of Grey's cutting down, cutting jobs. They're scared, and they've every right to be.'

There was a jumble of voices, audible to Sally but indistinguishable, as if Amanda and Ian were both talking at once.

Presently, Dan said, 'We are talking calmly. At least, I am.'

Pause. 'Yes, I am talking calmly. You say there's going to be a fight? Seems to me you're spoiling for one right now. I don't know what's come over either of you. I surely don't want a fight. I wish we could talk to Oliver . . . Yes, I heard him say he doesn't want to be involved, but . . . All right, then, let's bring Clive in . . . Dammit, Ian, can't we have some order here? Amanda? Speak louder, Amanda. I'm not hearing you . . . What? She hung up? Good God, you're both crazy. Okay, I'm stubborn, but so are you. I don't know how to deal with you, either, Ian. That performance this afternoon . . .'

Dan turned away from the telephone. 'Ian hung up on me.'

'Can't Clive do anything? No matter what else Ian may think of him, he respects his intelligence. He's almost in awe of it.'

'Yes and no. Didn't you hear me ask about Clive just now? "Never made a nickel on his own in his life" was Ian's answer. "Doesn't know a thing about business. A math whiz with a computer in his head. And anyway, he's coughing himself to death." So much for Ian.'

'Maybe you should go to Uncle Oliver after all.'

'I can't force him to take sides when his own son is involved, can I? It wouldn't be fair to the man. Besides, he's not young anymore.'

'Poor Dan. Where's this going to end?'

'Oh, somehow. I'm not going to be beaten, Sally, although I may look it this minute.'

'Happy's worried about Ian. She's never said a word to me before about anything that personal, so she surprised me. She said he's been in a terrible mood for the last few weeks. She doesn't recognize him.'

'He gets like that sometimes,' Dan said. 'Come on, let's get something to eat. It's half-past six, and the end of a rotten day, but still I'm hungry.'

CHAPTER

—— 7 ——

At half-past six Roxanne emptied a bag of take-out chicken on two paper plates and handed one to Michelle. On the rickety table between the two beds stood a six-pack of Coke and a box of donuts.

'There. A whole lot better than eating with that brawling crew downstairs. Pop's in a foul mood, the kids are fighting, and I'm sick of them all.'

Settled against the headboard of the bed, she was able to see herself in the dresser's mirror. It was interesting, instructive also, to watch the changes in herself as she talked and gestured, letting her hair fall carelessly in a becoming loop over her cheek or laughing so that her fine teeth showed and dimples formed.

Then, frowning, her glance fell on the faded green rag rug in front of her dresser and roved from Michelle's cheap cupboard, covered in yellow varnish and missing a handle, to the washed-out curtains at the single window. The cramped little room reminded her of those dingy motels, or looked even worse than they did because it was littered with possessions: clothes, music tapes, and Michelle's schoolbooks covered every flat surface.

'This place is a dump,' she said, startling Michelle. 'I want to get out of here.'

'You could fix it up.'

'I could? With what? Unless you've got money stashed away someplace.'

'Well.' The younger girl gave Roxanne a significant, ironic smile. 'No, but you can always get money.'

'That's what you think. You're wrong.'

'He phoned again, right after I got home from school. I picked it up before anybody else got to it.'

'Thanks. Did he say anything?'

'Just said, "Roxanne there?" I said what you told me to say. "She's not home and I don't know when she will be."'

'Good. He's going crazy, and it serves him right.'

'It's the fourth time he's called since Sunday.'

'Serves him right, I said.'

'What's he done to make you so mad?'

'He won't marry me, that's what. I don't like this arrangement. I don't want to live this way. It's been too long. I won't be used anymore. Sure it's great right now, but – and you listen to me, Michelle, you take it from me – only a damn fool would go on indefinitely with something that can be ended whenever the guy wants to end it. Apartments, cars, the whole works can be cut off in two seconds, and you're right back where you started, except that you're older. No, I'm sick of it, and I'm through.'

'Why don't you threaten to tell his wife?'

'You think he'd thank me for that? You think he'd buy me a ring and move me into his house after a messy divorce? Me? How dumb can you be? It would only wreck the woman and do nothing for me.'

As she flung her arm out, Roxanne's plate slipped, dropping a greasy chicken leg and a heap of coleslaw onto the bedspread. This accident was the last straw. It broke her control, and she burst into tears.

'Oh, damn! I really loved him. I made him so happy, and he – I don't know, Michelle. I think I'll remember him every day of my life, the times we've had, it wasn't the money, you probably think that's all it was, but it wasn't all. I loved him – '

'Then you're just cutting off your nose to spite your face.'

'Honey, it's too complicated. You don't understand. You simply don't.'

'I'm fifteen years old, and I understand more than you think.'

Someone was knocking at the door and calling, 'Rosemarie, oh Rosemarie!'

'Go away, Grampa. I'm busy.'

'Open the door. I want to sing to you, Oh Rosemarie, I love you, I'm always dreaming of you – '

'Old fool,' Roxanne muttered, wiping her eyes. 'I don't want him to see me like this. He'll go tattling all over the house.'

'He's been drinking beer all afternoon,' Michelle said.

The doorknob rattled. 'Unlock the door, I want to see you.'

'Go on, open the door a crack, Michelle, before he breaks the knob. Here, give him a donut to quiet him.'

The silly, pathetic face of the drunken old man grinned at them from the doorway. He drooled. 'I only wanted to see you. They're at it again down there, you know.'

Sure enough, the familiar strident bickering of Pop and his young wife came floating up the stairwell.

'So what's new?' asked Roxanne.

'I didn't have my supper, Rosemarie.'

'Give him a piece of chicken, Michelle. Take it and go away, Grampa. Be good, now.'

Michelle locked the door. Roxanne groaned. 'God almighty, this is a loony bin if there ever was one. No, we absolutely have to get out of here.'

Michelle sat down on the bed again, regarding her sister with interest. 'How's that going to happen?'

Roxanne considered for a moment or two before replying. 'Well, as you say, you're old enough. I guess there's not much you haven't heard, so here goes. Look on my side of the closet, back against the wall.'

'These brown pants?' asked Michelle.

'Don't you know riding breeches when you see them? Now look on the floor.'

'Boots.'

'Jodhpur boots. Your sister has become an e-quest-rienne. How does that sound?'

'So far, pretty crazy. You don't know anything about horses.'

'Two weeks ago, I didn't. Now I do. You'd be surprised how fast you can learn a thing if you put your mind to it. Sit down, and I'll tell you.

'It's this way. He's got a brother. The brother – name's Clive – is nuts about horses. When he's not working or sleeping, he's sitting on a horse. So one night when I was lying here thinking, I suddenly had a brainstorm. Why don't I go meet the brother, I thought. I remembered him from the night I met *him* at that restaurant. You know I don't forget faces. And besides, I heard so much about him that I could have practically drawn his picture. Short guy, about up to my shoulder, face not much to look at, and going bald, just starting. You'd never take them for brothers.' She reflected. 'God, he must hate Ian. *Him*. Only natural, looking like that. I'll bet he never had a love affair, and he must be thirty-five.'

'What is he, a fag?'

'Don't talk that way, Michelle, it's common.'

'Jeez, pardon *me*!'

'And don't say "jeez", either.'

Michelle rolled her eyes upward. 'Will you please go on with the story?'

'You interrupted me. I lost my track. Yes, well, I went downtown to a fancy store and bought the outfit – '

'Aren't you supposed to have a jacket?'

'You keep interrupting me. Yes, when it's cold. In the summer, you wear a shirt, the woman said. I bought two. They're in the drawer. Now will you let me finish? So I decided to go out to the riding academy up near the Greys' place and take a lesson. I figured I'd go on Sunday because if this guy's so nuts about riding, wouldn't he do it on Sunday? There was a kid there who gave me a lesson. I caught on without any trouble. It's fun. So while we were walking the horses through the woods, taking it slow my first time, we were talking, and I just happened to mention that I thought Clive Grey rode here on Sundays. The kid said yes, he does, but he comes later, after church. So to make a long story short, I hung around ready to hire the horse for another lesson, but the kid said he was too booked up. And just then, can you believe it, Clive Grey walked over and said, "I see you're disappointed. I'll be glad to give you a lesson if you like." And the kid said, "Lucky you, Mr. Grey's an expert." And that's the beginning.'

'Beginning?'

'We've been out five times, two Sundays and three evenings after work while it's still light.'

'Hmm,' said Michelle. 'So what's next?'

'Whatever I want. I can make anything happen. He fell for me. He looks at me and giggles like a baby.'

Michelle made a face. 'He sounds gross.'

'He isn't really. He's awfully smart, sometimes like a genius, a whiz kid, I heard. And very friendly, very nice. You can't help feeling sorry for him.'

'If you feel so sorry for him, why are you kidding around with him? It's kind of cruel, I think.'

Roxanne got up, sat on Michelle's bed, and put her arm around her, pleading, 'I'm not cruel. I wouldn't hurt anybody, not even a ladybug, would I? Remember a couple of nights ago when I found two in the bathroom and went downstairs to put them out on the grass? I want nice things for you. You're smart and you're pretty. I don't want you growing up and going to work at Grey's like the rest of us. I want to send you to a good boarding school – '

'Boarding school! Where'd you get that idea? Who goes to boarding school?'

'People do. They've got a sister or cousin in that family who went when she was younger than you.' She paused, and went on, '*He* was willing to send you.'

'Seems you've got a lot of ideas from him. So now you think this one will do it, too, is that it?'

'Only if I get him to marry me, and I'm sure I can.' She paused again. 'God! That'll be the surprise of Ian's life. It'll kill him.'

Michelle's eyes were wide with astonishment. 'Only you,' she murmured, 'only you, I swear. Who else would think of a scheme like this?'

'Plenty of people. Up there on the hill in those big houses, don't you think they know darn well what they're doing when they marry? Hey, don't you think Diana did plenty of scheming to get hold of Charles?'

'Well, I hope whatever you do, it turns out better than that.'

'It will. I'll give him the best time in bed, I'll do whatever he wants, I'm good-natured and easy to get along with. I'll make him the happiest man alive. Why wouldn't it turn out?'

Michelle gave a little shudder. 'But the way he looks, the way you described him.'

'He's clean. Immaculate. That's all that matters. As for the rest, I don't have to stare at him.' A sudden thought made Roxanne spring up and go to the closet. 'Here, I've got new shoes for you. I only wore these black patents once. You're an A width, aren't you? I'm double A, but you can have them stretched. And these whites from last summer are spick-and-span. My present to you. Might as well throw the old ones out, unless you want to keep a pair for the rain.'

'What the hell are you doing this for?'

'Because he's half a head too short.' Roxanne laughed. 'Or you could say I'm half a head too tall. So I'll wear flats from now on. By the way, watch your language. You don't have to say "hell" all the time, Michelle.'

'Oh, pardon *me*!'

'I'll pardon you. I mean it, though. I've noticed he

don't – doesn't – talk that way. He has nice manners. So watch yourself, please, when he comes. I don't care what they do downstairs because I've already explained to him about them.'

'When he comes?'

'He's taking me out to a movie and dinner on Saturday.'

'He's calling for you here? In this dump?'

'He won't mind. He's that type. Things like that aren't important to him.'

After the movie, they went to dinner.

'There's a good place out on Summer Street. Christie's,' Clive suggested. 'It has a great circular salad bar, lobster, giant shrimp, and the best desserts in town. How does it sound to you?'

'Oh, I'd love it. I've been there. There's only one problem. An ex-boyfriend of mine goes there a lot. We broke up on bad terms, and it would be awfully embarrassing to meet him. Do you mind if I pick a place where we won't see any of the crowd he goes around with?'

'Not at all. Just tell me where.'

The twinkling lights of a sign alongside the road a few miles from the city spelled out BOBBY'S BAR AND GRILL, and Roxanne said, 'Bobby's. This'll be fine. They have good steaks, that is, if you want steak?'

'Well, sure. I thought I'd take you to something more – more gala than this.'

'I know it doesn't look like much from the outside, but the food is the thing, isn't it? And the company,' she added, giving him the warm flash of her smile.

From their booth, as far away as was possible from the thump of the three-piece band, they had a clear view of the dance floor, where girls in cutoffs and jeans were gyrating with fellows in shirtsleeves.

'A blue-collar place,' Roxanne said. 'Maybe you don't like it?'

'Why shouldn't I? It's interesting.'

'Well, you being a Grey, and all. I was just thinking maybe I've made a mistake. You're not used to places like this, and I am. I'm blue collar.'

'You don't know me, Roxanne. What does it mean, "being a Grey"? It means that I have more money than these people have, which is no credit to me. I was just smart enough to pick the right grandparents.' He laughed. 'No. Great-grandparents.'

'That's what I like about you, Clive. Your honesty. You're plain and straightforward.'

'And that's what I like about you, among other things.'

The lighting was blue, but not too misty to hide the gleam of Roxanne's eyes and her teeth, or the glitter of the rhinestone pendant that lay between the round breasts under the red satin blouse. A strong scent of flowers drifted across the table.

'I like your perfume,' Clive said.

'Do you? It's French. My one extravagance. I love perfume. It makes me feel happy when I wear it.'

'I imagine you feel happy most of the time.'

When she leaned toward him, the pendant swung outward, revealing a half inch, a mere glimpse, of cleavage.

'Do you? What makes you imagine so?'

'Oh, everything about you. The way you took to riding, for instance. You loved it right away.'

'Oh, I did, I do. It's so free, being out there in the wind. It must be wonderful to have your own horse, the same one every time. I guess you get to know each other, almost like friends.'

'You do,' Clive said gravely. 'Maybe someday you'll have your own horse.'

'I hope so. How's your steak?'

'Good. Just right.'

'And the fries? Not greasy?'

'No, no, everything's fine.'

'I'm glad because I feel responsible for bringing you here. I'd feel terrible if I spoiled your evening.'

'Spoiled? I'm having a marvelous time, Roxanne. You know something? I have a definite feeling that I've seen you once before. I can't remember where or when, but I'm good at recalling faces, and, of course, yours is the kind of face that a man remembers. Have I ever seen you?'

'Not that I know of. But thank you, anyway. You're very gracious, Clive.'

The music went wild. On the dance floor they were whirling and sweating. Roxanne pointed out a couple whose twists and bumps, in perfect rhythm, were professionally expert.

'Would you look at them! Aren't they great? I wish I was that good. I love to dance,' she said, tapping her foot.

'I'd like to oblige, but the fact is I hardly ever dance. Almost never, really. I'm afraid I'd step all over your feet.'

'I'll take that chance.'

'Besides, to tell you the truth, I don't know how we'd look together. I'm short, too short for you.'

'Are you? I didn't notice. Anyway, even if you are, what's the difference?'

'Women don't like men to be shorter. On the dance floor,' he amended.

'What has height got to do with dancing or anything else? Napoleon was short, and women were wild about him. Come on, let's dance.'

'Okay. You'll have to teach me the steps, though,' he said as they left the booth.

'There are no steps. You're on your own. Just hang loose and move to the music, any way you want. Watch me.'

She was as lithe as a whip, with her feet coming down hard right on the beat, her hips and her arms swinging free.

She encouraged him. 'That's the way, Clive. You're getting there. Come on, grab my hands, turn me. That's it. Say, you've got it, that's the way. Do it again, you're great.' She smiled. Her bright face sparkled at him. 'Didn't think you could do it, did you? Who said you don't know how to dance?' She grinned at him. 'Isn't this fun?'

And it was fun. Nobody here knew him, nobody would be able later to gossip about how foolish he must look, jumping and spinning in his dark blue suit and proper striped tie, with the music crashing on his eardrums. His blood was pumping. It felt good. He let himself go.

All at once, he began to cough, the cough catching him in mid-spin so that he stumbled and lost breath. He had to break loose and sit down, gasping, until his eyes teared. Alarmed, Roxanne followed.

'You all right? All right?'

He nodded, wiped his eyes and, still unable to speak, pointed at the ashtray, which was full of cigarette butts.

'Ah, so that's the reason!' And when finally the cough subsided, she said seriously, 'Hey, you should quit that. Have you tried wearing a patch?'

He nodded again. 'Tried everything, and it's no use. So I've decided to smoke and cough. This only happens now and then,' he apologized.

'The more you smoke, the more it'll happen.'

'So they tell me. My whole family keeps at me, and I know they're right, but I'm not going to listen to them. I hate being nagged about it.'

'Okay, I won't say another word.' She regarded him seriously. 'You only have a father and some brothers, right?'

'One brother. And a cousin, who grew up in the house, so he's like a brother.'

'That's nice. And you all get along very well. Very nice.'

'What makes you think that?'

'Well, you're all in the business together, so I should think you must get along.'

'Oh, we do, well enough, although they're not like me. Or I should say, I'm not like them. I'm a loser. They're not. My brother, especially, is not. He's good-looking, popular, travels, gambles, has fun. Not like me.'

Roxanne reached across the table and touched Clive's hand. 'That's too sad.'

'No, just realistic.'

'People are different, Clive. You're very attractive. You could travel if you wanted to, you could gamble if you wanted to, but it's plain you're not the type, and you can have all the fun you want, in a different way. I've heard a lot of great things about you, about your head for math. I really admire that. Math was always my worst subject. Why, you could be a big genius at Harvard or someplace, teaching – '

'Who told you that?'

'I – people in the company talk, you know,' she said hastily. 'Even as far down as the shipping department, we hear things from the top. Harmless gossip, you know. In your case, compliments.'

'You're a sweet person, Roxanne.'

'Why, thank you, and the same to you.'

'I feel at home with you. I can talk to you as if I'd known you a long time.'

'I'm glad, Clive.'

'I hope I'll be able to see a lot of you.'

'Anytime you want. I feel honored.'

'Don't feel honored. Just feel that you've found a friend.'

'Oh, I feel that already.'

'Would you like to skip our ride tomorrow and drive to the country with me instead? I'll show you the cottage I'm building on Father's place at Red Hill.'

'But your family . . . I don't want to go if any of them will be there.'

'Why? What difference would that make?'

'I don't know. I'd feel awkward, that's all.'

'You're the last person in the world who'd need to feel awkward anywhere, Roxanne.'

'I can't help it. I'll only go if you promise me no one else will be there.'

'I promise. Father's in Boston, and Ian's at his sister-in-law's wedding.'

'That's okay, then. I'll go. I'd love to.'

'Okay. Tomorrow I'll call for you around noon. Don't dress up. Wear sneakers. It's out in the woods.'

The foundation and two walls had been completed in a stand of oaks that must be, Clive explained, at least seventy-five years old, perhaps a hundred. Drawing a blueprint out of the glove compartment, he described the house that he had designed.

'Nothing fancy, just a house in the woods. A private little place that belongs only to me. I can come and go when I want and do what I want.'

They got out and walked through rough, knee-high grass.

'I'll probably have a scrap of lawn to hold some chairs and a hammock to read in. Other than that, the woods. There'll be a great big room with a stone fireplace at either end, a kitchenette, a little bedroom for me, and another for a guest. My cousin Tina will be the first guest when it's finished. I promised her. My beautiful cousin Tina.' And Clive smiled, enjoying his little mystery. 'You don't ask about Tina?'

'Am I supposed to ask? All right, tell me about her.'

'She's five years old, and she already loves horses.'

Roxanne asked where the horses stayed.

'The stables are at Father's place. You can't see from here, but it's only a two-minute walk. Come, I'll show you.'

The narrow path led over an abrupt, leafy rise. Obliquely, not wanting to be caught staring too eagerly, he watched her. In jeans and shirt, as in riding breeches, she was even more appealing than she had been last night in her red satin dress. It, after all, had been fairly awful. He found himself thinking about her potential. With the right teaching, she would learn about simplicity. He found himself thinking that he had never seen a human being so joyously alive – except perhaps his brother.

At the top of the rise, the land spread out, a vast, level circle rimmed by forest. There stood the compound, stables, servants' house, and, at the end of a well-tended, oblong flower garden, the main house, built of logs, yet undeniably a mansion, a small mansion.

Roxanne was overwhelmed. 'Say! What about this!'

'So you like it.'

'Who wouldn't?'

'If you want to know, I prefer the house I'm building.'

She shook her head. 'Uh-uh. I'll take this any time.'

'Fair enough. I understand.'

He understood everything, her entirely natural awe of wealth, as well as her willingness to be here with him today. Read history: Old, ugly kings have beautiful young women around them. It was as simple as that.

'If you've seen enough, shall we take a ride?'

'Horseback?'

'No, car. I thought maybe you'd like to go up past Mount Bliss and have dinner at a little country hotel. It's a nice place.'

'Good grief, the way I look?'

'You're dressed just right for it. Take my word.'

'Okay, then. It sounds great.'

He thought, I suppose if I said let's go parachute jumping, she'd say that would be great, too. When the thought brought forth a laugh – a damned nervous giggle – she asked him what was funny.

'You're funny,' she said when he told her. 'Funny nice. I can tell you have a great sense of humor.'

That he had. But it was sardonic and silent, kept inside himself.

'I laugh inside,' he said. 'Can you understand that?'

She looked all of a sudden almost sad. 'Oh, yes. It's the way I feel sometimes when we're at supper and everybody's arguing about something stupid, and somebody gets excited and knocks over the catsup bottle. I have to laugh at them all, they're so ridiculous. But I keep it inside because they'd never understand how stupid they are. I guess that's why I like to be out with people, away from home.'

'It's different for me. There are just Father and me in the house now, and we get along fine. He's a wonderful man, my father.'

'Then why are you building this separate house?'

'One wants one's privacy sometimes.'

Roxanne said, 'When you told me yesterday that you feel you've known me for a long time, I thought it's the same with me. I fell asleep last night thinking about it.'

He felt so happy. He had never before had such revealing, intimate conversation with a woman or with a man, either, for that matter. Revealing yourself to people, you became vulnerable. Or, he should say, more vulnerable. He was already that every time he walked into a crowded room; tall, well-dressed women stared for half an instant at him and at once put on their correct social masks. As if he were some freak ... Of course he was no freak; he was merely a person not to be desired. But amazingly, this girl didn't make him feel that way. Her honesty was natural, kind and blunt. *Napoleon was short*. He felt so happy.

The restaurant was empty except for two or three old couples dining at the other end of the room. The gingham tablecloth, the bottle of inexpensive California red set out on the table, and the display of homemade pies were cozy. This was their second dinner together, two in a row. It gave him a free-and-easy feeling. He let himself imagine that this happened every night.

Between them they finished an enormous order of spaghetti carbonara, all cream and bacon.

'To hell with cholesterol,' Roxanne said.

Between them they finished the bottle. Her face was hot pink, and she had a laughing fit. 'First thing tomorrow morning, Alcoholics Anonymous. Here. Have the last in my glass. I'm finished.'

Laughter, catching in Clive's throat along with those last few drops, brought on a coughing spell. *Oh Lord, don't let it be*

*one of those choking ones, sputtering and disgusting, making a
spectacle of myself in front of her.*

His luck was with him. He got through briefly with
minimal noise, and Roxanne did not give him a lecture
about smoking. So, relaxing after the exertion, he lit a
cigarette.

The low sun, now visible through the trees at the window where she sat, put copper lights in her hair, and
when she moved her neck, made a blinding dazzle of
the rhinestone pendant. Clive was hardly a man to pay
much attention to women's jewelry, although last night
he had noticed her bracelets, handsome ones in gold and
diamonds. Of course, they could not have been real,
but they were at least tasteful. This thing was gaudy,
particularly out of place with a T-shirt in daylight. And
he was moved unexpectedly to a kind of tenderness. It
was probably her special treasure, the best she had, poor
young thing.

An elderly couple on their way out seemed as they passed
to be smiling at Roxanne, illuminated by the sun's last
glow. The man's glance seemed to last a moment too
long. And so it should; a thing of beauty was to be
admired. If Ian could see me now, Clive thought, he with
his women . . .

There were deck chairs on the lawn, a pleasant place to
sit in the quiet dusk. No cars passed on the road. Even the
birds' late twitterings were dying away.

He ventured to say, 'I don't suppose you're in any hurry
to get back?'

'Not at all. I leave it to you.'

The chairs were so close that the wooden arms touched,
and the human arms that rested on them could, if anyone
wished, touch too. When Clive moved his, she did not move
hers away. After a minute, he slid his hand down and took
hold of her hand. Their fingers interlaced, hers guiding his,
quickening his heartbeat.

Could he? Would she? A false move might drive her away. He wondered whether he dared risk it. It had never been much of a risk at other times because he had always been sure that the woman was desperate. But a woman like this one was hardly desperate! He wished he knew what to do. The vivacious mood at the dinner table, with her tipsy, pretty laughter, was now silenced. He was afraid she was bored.

'So quiet,' he murmured, needing to say something. 'They can't be doing much business. They have rooms upstairs, you know.'

'Oh, have you ever stayed here?'

'Friends of mine have,' he lied. 'They say it's very comfortable, a plain country inn.'

'I love the country. I should have been a farmer's daughter.'

'Really? I don't see you like that.'

'How do you see me?'

'In a more lively place than a farm. Still, maybe I shouldn't judge. I don't know you well enough to judge.'

'Not yet. After you know me awhile, you'll see I can be very happy anywhere. I'm not at all demanding. You could set me down right here, and I'd love it.'

'You mean you'd enjoy a weekend here, for instance?'

'Anytime, long or short.'

By now his heart was pumping hard, and he could feel the pulse in his temples. The last couple out of the restaurant, and the last car drove away. It was almost totally dark. If he only knew whether he dared.

'It's almost too late to drive home.' Roxanne's voice came out of the summer night with a dreamy intonation.

'You sound sleepy,' Clive said.

'Not so much sleepy as just tired. I'd love to stretch out.'

He hesitated, and at last dared. 'It's a long drive back. I don't mind staying till morning if you don't mind.'

'I think that's a great idea, Clive.'

Suddenly as her fingers tightened, he realized that they had been holding hands all this time. And he jumped up, pulled her up, and said, 'We'll need an overnight bag. It won't look right otherwise. I've got a small duffel in the car. It's empty, though.'

Then it occurred to him that she might expect two rooms, although probably not. For God's sake, this was 1990.

And that was what he said himself only a few minutes later, after the graying lady at the registration desk had given them a look. Once in the room with the door shut, he laughed.

'Did you see her face? I was dying to say, "Hey, lady, this is 1990. You're in the wrong century."'

Only then did it come to him that the look had been one of curiosity. *The showgirl, the beauty, and me.*

The room was neatly furnished with hooked scatter rugs, two rocking chairs, and a Victorian chest. The bed was freshly made, crisp and white. He looked at it for a moment and, overcome by a familiar, tingling hot embarrassment, sat down in one of the rocking chairs.

Roxanne broke out laughing, and then, glancing at Clive, quickly broke off to explain herself. 'I'm laughing because I haven't even got a toothbrush. Haven't got a nightgown, haven't got anything. Isn't that ridiculous?'

Thinking that he understood her shyness, he offered to turn the light off.

'Only if it makes you more comfortable,' she said, ripping the T-shirt off. 'As for me, I'm natural. Nothing to hide.'

She wore a black lace bra. And while he sat and stared, the jeans came off. Under them, there was a black lace bikini.

'Well,' she said, 'this is the last. Here goes.'

He had never seen anything so beautiful, had never known

that there could be a woman so beautiful. Words stuck in his throat.

When she lay down on the bed, the faint light from the worn-out bulb on the nightstand turned her skin to dusty pink. All creamy rose, he thought, getting up from the chair. Camellia petals, moist like them, but not, like them, cool. No, warm. Hot. Burning hot. He reached over and turned out the light.

'Was it good?' he asked in the morning.

'Idiot!' she said. 'You know it was.'

He liked that she called him 'idiot' and tousled his hair. It was affectionate. First came passion, next affection, and then passion again.

'Shall we do it once more?'

'Idiot. Of course. What else?'

A marvelous day! Love in the morning, in the sunlight. He could not believe his happiness. He had won the Nobel prize, or been crowned king. He did not recognize himself.

On the way back in the car, he repeated, 'Shall we do it again?'

'What? Now?' she answered, pretending, as he knew, to misunderstand.

'No, idiot,' he responded.

'Honey, I knew what you meant. And you know I'll do it again. It was wonderful. But,' she said seriously, 'you have to promise not to let anything accidentally slip. My father's very religious. You wouldn't think a man with such a mean temper could be religious, but he is. And he's suspicious. I'll say I was at a girlfriend's house last night and hope to get away with it. I usually do.'

Clive had a moment of jealousy. How many men had she had before him? But he had no right to look back. Now was what counted.

She spoke hesitantly. 'You don't – don't confide in anybody at home, do you?'

'Me? Of course not. I'm the most closemouthed man there could be.'

Relieved, she sighed. 'That's good. It's nobody's business but ours. Yours and mine.'

CHAPTER
—— 8 ——

June 1990

He would give anything, anything in the world, to feel like that again. No matter what you might experience or read about or fantasize about, nothing could possibly describe the reality of what he had felt.

She has bewitched me, Clive thought, after that night and after the few that rapidly followed each other during the next two weeks. There was a weekend, two nights back at the first hotel, and then three short, quick evenings at an inn not far from town.

Roxanne had been worried about her father and about being too close to home. Clive had countered boldly, with a still unspoken idea beginning to form.

'I don't give a damn who finds out. I'll see that you're protected whatever happens and no matter who objects.'

He would protect her . . . In his bed, in his car, and at his desk, she filled his thoughts. Her image floated in front of his eyes; her face and her incomparable, life-giving body took shape in the empty air. He knew perfectly well that the name for this bewitchment was 'infatuation', but what difference did it make what you called it? There were myriad definitions of 'love', too, and love usually began with infatuation. People tended to disparage 'love at first sight', yet only recently he had come across a semi-learned article in which it said that love at first sight was very common indeed and had as much chance of lasting as love at hundredth's sight.

He was almost certain that if he were to ask her to marry

113

him, she would. And he told himself again, as he had on that day at Red Hill, that if money played a part in her decision, it would make no difference. That was merely the way of the world and always had been.

Then he thought, in his bed at one o'clock in the morning, and at two, with his mind still weaving and planning, that there must also be considerable feeling for him on her part. Surely no woman could be so passionate if she did not mean it! And in addition, she was so tenderly loving. In this short time, she already remembered that he would not eat cauliflower, that he liked steak done medium rare, and that he did not want to be warned against smoking.

Oh, she was a treasure, and he must not lose her, must hurry before something happened, some younger man came along. And this possibility – no, the probability – sent him into a panic.

In war a successful general concentrates all his forces into one quick surprise attack. So he would present her, in a single hour, with a total plan for living: wedding date, ring, and house.

The date was to be immediate. The ceremony was to be a simple one in front of a justice of the peace, and secret. There was no sense in preparing Father. For loving, prudent, and wise as he was, he would inevitably try to talk his son out of taking such a drastic step.

'The girl is twenty-two and you are past thirty-eight. That's a big difference, Clive. And you've known her less than a month. It makes no sense for you, Clive, and none for her, either.'

They would be sitting in the library after dinner. Father would listen, nod, and in his grave, kind way, would reason with his son. Since the effort would only be wasted, it made more sense to bypass it. Save energy.

'Because my mind is made up,' Clive said aloud. 'Now for the ring.'

In all of Scythia there was no jeweler who was able to supply him with what he wanted. He had never paid attention to women's jewels any more than to their fashions; nevertheless, he was aware that Happy and Sally each wore a ring that winked and shimmered as they moved their hands at the dinner table. By dint of inquiry and comparisons at Scythia's various jewelers, he learned that the diamond he had in mind weighed probably six or seven carats. Such stones were not kept in stock but could be ordered on approval. He would have to wait about ten days.

Haste was driving him. He walked faster and faster and talked faster; he was in a fever of fear. He kept reminding himself that the delay might lose the prize. So he telephoned to a Fifth Avenue jeweler and, to the barely concealed astonishment of the salesman who took his call, ordered a ring.

'Pick out for me what you would buy. Your taste is certainly better than mine.'

'Well, a round setting's especially brilliant, I always think.'

The price was staggering; he had had no idea what such baubles cost. But it was also rather thrilling to be spending so much and to be able to spend it. For all his working life, having so few expenses, he had only been saving. The most costly gift he had ever made was Tina's pony.

'I suppose the credit card people will hold this up to investigate before they accept it,' he said. 'Just fax my bank, please, and they will accept. Then can you have it sent by overnight mail? I'm in a hurry.'

It amused him to think that the salesman was wondering whether this customer was a maniac. Well, he would find out otherwise when he spoke to the bank.

'May I ask, sir, whether this is an engagement ring?'

'Yes, yes, it is.'

'Then may I suggest – perhaps the wedding band?'

'Oh good Lord, yes, I forgot it. Yes, send that, too. Whatever you select.'

'It should be very simple. The simplest, so as not to detract from a ring like this.'

'I leave it to you.'

'Thank you very much, sir. Congratulations to you and the lady.'

The lady. Oh my God, what would she say, what would she do, when he handed her the treasure in its little velvet box? She would be stunned. It was funny, what a fuss women, and some men, made over what was after all a piece of ancient carbon. Funny. But it was the convention, a symbol of permanence, to wear one.

And then he had an old flash of memory, of his father's removing the velvet boxes from the wall safe in the bedroom after his mother died. For a moment, sorrow pierced through his jubilation. Yet sorrow told you something, too; it told you to grab hold of joy wherever you found it and hold on to it.

So he would hold Roxanne. He would fasten her to him, root her in one place, and nurture her like some rare, gorgeous specimen tree in a garden. And for that, a house was needed. It would be no little hideout like the one he was building at Red Hill, but a simple family house, for probably there would be children. It would be a dignified home, not as elaborate as the one Ian had chosen and Happy very likely had not wanted, but something tasteful like Sally and Dan's. While this house took shape in his head, he was already searching in the telephone book for a real estate agent.

'What is your price range?' the woman inquired.

'That's not the first consideration. The first is that I have to like it, and the second is that I want to move in no later than two months from now.'

'That will be difficult – Mr. – '

'Grey. Clive Grey. You can reach me at Hawthorne when you have something to show me. I'm assuming you'll get busy on it right away.'

'Oh. I'll do my best, Mr. Grey.'

Never in his life had he spoken to anyone with so much

authority. And he leaned back in his desk chair, chuckling: 'Hey, Clive, you don't even recognize yourself, do you?'

For two days he rode around the area with the agent, considering this house and dismissing that one. Some he even refused to enter. This, his first foray into ownership and domesticity, must be nothing less than perfect. Here the grounds were too small to fit the house. There the architecture was a hodgepodge. Another house was ostentatious. Still another was cold and unfriendly. Finally, he made his choice, a classic Georgian, old, rosy brick trimmed in white. It was neither too large nor too small, with spacious grounds. There was a splendid stand of full-grown blue spruce. He went through once, finding it all delightful, especially the master bedroom, where the bed would face a fireplace. On winter evenings they would go early to bed and watch the dreamy flickering . . .

'I'll take it,' he told the agent.

She looked a little doubtful. 'That's a quick decision, Mr. Grey. Are you quite sure?'

'Quite sure, provided I can have it in a month. I'm going away, and I want to move in as soon as I return.'

She still looked doubtful. 'I have to see whether they're willing. The closing and the moving don't go that fast. But I'll ask.'

The first asking was unsatisfactory, but as soon as the owners learned there would be no haggling over the price, that, indeed, Mr. Grey was prepared to pay even more if they should insist, a satisfactory answer was given, and Clive would have his house on time.

He said nothing about it to anybody. One evening, though, he found an excuse to stop in at Dan and Sally's with the real intention of examining their furnishings.

In the broad entrance hall and all up the staircase, the walls were hung with Sally's photographs, not the professional portraits, but assorted subjects that had appealed to her in the ordinary round of life: two horses out on a field in the rain, a close-up of a bee in the cup of a honeysuckle flower, an old man, bearded like some medieval scholar, gazing out of a tenement house window.

'You're an artist, Sally,' Clive said, meaning it wholly. Yet at the same time, he had been absorbed in the elements of the house's style.

Light, plenty of light from unencumbered windows and pastel walls. Fresh flowers, books, and comfortable spaces among objects.

'That's a handsome cabinet,' he observed.

'It was my grandmother's,' Sally said. 'Half the things in this house are hers, antique or good reproductions. The modern stuff is what we added.'

'That would take skill, I imagine.'

She nodded. 'Oh, yes. Thank goodness for Lila Burns. We had plenty of help. She's a marvelous decorator who knew how to put the whole thing together in almost no time and saved us money in the long run. I surely couldn't have done it alone.'

'Is she from around here?'

'Why, yes.' Sally stopped and regarded Clive with curiosity. 'Since when are you, Clive Grey, so interested in decorators?'

'I'm not. I was only admiring.'

'Well, thank you. By the way, you haven't been riding lately. Tina's missed you.'

'I know. I've missed her, too. Things have picked up in the office. I had a head cold, and – ' Faltering absurdly, he stopped, then added, 'But I'll get back on track.'

'Good. We've put her in a beginners' class at the academy, anyway. It seems to help her shyness.' Now Sally hesitated. He was wondering why when she continued, 'I know Dan mentioned once that we were having problems with her. Of course, they're just the usual upsets when a new baby comes into the family.'

'Of course,' he agreed, and wondered why she was so earnest, so emphatic.

Presently, Dan brought cold drinks. They sat awhile in pleasant conversation about nothing in particular until Dan brought up the matter of the consortium, Amanda, and Grey's Woods.

'I still can't see why Uncle Oliver doesn't take a stand,' he complained. 'That land is his spiritual treasure. Hell, I grew up knowing it was part of his religion. The preservation of the wilderness – now he leaves it to us to squabble over it. And we're heading nowhere except into trouble.'

To Clive on this evening, nothing could have mattered less than the wilderness, the consortium, or Amanda. So as soon as he decently could, he said good night and departed. Once in the car, before he could forget, he scribbled the name of Lila Burns. The minute the house was in his hands, he would call her with instructions to do the entire place, using Dan's house not to copy but for inspiration. He was certainly not capable of doing it himself. Nor, he thought with his usual tenderness, was Roxanne. Not yet. For she would learn.

And he thought of Pygmalion. He would show her many things that she had had no chance to see or hear. How bright, how quick she was.

They would have their honeymoon in the Greek islands. He scribbled another note: *travel agent*, *deluxe suite on upper deck*. They would dine, dance, and make love. They would sail the blue waters and he would explain the islands' history, tell her about Ulysses and Athena, and – He scribbled another note: *Replace scuffed luggage for self*. New set for Roxanne. She would need clothes, too. He would take a whole day for that. With her figure, she was surely a perfect size. A day would be sufficient to outfit her.

Today was Tuesday. Let's see, he thought. By Friday, everything will have fallen into place. The ring is already here, the ticket reservations will be complete, and I'll get permission to show her the house. So Friday is our day.

He had no doubts and no qualms. He was supremely confident, supremely happy.

CHAPTER

——— 9 ———

Late June 1990

The heavy red silk curtains that were protective on a winter's night now merely concealed the glorious noon outside. From above the mantel Lucille Grey in her white gown and pearl choker cast her melancholy, lovely eyes upon the luncheon table. Conversation, courteous as always, was desultory in spite of Oliver's brisk efforts to create a warm 'family' atmosphere.

Every one of us here, Sally was thinking, would rather be someplace else on a summer afternoon, reading the paper, taking a swim, or having a nap in the hammock. Certainly Tina had been convinced to come only by Uncle Oliver's announcement that he had a Japanese doll to give her. Now, sullen and silent, she sat between her parents eating cake while clutching the yellow silk doll in the other hand.

It was, however, hardly nice of them all to feel put-upon. To Oliver it was important to keep the ritual of midday dinner on Sunday, a ritual that like so many others in the last half of this century most people had long abandoned. But it made him so happy to see them all gathered at his table. It didn't take much to please him, after all.

She hoped he wasn't noticing the barely perceptible coolness that had existed between Ian and Dan ever since the time Ian had hung up on Dan. At the office, Dan reported, work was going on as usual. Ian's mood was still dark, but they had avoided their dispute. Or, to be more accurate, postponed it. Happy was probably aware of what had happened, but neither she nor Sally would ever think of mentioning it. They were friends. Let the men fight it out by themselves.

As it was, the two men were letting the women take the conversational initiative. Happy, always garrulous and cheerful, wondered aloud whether Clive was out riding so early today.

'I mean, he's always here at dinner.'

'He wasn't home last night,' Oliver said.

'Out with the girls again,' Ian said, grinning.

'Why not?' Dan countered. 'He's not married.'

Ian changed the subject. 'This new cook of yours is something else, Father. You can't get better pastry in Paris.'

Oliver was pleased. 'My sons with their sweet teeth! Your mother had a sweet tooth, too, thin as she was. Well, shall we have our coffee on the porch?'

The party transferred itself to the screened porch, which was furnished in white wicker, and shaded by green-striped awnings. Through the trees there blew a mild, soporific breeze; lying back on soft upholstery after a heavy meal, it was hard not to yawn. Only Oliver in his linen suit sat upright.

'There's nothing to play with,' whined Tina, who was understandably bored.

'You might take the new doll for a walk. Show her the pigeon house,' Sally suggested for lack of a better idea.

'I don't want to. I hate this doll.' And Tina threw it on the floor.

Dan intervened. 'It's naughty to treat a beautiful present like that and when Uncle Oliver is so nice to you. You should tell him you're sorry.'

'I won't. I'm not sorry. It's an awful doll. It's ugly.'

Happy and Ian were considerately looking the other way. Their consideration made Sally's embarrassment more painful. It wasn't hard to guess what they were thinking about Tina.

'I'll be glad to get you a different one,' said Oliver. 'The minute I saw this one in the window, I thought you'd like it. But that's all right. Just tell me what you'd rather have.'

'Uncle – ' began Sally, wanting to suggest that he not reward the child's behavior.

But she was interrupted by Oliver. 'Tell me, Tina. Come here and whisper it in my ear.'

'No, I said. You're deaf. No, I said.'

Oliver walked across the porch and, lifting the shrieking child, coaxed, 'Listen to me – '

In the midst of this disturbance came the sound of voices on the gravel path.

'Guests, Father?' asked Happy.

Oliver put Tina down and looked across the lawn. 'I'm not expecting any. Why, it's Clive! Clive with somebody.'

Up the steps and onto the porch came Clive, holding by the hand an astonishingly beautiful young woman who wore a fine, cream-colored silk suit and a matching straw hat above a magnificent cascade of burnished red-brown hair. They stopped before Oliver, and Clive spoke.

'Father,' he said in a loud, clear voice, 'I've brought you a surprise. This is Roxanne Grey. We were married last night.'

'A surprise,' said Oliver. 'A surprise. You're quite serious? Not joking?' he cried.

At this the girl stretched out her hand up to the level of Oliver's face. 'Not on your life. And here's the ring to prove it.'

Oliver blinked and sat down. Shock overwhelmed the little group on the porch. It was as if a giant wave had crashed upon a beach and then receded into silence.

No more than a few seconds could have passed, but it seemed like a long time before Clive said gaily, 'I've dropped a bomb, haven't I? This is the last thing you expected me to do, and to tell you the truth, I never expected to do it, either. Until I met Roxanne.'

Wicker creaked in the stillness as the little group shifted

in their chairs, waiting for the head of the family to respond.

'Of course, we wish you all the happiness in the world,' Oliver said in his formal way. 'But there was no need for secrecy like this.'

'Not secrecy, Father. Haste. Impulse. Blame it on me. I didn't have patience for the usual fuss and delay.'

Disjointed thoughts sped through Sally's mind. The pair looked awkward there, like people who perch uncertainly in dentists' waiting rooms or unemployment offices. It's strange that not one of us has cried out in amazement or with curiosity, or stood up to make some attempt at congratulations. A handshake or a hug. We're all numb as stones. It would make a stunning photo, forbidding in a way, like the painting 'American Gothic', stiff and painful.

Dan's astonished eyebrows were practically up at his hairline, and Happy's mouth had dropped open. Ian raised himself from his chair and fell back. His face was a raging crimson. With that temper, he would have a premature stroke one day. It's no business of his, anyhow, that his brother decided to elope, Sally thought indignantly.

And somebody really ought to *welcome* the girl! So, saying the first trivial thing that came to her head, she addressed her.

'Roxanne! What a pretty name.' She went over and took Roxanne's hand. 'We might as well introduce ourselves. It seems that the bridegroom, like all bridegrooms, is too flustered to do it.' And dropping a kiss onto Clive's forehead, she continued, 'I'm Sally. This is my husband, Dan.' For Dan, too, had risen and gone over to shake hands.

Now everyone stood, and things began to fall into place.

'This is Happy – her real name is Elizabeth – but everyone calls her Happy, and this is her husband, Ian.'

Ian bowed over the extended hand. 'Roxanne. Do people call you Roxy?'

'No,' said the bride with a sweet smile, 'no, they never do.'

How ridiculous of him to bow like that as if he were a viscount greeting a baroness! The gesture had been almost ironic.

'And this is Tina, our daughter.'

'What a pretty girl,' said Roxanne.

'I'm not,' Tina said crossly.

'That's not polite,' Dan remonstrated. 'You should say thank you and shake hands.'

Tina bellowed, 'I don't want to shake her hand.'

'She doesn't have to,' Roxanne said.

It was distressing. You got tired of it after a while. Other children didn't behave like this. Distressing.

'Don't feel bad,' Roxanne said gently. 'I've been around kids. Mothers always feel bad when kids act up.'

At this point Oliver resumed charge. 'Well, Clive, I must say you have good taste. Now that we've seen your beautiful wife, you must tell us something about her. Are you from Scythia, my dear?'

'Oh, yes. My family's always lived here. We've all worked at Grey's. I work in the shipping department.' She spoke easily and frankly.

Sally liked that. Most girls coming into Hawthorne in these circumstances would be intimidated. Obviously, this girl was sure of her own worth. She had traded her exquisite body for the right to be here. That was evident enough. You might not approve, but you had no right either to condemn. At any rate, the situation was interesting, a minor drama.

Clive put his hand over Roxanne's and corrected her. 'You did work there. In the shipping department. You don't anymore. We have bought a house, Father. It's not far from here, on Brookside Road, about two miles out.'

'I'm flabbergasted.' And Oliver shook his head in bewilderment.

Dan looked at Sally. *He must be*, the look said.

'We'll take possession next month. In the meanwhile, I have someone working on the furniture.'

'Oh, it's simply gorgeous,' Roxanne cried.

'And in the meantime you'll be staying here?' asked Oliver. 'Or with your parents, Roxanne?'

'Parents? I only have my father, and I darn sure don't want to go back to him.' She gave a hearty laugh with her head thrown back. 'No, I'm starting a whole new life with Clive.'

No comments were made, no one spoke, until Clive entered the silence with an announcement that they would be away on their honeymoon during the next month.

'We're going on a cruise of the Greek islands. After that, Italy. Venice and the lakes, Como and Maggiore.'

'Ideal choices for a honeymoon. Some of the most beautiful places in the world,' Oliver said agreeably.

Unlike Ian, whose outrage was almost palpable, Oliver had, typically, regained his equilibrium in these few moments. His thoughts, however, could only be imagined as he regarded his son and his new daughter, the son so exceptionally unattractive at the moment, sweating in collar and tie through the midday heat, half slumped on the sofa and dwarfed beside the cool, graceful girl. The contrast was grotesque. Characters out of Dickens, Sally thought.

'If only you had come earlier and had dinner,' Oliver said. 'But we must have some sort of celebration, anyway. A little supper tonight instead.'

'We'll have to postpone it till next month, Father. From here we're going to drop in at Roxanne's father's for a minute and then catch the plane to New York to spend the night before we fly overseas tomorrow.'

'Very well, but we can't let you go without some festivity. Ian, will you go to the kitchen, please, and ask them to bring up the champagne from the cellar? And plenty of it. Perhaps some little cakes or biscuits or whatever they have. You're boiling red, Ian. Don't you feel well?'

But Ian had already rushed out of hearing.

Meanwhile, Happy invited Roxanne to take a short tour of the house. 'Women always like to see houses, don't they? And this is the kind that will never be built again, I'm afraid.'

'Oh, I'd love to. I said to Clive when we were coming up the driveway, this place must have cost a fortune. More than a million, I'll bet. Not counting the furniture, I mean. Am I right?' Roxanne asked, turning to Oliver. 'A million at least?'

'I really can't say. It was built right after the Civil War. The value of money has changed considerably since then.' Graciously, he smiled.

And again, Dan's glance met Sally's. It was as though they were automatically exchanging their similar impressions. Oliver would in his propriety be shrinking inside at such a question concerning his home. But considerate gentleman that he also was, he would accept an accomplished fact. He would make the best of this marriage.

Gathered now in the library, they waited for Oliver's 'festivity' to begin. Growing slightly impatient, he asked what Ian was doing.

'Gone for the champagne,' Dan reminded him.

'I didn't expect him to bring it up himself.'

'Oh, this is a gorgeous house. And this is a gorgeous room,' cried Roxanne, looking around at the carved stone mantel, the beamed ceiling, and the tall shelves crammed with curios and books.

'Yes, isn't it?' Happy agreed. 'It's my favorite room in the house.'

'My brother and I used to hate it because we had our piano lessons here, and neither of us was very good at piano. In fact, we were terrible. But your mother, Clive, was a pretty fair pianist and spent many evenings at that piano. Of course, you fellows didn't appreciate it then,' Oliver said with a kind of twinkle toward Clive and Dan, 'but you did develop an ear for music by listening to her. Even in the one year you spent here before she died, Dan. Yes, this room is filled with memories,' he finished gravely.

Then abruptly, he turned cross. 'Where the dickens is Ian anyway?'

Dan rose. 'Shall I go see?'

'No, no, sit still.'

There followed a few seconds of another stilted silence. Roxanne was the one to break it, murmuring as she looked toward Oliver, 'So many books! I guess you must have a book about everything in the world.'

'Not quite. But more than I'll have time to read during my lifetime.'

'Oh, you shouldn't say that, a man as young and healthy as you.'

Sally felt a sudden sympathy for the girl, which was odd because, gold digger that she must be, she had dug so successfully and wasn't in need of anybody's sympathy. Yet Roxanne was on display, at the judgment seat, and she was trying very hard.

Dan would be amused to know of her sympathy. 'You'd take pity on a man who mugged you,' he always said.

'Father has a book that tells about Scythia almost two hundred years ago. Would you like to see it?' she started to say, but Happy, who had the greater talent for making conversation, was ahead of her.

'Father's been all over the world, Roxanne, and he's brought back some wonderful things. Come look at these. Every coin in this tray is from Rome, before Christ.'

'I don't believe it,' said Roxanne with appropriate awe.

'Oh, yes. And look over here at these porcelain flowers. This rose is my favorite. There's even a drop of dew on it. Isn't it lovely? And daisies with a petal beginning to curl. And over here, why – where's the carousel, I wonder? There's the most marvelous car – merry-go-round. Where has it gone?'

Tina cried out, 'In my house. It's mine.'

'Yours, darling. Really?'

'Yes, it's in our house,' Sally said. 'A present for Tina.'

'Mine, mine, mine!' Tina shouted, jumping up and down. 'And you can't have it,' she whimpered.

'Of course it's yours,' Clive reassured her. 'A present for a sweet girl. Come sit on my lap the way you always do, and don't cry.'

'I don't want to sit on your lap. I don't like you.'

'She doesn't mean it, Clive,' Dan had said, seeing that he was injured. 'You know her better than that. That damn carousel,' he muttered aside to Sally, 'has made more trouble. The child's obsessed with the thing.'

'Well, here we are,' said Oliver at sight of Ian, followed by the cook and the houseman, who had very likely been roused from an afternoon nap. Between them they rolled a two-tiered cart with a double-sized bucket containing three bottles of champagne in ice and a silver tray of assorted biscuits and miniature iced cakes. The newlyweds were brought to the fore so that the two servants might give congratulations and receive thanks, after which they disappeared. The family festivities began.

It was Ian rather than Oliver who suddenly undertook the role of host. It was he who filled each flute, who had remembered a glass of lemonade for Tina and who made the toast.

'To the lovely, happy bride,' he cried, raising his glass. 'May her dreams come true. Trite but traditional. Right?'

Softly, his father corrected him. 'It seems that you've forgotten the groom, Ian.'

'Oh, have I? Sorry, Brother. Accept my apologies. I'm always so moved by the sight of an innocent young bride that I don't think straight. Here, let me replenish your glasses. Not ready yet? Well, I am. Here goes. To Clive, hardworking, faithful, brilliant Clive. You deserve the best, and we can all see that you now have it. Good luck, Brother, from the bottom of my heart.' And he gave Clive a hearty slap on the back.

What was this all about? And Sally saw that Happy also was bewildered.

Clive rose with dignity and began, 'It's hard to put into words how I feel and I know Roxanne feels, too. It's like a dream – '

A cough convulsed him. Gasping and choking, bent in two, he was racked from head to foot. Roxanne sprang toward him, but Oliver waved her away, saying calmly, 'Let him be. He does better alone.'

When Clive ran from the room, Dan remarked, 'He'll have these spells until he stops smoking.'

'He'll never stop,' Ian retorted, 'unless he develops cancer or something.'

To Sally the remark was nothing less than brutal. A fine thing to tell a bride! Yet Ian had always been capable on occasion of such insensitivity. And probably Roxanne, to judge by her remark about her father, was used to it, for she gave no sign but merely waited for Clive to come back. After two or three minutes, teary-eyed and exhausted, he returned.

'Okay now?' she asked him pleasantly.

He gave a weak smile. 'Okay. Sorry, everybody. Let's go on with the party.'

Happy and Sally passed plates of biscuits and cakes. When Tina took three at a time instead of one, Sally did not remonstrate; there had been enough commotion for one day.

Ian was still presiding over the champagne, urging everyone in a loud and bullying voice to drink up. 'Come on, what is this, a meeting of the temperance society? It's a wedding feast, folks. This is Taittinger that we've got here, and you're letting it go to waste. Well, if you won't, I will.'

Gently enough, Happy protested. 'You're getting drunk, Ian.'

'Well, I need liquor to wash these biscuits down. It's a man's privilege to get drunk if he wants to. At weddings you're supposed to get drunk, anyway. And I don't give a damn.'

Oliver said sternly, 'But I do. This is no way to behave, to welcome – '

'Welcome!' Ian cried, not seeing his father's grim expression. 'That's it! I haven't welcomed the bride. May I kiss the bride, Clive? A chaste, brotherly kiss? You won't mind?'

'I should say that's up to the bride,' Clive replied.

Although Roxanne had pulled away, Ian seized her and, turning her resisting head with both hands, kissed her roughly on the mouth.

'Ian!' gasped Happy.

Oliver took Ian by the shoulders. 'Now, sit down and cool off,' he said. His anger, although he did not raise his voice, was powerful. 'My son is not a drinker,' he explained to Roxanne, 'and I apologize for him. The champagne has gone to his head.' He smiled wryly. 'Champagne has a way of doing that.'

'It's all right. All well meant,' she replied nicely.

With Ian restrained and safely planted in a chair next to his father's, Oliver steered the conversation toward Greece and Italy.

'Since you're going to the lakes, be sure not to miss Isola Bella. Take the morning boat,' he recommended, 'before it gets too hot. I hope you have brought or will find a shady hat, Roxanne. You will need it.'

'I've already thought of that,' said Clive. 'But thank you, Father.'

'Clive thinks of everything,' said Roxanne, squeezing his arm.

Sally thought, Every move she makes is seductive. Is it an art or are you born with it? Some of both, probably. I would photograph her from the back with that long neck and a quarter face, eyes almost shut to show those lashes –

Ian made a dreadful sound. His face had gone from bursting red to greenish white. He got up and ran. Then when they heard a crash in the hall, everyone else got up and ran.

''S'all right,' he said, stumbling up. 'I tripped. Need bathroom.'

Dan took him by the arm, saying quietly, 'He'll be fine. Let me take care of him.'

Happy wrung her hands. 'I can't imagine what's got into him. He's never in all our years been drunk like this. He doesn't even like liquor all that much.'

'Only gambling,' Oliver said, trying to laugh, trying to inject some humor into the situation.

They all went back and sat down.

'Let's see, where were we? Oh, at Isola Bella. Now, when you drive from there to Venice, you must show Juliet's balcony to Roxanne.'

'The real one?' Roxanne was excited. 'It's still there?'

'Well, so they say,' replied Oliver. 'But Juliet was only a character in a play, you know.'

And the conversation, like the proverbial ball, went gently back and forth with everyone making sure to toss enough balls, easy balls, to Roxanne.

Presently Dan returned with a report. 'He's all right. When he threw up, he felt better. I made him lie down for a while, then I gave him coffee, and he's gone home. He left apologies to you all. We'll drive you back with us, Happy.'

'My God, you didn't let him drive? You should have called me to take him.'

'He insisted, Happy. And he says it wasn't only the champagne. He hadn't been feeling well before he drank it. He thinks it's a stomach virus, and he'll be perfectly fine resting at home.'

'Well, I don't know – '

'He was quite able to drive, Happy, otherwise I wouldn't have let him go.'

The party had wound down; Roxanne was looking at the gold watch on her wrist, and Clive was making a little speech of thanks. Everyone went out to the driveway to see them off, and as soon as their car was out of sight, went back to the porch to discuss them.

Oliver began. 'Well, I must say, I was stunned. Somehow one never – at least I don't – think of Clive as a man who would do something so impetuous.' No one present was able to disagree with that. And Oliver continued, ruminating with his eyes fixed on the trees at the far end of the lawn, 'How can they possibly have met? She doesn't seem uh, uh, the kind of girl he would – well, not like you two,' he finished, turning toward Happy and Sally.

Happy's remark was typical of her. 'She's certainly a friendly person, not that you would expect her to be unfriendly, coming here like this. I mean – well, I mean she wasn't shy, was she? I remember when I came to visit you, Father, I was scared to death.'

Oliver smiled. 'Worlds apart. But she's Clive's choice. We must only hope she makes him happy.'

'Oh, I do hope it will work out,' Happy repeated.

'I have a hunch it will,' said Dan. 'She's so vivacious that she may draw him out of himself. Besides, face it, it's in her interest to make him happy.'

'Time will tell,' said Oliver. 'We will all do our best to smooth their way, I'm sure.'

Sally exclaimed, 'No wonder he was so interested in decorations the other evening at our house! It seemed so out of character. He seemed tense, too, as I think of it. Tense, and excited.'

'Yes,' said Oliver. He sighed. 'Clive has always held a special place in my heart. Not a warmer place than your husband, Happy, just different.'

'I understand,' she said soberly.

'I know. Working with children as you do, of course you understand.' He looked out again toward the far trees. 'The thing is, Clive was never a joyous child, never one who did much laughing. Nor does he do so now. Ian was the rascal who gave me more trouble as an adolescent. Clive never gave trouble. But I never worried about Ian. I always knew he'd turn out fine. Life was an adventure for him, everything came easily, athletics, popularity, and graduation with honors. And finally, a wife like you, Happy. Clive, well, Clive was different, as we all know.'

'Still, I'm worried about Ian, Father,' Happy said. 'He certainly wasn't himself today. He hasn't been for weeks now. Ask Dan. You must have noticed something at the office, Dan, and been puzzled, I imagine.'

'I noticed,' Dan admitted, 'but I won't say I'm so puzzled. Shall I speak frankly, Uncle Oliver? I know it upsets you to hear about business arguments. You want things to run as smoothly as they did when you and my father had the business, and when you had it later, alone. But they're not running smoothly now.'

Sally longed to speak her mind, but it was not her place to give public opinions about Grey's Foods any more than it would be Dan's place to interfere in her work. She could have her private opinions, though, and she very well had them. Ian, efficient and industrious as he was, had streaks of laziness and greed. Big, wide streaks.

'He's still growing up. He hasn't quite gotten there yet,' she had once remarked to Dan. And laughing, he had asked her whether she thought he ever would.

'But he's a good guy at heart,' Dan said, 'good-natured, kind to the employees, and wonderful to Happy.'

True enough, but the performance this afternoon had been horrible, not so much that he had drunk too much, but because he had been mean. Yes, mean. Even if the marriage had looked ridiculous to his eyes, it was disgraceful to let it show like that.

'Ian's determined to sell to the foreign buyers, and my sister encourages him,' Dan said emphatically. 'She's giving him another reason, with her demands for money that we can't afford, to press for the sale. If it weren't for her,

I really think Ian might be talked out of it.' And Dan pressed on, perhaps too boldly, Sally thought. 'We all know how precious that forest is to you, Uncle. Your grandfather bought that land piece by piece. And it's precious to me, too. We think alike on that subject. We'd do anything to preserve it. If only you would talk to Amanda, I believe it would help so much. Some words from you – '

Oliver twisted in the chair to face Dan. 'Amanda is – but I don't want to speak against your sister, Dan,' he said.

'You won't hurt me if you do. Anything you say will be fair, I'm sure. It always is.'

'Dan, I'm sorry. This isn't the time. In fairness to us and to the women here, we've been all talked out this afternoon. And I'm sure Happy wants to get home to Ian.'

All at once, Sally gave a cry. 'Oh my God, where's Tina?'

'I don't know,' Dan said, looking puzzled. 'She was just here, wasn't she?'

'She must be inside,' Happy said calmly. 'She's probably eating the last of the pastries.'

In the commotion that Clive had brought about, they had quite forgotten the child. Now Dan and Sally went back into the house, first to the library, where they did not find her, then calling through the rooms, living room, dining room, front hall, back hall, even Oliver's den, still calling. There was no answer.

'Did you look upstairs?' asked Happy.

All three clambered up the stairs into bedrooms, sitting rooms, and bathrooms. Now they looked in alarm at each other.

'She must have gone outside,' said Oliver, who waited at the foot of the stairs. 'Let's not get frantic. She has to be here.'

The pool, thought Sally. Dan, obviously with the same thought in mind, had already raced toward it. But there it lay, bright blue in the strong light, and so unruffled that the bottom was clearly seen.

Without a word now, the four adults spread out through the grounds. Hawthorne had greenhouses, garages, vegetable and flower gardens, and in the center of the rose garden, it had a little summerhouse. So they went calling and calling everywhere, while their terror mounted.

'Let's try the house once more,' suggested Happy. 'Perhaps she's hiding. Children think that's so funny. It's a game.'

They found her sitting under the piano, concealed by the heavy curtain that fell behind it. She was just sitting there, sucking her thumb.

'What are you doing? You scared the life out of us,' Dan cried.

'Yes,' Sally said. 'We called and called. You should have answered us.'

Happy tried to soothe. 'You were making a little house for yourself to hide in, weren't you, honey?'

Tina gave Happy a blank stare and did not answer. Evidently, this was no jolly game.

Sally knelt down. 'Do you feel all right?' she asked, putting her hand on her daughter's forehead. 'Maybe you had too many of those cakes. Does your tummy feel all right?'

Tina looked up at the adults and did not answer.

Happy, who sometimes spoke to children as her grandmother had spoken to her, said kindly, 'Cat got your tongue?'

'What's wrong with you?' demanded Dan.

Tina was not only refusing to answer, it seemed almost as though she wasn't hearing.

'This isn't funny,' Sally said, although no one was even smiling. And a chill went through her. The little girl had withdrawn herself from them all. Perhaps no one else but a mother could sense that something very strange was happening to Tina.

'She's tired, that's all it is,' said Oliver, after a few minutes of fruitless appeals and commands. 'Better pick her up, Dan, and take her home.'

Then Tina was picked up, unprotesting, and was carried home, still without having spoken a word.

CHAPTER

—— 10 ——

'Oh, you darling!' Sally said.

Susannah had sat up straight for the first time without toppling over backward. Pleased with herself and with her new perspective of the world, she gurgled. What a love she was, plump and pink and bare, except for her diaper. With the creases at her elbows and dimples on her knees! Her eyes, almond-shaped and light like Dan's, not green nor gray nor blue, but a little of all, were fixed on Sally in a studious gaze, as if she were thinking, You look so different from the way you did when I was lying down looking up at you.

Sally took her out of the crib and kissed the back of her neck. 'You darling,' she said, 'I love you, I love you. Do you know how much? No, of course you don't. And what's more, you never will until you have your own baby.'

Far, far in the future that will be. And in the meantime, we will watch you, sweet Susannah, care for you and guard you every minute of your life. Please God, let nothing ever harm you.

Last week a baby bird had fallen out of the nest in the curve where the roof met the roof of the kitchen wing. Every year a new family had made a house in that spot. Every year she and Dan had watched the dun-colored mother sit patiently for two long weeks on her eggs, while the rosy-headed father flew back and forth on his errands. When tragedy struck, Sally watched the two parents' frantic flutterings over the blind, naked weakling, half the size of a human thumb, that lay

139

struggling and dying on the grass. She watched their vigil, heard their peeping cries and recognized their grief. You might not call it grief in a human sense, and yet they had wanted to save their baby.

To lose a child to sickness or to death is the worst thing, the very worst . . .

'Mrs. Grey,' Nanny said. 'She's got another one of her no-talking spells. I can't get a word out of her this morning.'

'It's the second time this week, isn't it?'

'The third. I can't for the life of me figure it out. I've never seen a child behave this way.'

She must not show alarm to Nanny because it was contagious, and everyone in the house must clearly ignore what Tina was doing. Those were Dr. Vanderwater's instructions. Tina's refusal to speak was simply a device for getting attention, and the way to stop her was not to pay attention. Ultimately, she would find it didn't work.

'I simply don't know what to do, Mrs. Grey.'

Sally said quietly, 'You do know what to do. Nothing.'

'What's the trouble?' asked Dan, who was late for work.

'The same. She won't talk.'

His slight frown deepened the pair of vertical short lines between his eyebrows. 'I don't know,' he murmured, as if to himself, and reached out to caress Susannah's head. Nanny, seeing that there was no helpful advice forthcoming, went back downstairs to take care of Tina's breakfast, leaving Sally and Dan alone. They were both looking at the baby; neither spoke until Dan began.

'We're seeing the same thing. She looks just like Tina at that age.'

'Yes.' And then a painful cry flew out of Sally's mouth. 'Oh Dan, what are we going to do?'

'I don't see what else we can do but follow instructions as we are doing.'

'These silences of hers are so *senseless*. I can only think, sometimes it seems as if she wants to punish us.'

'Punish! For what? What in God's name have we done?'

'I don't know. She seems so defiant. The way she looks back at me when I say something and she simply refuses to answer.'

'Ah, Sally. Defiant? She's five years old.'

'It's possible. Children defy you when they're two. And yet sometimes I do think it's not defiance. I think she's just plain scared.'

'Of what? There's nothing to be scared of. Unless Susannah's done it to her. That's what we've all decided, isn't it?'

'Tina's getting worse, Dan. Let's face it. And if the new baby's the reason, I should think she'd be getting better instead.'

'Not necessarily. Not at all.'

'Well, then, give me your reasoning.'

'No, you give me your theory.'

At the changing table, Sally was diapering Susannah. For a moment she did not answer him. Then, although not quite certain of her answer, she gave it anyway.

'Sometimes I think we should take her back to Dr. Lisle.'

'No, and again no. That makes no sense.'

'Why? Dr. Vanderwater isn't getting anywhere.'

'Everyone knows that behavior problems aren't like a broken leg. You can't say, "In six weeks," or whatever, "we'll be ready to take the cast off." Give the man a chance.'

'I have a hunch he's worried himself. Or perhaps, baffled would be more accurate.'

'Hunches aren't worth much. And I doubt that Vanderwater is very often baffled, either. He's the best man in his field that we have here. Dr. Lisle can't come close. She's not in his league.'

Sally felt hopeless. The day wasn't an hour old, and already she was spent. When, after laying the baby in the playpen, she turned her face to Dan, he saw that her eyes were filled with tears.

141

'Ah, Sally.' And putting his arms around her, he pleaded, 'It kills me to see you like this. It's not like you. Listen, honey. We have no choice. Patience is what this is all about. And thank God we don't have a Down's syndrome or one dying of cancer.'

Sally shuddered against his shoulder. 'I know. But there are other things. Not like those, but other things.'

'I hope you don't mean that stuff Dr. Lisle put in your head.'

'I'm not sure. I keep having crazy thoughts.'

'Yes, and they are pretty crazy. I thought you'd gotten rid of them.'

'I thought I had, too.'

'We're not going to make any changes, Sally. You can't keep shifting a child from one doctor to another every time another idea pops up in your head.'

'I don't like to leave you so despondent, but I have to go to work,' Dan said, releasing her.

'I'm seeing Dr. Vanderwater this morning, you know.'

'Good. I hope he'll ease your mind.'

Each time her eyes left the doctor's face, they met the four sturdy, curly-haired boys in the photograph. Wholesome, they were, grinning and twinkling. The youngest, holding a ball between chubby hands, was laughing wide, showing his neat baby teeth. Tina had used to look like that not very long ago . . .

'With all respect to you, Doctor,' Sally said. 'I have to admit that I haven't entirely put out of mind that other possibility.' She stopped. It was difficult to go on, and this very hesitance on her part made her angry. She, Sally Grey, who had always made her own way in the world and who had trembled before nobody and no situation. Now look at her!

And in a quivering voice, she went on, 'I have such dreadful dreams, Doctor. Tina was standing in some high place, a window ledge or a precipice, and I wanted to catch her or call to her, but I was afraid that if I should startle her, she would fall, and anyway, I wasn't able to move, my voice wouldn't work – ' She broke off. 'I'm sorry. My dreams are hardly relevant. It's only that I'm so afraid.'

'Because of that other diagnosis?'

She looked away from the man's serious scrutiny to the wholesome boys and said very low, 'My husband thinks it's absolutely ridiculous, and he's very smart, so maybe it is ridiculous.'

'Well, tell me why you can't put the idea out of your mind other than what you've already told me, that Tina is no better than when she first came to me.'

She said hastily, 'Oh, I don't mean to complain – ' when Dr. Vanderwater interrupted, 'I'm not sensitive. If you have a complaint, say what it is.'

'That's just the trouble. I know these things take time. I know it perfectly well. But there have been changes. Not wanting people to touch her. For instance, my husband has a cousin, a man she used to love. Now she won't go near him.'

'You said she doesn't want "people" to touch her. Do I understand that you are singling out this man?'

'Well, yes and no.'

The doctor smiled slightly. 'In my experience, an answer like that generally means yes. What is it about him in particular?'

She was feeling inept. What she had to say was vaporous and unconvincing, even to herself.

'He's odd,' she said lamely. 'Unmarried until a few weeks ago. Reclusive. Just – just queer, that's all.'

'Your description fits a good many of the world's geniuses. It hasn't anything to do with being a sexual psychopath.'

'I know. But he's always paid so much attention to Tina, hugs her and puts her on his lap and gives her presents. I'm not making it clear,' she apologized. She was making Clive sound like Santa Claus.

'I understand you. I haven't changed my own opinion at all, but since you have these feelings, the most I can suggest is what I suggested before: Keep watch over the child, as I'm sure you do. I certainly don't want to close off any possibilities. Evil does spring up in unexpected places. It can be anyone, even fathers, although I don't think it is anyone.'

She was horrified. See the dank, dark pit where my thoughts have led me. The shame, that even for the fraction of a second such a thing should flash into a person's head. And she closed her mind, snapping it shut as if she were locking a box, and throwing away the key.

'I'm going on vacation for a month, Mrs. Grey. Meanwhile, you know what to do. Try not to let yourself act too disturbed, either by tantrums or silences. As your husband wisely said, patience is everything.'

Yes, she had probably sounded foolish to have mentioned without any evidence worth a penny her 'husband's cousin', and she was overcome with shame. Poor Clive, married now and apparently, for the first time in his life, really, really enjoying life. 'He walks around the office now as if he'd won either the Congressional Medal or the lottery,' Dan had said. On the other hand, a man could be married and still –

Then she thought, This is preposterous. The seed Dr. Lisle had sown had grown into a giant, strangling jungle weed inside her head. Clive, Ian, Uncle Oliver, Nanny's nice son who comes to visit, the handyman who brings his little boy, that neighbor near her parents' last summer – preposterous all. Yet what about the father of Tina's friend Emma down the road? He's a strange, unfriendly, dour man. I never really liked him –

'Oh my God, stop it, Sally!' she cried aloud.

Clive's house was charming. Lila Burns had performed a miracle in little less than a month, Sally thought as Roxanne showed Happy and her through the completed rooms. Lila, given the magic wand of money almost unlimited, had filled the house with oriental rugs and handwoven carpets, with polished brass, English silver, and French porcelains, with eighteenth-century mahogany and curly maple, and nineteenth-century genre paintings. Clive had known what he wanted, and Lila had understood perfectly. In the dark red den, one wall was almost covered with gilt-framed horses. In the blue and white living room, the fireplace was bordered with flowered tiles. Scarlet gladioli stood in a jug on a chest between the windows.

Roxanne put a tray with iced tea and cookies on the table and sat down. The August day was miserably humid; one felt it even in the air-conditioned room. Sally's skin was clammy, and her dress clung to her, yet Roxanne in white linen looked fresh.

'I love your dress,' Happy said.

'Do you? It's from my trousseau. Clive picked it out. He buys everything for me.'

'You're lucky he has good taste,' Sally observed. 'Now, if I had to depend on Dan, oh, that would be something! He says, "That's a nice dress, is it new?" "No," I say, "it's four years old."'

The women laughed. Conversations were moving easily among them. Ever since Roxanne and Clive had returned from their wedding trip, the two older women had made an effort to welcome her. And Sally, who always tended to analyze motives, her own as well as other people's, concluded that this particular motive stemmed from well-bred courtesy, a practical need for family peace, from curiosity, and from compassion. A strange mixture!

And so, with that compassion, she tried to imagine the need that had propelled Clive into this sudden marriage. She tried to imagine the kinds of deprivation that had turned the young woman sitting opposite into one who would 'settle' for a house and some jewelry in return for Clive. She was surely not in love! It could not possibly be for her what it had been for Sally Grey on that day in Paris six years ago, and still was.

Roxanne remarked, 'Don't summer afternoons make you lazy!'

Summer afternoons. Henry James had called those the most beautiful words in the English language. But that depended somewhat, didn't it, on where you were spending the afternoon, on who and where you were: a girl packing cartons in a vast, noisy shipping shed, or a lady drinking iced tea in her own cool, blue and white room. And a rush of pity, contradictory and perverse, traveled through Sally's veins.

'Sometimes I don't know myself,' Roxanne remarked. 'Sometimes I wake up and for a minute, I don't know where I am. Or, if I do know, I think that this can't ever last. All this money Clive spent – ' She clapped her hand over her mouth. 'Sorry. He says you aren't supposed to talk about what things cost.'

Sally laughed. 'That's right. Don't talk about it. Just let people see it.'

'What I like about you,' Roxanne said, 'is your sense of humor. You see right through things.' She paused, looking thoughtful. 'Oh, I do want to do everything right! Clive's been so good to me. Did you know he's paid for my sister to go to camp this month? And he's arranging to send her away to school. She wants to go to Florida, so he's asking about a school down there. He's been so good to us.'

'It works both ways,' Sally said. 'Dan tells me Clive's a different man in the office. He used to be' – and about to say 'laconic', she changed to 'quiet' instead – 'very much to himself, you know. But now he tells about how you feed him, what a great cook you are and how you took care of him when he got sick on the ship, and – '

Happy interrupted. 'Clive was sick? I didn't know that.'

'He was having coughing spells, as usual, but one night he really couldn't stop, so we got the ship's doctor to give him some medicine. The cough stopped, but he had some fever with it, and his ribs hurt. "Smoker's cough," Clive said.'

Happy loved medical conversations. At home she had a

shelf filled with popular books of medical advice. She said now, 'I disapprove. What Clive said doesn't matter at all. It's what the doctors say that matters. He ought to look into it, Roxanne.'

'Well, the doctor told him to do that as soon as he got home, but he's stubborn, he hasn't gone yet. I think he's having too good a time with this house.'

And with some other things, too, Sally thought, a small, ribald smile barely touching her mouth.

'Clive said you had a special recipe for chocolate cake, Happy. I was wondering whether you'd give it to me. I love to cook, you know.'

'Why, of course I will. Get me a pencil and paper. I'll give it to you right now. Those two brothers are perfect fiends for chocolate.'

'She certainly doesn't look domestic, but you never know,' said Happy as the two visitors drove away together.

'She's a fast learner. Did you notice what she said about not mentioning the price of things? Clive's transforming her. Even her speech is changing. She didn't use one swear word all the time we were there.'

'She'll soon be too elegant for you and me,' Happy laughed. 'You should have heard me the other night when I cracked my elbow on the corner of the bathroom counter.'

'Remember what she said about her father that first day? She must have had a horrible life.'

'I was awfully embarrassed not to know that Clive had been sick while they were away. That's Ian's fault. He's so annoyed about that marriage that he won't mention anything concerning Clive. And it's not as if Ian were the kind of man who'd care about a society match or anything.'

'No. Although he did make one himself, didn't he?' Sally teased.

'Big deal. You know what I meant. With all respects to Oliver, Ian's not like Oliver in that way. I can't understand why he's acting like this. He hasn't even been in Clive's house, and it's over a month now. I've told him he's being damned rude. Practically everybody we know has been there. Of course, they're all curious, we know that. But what's the difference?'

'Does he explain himself at all?'

'Oh, he hinted something once about a man's buying a wife, and if that's what a man wants to do, good luck to him.'

'I hope so, and to her, too. You really can't dislike her. At least, I can't.'

'I have a feeling it's not going to be easy sailing for them. I have a feeling that Clive's a sick man, sicker than he wants to admit.'

It crossed Sally's mind that Happy might also have feelings about Tina. She had, after all, seen and heard plenty at the nursery school. But Happy would be too polite to speak of the subject unless spoken to. And Sally, resolved to preserve Tina's privacy, had no intention of speaking to anyone.

Back to the current subject of Clive's marriage, she reflected, 'It's really extraordinary. Dan never expected him to be married at all, while I never ruled it out. People marry so much later these days, although goodness knows we didn't. I expected him to bring back some quiet, unobtrusive intellectual out of a library or a laboratory.'

'Well,' said Happy, repeating in her careful way, 'it just goes to show, you never, never know, do you?'

In the airy, mirrored dressing room, Roxanne stood looking at herself. Clive was right. Simplicity was richer-looking. And with a grimace, she remembered the red satin dress, too slippery, too loud, too ruffled, too low-cut, that she had worn at their first dinner. This plain white linen, which had cost three times as much as the other, was far more flattering to her skin, her figure, and her hair.

Carefully, guarding against lipstick stains, she took it off and put it away. Three sides of the large closet were lined with clothes, silks, cottons, linens, a Scottish tweed suit ready for fall, a leather jacket bought in Italy, and shoes and bags and the pale straw hat in which she had been married. Three or four times during every day she was drawn to this closet simply to look again at all her beautiful things. They made her so happy! As she had said, it was like a dream.

Yet, when you wake up from such dreams, you are not always happy . . . She thought: The truth is that I feel – well, I feel nasty. I feel as if I had stolen all this. Well, haven't I? Can he really believe I went mad with love for him? Or that I am dying for night to come so that we can get into that Chippendale or whatever-you-call-it bed together? It isn't exactly comfortable to know that you're a liar or to put on a smiling act when you're taking a walk or eating your dinner, a passionate act when you're in bed. Yes, I feel nasty.

She walked to the window. Below lay the rolling lawn and the stand of spruce with which Clive said he had 'fallen in love'. Colorado blue spruce, they were. Well, a tree was a tree. But they were pretty.

She walked back thinking, as long as he didn't know the truth, as long as he was never hurt, was it so bad of her, after all? Poor guy. He tried so hard to please. There was so much kindness in him. It made you want to be good to him. She would never hurt him, never take his happiness away. It would be, as they said, like taking candy from a baby. No. She would satisfy him in every way. She would pay her bill fairly.

The visit today had gone very well. They were nice women, not snobs at all. A lot of women in their place would be. Damn right they would be. Women were cats, especially if you were better-looking than they were. But these two were not cats.

It took some acting, though, to be natural in front of Ian's wife. Now came that nasty feeling again. Funny, it had never bothered her before to think about her. But seeing the woman was another matter. Still, things like this happened every day. You read about it in the advice columns all the time: The wife goes to the office party and shakes hands with the polite secretary, while the husband looks on . . .

But what a wonderful thing it would be to have this house and Ian, too! There was a simmering in Roxanne's chest, as if her blood were heating up when she thought of what could have been – if only he had been willing. What was wrong with the man? They were mad about each other, couldn't stay away from each other. Her blood began to boil . . . She had to calm herself.

'Calm down, Roxanne,' she said. 'Put on a pair of shorts and go lie in the hammock with a magazine.'

It was growing cooler now. A wind was making a delightful, sleepy sound above her head. Slowly, she began to feel the loveliness of this green peace. Slowly, it was bringing ease to the tumult within her. After all, you couldn't have *everything*, could you? So she would close her eyes for a while, then get up and make a chocolate cake, a surprise for Clive's dessert. It was a pleasure to see how he enjoyed desserts.

'Well, well, Sleeping Beauty. Wake up, you bitch.'

Ian, wearing a business suit, had set his attaché case on the ground and folded his arms across his chest. He glowered. For a second when he moved, she thought he was going to strike her.

'Don't look so scared, I'm not going to kill you, although you deserve it. But you're not worth my spending a lifetime in prison,' he said.

Her heart was hammering and pains like pinpricks darted all through her body from arms to legs.

'Well, have you got anything to say for yourself?'

She had to wet her lips, her mouth was so dry, before she was able to reply. 'I could ask you the same.'

'Go ahead and ask it. This is what I have to say for myself: *I* never lied to *you*. *I* never tricked *you*. I said what I meant, and I meant what I said.'

He was so strong, standing there as if he owned the earth. Like a prince, a lord, with his mouth set hard and his eyes flashing, he defied her. As he always had.

And suddenly, with the pain still pricking, she was emboldened. 'I never tricked you. I told you on that last night that if you weren't willing to marry me, you could go to hell. Plain and simple, Ian.'

'And then you did this. You tricked poor Clive. A bastard's trick.'

'Don't you call me a bastard.' She got up from the hammock and stood tall. 'I haven't tricked him any more than you've tricked Happy.'

'There's no comparison, you fool, you sneak thief,' Ian shouted.

'I think there is. And anyway, shut up. Clive may be coming home any minute.'

'What difference does that make? I have a right to visit my sister-in-law at her new home,' he sneered.

'I wondered how long it was going to take for you to get up enough courage to pay a visit. It was beginning to look mighty queer.'

'I was afraid you'd have a heart attack when you saw me.'

'You're the one who seemed more apt to have one the day we went to your father's house.'

'That wasn't my heart. It was an attack of nausea. I wanted to vomit. I did vomit. That any woman could be so foul as to pull a dirty stunt on a poor, unsuspecting jerk like my brother – '

'"Jerk"? You used to tell me he was a genius.'

'In mathematics. You know damn well what I mean.'

'Well, I don't call him a jerk. The only word you used exactly right just now is "unsuspecting".'

'You mean he has no idea we ever even met before?'

'What are you, a retard? Of course that's what I mean.'

'And what's more he never will know?'

'Of course that's what I mean.'

'Don't be too sure of it. Maybe he ought to know.'

Roxanne waggled her finger, the left-hand finger that wore the diamond. 'Uh-uh. Never. You don't want Happy to find out, so you'll never, never open your mouth. I have no fear of that.'

When Ian was silent, she poked his chest gently with her finger, this time the forefinger, and gave him a smile. 'Come on, let's get along. Here we are, nice and cozy, and your brother's happy as a clam.'

'Make that a lark. It sounds better.'

'You see he's a new person, don't you? He's getting something out of life.'

'And of course you aren't getting anything, are you?' said Ian, looking toward the glassed-in garden room and the little goldfish pool under the willows.

'Oh, I'm getting plenty. I don't deny that's what it's about. But I've made a bargain, and I'll stick with it. He treats me like a queen. And I don't mean only because he buys things like this house. There's a lot more to it than that. He respects me. That's why I'm really fond of him. He trusts me, and I'll never let him down. I swear I won't.'

For a few silent minutes they stood facing each other, facing in each an unbelievable new reality. Ian looked Roxanne up and down from head to foot and back. Unflinching, she looked straight into his eyes.

'By God!' he exclaimed. 'Maybe I do believe you. Maybe miracles do happen.'

'You can believe me.'

'He never asks any questions?'

'What kind does he have any reason to ask?'

'Well, about your mink, for instance.'

'He hasn't seen it. This is August. Anyway, I gave it to my stepmother. It earned respect. My relatives won't dare drop in here or bother us. They'll wait till they're invited. They know there'll be more goodies now and then if they behave.'

'You think of everything.'

'I want to make a nice life here. The neighbors are very friendly. I was surprised how friendly the women were to me the minute we moved in.'

'The Grey name helps a bit, don't forget.'

'I don't ever forget that, Ian.'

'I guess not. Clive spent a bundle here, I didn't know he had it in him.' And picking up the attaché case, he sighed. 'Well, I guess I might as well be getting along home. There's plenty more I could say, but there's not much point in hashing things over. Nothing would come of it. Not that there's much good to come of this mess, anyway.'

'Okay. I have to get working on the dinner, anyhow.'

'So you're an expert in the kitchen, too?'

'What do you mean "too"?'

'You know damn well what I mean. You've hit me where it hurts, Roxy. I can't imagine you and Clive – '

'Cut it out,' she said smoothly. 'I don't want to hear that. Yes, I'm a good cook. I had to be if I wanted anything but take-out food at home.'

'So, what are you having tonight?'

She knew that he was lingering, finding it hard to pull himself away. And it hurt her because she was feeling the same.

Yet, mingling with the ache, there was a sweet thrill of mean revenge as she said calmly, 'We're having boeuf à la mode with horseradish sauce.'

'Gee, you even pronounced it right. Gee!'

'And chocolate cake,' she added, ignoring the sarcasm. 'It's your wife's recipe. She said it's your favorite.'

Ian looked her up and down again. 'You *are* the god-damned limit! Who could ever dream up a human being like you! So you're chummy with my wife, are you?'

'I like your wife. Sally and she have been very nice. Sometimes, though, it does make me feel awful when I look at her and think of what I did.'

'You don't mean that.'

'Yes, I do. And then sometimes, I don't.'

'I'm not going to see you anymore,' he said. 'Ever. You understand that, I hope.'

'But you'll have to, won't you? I'm in the family.'

'No. The men see each other every day at the office, and the women can do what they want. We don't need to meet at night. It comes down to only three times a year, Thanksgiving, Christmas, and Father's birthday. I guess we can manage those.'

'I'm sure we can.'

'So long, Roxanne.'

'So long.'

For a minute or two, she watched his car go down the driveway and pass out of sight. Then she turned around and went into the house to bake the chocolate cake.

He asked himself how he would describe his feelings if he had to. They were a sickening meld of outrage, quiet disgust, and sadness. To think of that sweet flesh, pink as a melon or a peach, to think of all that vitality in Clive Grey's meager arms. It was a physical agony. And with his right fist, Ian pounded the dashboard.

It was wrong, though, to rage at Clive, who was as much a victim as he was. Rage at the victimizer instead, the infuriating victimizer in her white shorts and halter, now safely ensconced in her nest of luxuries.

I like your wife. The gall, the unbelievable gall! Clive said they met at the riding academy. She knew where to find him, all right. Damn her, she must have memorized every casual remark I ever made. She has all the qualities of a great CEO, the spunk, the ingenuity, the determined drive. And what a lover, besides. And what an actress. She has Clive enchanted. He's actually been born again, the dour little man who used to hunch over his desk, who now struts, whistling, down the corridor. In the men's room, they tell jokes about him, the kind of jokes you hear at bachelor parties the night before the wedding.

Yes, she would pull it off, he thought. As she said, she'd made her bargain. She'd slip right into the family and the life, and nobody would be any the wiser. Except himself. And he would keep a thousand miles away from her. She was poison. The most delicious poison . . . And again, he struck the dashboard.

He had almost reached the crossroad leading to his own house, when he had a vision of Happy. He seemed to see her face on the other side of the windshield, hovering there ahead of him with the most lovely expression, that small smile about her eyes that was so familiar. And he thought of her being 'nice' to Roxanne, all innocently being 'nice', all ignorant of her own humiliation before the other woman.

And yet, was it not he rather than Happy who had been humiliated?

Sweating now, he removed his jacket and turned the car around, heading back to the suburban shopping center, where he remembered there was a flower shop. There he ordered two dozen roses.

'Those?' he questioned. 'Those little pink ones?'

'Apricot,' the old man said. 'Old-fashioned, very fragrant.'

'Or maybe those flashy red ones would be better?'

'That depends on the woman. There's the red type, the flashy red, and we all know her. The apricot is for the sweet woman, the one that lasts.'

'Since you're a philosopher,' Ian said, 'tell me. What about some of each?'

The man laughed. He was a very, very old man. 'It never works that way. We all know that, too.'

At home Happy would be at her desk, preparing for the opening of school in September. Her eyes would light when he brought the roses.

'Ian, how beautiful!' she would cry, and then, 'Is it some special day that I've forgotten?'

Yes. Special in its own way.

'I'll take the apricot,' Ian said. 'The sweet one that lasts.'

155

CHAPTER
—— 11 ——

September 1990

In the first weeks of September, through the woods that climbed the hills behind the house, a splash of emerald still lingered here and there among the dusty reddish browns and golden maples. The mild air was filled with the smoky, subtle aroma of fall.

Sally, letting the book drop shut, gazed out of the window toward the yard, where Nanny was entertaining the children. She was leaning down to hold Susannah's hand; now merely a few days past her ninth month, this tiny person was taking her first steps. When she looked up at Nanny, there was astonishment on her face: *Look what I can do*!

Sally had to smile, for most babies begin to walk at twelve months or even later. Then, as quickly as it had come, the smile shrank on her lips. Tina also had started at nine months. Now whenever there was cause for some new pleasure in this second baby, her chortling laugh, or the growing thickness of her dark hair, it was only to be reminded that Tina had done, or been, the same.

At that moment, Tina, no doubt to Nanny's great relief, was occupied in the sandbox. Thank heaven for Nanny, Sally thought. Tina herself was almost a full-time job these days, leaving not nearly enough time for enjoyment of Susannah. But Tina needed her so badly.

Now that the school year had begun, every morning was a battle that the mother sometimes won and the daughter sometimes won. The kindergarten teacher was a young man,

157

one of the new breed of teachers. He was by all reports a talented young man, with a genuine feel for little children's needs. And yet, Tina feared him. There was no reasoning with her.

Dr. Vanderwater, having been informed of this, had been working on the problem. Abruptly then, a week ago, Tina announced that she would not go again to 'play' with Dr. Vanderwater. So where does that leave us? Sally asked herself. You can't very well pick up a child and carry her, kicking and screaming, to where she doesn't want to go.

The only thing Tina really wanted to do was to ride her pony, Rosalie. However, she would go only if Sally would rent a horse and ride with her. Uncle Clive was no longer an acceptable companion.

'I won't. I won't go with him. I don't like him,' she said with, as usual, a stamping of her feet.

There was no need to argue the point even if anyone had wanted to argue it, for Clive had been taken to the hospital three days before with a severe case of pneumonia.

'Don't coax or try to reason,' advised Dr. Vanderwater. 'Stay loose. Let things take their course. If she doesn't want to see me now, let her be. She'll decide to come back. She'll see me as her friend as long as you don't press the point.'

It was plausible advice from an expert. Then why was she so doubtful? The morning's ride, followed by the usual household errands and the unfortunately usual lunchtime tensions, had tired her out, and she wasn't one to tire easily, she who thought nothing of a ten-mile hike. But Saturdays and Sundays were the very devil lately. And retrieving the book, which had slid to the floor, Sally tried once more to read. The book only slid to the floor again while she sat gazing at, although not seeing, the glaze of foliage on the hills.

'You look as if you'd lost your last friend,' Dan said as he came in.

She thought she detected a touch of scorn in his voice. When she turned to him, she saw that it had indeed been there.

'Not my last friend, but I have lost something.'

He gave a long, purposely exasperated sigh. 'Not again, Sally. Or should I say, still? You'd think somebody had died in the house. Buck up, will you?'

Resentful of this rough intrusion, she mocked, '"Buck up." If there's any more stupid expression! What do you think I'm doing? You at least can get away from this trouble for a few hours every day, while I'm here trying to, trying to – ' She groped for words. How to express what she was trying to do?

'I suppose there's no trouble at the office. I suppose all do is sit there, answer telephone calls, write charming letters and sign them, then wait for the checks to roll in. Nothing to it at all.'

'You know I didn't mean that. All the same, anything you may have to cope with is nothing' – And with thumb and forefinger she made an 'O' – 'nothing compared with this heartache. Tina's getting worse, don't you see that?'

'No, I don't. As a matter of fact, she seems a little better.'

'You don't believe that, Dan. It's only your congenital optimism that's talking.'

'Oh, you object to optimism?'

'Yes, when it's just a way of shielding yourself from facts you can plainly see and don't want to see. It's the one trait in you that I frankly can't stand.'

'The trouble with you is you want what you want right now. You want it yesterday. With all your education, you ought to know better. You surprise me, Sally.'

'With all that education, my friend, I do know better. What I know is that your nice Dr. Vanderwater is too casual about what's happening to Tina.'

'Too casual? Are you a judge? What medical school did you graduate from?'

'You don't have to be sarcastic, Dan.' She stood up. 'Listen. I want to go back to Dr. Lisle. I've this minute made up my mind.'

'Then you're out of your mind. What did we accomplish with her? Nothing. Worse than nothing.'

'We didn't give her a chance.'

'Listen to me. The only thing that woman was able to come up with was some sensational horror based on an airy theory. Good God, we've been all over this a hundred times, and I'm sick of it. I don't want to hear any more of it.'

'You're pretty dictatorial this morning, aren't you?'

'No, I'm commonsensical, and I'm the child's father.'

'I'm her mother. Doesn't that count for anything?'

'Really? I thought Mrs. Monks down the road was her mother.'

'Don't be funny. We've got to do something with this child, don't you care?'

'No, I don't care,' Dan drawled. 'My children don't interest me at all.'

'Don't mock me, Dan Grey. I won't stand for it. I have as much right to make decisions in this family as you have.'

'Seems to me you make plenty of decisions. I never stop you.'

'So I want to take Tina back to Dr. Lisle, or somebody else. I want to change, and you're trying to stop me. So don't say you never do.'

'Then this will be the exception.'

'Who says?'

'I say.'

Tears of anger brimmed over onto Sally's cheeks.

'Damn you!' she cried as Dan left the room.

Frustrated and furious, she did not know what to do with herself. She moved away from the window so that Tina would not see her and come in to demand attention that she was in no mood to give. Perhaps a walk, a long, demanding climb up into the hills, would relieve the worry and the anger. She went upstairs to change from heels into sneakers, comb her hair – she did look woebegone, uncared-for – and came very gently down to avoid Dan's notice. Damn him!

She had just reached the front door when he came out into the hall, looking more like his usual self.

'Sit down,' he said, and as she followed him into the living room, continued, 'This is all wrong. We're both worried and unsure, so we're taking it out on each other. We both know,' he said ruefully, 'that this is quite normal. It's what people do, unfortunately, when they're half out of their minds with worry. I'm sorry it happened. Forgive me, Sally.'

Instantly softened, she admitted, 'I'm sorry, too. I've not always been the sweetest lately either.'

'I've thought of something. This is September. Let's be both fair and practical. Let's give this man until the first of the year to work with Tina, and then if we don't find any change for the better, we'll go elsewhere. Either to Dr. Lisle if you wish, or look for somebody. How does that sound?'

'It sounds fine if Tina will go back,' Sally said with some doubt.

'Well, if she refuses, then we'll know for sure that he's not the right person. Maybe it's even possible that between you and me and Nanny, in time she'll straighten out. Shall we try?'

Still doubtful, she nevertheless assented. The suggestion was reasonable enough.

'There's something else that's got me disturbed. Ian and I each had a piece of overnight mail, and that's what took us both to the office on a Saturday morning.'

'I wondered why you went out this morning. What happened?'

'It's Amanda again. Here, I'll read. "I have waited too long already. I made you a proposition last March, and I've heard nothing from you, Dan, but a rejection, a very final-sounding one, and from you, Ian, yet another request for patience. Well, I think I have been very patient. From Clive I never get any answers except that he doesn't take sides, which is ridiculous. I'm tired of waiting for your foreign investors, who may, after all, change their minds. And even if they do not change their minds, who is to say, with you people unable to agree, how much longer I will have to wait for you to straighten out your affairs? No, you'll have to buy me out at the market price or I'll sell my shares to strangers. I've told you that before, but you haven't believed me. My new law firm in New York advises me now –" and so on and so on,' Dan concluded, wiping his forehead. 'So that's another reason why I was in a bad humor, Sally. Things are coming to a head, and I'm so worried, I can't see straight.'

'So you saw Ian. What then?'

'It was bad,' he said gloomily. 'We had a knock-down fight. Oh, a verbal one, but it was bad. Bad. He attacked me as if he had caught me robbing him. Well, the bottom line is that Ian can't resist that offer. He says so himself. "They've made an offer we can't resist." Simply put, it's greed. Never in his life has he complained about overwork! He always loved the challenges. Now he says he's sick of a strike in South America holding up deliveries, and our chocolate business slumping because there's a new European brand in competition and rising costs, and on and on. So if we sell the forest, we can afford to get rid of the business with all the headaches – well, you know,' Dan said, breaking off.

The sight of his distress brought forth Sally's deepest loyalty. 'I think he's disgusting,' she cried. 'To take an inheritance like this and throw it away in the trash!'

'To say nothing of any allegiance to the workers and the community.'

'When is Oliver coming back from France?'

'Not until close to Christmas. He's been invited to stay with friends at their house in the Alps. But it wouldn't make any difference if he were here. He wants no part of this decision, so that's that.'

'Oh dear, are you and Ian really on the outs now? Not speaking to each other? I hate to see discord like this, especially since Happy and I are such friends.'

'It needn't have anything to do with you two. As for me, I

don't see Ian and me having much to say to each other from now on.'

The falling cadence of Dan's voice saddened the room, that room so filled with life, in which chrysanthemums and the last of the roses stood among books and photographs, where a rag doll lay on the floor and an enormous jigsaw puzzle lay on a table. A stranger, walking in, would never imagine that any family who possessed so much could have such troubles.

'I think,' Dan suddenly said, 'I'll run down to the hospital and visit Clive. He's going home tomorrow, so I don't see any harm can come by just filling him in on our fight this morning and maybe getting his opinion. It's time he declared himself, anyhow, one way or the other.'

Clive, sitting up in bed, was glad to see Dan come in.

'I thought you'd be walking up and down the hall, getting ready to go home tomorrow.'

'No, I'm resting.'

'Sure. Pneumonia takes a lot out of you.'

'That it does. You never had it?'

'Not yet.'

'You'll live to a hundred. You're what they call the picture of health, Dan.'

It was true. Fair, pink-cheeked, tall and muscular, Dan was 'the very model of a man', thought Clive. And yet he had never resented that superiority. There was a decency in Dan that made it impossible to feel anything but goodwill toward him. Still, at this moment he saw something in the other's expression that caused him to ask, 'Is anything wrong?'

'No. Why? I only came to see you.'

Clive narrowed his eyes. 'Something's upset you. I see it in your face.'

Dan smiled. 'Pretty shrewd, you are. Yes, Ian and I had a blowup this morning. The same business about the consortium and my difficult sister. Amanda wrote a letter. Or should I say, an ultimatum? I wouldn't be bringing this trouble to you today if I hadn't known you were okay again and going home tomorrow.'

'That's all right. You need to know where I stand.'

'Yes, I realize, of course, that this foreign offer may blow away like hot air, but still we must know where we all stand, every one of us.'

'It's not going away. I've gone over the figures, and from the investment standpoint, they make sense. Those people are very eager.'

'People in town are anxious. Anxious about the Greys splitting up. The news has gotten around.'

'I know. One of the nurses here was worried about it. People, except for the usual merchants and contractors, don't want any new community, and they don't want to lose Grey's Foods, she tells me.'

'Well, then?'

Clive reflected: 'To Father and Dan, the wilderness is everything. Every tree, every little animal is precious. For me, it's not so. As long as I can have a small part of it where my horse and I can be alone, that's enough. But for them, it's everything. If I vote with Dan against Ian and Amanda, the family and the firm will be torn apart. Two against two, through every court in the land. But if I vote with Ian, it will break Father's heart. Either way, it will break his heart.'

Dan, waiting, could not restrain himself. 'I can't understand what's happened to Ian. Although I told Sally it was temptation, the sheer size of the offer, I still can't get it through my head.'

'Power and prestige. This is a tremendous, innovative project. It will be written about.'

'I wish I knew why your father stays aloof. Is it because he really doesn't care?'

'He cares.'

'Then why won't he say so?'

'I don't know.'

'You've stayed aloof, too, Clive, unwilling to declare yourself. May I ask you why?'

Why? Because I was the odd man. Because it was easier not to be involved, to do my work magnificently – so they told me, and I knew it anyway – to live quietly with Father and let them all do what they wanted with the business. It made no difference to me. I needed nothing, a new suit now and then, books, a trip abroad now and then, that's all. It's different now. I have Roxanne. Now I am involved. Now I will speak.

'I'll stand with you, Dan. I'll vote with you. We'll fight it out if we have to, and it looks as though we'll have to.'

Dan grasped his hand. 'By God,' he said, laughing, 'by God, we will. I can't tell you what this means to me.'

'I know what it means to you,' Clive told him.

'We ought to have a meeting with Ian and discuss it, and discuss the next step.'

'Are you sure you're on speaking terms?'

'We're not children, and we'll have to be. We'll certainly have to talk business, as well as keep the firm on an even keel until – well, until when. We can meet at your house any day this week that you feel up to it.'

Clive braced himself. He had not told anyone yet, had not spoken to anyone since the two doctors had left the room an hour ago.

'Not this week, Dan,' he said, wondering how the words were going to sound out loud on his lips. 'Naturally, when you have pneumonia, they take X rays of your lungs. They found a spot in the right lung, a fairly large one, in the right hilum. So then they did an open biopsy. The pathologist did a frozen section and came back in half an hour with the news. It's cancer.'

Cancer. Now he had said it.

'My doctor brought a pulmonary specialist just now to talk to me. They'll have to remove my lung.'

Dan's eyes were wide and sad. It was clear that he was

feeling a genuine compassion. So many people merely act appropriately, Clive thought, merely act.

'I told him I wanted to know the truth, always. If it's spread beyond the lung, I want to know the truth, and he gave me his word.'

'Don't leap ahead.' Dan spoke softly. He reached over to touch Clive's hand. 'It happens far more often that things turn out well than that they turn out badly. That's statistically correct.'

Clive smiled. 'Always the optimist, Dan.'

'No, I'm a realist. Can I do anything for you, anything at all?'

'Only in a negative way. Roxanne will be here any minute. Don't say anything. I want to tell her myself when we're alone. Poor girl.'

'I won't say a word.'

'Tell me, how's my Tina? I've missed her and Rosalie these past few weeks.'

'She's fine. Sally's been riding with her.'

'That's good, but I know she'll be happy to go with me again. I love that little girl. As soon as I get on my feet, we'll have her up at Red Hill, now that the little house is finished. You see, your optimism is catching, Dan.'

CHAPTER

—— 12 ——

September 1990

Clive was an oblong white bundle on the bed, connected to machines by a series of tubes. The intravenous tube was attached to his arm. From the area of his ribs, draining through a larger tube, came a yellow fluid, slightly bloody. Inserted in his mouth was still another tube leading to the respirator that, standing beside the bed, emitted a gentle, rhythmic sound. Pitying, Ian stood looking down at his brother. The man seemed smaller than ever, even shrunken, and his face was a sickly green. Still, what else would you expect of a man who had just had a lung removed? Poor guy. He didn't deserve this.

Desperately, with pleading eyes, Clive was pointing to the tube in his mouth.

'Not yet, Mr. Grey,' the nurse said kindly. 'Twenty-four hours from now we'll take it away and you'll be able to talk all you want.'

Roxanne was on the other side of the bed, looking scared. He hadn't seen her since the day he had gone to the house and found her lying in the hammock dressed in those very short white shorts. Today she was a proper suburban lady, discreet and smart in a gray fall suit with a coral scarf over her shoulders. Having a keen eye for women's clothes, he noted her fine dark brown bag and pumps, the simple gold earrings, and the pale glow of her nails. Recalling the long, dark red claws that she had taken care to display as she rested her hand on a tablecloth, he had to smile to himself.

He had always known she was a fast learner, but this was extraordinary speed indeed.

'Poor man,' she mourned. 'My poor man.'

She laid her hand, the one with the fiery diamond, over the limp hand that lay on the sheet. Ian was thinking, That ring cost him a bundle of money. It makes Happy's look insignificant, and I know what I paid for hers.

'You must have lost ten pounds. But you'll be out of here by Monday, and then I'll fatten you up. I make the best potato soup. Maybe I'll bring you some tomorrow if they'll let you have it.'

Ian said sharply, 'Monday? Who said Monday?'

'Why, the doctor, of course.'

He stood up and went to the door. 'I need to talk to him. I'll go see whether he's in the building.'

'You don't need to. I've already talked to him, and I'm Clive's wife.'

'And I'm his brother,' Ian said, still sharply.

'I know you've already spoken to Mrs. Grey' – this title did not come easily to his tongue – 'but she's only been his wife for three months, while I've been his brother all his life.'

When the doctor's eyebrows went up, Ian knew that he had spoken with asperity, that he had denigrated Roxanne. But the very thought of her taking the position of *wife* to any man named Grey had stabbed him, here in this building where serious matters were treated. His feeling of responsibility for his brother, his feeling of blood tie, had already come to the fore. But he softened his tone.

'You've removed his lung, so my question is, naturally, what is the prognosis?'

The doctor spoke precisely. 'The spot on Mr. Grey's lung revealed, as you know, carcinoma. When we removed the lung, we also removed nodes in the hilum area. We're pretty sure we've made a clean job, gotten rid of everything in the lung area.'

'So that's it?'

'Not quite. He'll need a course of chemotherapy to be on the safe side. Two or three months' worth. And naturally we'll keep in touch with him, taking some bone scans, an MRI, tests as indicated. If we find nothing anywhere else as time goes on, we'll congratulate ourselves that we have succeeded.'

'And that will mean a complete cure? Is that what you're saying?'

'Mr. Grey, there can always be straying, microscopic cells anywhere in the human body that can't be seen. But if after the most sophisticated tests that presently exist we find nothing, we shall emphasize the positive and rejoice.'

'Good. I want to be able to cable something positive to our father. He's on vacation in Europe, and my brother absolutely forbade me to say anything that would bring him home unnecessarily.'

Back in the room, the nurse was washing Clive's face with a cool cloth. The two stood there watching, uncertain, feeling superfluous.

'I think,' the nurse said, 'he'll be going to sleep soon. There's really no reason for you people to stay here unless you want to. He'll be just fine.'

'Well, in that case,' said Ian, 'I'll be going along. You have Mrs. Grey's telephone and my number, too, in case you need us.'

'I wonder whether you might give me a lift home, Ian,' said Roxanne. 'I'm without a car. Yes, dear,' she explained to Clive, whose eyebrows had formed a question. 'Both cars conked out. Yours is still in for a tune-up, and my battery went dead this morning. They told me I'd have to wait an hour and a half for them to come, and since I wanted to get here, I called a taxi. So can you take me, Ian?'

'Of course, no trouble.'

But it would be. Half an hour's ride making conversation with her. He had nothing to say. He had everything to say: you conniver, you second-rate actress – but she was far from second-rate. She was superb. See her now, bending over that poor, balding, sweating head and clinging to that innocent hand. Hear her now.

'Good-bye, honey. Have a good night's sleep. I'm sure they'll give you something to help you sleep if you need it, but look, your eyes are closing already.'

She tiptoed out, whispering in the hall, 'Poor Clive. He looks terrible, doesn't he?'

'What did you expect, to see him dolled up for a day in the country?'

'You have no heart. He looks awful, and I'm worried about him.'

'I have a heart and you give a perfect imitation of a worried wife.'

'Listen, if you're going to yell at me all the way home, I'll take a taxi,' she said as they stood at the curb.

'Who's yelling? I never yell.'

'Well, scolding. I don't have to take it from you.'

'Then don't take it.'

Two young men passing slowly in a red soft-top with the top down looked and whistled.

'Fresh,' she said, tossing her head, then turning to Ian. 'I could take a lift from them, you know.'

'I wouldn't be surprised if you did. Come on,' he growled, 'get in the car.'

She sat down, carefully adjusted the seat belt to prevent a wrinkle in her suit, crossed her legs neatly at the ankle, and rested her hands in her lap. It was a prissy-lady pose for her, whereas for women like Happy or Sally it was simply natural with nothing prissy about it. The comparison amused him. People in their million subtle variations were an endless amusement. Often he did not mind being delayed in an airport because he could always watch people. 'The proper study of mankind is man,' he thought. Or woman . . .

She was staring straight ahead with an intent expression, watching everything, drab women coming out of the cheap downtown stores, clutching their bundles, or sweating men, loading and unloading trucks. Traffic thickened as workers, their long day ending, hurried home. Only yesterday she had been part of all this hard life.

And he thought that she must sometimes awaken in the middle of the night with Clive beside her in the fancy bedroom that he had not seen but could imagine, awaken and be struck with amazement, or with horror at what she had done.

She said suddenly, 'You don't have to sulk.'

'I'm not. I'm driving a car.'

'You haven't said a word.'

'Neither have you. You were looking very solemn.'

'I was thinking, it feels strange to be sitting here with you. And still, not so strange.'

'Let's not go into that, Roxanne.'

'You're right. Would you mind stopping off at the deli for a second? I want to pick up a sandwich for my dinner.'

'I don't mind. That's not much of a dinner.'

'I'm not in a mood to cook for myself. It's too lonesome. This way, I can sit in front of the TV, eat and go to bed.'

He made no comment.

'At lunch it doesn't matter, but there's something about eating by yourself in the evening that is so depressing.'

'Yes,' he said.

Actually, he had not given any thought to his own dinner. Happy had gone to Rhode Island for a couple of days to see her sister and her newborn baby. She would certainly have prepared plenty of food for him, but the prospect of poking around the refrigerator and heating the stuff, then cleaning up afterward, was dispiriting.

While he was thinking this, the traffic light turned red at the very corner where stood the best restaurant in the city. And suddenly he knew he was starved; his mouth was watering.

'I could use a good steak,' he said, 'or maybe a veal parmigiana. Want to go in?' And then, too late, he remembered that this was the place where they had met almost three years ago.

'Yes, but – '

'But what?'

'We shouldn't be seen together.'

'That's ridiculous. Will you get it into your head that I have no designs on you, that there's absolutely nothing to conceal – anything that happens from now on, I mean. Nothing is happening now except that my wife's away and your husband, who is my brother, is in the hospital, and we are having dinner because I'm hungry. I'm assuming you are, too. Are you?'

'Yes, I'm hungry.'

'So. Okay. Let's go eat.'

When other women, not just men, look at a woman, you know she's a knockout, Ian thought as they walked to their table.

'Shall we go to the salad bar first?' he asked.

'No, I'll just order an entree. It's – ' She gave a pretty shrug. 'It's too sad to stand up there. Do you know, I've never been here since I told Clive I don't like this place.'

'Now, what sense does that make? You made your plans, you've got what you wanted, so there's no need for this sentimental moping. I don't want to hear it, Roxanne. I came here to eat.'

'Okay, okay. You don't need to get so upset about it.'

'I'm not upset. Let's order.'

The food was as good as ever, the steak just right, the french fries crisp, and the mélange of vegetables as succulent as any ratatouille he had ever had in France. Without thinking very much of anything, he ate steadily and drank his wine with his gaze fixed on the air behind Roxanne's head.

'We can't simply sit like this without talking,' she said after a while.

'Why not?'

She made an attempt at a joke. 'It makes us look like a married couple.'

No doubt that was true of some married pairs, although it was definitely not true of Happy and himself. She always had things to tell him, not mere time-filling things, either.

Happy was *interesting*. He was uncomfortable in this place, thinking of her. He should not have come here or gone anywhere with Roxanne, and damn it! he knew it. Why had he done it?

'All right,' he said, 'since we certainly are not a couple, we don't want to look like one. So let's talk.'

'What shall we talk about?'

'I don't care. Politics. Anything. What's going on in town?'

She thought for a moment before asking, 'What about that big deal, that forest business? Clive's told me you and Dan are sore at each other because of it.'

'Yes, it's a shame. I don't want to be sore at him, and I don't suppose he wants to be sore at me. He's being a fool, though, turning up his nose at money like that.'

'Clive hasn't said how much it is. He doesn't tell me much of anything about the business.'

So Clive had not gone completely crazy. The last thing this lady needed to know about was the financial condition of Grey's Foods. It would be all over the city the next morning. On the other hand, though, she was too shrewd to do that. Anyway, the less said, the better.

'Well, it's a great offer. I assume Clive intends to stick with me?'

'I don't know. He hasn't said. What about this Amanda person?'

'I can do business with her.'

She reminds me of a hornet, he thought. Buzzes and stings. But there's no mystery about what she wants: money. What else? It's what everybody wants except types like Dan. A nice fat lump of money. Travel, see the world, no worries, no sweat. The thing is, be sure of her vote. Be sure she understands that's the only way she can get her money. Keep after her. She's as slippery as an eel.

'Amanda's a bitch,' he said. 'But there are bitches and bitches. Different kinds.'

'You surely don't mean me!'

'Don't twinkle at me. Yes, I do mean you, but you're no Amanda. The only thing you have in common with her is that you're both tough. Smart and sharp-witted. You look after yourselves.'

'We have to, when you deal with men. Excuse me, I'm going to the ladies' room.'

When she had gone, a man came over to his table and whispered, 'Hey, who's that with you? What's going on?'

An old familiar from the tennis club, he had a right to be intimate, and Ian answered with a laugh, 'Nothing's going on. She's my sister-in-law. Did you know Clive's in the hospital?'

'Sure. I've already sent him a get-well card. How is he?'

'Thanks, he'll be all right.'

'I don't get it. Your sister-in-law – you don't mean that's Clive's wife?'

'I do mean.'

'Wow! I wouldn't have thought it of Clive. No harm meant,' he added immediately, as Ian stiffened.

And Ian knew that anger must be showing in his eyes, not anger at this clumsy man, but at the situation. Better get the hell out of here, he thought, before there are any more questions.

Back in the car, there was another silence until Roxanne leaned forward and turned on the radio.

'Do you mind?'

'No, go ahead.'

They were playing old show tunes from the forties and fifties, music from *South Pacific* and *My Fair Lady*. She liked that sort of thing, melody that made you want to sing with it, and lyrics with words like 'spring' and 'moonlight'. Well, you had to admit there was a sweetness to the old songs.

Her hair smelled sweet, too. It had grown chilly, so that

the windows were closed, and in the car's confined space, the perfume was unmistakable. It was a new scent, one that he did not recognize.

'Did you know,' she said, 'that Clive bought me a puppy?'

'No.' What did she think, that men sat around in an office talking about presents and puppies?

'Yes. It's a darling pug, fawn color with blackish cheeks. Pugs were the Windsors' favorite dogs, you know. They had lots of them.'

'Is that so?'

She was so clever, she was so shrewd, and she could prattle like an idiot.

'Well, here we are,' she said as the tires crunched gravel. 'Would you like to come in a minute and see him? He's been alone most of the day, but I couldn't help it on account of Clive.'

That fragrance was overpowering . . . The weather had changed into a real fall night. It was gloomy in these shortening days with winter looming. Funny, he liked winter once it was here. Of course, he loved spring and summer; it was only fall that depressed him. He didn't feel like going home to an empty house, not yet . . . All this went through his mind while Roxanne, already out on the driveway, held the car's door open.

'Coming in?' she asked.

'Okay. You can show me the house.' He could have added, 'Happy says it's beautiful,' but he could not bring himself even to think of her name in this place.

The first thing he remarked was the curving stairway with its wide treads and shallow risers. They didn't build that way anymore. Couldn't afford to. The house was definitely prewar, pre-World War II. The wallpaper looked like Williamsburg, pre-Revolution. It was unmistakably Clive's taste, a little too historical, but very good taste all the same.

There was nothing historical, though, about the kitchen.

Its glossy white porcelain and gleaming copper were all state-of-the-art, newer than new. Clive had spared no cost.

A round, fat puppy that had been lying on its bed in the corner got up and waddled toward Roxanne, yapping a shrill welcome. She picked it up and held it to her cheek.

'Poor Angel. That's his name, you know. Angel. It was my idea and probably silly because angels are girls, aren't they, and he is definitely a rambunctious boy.'

'Don't worry about it. He's well named. Angels are male.'

'They are? That's what Clive said, only I didn't believe it. He wants his dinner. Look, he's piddled on the paper. He's learning fast. Would you like a brandy, Ian? It's in the bar cupboard in the den. The light is on.'

She was talking fast, eager to keep him, afraid he was going to say something like 'No, I'll just stay a minute.' He was, however, quite willing to have his usual brandy in comfort before hurrying home. If she thought there was going to be anything more than that, she was dead wrong. But he really did not believe she had any intention of risking her gains for a night of sex.

The den was warm, as a den should be. Its colors blended as in a stained-glass window; the colors of rugs and chintz and books all ran pleasantly together. Holding the brandy snifter – fine French crystal, too – he walked about examining the room. Out of curiosity he peered at two or three of Clive's books: mathematics, physics, black holes, nanoseconds – he replaced them carefully in their original alphabetical order.

Then, for the first time, it came to him that Clive had never had a place of his own, and his heart was touched. Clive had been holed up at Hawthorne all his life in his father's house. Yet, it had been no one's fault. Or maybe 'fault' was the wrong word, it being no choice of Clive's or anyone's that he had been made as he was. He never liked me, Ian thought, not from the very start before either of us was old enough to go to school. And I? I never paid much attention to him, to tell the truth.

He was just not that important. I hope to God things work out for him now. I hope this dizzy woman will do what's right for him. I hope he isn't as sick as he looked today.

And restlessly, he continued his round of the room, warming the brandy between his hands, observing two very nice landscapes and a photograph of his parents, young and proud together. On another table stood a recent photo of Clive with Dan's little girl on the pony he had given her. The child was already a beauty, he was thinking when Roxanne returned.

She had changed into a short, loose dress of some thin apple-green material, left from summer. Her hair, which had been fastened back with a flat ribbon bow at the nape of her neck, now hung loose.

'I promised to make potato soup for Clive. He'll be able to swallow it tomorrow, I think, once they take the thing out of his mouth. And I couldn't very well start cooking with that suit on, could I?'

Her breasts swayed slightly when she walked. By God, she had no clothes on under that dress or whatever you called the thing. He took up the photograph, saying, 'Nice picture of him with Tina.'

'He's crazy about that kid.'

'She's a beautiful child. She's going to be prettier than her mother, and that's saying something. I always admired Sally,' he said, thinking: Let this one know she's not the only one men look at.

'Yes, but there's something wrong with Tina.'

'Wrong?' he repeated. 'She's ornery, a little bit spoiled, that's all. Lots of kids are and they turn out fine.'

'No, it's more than that. I've been around kids and I have a feeling for them. I went over one day when Sally invited me to look at something that woman did in their house, the same woman Clive got to fix up this house, and the kid wouldn't talk. Wouldn't talk to me or Sally or anybody. I was there an hour and all she did was play tunes on some damn merry-go-round she had.'

It offended Ian to think that any child belonging to the Grey family, even a child whom he himself had thought of as a brat, could have anything 'wrong' with her. Happy had made some remarks to him about Tina, about something going on at Dan and Sally's house, some kind of trouble with their girl. She didn't know what it was exactly; she had only mentioned that they should probably be taking Tina for 'help' – the euphemism for what you did when you were at your wit's end with an unmanageable kid. It seemed that she had been a real brat at the party Happy had given for the nursery school. Too bad. She was a beautiful kid, too, with Dan's light eyes and Sally's thick black hair. You wouldn't think a child only five years old could prefigure the intensely feminine woman she would become.

'I'm no shrink, but –' Roxanne began, when he interrupted, cutting her short.

'You're right, you're not. So let's drop it.'

'Clive wants us to have a baby, you know. He'd like to have a little girl of his own.'

'So? What's to stop you? You've got a ring on your finger. You're all set.'

He knew he was being nasty, nasty and cold. As always, the thought of Clive and her clinging together enraged him.

'I don't know. I suppose I should. I'll have to. Only I do so wish it could be yours. Ours.' And with wet eyes, Roxanne gave him a rueful look of appeal.

He set down the half-finished brandy. 'I told you – ' he began.

'All right, all right. I'm sorry. But you must admit it would be very nice. We'd have a gorgeous baby, the way we both look.'

Ian was thinking, I've always wanted a kid. A boy, especially. But mine would have to be Happy's, never Roxanne's. Why? Because of that streak in her. Not the greed – because, he thought with a bitter unseen laugh, because I guess I'm pretty greedy too – but the streak of *cunning*. I wouldn't want a child of mine to be *cunning*.

'Tell me,' he asked curiously, 'now that you have all this, are you comfortable being a part of this family? You've made yourself into a new person, like the talented actress you are.'

For a moment, she considered the question, and then said seriously, 'I would be more than just "comfortable" if this house belonged to you. Because that would be living with love, wouldn't it?' And seeing his disapproval, she tried a defiant gaiety. 'God knows I don't belong back in my father's house, so since I'm here, I'll make the best of it.'

It came to him that he did not like her at all. And he said wryly, 'A poor best. You poor soul.'

'You always have to be sarcastic.'

'Not always.' He yawned. 'You'll have to excuse me. It's been a long day for both of us. I'm going home.'

'I thought you wanted to see the house. Come upstairs and I'll show you. It'll only take a minute.'

With partial reluctance and partial interest, he followed her while the puppy leaped behind them.

'Let me show you his bed,' she said. 'In here at the foot of ours.'

The low, queen-size bed was dressed in some soft, yellow-flowered cloth, and the dog's bed matched.

'Isn't that adorable? I saw in a magazine that there's a place where they'll make a dog's bed to match your own. Look, he even has a pillow.'

Ian was looking not at the dog's bed but at the other one, the 'nuptial' bed. And the rage, that rage which ever since June he had been fighting so hard that he had almost beaten it down for good – almost – now came surging back. He could taste it in his mouth, stinging and hot as pepper.

'Come look at the bathroom. It's bigger than the bedroom

I had at home. It's got a Jacuzzi and Clive had a skylight put in. What's the matter, don't you like it?'

'Of course I do. There's nothing not to like.'

'Now listen to this. No, come in here. Listen. Even in the guest rooms.' She flipped a switch, and music came pouring out. 'All over the house, anyplace you want it,' Roxanne announced as though nobody had ever heard of such a thing before.

Well, probably she had not. 'Very nice,' he said.

'Clive likes to hear music in bed. It's nice, except that we don't enjoy the same kind. He likes Moz – moz?' she finished, uncertainly.

'Mozart.'

'But he likes to listen to what I like, too. Sometimes we dance. I've taught him. Watch.'

She raised the volume so that the hall and all the rooms were filled with the rock and boom of a band. And moving into the rhythm, she made a glissade down the long hall and returned to Ian, whirling, shaking her breasts, tossing the short, full skirt to reveal what he had known, that she was naked underneath it.

'Well, how about that?' Her eyes sparkled. And suddenly, she flung herself on him. 'One kiss. I order it. Come on. It won't cost you anything.'

The perfume was roses, pine, new hay, warm fruit, warm woman. Her mouth tasted like raspberries. He tried to free himself of her tight hold and wasn't able to because she was strong; then, though he surely was the stronger, he still wasn't able to, and then didn't want to. Even at gunpoint he could not have stopped what had begun. And still with her lips attached to his he picked her up and carried her to the guest room's bed.

The one sane thought that fled through his mind was, Not in there. Not where she lies with him. Then all thought fled.

When he woke up, it was almost midnight by his wrist-watch. Roxanne had been watching him sleep. He rose on his elbow and frowned.

'Don't you know people don't like being stared at while they're asleep?'

'How can you not like it when you're asleep and don't know they're doing it?'

'Ah, don't be stupid.'

'Men always like to think women are stupid.'

He had to smile. Be darned if she didn't sound like Amanda Grey.

'You're so sweet when you smile, Ian.'

At once his smile receded. What had he done? What a dirty business this was! He had felt enough guilt these past years on account of Happy, but now he had committed a double offense. My God, if this business tonight had given Roxanne any ideas, he would have wrecked poor Clive's life. And in what might turn out to be his last few years, too.

'Don't look so miserable, Ian,' she said, reading his mind. 'We're not taking anything away from anybody.'

He got up hurriedly to put on his clothes. He was terribly anxious.

'You said, that day I came here, that you intended to keep faith with Clive and the bargain you made with yourself. If you don't, if you dare – '

'I intend to keep it, Ian. I've grown fond of Clive. But this has nothing to do with him. He'll never, never know,' she said calmly, putting the green dress back on.

How queer it all was! A few hours ago she had driven him to her will, making her will his own, while now he was only tired, fearful, and in a rush to get away from her. And foolishly he stammered, seeking words.

'You – you *actress*!'

'I wasn't an actress just now,' she said. 'That was the real thing.' She looked into his eyes. 'And you know it.'

He almost ran down the stairs. At the bottom she caught up with him.

'You know you'll want to do this again. We owe it to ourselves, Ian. When can we?'

'When your husband's in the hospital.'

'He's coming out soon, so what then?'

'You've got your answer.'

'But we owe it to ourselves. It's not hurting anybody,' she pleaded.

'You forgot to make the potato soup,' he called back when he was halfway out the door.

'Oh my God!'

From the driveway as he got into his car, he saw through the lighted kitchen window that she had put a little heap of potatoes on the table and was peeling them. She was crying.

Well, it was a mess, that's all.

When he let himself into his empty house, the silence roared up at him. Even the dog was gone, for Happy had taken it along so it would not be home alone all day.

When he saw the blinking light on the answering machine, he knew that the voice would be Happy's. 'It's eleven o'clock and I still haven't heard from you, so I think that must mean it hasn't gone well for Clive. I know you won't wake this household after midnight, but please call me first thing in the morning, as early as six. I love you. Good night.'

He clapped both hands to his head. Oh, damn, damn, damn. Then he went up to bed and lay awake, going over the day and the night just past.

It seemed to him that he was like an alcoholic, the kind of fellow who gets along fine without a drink but cannot refrain if he's left alone in a room with a bottle on the table in front of him. Or it seemed to him that maybe he had not reached his chronological age, that he had lingered behind in the collegiate years. To be a steady guy like Dan must be much less complicated . . . Not that Dan was perfect; he was a stubborn bastard. Take this business of Grey's Woods. Stubborn, stupid, sentimental fool.

His mind was hopping from one thing to the other, all these disturbances, Clive with cancer, all crowding in. How could a man sleep? He went downstairs and got the morning paper from the hall table, came back to bed and tried to read it.

The paper was full of trouble. Naturally. Troubles made news. Damn right they made news. He shuddered. He wondered whether Roxanne was any danger in that respect. Probably not. But on the other hand, maybe. She was emotional, quick-tempered, and sorry afterward. He really, really, really did not want to be alone with her ever again.

Yet he knew, and this is what scared him so, that very probably he would be, and then – white legs dancing, huge eyes dancing, mocking, laughing, taste of raspberries on her lips – where are we all going? he wondered. Nothing stays the same, that one knows. Something has to happen. But what?

'Ahhh,' he cried, threw the paper on the floor, and turned off the light. Dawn was already rising at the window.

CHAPTER
—— 13 ——

December 1990

A storm was mounting. Its winds already threatened gale force. Or you might say that a fire, begun with a low crackle in the underbrush, would soon be roaring through the treetops. Unless we can call a halt, Ian thought. But how?

He turned on the desk light and went over the newspaper for the third time that morning.

'It is reported' – and here he gave a snort of contempt for reporters' reports, nasty snoopers all – 'that the two cousins, Ian and Daniel Grey, are no longer speaking to each other but send messages through their secretaries.'

Well, that was partially true. His eyes then skipped to the editorial and read:

> The situation has become complicated by the offer coming from a group of European investors to build a community in the southern section of the woodlands that have been held by the Grey family for considerably more than a century. Added, then, to the family's internal disputes about which rumors are rife, as is only to be expected, given the prominence of the family, is the conflict between preservationists and the proponents of unfettered free enterprise. What concerns us here more than either of the above is the survival of this respected firm that has for so long filled a dominant position in our economic, our cultural, and our philanthropic life. Scythia, and indeed the entire region, farmers, workers, and families, cannot afford the demise or crippling of Grey's Foods. We can only pray that cool heads will prevail to prevent either.

'Cool heads' indeed. How many of you good citizens would turn down a twenty-eight-million-dollar offer so that you would never need to get up by the clock and go to work, never again for the rest of your life? How many, hey? And yet you expect me to do it.

Across from the editorials came a full-page paid advertisement signed by various 'concerned citizens' who had established a Committee to Save Grey's Woods. On the next page came letters to the editor from nature lovers and lovers of free enterprise alike, most of them indignant and even caustic.

He shoved the paper aside and picked up a sheaf of letters, muttering as he read. There was one from Amanda again, an ultimatum until the first of the year, when she would be coming east herself. There was one from her New York lawyers, a top firm, five hundred dollars an hour; she meant business, to spend all that much. Ian's temples pounded. There was one from the consortium's New York lawyers with a photostatic enclosure from Sweden; they, too, wanted immediate action after the first of the year. Even so, they warned, the deal was not to be taken for granted because there were a good many items to be ironed out before conclusion. The last letter came from Grey's Foods' own counsel, three solid pages of cautious analysis.

And tossing them all aside, he jumped up and left the room, banging the door so loudly that his secretary in the outer office looked up in dismay. He strode down the hall and without knocking, burst into Dan's room, shouting.

'Well? Have you done your reading this morning?'

'I assume you mean Amanda's letter.'

'Yes. Two-gun Amanda. And from her lawyers. She'll ruin us.'

'Not necessarily. I'm not yet willing to concede. There must be a way out.'

Dan made him sick sometimes with his calm, blind, stupid optimism.

'The only way out is to go along with Sweden, as I've explained to you a hundred times by now. With this cash, we – '

Dan raised his hand. 'Please. Not again.'

'Well, why the hell don't you listen to me, then? It's our last chance. They're tired of the shilly-shallying. And you sit there like an imbecile! I can't get anywhere with Clive, can't press him, can't even talk to him because he's too sick. So it's two against two, and that's an impasse, and we'll lose the deal but still have Amanda to contend with. We're going to crash. You know something? Grey's Foods is going to crash.'

Dan said with some bitterness, 'I thought you wanted to get rid of it anyway, so you could have a free life while you're young enough to enjoy it, you said.'

'No. I'm perfectly willing to pay for my share and let you run it with Clive.'

'You know Clive and I couldn't run this thing alone even if he were well.'

'He's getting back on his feet. He's only got another month of chemotherapy, if that. And I do think that you two could run it.'

'Well, we can't. And you just said before that he's too sick for you to talk to him, chemotherapy or not.'

'Will you stop nitpicking? All right, so you and Clive can't run it, and it closes up. Liquidates. There's a big difference between that and collapsing because Amanda drives it to the wall.'

'Liquidates,' Dan repeated. He got up from his desk and walked to the window, from which one saw the new office wing, the warehouses, a railroad siding, a load of tomatoes coming by truck from the farm, three trucks departing with cartons bound all over the country, and old Felix, the retired pensioner who still hung about because Grey's was home. A panorama.

Without looking, Ian knew what Dan was seeing. And he knew, too, what Dan was thinking because he had heard it often enough. *All this, so long abuilding, to pass into strange hands. Or, worse yet, and more probably, to be absorbed by some megacorporation, sold off in pieces, and moved away.* There was truth in it as well as pain. Ian felt twinges of pain himself.

But twenty-eight million dollars!

'Let it at least go down with dignity, Dan, if it has to. Better that than letting Amanda wreck it.'

Even from where he stood on the other side of the room, he could hear the long sigh. After a minute or two, Dan turned around. He looked as sad as anyone Ian had ever seen, stricken and sad. But he spoke quietly.

'All right, Ian, I give up. Take charge. Do whatever you think best.'

The afternoon was extraordinarily mild, considering that this was the first week in December. The last few leaves fell straight down in the windless air. Sally and Dan, with Clive between them, walked slowly around the paddock at the riding academy.

'Let's take Clive out Saturday afternoon,' Dan had suggested. 'He's been wanting to visit his horse, and Roxanne apparently has to go someplace.'

He looks terrible, Sally thought. It was not just the baldness, for Clive had lost all his hair except for a sparse circle around a naked dome; it was the color, the fish-white pallor. But they said he was doing very well, as he himself proclaimed. He had been going to the office three times a week after the rest at home that followed each treatment.

'How are you doing?' asked Dan. 'We can sit on a bench for a while if you want to.'

'I guess maybe I will. I'm still kind of weak. It seems years since I was last on a horse's back.'

'You'll be on horseback sooner than you think,' Dan said.

'Oh, I do think. I know it.'

Clive had courage. He didn't want to be pitied. Yet Sally

pitied. When people were brave, your heart went out to them even more.

'I thought you'd bring Tina,' he said now. 'I never see her anymore.'

They had asked Tina to come along today, but she had been going through one of her silent spells, and they had not pressed the matter. Dear God, how much longer, Sally wondered, and lied cheerfully, 'We'll bring her next time. She had a friend over to play, and they were having fun, so we didn't disturb them.'

'Of course not,' Clive said.

They sat for a while watching the horses. The very sick or even those who are recovering are in another world for a while, Sally reflected, imagining that the healthy animals and the clean, healthy air must be a gift of renewal for Clive, that he was sitting there quietly being grateful.

'Father's coming home next week. He telephones every day to find out how I am.'

'Big phone bill,' Dan said, being jocular.

'He wants a few days before Christmas up at Red Hill, did you know?'

'I heard. It'll be fun for a change.'

'I'm glad. I've been wanting to stay at the new cottage. Roxanne and I will sleep there and walk over to the main house to eat. Our first Christmas for Roxanne and me.' He went on ruminating, 'I wish I looked better, though. When I pass a mirror, I get sick all over again. Not that I ever was anything to look at, but now – '

Sally said quickly, 'The hair, you mean? Why, that'll grow back in no time. Don't worry about it.'

Clive turned to her. 'You're very good to me, Sally. I don't believe I've ever told you or thanked you for welcoming Roxanne. You and Happy, too. Ian I don't understand. He came to the hospital, couldn't do enough and still does plenty for me, but he never comes to our house, never asks about my wife. I know he was shocked by the marriage, I'm

189

sure you all were, but that's no reason to be like this. I don't understand.'

'He's been terribly upset,' Dan said. 'I don't know whether you know.'

'I know. I read the paper just this morning.' Clive smiled. 'I know about the letters, too. I found my secretary trying to hide my copies, and I made her give them to me.'

'We didn't want you to have anything to worry about,' Dan said.

'I understand.' Clive paused. 'I know I can speak frankly to you both, so I'll say it. Amanda's another one I don't understand. Of course, I scarcely know her. But greed, hers and Ian's, is beyond me. They already have so much.'

'It's beyond me, too,' said Dan.

'Ian, I'm afraid, is immovable. But maybe Father will be able to convince Amanda when she comes.'

'Maybe,' Dan said.

He knows better, Sally thought. She was so sad for him, and as she looked now into the silent depths of the ancient forest, sad for it, too.

Dan cleared his throat and said abruptly, 'Clive, I've decided. I've thrown in the towel. The Swedes and their crowd, Ian, Amanda – it's a losing battle no matter how you turn. There's no way out.'

'What are you saying?'

'I'm saying that I've told Ian to do what he thinks best. I'm finished with the struggle. And I release you from your promise. Let's make it unanimous with Ian and see what happens.'

'Dan, you can't do that.'

'Can I keep banging my head on a stone wall? Not one wall, but two?'

'I vote for Grey's Woods. I vote against the consortium. It would break Father's heart, and yours, too.'

'Oliver hasn't taken sides, Clive.'

'Only because he doesn't want to hurt anybody. That's how

he is. But I know what's in his heart. I know.' Clive raised his head defiantly. 'I may not look it, but I'm a fighter.' Then he laughed. 'Funny, Roxanne has for some reason been broaching the subject lately. I never thought she was interested, but I guess Happy must have told her something. She thinks I should vote with Ian for the consortium.'

That's odd, thought Sally. Happy never discusses the business with me. It's our unspoken agreement.

'It must be the tempting money,' Clive said, still laughing a little. 'Twenty-eight million. It's a staggering sum by anybody's standards, and I guess when you never had anything – How she appreciates things! It's a pleasure to watch her in the house, bustling around, cooking. She's a marvelous cook, a homemaker.'

Sally was glad that the subject had veered from the business. It had been grinding Dan down, that and the frantic worry over their child.

'She loves being home. Sometimes when she disappears on an afternoon, I miss her so. The house is too quiet until she comes back.'

He seemed so happy, with that tranquil look on his face. Sally had never before heard him speak so openly about himself. It was completely uncharacteristic. And Roxanne, of all people, had done it.

'You know,' Clive went on, 'I never realized how splendid life can be. Just six months ago it all began. Can you picture those fireworks on the Fourth of July, that fierce burst that seems to spread flowers all over the sky? Well, that's what has happened to my life.'

Such poetic imagery coming from this man was astounding. You never knew what you might discover in the most unlikely people! And with shame, she recalled the evil thoughts she had once had about Clive Grey.

He said shyly, 'I have to trust you both with a secret. Roxanne is pregnant. It's very early, and she doesn't want it told yet, but I have to tell someone.'

Dan said promptly, 'Congratulations! That's great. That's just great.'

'I'm thrilled,' Sally said, wondering about the consequences, a father who might die before the child was even born, although they said he wouldn't. But he looked so dreadful.

'I hope it doesn't look like me,' Clive said, not joking.

'There's nothing wrong with the way you look. And it doesn't matter what a child looks like, anyway, as long as it's healthy,' Sally assured him, and meant that from the bottom of her worried heart.

The short winter afternoon was ending. It was time to take Clive home. For a minute they sat in the car watching him as he moved slowly, almost at a shuffle, up the hill, fumbled with the key and let himself in at the door of his gracious house.

'My God, Dan, how sad.'

'Yes. But how he's changed. As dry and sharp-tongued as he used to be, now he's absolutely soft. I don't recognize him. Is it the illness or the woman?'

'Some of each, I suppose.'

At the highest point in the road, where through the bare trees the city's lights were beginning to show, Dan slowed the car.

'My father worked down there, too,' he murmured, 'and his father before him.'

Sally touched his arm without speaking, for she understood that he was already mourning the death of Grey's Foods.

'I'm flying to Scotland the week after next for five days,' he said. 'I have to see about a new product, some sort of mincemeat. Pie stuffing. I'll be back long before Christmas, of course.'

'So you haven't quite given up?'

'We're not buried yet, although I daresay we will be soon, but as long as we're above ground, I'll keep on feeding the business.'

'You have what they call guts, Dan Grey.'

'The first of the year. By then, things will come to a head.'

She could have reminded him of his promise that if by then Tina had not improved, they would make some kind of drastic new effort by the first of the year. She could have told him that only yesterday morning when Happy had come by on an errand and found Tina having a frightful tantrum about going to school, she had gently suggested that perhaps they should see a doctor. 'Have you taken her anywhere?' Happy had asked, and when Sally had answered, 'Not yet,' had repeated the name of Dr. Lisle. 'She's supposed to be excellent,' she had said, and Sally had not replied.

She could have told him all this, but she did not. The day was growing cold and dying. The year was dying. Let it go quietly. After this new year, as Dan had predicted, things would come to a head.

CHAPTER

—— 14 ——

Ian raised the grimy shade and looked out at the parking lot. A wind was coming up so hard that he could almost hear the creak of the Happy Hours Motel sign as it swung. It was only a quarter to four, but the day had ended and the tinselly Christmas festoons around the property were already lit.

He hated an afternoon assignation. It lacked the festive excitement of the night that could give charm to even such a tawdry and depressing place as this.

Roxanne was sitting up in the bed shivering. 'It's as damp as the inside of a goddamn icebox. You'd think they could at least give you some heat for your money.'

Her clothes, as always, had been tossed on a chair. He picked up her new mink coat and read the label of a fashionable New York furrier. This coat was a decided improvement over the one he had given her.

'Here, wrap it around yourself,' he said brusquely. 'By the way, didn't you tell me you had stopped swearing every second word?'

She laughed. 'I only swear when I'm with you. With you I can be myself.'

He knew he was supposed to acknowledge the intimacy in some endearing way. But because a somber mood had come upon him, he did not do it. *After coitus, man is sad.* He remembered having read that in the original Latin when he was in school and snickering over it with his best friends. In all the years since then, he himself had rarely experienced any

195

such sadness, and certainly not after Roxanne. Nevertheless, here it was, a cloud before his eyes and a weight on his shoulders.

Like a robed queen, she now sat wrapped in fawn-colored fur with a narrow gold collar gleaming at the V-neck. After the satisfaction of desire – and make no mistake, Ian, he told himself, you were just as eager as she was – she had settled in for a long, cozy talk.

'Get up,' he said. 'I don't know about you, but I have to go home in time for dinner. We're having guests.'

'I thought you were staying with your father at Red Hill for this week. We went up there last night. I took this afternoon off to see the dentist, ha, ha.'

Roxanne had not yet brought herself to say 'Father', as Happy did. Perhaps it was because she had her own father. Yet Happy had one, too, whom she called 'Dad'. More likely it was that Roxanne was too much in awe of Oliver to say the word. Most people were in awe of Oliver, even when he was at his most kindly.

'We're driving up there tonight after the guests leave.'

This whole business had been Clive's idea, and it was a nuisance. Still, the poor guy had never asked for anything, and actually wasn't asking for much now. Maybe he was thinking that this Christmas season was to be his last. And he imagined Clive sitting there in front of a fire, reading.

'This Christmas will be my first of those family get-togethers that you dread so much. But don't worry, I shall be perfect,' Roxanne said with a little gesture, fingertips to her lips as if kissing, that she often made.

This, too, annoyed Ian. 'Come on, will you get moving? I have to go pay the bill, and I can't while you're still in the room.'

'Okay, okay.' She yawned, stretched, and slid naked out of the bed. As she bent over to pick up her clothes, as she fastened the brassiere in the back with arms akimbo and breasts outthrust, as she raised her arms to put on her sweater, every slow, graceful motion was as studied as those of a striptease performer.

'You don't show yet,' he said.

'Of course not. It's only two months.'

Three weeks ago she had informed him that she was pregnant, and he was still having moments when he was sure he had dreamed it.

'Are you certain it's no mistake? For God's sake, are you certain?' he pleaded.

'I told you I went to the doctor. It's no mistake.'

'I meant, whose it is,' he said, swallowing his disgust at the words.

'You've got some nerve asking me that again, Ian.'

'I have a right to ask. We've only been together three times, once that night at your house, and twice here.'

'Once is enough, my friend. And what is this third degree, anyway? Look at the man! I haven't been with him for the last three months. How could I? Use your head. Yes,' she said, clasping a velvet band on her hair, 'it's been a short, short honeymoon.'

'Don't,' he said.

It was revolting. And he stared back out the window where Roxanne's BMW was parked in full sight. 'He treats you pretty well, doesn't he?'

'What are you looking at, the car? Yes, he does. He treats me better than you did when you had the chance.'

'Don't,' he said again. And he saw Clive lying in the hospital, fastened down by all those tubes, saw Clive lying in a coffin, and whirled around crying out, 'I am so ashamed, Roxanne!'

She was repairing her lipstick. When she was finished blotting it carefully, she answered him.

'It's a little bit late for that now, isn't it? I'll tell you what, Ian. Your trouble is too much conscience. If you had married me when you could have, we wouldn't be in this pickle now.'

Fear drained him. He could feel it pouring through him like ice water, descending into his vitals. 'Doesn't he – won't he question the dates?' he asked.

'No. I've had to let him fool around a little whenever he felt a bit better, but he barely could. It was all in his head. It was nothing. But he doesn't know enough to realize that. Anyway, this is the last thing he'd ever suspect.'

'I feel like dirt, Roxanne.'

'You might at least say something glad about the child I'm going to give you. You must have been wanting one all this time. Most men do.'

'Women think more about it,' he said, dodging around the subject. 'Of course, I hope it will be well, and that you will be, too.'

'You haven't suggested an abortion, I notice.'

'It is not my choice.'

She pressed the subject. 'You could act a little bit glad about the baby.'

Fool. How could he be glad? 'It's the situation, Roxanne. I'm terribly, terribly worried.'

They stood there facing each other, ready to go and yet held back. Yes, he was thinking, I have wanted a child. But not hers. There lay the bitter irony. If it should turn out to be the finest boy in the world, it still would not be his, it would be Clive's. And if Clive should die, she would marry again in a couple of years. Transformed as she now was, the beautiful widowed Mrs. Grey would have no shortage of takers. His thoughts moved swiftly, as swiftly, he thought grimly, as the nanoseconds in Clive's physics books. Suppose, for some reason, she did not want to marry but preferred to cling to him? He would be trapped and tied to her. She would have a hold upon him till the last day of his life or beyond, when the hold would be transferred to Happy. At that last thought, he groaned inside.

'You look like death,' she said.

'Right now I feel like it.'

He was hearing his father's voice: *Your brother's wife!*
That slut . . . And your own wonderful wife, Elizabeth . . .
I should have thought you'd gotten that sort of thing out of
your system before you married. . . I lived a clean life, I had
my fun, although not with my brother's wife. And after that,
your mother was the only one . . .

That was Father in one of his lofty Victorian moments. As
if Victorians actually lived the way they talked! And still, his
father would be rightly horrified by this.

'If you ever let anybody know and Clive finds out, you'll
kill him,' he said.

'Are you crazy? What do you think I'm going to do, put
an announcement in the paper?'

Her eyes were hard. She was angry at him, and he
understood why. A pregnant woman wanted attention and
praise, some acknowledgment from the father of the coming
miracle. And he remembered Dan's pride.

So he said to her very gently, 'Don't be angry at me. A part
of me is glad about the baby, while the other part is what you
see. I only meant, don't even confide in your sister. Don't trust
anybody. Can you imagine what will happen if this leaks out?
Father and Clive and Happy – '

Now she interrupted. 'For her sake alone – not to
mention Clive, whom I care about more than you may
believe – I'd be careful. I'm not as rotten as you may
think I am.'

He interrupted, 'I don't think you're rotten, Roxanne!'

No, she wasn't a 'good' person like Happy or Sally, but she
certainly wasn't 'bad', either.

'She's been very nice to me, giving me her recipes and
everything, when she could have snubbed me. You don't
have to worry, Ian.' She tossed her head. 'Besides, if you
don't believe how good I can be, you sure as hell know that
I know where my bread is buttered.'

This was the more familiar side of her, and he nodded. 'Oh,
I've no doubt you do. None at all.'

She frowned. 'Speaking of that, though, how is my bread going to be buttered if Clive should die?'

'Don't bury the man yet, please.'

'I'm not doing anything of the kind. But people die. And he's sick, and I'm having a baby, so I ought to know.'

'What you're asking me is what's in his will,' Ian said bluntly. 'I don't know what's in it. Ask him.'

People were not supposed to think about wills – although of course they did and always had done so – until someone died. Then they found out what had been left to them.

'That's a hell of a thing to ask a man in the shape he's in. Don't tell me you have no idea what he's done about it. You do have an idea and you just don't want to tell me.'

To Ian, the subject was most distasteful. 'Well,' he said reluctantly, 'he's always said that he wanted to leave something to Tina, and I suppose he must have added Susannah.'

The words had dropped inadvertently from his mouth, and in that very moment, he knew he had made a big mistake.

'The hell you say! Whatever he's got goes to me and *my* kid. Those girls have their own father, not my kid's father.'

My kid's father. Trouble had already started. Most certainly there would be no Grey's Foods stock for Roxanne if Clive should die. That stock was to be handed down, to be kept for the Greys' own blood, from generation to generation. So the question was how much Clive owned outside of the stock. He had always been a saver, and as a money man, he had undoubtedly made good investments. But he had also spent a fortune on that house. It was quite possible that he had spent himself dry. Infatuated to the point of madness, it was even probable. In that case, his widow – *But why do we speak as if he were dead or even soon to die? He might live to ninety, for all we know* – in that case, he would leave her the house, but you can't eat a house, nor can you live on the interest you'd get from selling it, live well enough to satisfy her, that is, now that she had had a taste of plenty. Ian's head was spinning. Roxanne would sue! Sue whom? Why, the father of her child, of course, Mr. Ian Grey.

He began to sweat. There in the chilly room, with his overcoat already on, he burned. Now suddenly this new possibility overshadowed every other trouble. What had been gloomy gray was now blackest black. His fear of losing the forest deal with its bag of gold and his fear of Amanda's raid on the company treasury had shrunk in comparison with this possible, or probable, menace of Roxanne.

She burst into tears. 'Ian! I'm scared. What's to become of me if Clive dies? I don't want to leave the house, everything will be taken away, I'd lose everything, I'd be like Cinderella at midnight.' And she flung herself at him, weeping against his shoulder. 'I know you think that's all there is to me, just two greedy hands, but you do know, don't you, that I've been good to him? I don't only take, I give. I make him happy. You can ask him, he'll tell you how very, very happy he is.'

He wouldn't be very happy if he could hear all this.

Deep, frightened sobs came from her chest; she was panicked. And he patted her back, soothing and murmuring.

'Nobody needs to ask. He tells people all the time.'

'Just when I've gotten used to everything, I have to think about losing it all.'

Unable to disengage himself from her leaning weight and her clinging arms, he stood there. And in spite of all the claims that were tearing at his brain, there was room for some faint pity; she had been plucked from the mud and placed on top of the mountain. No wonder she feared the fall. And he stood there, still stroking her back and murmuring. 'You're way ahead of yourself. You've no need to be afraid.'

She raised her head, reached for the handkerchief in his breast pocket, and dried her eyes, still sobbing, 'I love you, Ian. I always will.'

Mechanically, as if his hand were moving of its own accord, he kept on stroking her back. He was beginning to arrange his thoughts, not even looking at her.

You treat a problem logically, as in geometry. This results from that, and that from something else, and so it goes until you grasp the answer. Now, here what is needed is money enough to keep Roxanne quiet in any and every circumstance. What is needed is to buy out Amanda because if we do not, the result is obvious. So we get back to the forest deal. Now that, miracle of miracles, Dan's given up, the only holdout is Clive, who is convinced, and no doubt he's right, that the sale will break Father's heart. But Clive doesn't know that there's something else that would make a far bigger crack in Father's heart . . . That's what has to be prevented, and Roxanne is the only one who can do it.

'I love you so, Ian. You don't know how much.'

That's right, he thought, I don't know. Everything is in flux. Where money is the issue, who can know?

'I want to talk to you,' he said. 'Let's take off our coats and sit.'

'I have to get home. He's been sitting there alone all day, waiting for me, poor soul. I hardly ever leave him now. He needs me and I feel so guilty about him anyway. He thinks I've gone to the dentist and then to take my sister to lunch. She's back from school. I've got to hurry home.'

'This won't take long if you pay attention. Clive must have told you something about the business. About the people who want to build that new community in part of Grey's Woods.'

'Well, you've told me something, and I've read a little about it in the paper. Clive hasn't said much. I know you've been wanting him to agree with you, that's all.'

'All right, I'll explain more.'

When he had given her the outline of events, making them as simple as possible, she exclaimed, 'Who the hell is this Amanda person anyway, that you're all afraid of?'

'We're not afraid. We just don't want to be tied up in the courts for ten years.'

'Why can't your father talk some sense into her?'

That was a very good question. That Father, with all his prestige and his very bearing, which commanded so much respect in public places before he had even given his name, could not deal with an impetuous, eccentric young woman like Amanda was a puzzle.

'He has a bad heart, and the worst thing for him is to get involved in an argument' was his reply, all of which was true. 'So you see,' he concluded, 'how important it is that Clive not delay the forest deal. That way, we'll get the money to satisfy Amanda, and – ' Here he gave Roxanne a long, serious, significant look. 'There'll be plenty for you whether Clive dies or lives. Either way – and may he live long – we'll establish a trust for you and you'll be taken care of for life.'

Her eyes were wide and glowing, while a little smile went quite out of control and spread across her face.

'But only, only,' he warned sternly, emphatically and for the third or fourth time, 'if you can get Clive to go along. Now, get home and do it. I'm sure you can. You'll know how.'

'Don't worry. He does everything I ask, and he'll do this, too.'

Let us hope, he said to himself. Otherwise, he would have two albatrosses around his neck, Amanda and Roxanne both. Hungry for money, that's all they were. Hungry for money. The curse. The root of all evil. Believe it or not, he didn't even care about having that pot of gold for himself anymore. He needed it only to get rid of them.

'Now, hurry,' he said. 'It's late and they're predicting snow.'

Putting her arms around his neck, she raised her lips for a kiss.

'Roxanne, there's no time,' he said after brushing her lips.

'That wasn't a kiss! When I love you so! I get desperate for you sometimes, do you know that? You're everything to me. If I ever lose you – '

'Roxanne,' he said impatiently as he opened the door, 'come on, come on.'

Still she lingered a moment. 'I've even come to care for this awful room. After all, it's the only place where we can be alone together. When can we do it again?'

'First things first. I've told you what I need. I need you to go back and talk sense into Clive.'

In the parking lot they separated, and Ian sped away. He just wanted to get home to Happy, so smart and pretty and good, a woman who would let him alone, would be content and busy, not whining or crying for love or asking for money.

Clive had been lying on the sofa for most of the day, reading, dozing, reading some more, watching some television, and watching the fire. Now and then he got up to put on a fresh log. It was such a pleasure to see the rush of sparks, the orange flare and then the dying down into a steady, homelike snap and crackle. Once he went into the tiny, perfect kitchen and made himself a pot of herbal tea, which he carried back to the fireside to enjoy with some of Roxanne's lemon cookies.

He loved the cottage. In a very different way, it was just as satisfying to him as his fine house in suburban Scythia. It was a log cabin, an elemental structure, and he had conceived it himself. The forest was all around him, so close that when the windows were open, you were able to hear its rustle. Even on a still day, the forest rustled. Most people didn't know that. And his horses – there were two now, his own and Roxanne's – had stables just up the rise behind Father's house. There was so much to enjoy.

And he was getting better. He felt he was. Slowly, strength was returning. With a little luck, he'd soon be able to ride again. With a little more luck, his hair, such as there was of it, ought to be coming back. On sudden impulse, he went to the mirror in the bathroom. There was no sign of hair yet, only a shiny, knobby skull. When you had hair, you didn't know that a skull was not smoothly rounded like a ball. Oh, it was ugly. He was ugly. Now with his cheeks so thin and sunken, his chin appeared to have receded; even though that wasn't plausible, since chins don't move about, it seemed so. And his teeth looked enormous, like a horse's teeth.

Anxiety wrinkled his forehead. What could Roxanne, a ravishing, radiant woman like Roxanne, really think of him? Truly, in her heart of hearts, in the place that people, no matter how smiling and kind, never do reveal? He worried about it almost all the time. Yet there was no sense in worrying; worry didn't answer your questions. Better simply to enjoy what you had without analyzing the whys and wherefores.

She was having his baby. In spite of the sickness that had attacked him like some savage, lurking criminal, he had achieved this wonderful thing: a baby that belonged to him, to him and Roxanne.

They hadn't made love in weeks. Or was it longer? Between the surgery and all the treatments, he had lost track of time. It must be hard for a healthy young woman like her to go so long without any loving. Well, give him another couple of months, and he would be as good as new.

'I am so happy,' he said aloud, startling the pug Angel, who had been asleep in his fancy basket.

And he reflected that he should have had a home of his own years ago. He should have struck out into the world, maybe not have worked in the family firm at all, or at least not have lived at Hawthorne with his father. You make mistakes . . . Still, he knew quite well why he had made them. Hawthorne was shelter. As a boy, he had come back to it from prep school in misery. He had been no athlete, he had been inches shorter than anyone else, and in the pecking order he had naturally been at the bottom. The pit. Father, understanding, had let him go to the local school and come back to his shelter every night.

My son will be different, he thought. I hope he will look like Ian. But then, a little girl would be so nice, too, a little girl like Tina, chubby and pink. I haven't seen her for so long. I wish she wouldn't stay away.

A car moved into the shed that was attached to the house. She was home. Gladly, he got up to greet her.

'Where were you so long?' he asked. 'I've missed you.'

Now she would have to make boring explanations and answer a hundred questions about her sister's school and whether she'd have to see the dentist about that tooth again. He always wanted to know everything; he acted so *interested* in every little thing about her. It was as if he wanted to eat her up.

She was in very low spirits anyway. All the way home she had been reliving the day. Very definitely, something had changed. Ian had not been loving at all. He had only wanted quick sex, which was not enough; if that was the only thing a man and woman had together, then they had really nothing . . .

'I told you,' she began, and hearing the exasperation in her own voice, turned a smile to him. After all, she did care about Clive and mustn't take her bad mood out on the poor man.

'I went to the dentist, he fixed the filling, it was nothing. Then I met my sister, we had a late lunch, talked till three o'clock, and here I am.'

'So you had a good day. How is Michelle?'

'She's fine. She has a Florida tan.' And reminding herself to show appreciation, she added, 'She sends her love. She can't thank you enough. The school is great, her marks are good, and you're going to see a good report card.'

Clive almost beamed. 'That's wonderful,' he said.

It was plain to see that he really cared. And this surprised her, for why should he care about a girl he scarcely knew? He was full of puzzles.

'I had to creep home. It's just starting to snow, and I get nervous on slippery roads.'

'You look mighty dressed up for a trip to the dentist and lunch downtown.'

'I wanted Michelle to see the coat,' she explained as

she shook out a few melting snowflakes and hung it in the closet.

'Did she like it?'

He was a pest. It was as if he just had to talk, keep talking, to keep her with him, to keep her from walking away out of his sight. Today, she found him especially irritating. It was strange how you could be actually fond of a person, grateful and kind toward him, and still sometimes be so annoyed by his very presence.

'She loved it. And why shouldn't she? It's one of the most beautiful coats I've ever seen.'

'You look like a doll in it. You look like a doll in everything you put on. But you look best without anything on at all.'

Once more, she arranged an appropriate smile on her face and flirted. 'Think so, do you?'

'Yes, I do. I haven't been seeing you like that lately.'

'Of course not. You've been sick.'

'Well, I'm on the last lap. As soon as I reach the finish line, back to normal, I'll make up for lost time, I promise you.'

She flinched. He really believed that she had been missing his embraces, that she was impatient for more of them. But had she not given him every reason to believe that her passionate responses were true? Today, after having been with Ian again, she had to marvel at herself, to wonder how she had managed to fake those responses so well. Now he was becoming physically repulsive to her. She could hardly bear to touch him at all, poor thing.

'You must be starved,' she said. 'I'll have dinner ready in twenty minutes.'

'I thought we'd be eating up the hill with Father this week.'

'Starting tomorrow. I thought maybe you'd like me to give this little kitchen a workout for the first time.'

'You're right. You think of everything.'

Angel came pawing at her foot, and she picked him up to hug and kiss the top of his head. 'Sweet boy. He's hungry too,' she said.

'Come here and give me a kiss. I need one more than Angel does.'

Intending to drop one on the top of Clive's head, which was not silky like Angel's, she met instead an upturned face and pursed lips. They were wet, and when she withdrew from them, she had to force herself not to wipe her mouth with the back of her hand.

'Do let me get dinner,' she said gaily, since Clive seemed on the verge of more kissing.

The kitchen, intended for little more than the preparation of breakfast, a sandwich lunch, or cup of tea, was too small for him to sit down in. At home, he had lately acquired the habit of keeping her company while she cooked. It was enough to drive a person crazy, being watched like that. It would be a relief when he went back to work full time.

A new kind of fear had come upon her. For months she had been free of it; once she had mustered the courage to leave Ian and try her luck with Clive, she had felt relieved and safe, sure that she would be able to make a success out of being Clive's wife. Now fear, with a sickening jolt, had come back and lay inside her, quivering like something alive.

Her hands worked automatically to mix a salad, season the tuna steak, and slice the bread, but her mind was floundering.

You'll be taken care of for life, Ian had said. *But only if you can get him to go my way.* What, then, was the opposite? That she would lose all this . . . Unconsciously, her arm swung out to encompass the surroundings. If Clive should die, she might well lose it. These people knew their way with lawyers and courts. Yes, there was no doubt about it: She had been threatened this afternoon. It was Ian who had threatened her.

Go home and do it. You can do it. And he had sounded so harsh saying it, not like himself at all. It wasn't fair to drag her into their family fights or into their business; she knew nothing about either. By rights, he ought to be protecting her, the mother of his baby. And Roxanne put her hand on her stomach, feeling not tenderness toward whoever was growing there, but anger toward her situation, which she now understood quite clearly. She was losing Ian, his strong body, his power, his humor, his sweetness, his simple *maleness*.

And she loved him so! Her eyes filmed and she blinked hard before Clive should poke his head in at the door. I would have loved him if he had nothing, she thought, and immediately, frankly, demanded: Would I? For a minute she pondered that and concluded that even if his wealth did matter much to her, there was no harm in that, for after all, if she had been a fat, homely woman, would he have loved her? But it was over.

Still, it was not quite over yet! Yes, she was losing him and she was frantic, but perhaps if she could just get Clive to do what Ian wanted, she would not lose him.

In some way, she would have to do it. As she set the little round table opposite the fireside, where Clive had fallen into a doze with his mouth open, she encouraged herself. Slowly, confidence began to build. Clive had always given her what she wanted, so why not this, too? The problem was how to start the subject so that it would seem natural coming from her.

She touched him on the shoulder and announced with a lilt that dinner was ready. He woke at once. Seeing the table so nicely arranged with a pair of candles lit and a colorful platter of fish in a garland of vegetables, he exclaimed as always, 'You know how to do everything!'

'Well, I try,' she said prettily. 'I want to see you happy.'

He gave a luxurious sigh. 'Who wouldn't be happy here with you?'

They were ready for dessert, and Roxanne had not yet found a way to broach the subject. Then a gust of wind shook the window.

'I have an idea we're in for a real storm,' Clive said. 'We haven't had a big snow yet this season, so we're due for one. There's nothing like these woods on the morning after a storm, when the snow has stopped at two feet deep and there isn't a mark on it.'

Here was the opening. 'You do love these woods,' she said, and then, 'Is this the section those people want to buy?'

'Nowhere near here. They're looking at the other side of the river, down near Scythia.'

'That's not so bad, then.'

'Not so bad! I think it's terrible anywhere. These woods should be kept intact.'

'A lot of people don't think so. They say that that company will bring jobs and new businesses to serve all the new homes.'

'Yes, it'll be a short-term gain, but the forest can last forever if you don't touch it. Once you destroy it, you can't replace it.'

He spoke so positively that fear began its quivering again in her chest.

'But it's so large,' she said. 'There would be so much left untouched if you sold the part they want. So you could really have it both ways, couldn't you?'

'No,' Clive said. 'Once you start selling it off, you'll have created a bad precedent. Piece by piece it will disappear.'

'It wouldn't have to. You could say this is the only time we'll do it,' Roxanne persisted. But she had sounded weak, and she knew it.

Clive grinned. 'What's the matter? Are you in the building business?'

'No, but I'm interested. There's so much money involved.'

'Yes, I know. For the contractors.'

'For the Greys, I meant.'

'Since when are you worried about the Greys' finances?'

He looked amused. She knew it was because she had never talked about money before, and it didn't fit his idea of her.

'Well,' she said, 'now that I'm going to be a mother, I'm interested. Not worried, just interested.'

210

'Our baby will be well fed, clothed, housed, and loved. No problem,' he said, still amused.

'I was thinking, with Dan's sister making all that trouble, I was thinking maybe you shouldn't be so sure.'

The look of amusement turned to interest. 'What do you know about Dan's sister?'

Roxanne made a casual gesture, a little shrug. 'Nothing much. Just that she's a real troublemaker.'

'In what way?'

She began to feel uncomfortable, slightly flustered, trying to remember how much she might say without saying enough to entangle her.

'Well, she's demanding a lot of money, isn't she? Her share of the firm's stock. And if you sell to those people, you'll be able to pay her and get rid of her. It seems to me you should do it.'

'We're not selling!' Clive's voice rose. 'Not if I can prevent it. I'm the holdout. I vote against it. I'll tie things up in litigation for the next century if I have to. I don't give a damn. Father does not want it, and I will not do this to him. It's a disgrace. He doesn't deserve to be treated this way. I'm ashamed of them all, my brother, Dan, Amanda, the whole lot of them. Ashamed.' He was almost breathless. Then suddenly he frowned, 'How do you know all this, anyway? I never told you.'

Roxanne became aware of her heartbeat. She had gone too far, had said too much. 'Why, it was in the newspapers. I read it in the newspapers.'

'No. There was nothing about Amanda's demanding anything. There was never any mention of her name in the newspapers.'

'Well, I must be mixed up. I must be thinking of something I heard at Dan's house.'

'Dan said those things? I'm amazed. It's not like him to shoot his mouth off. When did this happen?'

'Not long ago. Only a couple of days, I guess, when I

dropped in at Sally's.' She had never seen Clive like this, never faced his keen scrutiny. And wanting to fill the silence, to divert that scrutiny, she stammered, 'Yes. Yes, it was Wednesday, I guess.'

'Are you sure?'

'Yes, Wednesday. Why are you looking at me like that?'

'It's very odd,' he said slowly, 'because Dan flew to Scotland on Monday.'

Her heart was really pounding now. 'Then it couldn't have been Wednesday,' she said lightly. 'I can't remember everything I hear or see or do. Suppose I ask you or anybody what they did a week ago Friday. They won't remember. People never do. Anyway, what difference does it make?'

'Only that you're lying to me, and I'm wondering why.'

'Clive Grey, I have never lied to you. "Lie" is a nasty word. It's rotten of you to accuse me like this. And such a fuss over who said what, when, and where. A stupid fuss. I'm going to bring the dessert, and let's have it in peace.'

In the kitchen she stacked the plates, got out the cake plate, and poured the coffee. Her knees were absolutely weak. 'You can do it,' Ian had assured her, but she had not done it. And Ian would be furious. Plainly, Clive had made up his mind. And now he, too, was angry at her. It was absurd that the anger of this sick weakling, clearly visible in his eyes, should so frighten her. Or maybe it was not absurd; she had, after all, so much to hide.

Then she decided to smile herself into a good humor. *Smile and the world smiles with you.* You start to feel better. It was possible that things weren't as bad as Ian had made them out to be . . . And she adopted a lively manner to joke Clive into a good humor.

'Here I come,' she cried, 'Madame Roxanne of the Palace Bakery with a selection of eclairs, napoleons –' The telephone rang. 'Sit still, sit still, dear. Let me put the tray down, and I'll answer it.'

Clive had already crossed the room and picked up the

phone. 'Michelle! How nice to hear from you. Roxanne was telling me how well you're doing. You have a Florida tan, she said. Be careful of your skin – '

Michelle. Quick, quick, before she says anything. And Roxanne reached the receiver, crying, 'My sister! Let me talk to her.'

Clive was holding tight to the phone. 'You what? You haven't seen her yet, so how does she know? Wait a minute, let me get this straight.'

'Give me the phone, Clive,' Roxanne insisted, with his elbow barring her.

'Then you did not meet Roxanne today. I see. A misunderstanding. Yes, of course. Well, it's nice to talk to you. No, she can't come to the phone this minute. She'll call you back. Fine. Take care, Michelle.'

Very slowly, very delicately, he replaced the receiver in the cradle. Without speaking a word, he turned and looked at Roxanne.

Unexplainable pictures rise to the surface of the mind and connections are made. In split seconds she found herself in a cave, deep, sunken, and dark, with endless, turning alleys and channels, lost, frantic, trying here, there, but trapped and finding no way out. 'Spelunking,' Clive had said while they watched a play on television. Queer word. Spelunking.

'Well? So you never lie to me.'

Her mouth went dry, and she was sick, nauseated, gasping. 'We did have a date, but I had to cancel it because the dentist took too long. I know it sounds silly, and I'm sorry, but I thought you'd be disappointed if I didn't have something to tell you about Michelle, so I made the lunch story up. You've been so good to her, so interested in her – '

'Please don't insult my intelligence, Roxanne.' Clive was very, very calm. 'Just tell me in a few simple, truthful words where you were all day.'

'Shopping. After I finally got finished with the dentist, there wasn't much time left, so I just went around the stores.'

'I don't believe you, Roxanne,' he said, still calmly.

'It's the truth. I can't help it if you don't believe me.'

'There's something here,' he said to himself, 'but I don't know what it is.'

Then he, too, sat down at the table, resting his chin on his hands and frowning. She watched him, took a bite of cake and, barely able to swallow it, pushed the plate away.

'There's something,' he muttered, still to himself, 'a trail . . . So much information, private information, and this afternoon's "going around the stores". In downtown Scythia dressed in a mink coat . . . Dressed . . .'

He looked over at her, observing the gold collar, which was handmade, twenty-two-carat Greek jewelry, his birthday present, taking in the rose-colored dress, scarcely concealed beneath the tiny apron, just bought a week before, worn today for the first time, as he well knew because he observed everything about her –

'Whom were you meeting today, Roxanne?'

'I met the dentist, for God's sake.'

'Dressed like that.'

'What do you want me to wear, a pair of overalls?'

'Who was the man, Roxanne?'

'Who, the dentist? It was she, Dr. Helen Kraus.'

'I'm not joking, Roxanne. Who is he?'

'You're insulting me. You've got no right to insult me. Who do you think you are?'

'I know who I am. What I'm wondering is, who are you?' He rubbed his forehead as though he were in pain.

'Listen, Clive,' she said, 'you're making a mountain out of a molehill. You'll make yourself sick. It's not worth it.'

'What's not worth it? My trust in you? I want to trust you. It's worth everything to me.' He stood up, grasping the table edge and leaning so far across it that his face approached hers. 'Everything to me, do you understand?'

'You can trust me, Clive,' she said gently.

'No. Not till I clear this up. You saw somebody this

afternoon. You were too late to have spent a whole long afternoon alone in the shops of downtown Scythia. There isn't a store anywhere there that would satisfy you, now that you've become used to better things.'

'You don't have to sneer at me, to remind me where I came from.'

'Don't dodge the issue. I only want you to tell me the truth about where you were today. And I also want to know who told you about Amanda and the company stock.'

He was breathing the smell of fish into her face. She pushed the chair back and stood away from him. He came closer and grasped her shoulders, not hard enough to hurt her but firmly, so that if she were to pull away, her dress would be torn.

'The truth. The truth, Roxanne. Clear this up for me. I don't want to have any doubts in my mind about you. Don't do this to me. I can't bear it.'

The passionate appeal was frightening. There was a look in his eyes that did not seem quite sane. And she whimpered, 'Let go of me.'

'No.' His hold tightened. 'You mustn't play games with me, mustn't do this to me. I love you, Roxanne.'

His hands slipped down to caress her breasts, and his mouth clamped down on hers. It was disgusting, unbearable, and she pushed him away, but not before he saw the grimace on her face.

'Do I disgust you that much because you're thinking of some other man? Yes, that must be it. I know the signs. You've found another man.'

'No. It's your behavior that's disgusting, your suspicions.'

'Then clear them up.'

He had backed her against the wall and was pressing against her from head to foot. For a man so ill, he was surprisingly strong. It came to her that for the rest of her life, she would have to submit to this intimacy. Yes, this revolting intimacy. And it was Ian's fault. When it could have been so different, so wonderful.

215

'Clear up my doubts,' Clive said, with his breath in her face. 'Go on, I'm waiting.'

All her rage, her fears and her grievous disappointment, collected into one explosion, and she burst out, 'I told you where I was this afternoon. As for the other business that you're upset over, I can't see why it's so awful for me to know a little something about the company's troubles. Anyway, for God's sake, what do you think – I mean, how much did he – ' She stopped.

'"He"? Who?' Clive's eyes bulged, and all the color, the sickly color, drained out of his face, which went gray.

So she had done it. In her stress, her stupid tongue had slipped. She was so stunned that for a few seconds there was no thought in her brain. It went blank.

'You've been talking to my brother,' he said.

Thought flowed again. Better come out with a half truth, then get in touch with Ian so their stories would mesh.

'Okay, yes, I met him accidentally and we got talking about the business.'

Clive slumped to a chair. She thought for a moment that he was going to have a heart attack and die right there in that chair. He laid his head back on the pillow and closed his eyes. She waited, still standing flat against the wall.

'He told you to talk me into the sale. Of course,' he said. 'How stupid I was not to have guessed it at once. And that's where you were today, all dressed up. How many todays have there been, Roxanne?'

His voice was dull. It seemed to have its own echo in it, as if he were speaking from far away. Or perhaps it was the pounding of the blood in her ears that made it sound like that.

'It was the only time,' she said.

'Lies and more lies!'

All her strength left, so that her arms dropped limply at her sides and even speech, the very forming of words, was an enormous effort. Her reply was faint. It was unbelievable and she knew it.

'I'm telling you again that I don't lie to you, Clive. This is a misunderstanding, that's all it is.'

If his eyes were darts, they would be penetrating her flesh, marking every entry point with a drop of her blood. She was unable to turn her head away from those eyes, and she stood there as if hypnotized, shivering.

'I'm telling *you* again, Roxanne, not to insult my intelligence. You met him "accidentally" and you "got talking", did you? "Accidentally", eh? Where? At the office, at his house? What do you take me for? Or perhaps you just passed each other on the highway bumping fenders. You, dressed for afternoon tea at the Waldorf-Astoria, except that there is no Waldorf-Astoria in Scythia. Answer me! Where?'

She tried to think fast. Never an accomplished liar, she was, in this terrifying moment, completely unprepared.

'Don't you understand that I know my brother? He never could keep his hands off a beautiful woman. So why should he have kept them off you?'

'He . . . no, you're wrong . . . we didn't . . . we only . . .'

'Ah, stop it, Roxanne. Save your breath. Tell me this, though, was it good with him? Yes, I'm sure it was. Far better than with me.'

And suddenly the angry light that had almost penetrated her body, died out of his eyes; in their place there seeped angry tears. Between the reddening, sore-looking lids, they puddled.

He was so ugly and so pitiable! And seeing him like this she had a revelation of horror at the sight of another human being so wretched. The man was being destroyed in front of her eyes.

She began to talk, hurrying, babbling, 'You mustn't take it like this. Please. There wasn't anything, honestly. We never did anything – '

Without warning then, he went mad. He sprang up, showing his fists. '"Did anything"! You . . . you . . . you lying bitch! As if I don't know, can't see you – you know what I'm going to do with you? I'm going to throw you out for good. I ought to throw you out in the snow right now. I should have known! That day I brought you to Hawthorne, the day after we were married, the way he behaved. I should have guessed something.' His sleeve brushed the coffee cup, which crashed into a brown puddle on the floor. He took the other cup and threw it deliberately to the floor. 'What the hell. The whole house can crash as far as I'm concerned,' he said.

She was aghast, alone there with him. When he confronted her, she cringed.

'I'm not going to hurt you. What do you think I am? But I am going to throw you out of the house, out of my life. If it weren't snowing, I'd do it tonight. You and the baby that isn't mine.'

'You're crazy,' she whispered.

'Then tell me it's mine. Swear on its life that it's mine.'

She could not speak. It came to her that there could be no mending here, that it was really over. Then she thought, I shall have to go to Ian. He's smart, he's resourceful. Yes, that's the word, resourceful. Ian will think of some way to mend this. Or if it can't be mended, he'll think of something else for me.

'Go on, swear on the baby's life.'

She had never been superstitious, yet she was not able to do that.

'No,' she said.

'Of course not. Well, it will be a better-looking child than I can give you, that's certain.'

His voice rang out. She was sure that the walls must be trembling from the force of his rage.

'Don't lie anymore! You're a bitch and you're making a fool of yourself. But you can never again make one out of me. Get out of my sight. I don't want to be in the same room with you. You ought to die. I could kill you. Get in there, where I don't have to breathe your air.'

She ran into the bedroom, the one Clive had so cheerfully

planned for guests. If there had been someplace to go, she would have fled from the house, but the snow was falling steadily, the windowpane was almost opaque with it, and the wind was roaring. She was caught between two dangers.

From the outer room there came the sound of dishes being smashed. In his blind fury, he might have stumbled against the table, or perhaps he was deliberately destroying the house. And remembering that she had not locked her door, she got up. Through the crack, she saw the ruination of the room, and then she saw Clive racing out into the storm. The outside door closed with a mighty slam and this time, the walls did shake with it.

She crept inside and sat down, huddled, on the edge of the bed, too numb now for any thought except how to survive this night.

CHAPTER
—— 15 ——

December 1990

Earlier that same afternoon, when the first tentative light snowflakes began to fall, Amanda Grey was having a cup of tea in Sally's living room.

'I'm so sorry Dan's not here,' she was saying, while Sally, who was curious about this woman whom she scarcely knew, observed her carefully. With the same strong, thick hair and the same lucid eyes, she was a feminine version of Dan. The tense manner and the too rapid speech were certainly not like him.

'My lawyer and accountant will be coming up from New York on Monday,' she said, 'but at the last minute, I had the idea that I'd come ahead of them and visit my brother and his family.'

Sally's lips tightened. The words 'brother' and 'family' seemed inappropriate in the mouth of a person who throughout the past year had been on the attack.

'I suppose I've startled you, barging in like this. I should have phoned ahead.'

Sally had indeed been startled, but she was not going to stoop to any possible argument, so she answered nicely, 'If you had, I wouldn't have wanted you to take a hotel room in downtown Scythia. You could have stayed here. The house is large enough.'

'Yes, I see. It's a lovely house. Your colors keep summer alive in weather like this.'

'This is no "weather", only a few flakes.'

'You're forgetting, and I forgot, how long I've been away.' For a few moments, Amanda paused. 'Yes, it's a long, long time.'

Her voice had the falling cadence that you hear when a very old person exclaims in wonderment at the passage of his years. It did not fit the young woman whose face was brightened by coral lipstick that matched her suit.

Suddenly she became brisk. 'So. Christmas is upon us. No time for looking backward. I tend to get sentimental, and I shouldn't.'

'I don't see why, if you feel that way.'

A pile of boxes in glossy wrappings lay on the sofa next to Amanda. 'Naturally, you won't open the presents yet,' she said, 'but I think I'd better tell you what they are so you can let me know if anything needs to be exchanged. The books are for Dan, and also a box of chocolate-covered orange peel; that was pure sentiment because I remember how when we were still with our parents he stole a boxful from the pantry and ate them all. I hope he still likes them. For Susannah, there's a rag doll with painted eyes, no buttons to swallow, and a baby doll with a whole wardrobe for Tina. Little girls, I remember, really prefer dolls they can wash and dress instead of the beautiful ones that you're not supposed to rumple up. And for you, Sally, there's a hand-knit sweater, black and white, because I remembered your coal-black hair. One of my girls made it. I've gotten her set up with a couple of others in a little children's wear shop. She has real talent, and I see quite a future for her.'

'You were too generous.'

Sally was feeling confusion in the face of this generosity on the part of a woman who was apparently determined to ruin them all. And deciding to be completely frank, she said, 'I have to tell you that I don't understand. I thought we were enemies, that you were very angry at Dan. And now you bring presents.'

'As far as the business is concerned, I am angry. In

fact, I'm furious. But that has nothing to do with Dan, my brother.'

'I'm sorry, but I'm still confused. You've made a distinction between Dan at work and Dan at home. Yet surely there's a wide overlap.'

'There is, but I can't let it stop me from getting my rights.'

'Nobody wants to deprive you of them, Amanda,' Sally said stiffly.

'Then you can't know what's been happening. All this stalling over some foreign deal, while I have to wait. I don't believe a word they say anymore. I've given them to the first of the year, and that's only ten days away, so – '

'I know all that, Amanda. There's no use telling me about it anyway. I have nothing to do with Grey's Foods.'

The woman was a nervous wreck. One foot was tapping the floor and one hand, in time with the foot, was tapping the arm of the sofa.

'Dan will be home tomorrow afternoon late. Perhaps,' Sally said, trying to placate her, 'when you meet face-to-face, you will be able to make peace. It's rather hard over the telephone.'

Amanda was silent, and Sally continued, 'I wish you would all come to terms. Dan's really sad about these arguments, and I know poor Oliver must be distraught, even though he keeps it all in.'

Amanda was staring into space as if she had not heard. With a sudden shiver, she hugged herself.

'Are you cold? There's a shawl on the chair, I'll get it,' Sally said, rising.

'No, it's not that kind of cold. It's inside me. I guess I shouldn't have come back here. I've never had a happy minute in Scythia since I lost my parents.'

People don't usually walk into a house and reveal themselves this way in the first thirty minutes, Sally thought. And she answered with sympathy, 'No wonder you have

---

no happy memories. You were a young girl who had just lost her parents! It must have been even harder for you than for a little boy like Dan. And to become the only female in a male household.'

'It wasn't all male. There was my aunt Lucille. Do you know anything about her?'

'Only the portrait in the dining room at Hawthorne.'

'She committed suicide, you know.'

Sally felt her mouth drop open. 'I never heard that!'

'Well, you wouldn't have. It is popularly supposed that she missed the bridge on a foggy winter afternoon and drove the car into the river. Or else that she had a heart attack. Take your choice. But I know better.'

'Are you saying that you are the only person who knows the truth?'

'Maybe not the *only* one, although I'm sure Dan doesn't suspect, or he would have told you.'

This woman was probably ill. The very mildest adjective one might use was 'eccentric'. Since she seemed to be expecting a comment, Sally made a brief one.

'It must have been terrible for you all.'

'I wasn't there. It happened the day after I left for boarding school. I wanted to go home for the funeral because I loved her, but they didn't think I should. The school thought it was too long a trip, since I had only just arrived, and my relatives – my mother had cousins in California, second or third cousins who took an interest in me – agreed. Aunt Lucille was a sweet, quiet woman, very gentle with me, and especially with Clive. He was a kind of misfit, I remember,' she said reflectively. 'Poor Clive.'

This last remark offended Sally in spite of the fact that she had always thought much the same of Clive. Now she defended him, saying decidedly, 'He isn't one now. He's happily married and doing well, even though he's been very ill. But he's recovering nicely.'

'I'm glad to hear it. I understand that he doesn't want to sell the forest to that group.'

'I don't know.' Sally did know, but she was annoyed at these attempts to draw her out. 'I told you, I don't get involved in the affairs of Grey's Foods.' And then, having given this blunt reply, she softened it by plucking something out of her memory. 'Dan boasts about your college commencement honors. He said you did wonderfully all the way through.'

'Oh yes, but I can't say I had a wonderful time doing it. I was never popular. I was really not very attractive.'

'I find that hard to believe. You're a lot more than merely attractive now.'

Sally was extremely uncomfortable. In truth, these intimate, gloomy revelations repelled her, and she moved to change the subject.

'Would you like to see the house? I'll give you the tour if you want.'

'The house and the children, of course.'

Amanda was appreciating Sally's row of photographs on the wall above Dan's desk in the upstairs office, when Susannah in her pink bathrobe came tottering into the room.

Nanny, following on her heels, cried out, 'Would you believe it? She's getting too fast for me. Hold on, miss, your hair's still wet. Let me dry it.' For Susannah was laughing, wrestling away from Nanny and the towel.

'There. Now go to your mommy.'

Sally picked her up. 'This is Amanda. Can you wave to her, like this?'

Five fingers wiggled toward Amanda, who wiggled back.

'May I hold her, or will she be terrified of me?'

'She'll go to you. Most babies this age are terrified of strangers, but for some reason, this one seldom is. Try her.'

Amanda held out her arms, and Susannah allowed herself to be transferred.

'The beauty!' Amanda cried. 'Look at you! You're adorable. She's adorable, Sally. How old is she?'

Sally said proudly, 'One, and she seems to have no fears.'

Amanda nodded. 'She'll meet life easily, I predict. Look at that smile. Now, where is Tina?'

Nanny answered. 'Playing. She's a bit cranky today,' and she directed a tactful look toward Sally. 'I'm trying to get her downstairs for supper.'

'Perhaps we'd better let her alone, then,' suggested Sally.

'Let's see her,' Amanda said. 'Who cares whether she's cranky? We all get like that. God knows, I do.'

Sally thought it more prudent to explain that something a bit more than 'cranky' was meant.

'We've been having a little problem with her lately. Nothing serious,' she quickly amended, 'but every now and then she has a stubborn spell when she simply refuses to talk. Nothing serious,' she repeated, 'just annoying.'

'I won't be annoyed,' Amanda said.

While crossing the hall, they heard the music-box tinkle of 'The Blue Danube' waltz.

Tina was standing beside the carousel. At the sight of her mother with a stranger, she ran straight out of the room.

'Tina, come back and say hello,' said Sally, knowing very well that no attention would be paid. She turned to Amanda and apologized. 'Yes, it's one of her cranky days. We'll let her go down with Nanny. She'll be in a better humor after her supper,' she explained, without being at all sure of any better humor.

The carousel was still playing. 'Damn thing,' she said, turning it off. 'It's a present from Hawthorne. I get so sick of hearing that tune.'

Amanda had covered her face with her hands. She was just standing there, trembling.

'What is it?' cried Sally.

'That awful thing. That awful thing was mine, a present to me.'

'I don't understand.'

Amanda was staring at the carousel as if she had been stricken and paralyzed.

Sally cried, 'What is it? What's wrong?'

Amanda shook her head. 'Nothing, nothing important. I'm sorry . . . I was just thinking. I'm sorry.'

'But you're ill! It has to be something. You're frightening the life out of me!'

'No, no, forget it. I don't want to come to your house and make trouble.' This was most strange behavior, and Sally wished Dan were there to cope with his sister.

Nevertheless, taking Amanda's arm, she said kindly, 'If I can help you, it will have been no trouble at all. But if you leave me with a mystery after scaring me so, I'll have to say it was a lot of trouble. Please, I need to know.'

'I – I was just stunned for a minute, that's all. It's dreadful for me to come to your house and do this to you. I'm awfully sorry.'

Amanda was looking at Sally with the expression people wear when they are making an estimate or considering a decision to purchase something. The brilliant eyes, Dan's eyes, met Sally's and stayed.

'I have never, never in all my life told this to anyone. And I'm wondering whether I should even tell you.'

'As you please. But whatever it is that can do to you what it did just now should be told to somebody before it goes off like a bomb and blows you apart.'

'I know. You're a very kind woman, Sally. I remember telling you that once after I had seen your photographs.'

'Thank you. I try to be kind.'

Two large, slow tears slid down Amanda's cheeks. 'Many, many times I've thought I must tell, but when the moment comes, I'm never able to.'

'Are you able now?'

Of course Sally was curious; anybody would be. Yet in another way, she did not want to hear more. Her own worries weighed heavily enough.

Amanda drew a long sigh. 'Yes,' she answered. 'I'm able.'
Then she gave a wry little laugh. 'You'd better make yourself
comfortable because it's not a short story.

'It was the sight of the carousel,' she began. 'It was given to
me when I was twelve, a bribe, the price of silence, although
I didn't need it. I would have kept silence anyway. And
I have.

'And there were so many people, friends and those distant
relatives who came to the memorial service for my parents, so
well meaning, so comforting. "You will be in the best home
a girl could have," they said, "living at Hawthorne in such a
family." I was told that over and over. Even the servants at
Hawthorne used to say so.

'Nobody understood why I cried so much all the year I
was there, why I was so rebellious and full of anger. But
I was scared, so scared. I used to sit alone in my room, or
sometimes under a tree with a book that I wasn't able to read
because the words all ran together.'

The words were all running together now, in a slow,
monotonous stream. Amanda's eyes were half shut, her
fingers playing with the clasp of her purse. And Sally was
mesmerized by the sight of her pain, as when seeing on
television a flood of refugees, the walking wounded, and
although you cannot bear the sight of them, you are unable
to look away.

'People tried for a plausible explanation of my behavior: the
horrible deaths of my father and mother, and I only twelve, at
the sensitive start of adolescence. Aunt Lucille could not have
been more gentle with me. Every day she spent hours trying
to distract me with walks, lessons, little trips, dresses and new
books. She didn't know about the nights, nights when she was
downstairs playing the piano or at the weekly meeting of her
women's club . . .'

Finish, finish, Sally said inaudibly. For God's sake hurry
and say what you have to say.

But the voice resumed its own dreamy pace. 'I was in my

bed. He came the first time just to sit on the edge of it and talk. He held my hand, and I was grateful for the warmth of his touch. "You're lonesome," he said, "I will come again." And he came again. The next time he held his hand over my mouth to keep me from screaming . . . At twelve a girl thinks she knows everything about life and sex, doesn't she? But she knows nothing. There's nothing written that can tell you what it is like to have – to have that happen.'

Sally was abruptly aware of her own body, of her heartbeat and rigid spine; leaning forward, as if to hear more clearly, she wrapped her long sweater in tight concealment of that body, as if to protect it. Her frightened eyes fastened themselves on the other woman, whose own drifting gaze went far beyond and away from this place.

'I cannot forget the smallest detail of that room. There was a branch that tapped at one of the windows all that winter. The curtains were white dotted Swiss. The tiebacks were held by painted metal pansies. The clock on the dresser clicked at the half hour and the hour. I used to lie awake to listen for it, listen for footsteps coming lightly down the hall, and then for the turn of the knob. There was no lock on the door.

'One night he brought me the silver carousel. I had admired it and played with it, so he gave it to me. Yes, it was a bribe. There were threats, too. "If you tell, Amanda, nobody will believe you. And God will punish you, anyway, for what you have done." That's how it was.'

A terrible anger surged into Sally's throat, and she thought she was tasting blood. If Clive had done this to Amanda, why not, then, Tina?

'Clive,' she said. 'Clive.'

Amanda raised her head. 'What? Clive? Ah, poor, sad Clive. Of course not. Don't you know that I've been talking about Oliver.'

For an instant, Sally's mind went blank and, uncomprehending, she stared back at Amanda.

'He was right,' Amanda said bitterly. 'He told me no one

would believe it, and I see you don't. You're thinking,' Amanda said, 'that I am hallucinating or that I've had what's called a "recovered memory", persuaded by some incompetent or dishonest therapist that this really happened to me. There are people who truly have recovered their buried memories, just as there are frauds and hysterics, but I'm none of them. I have lived consciously with this every day of my life since it happened, and I swear to you that it is all true.'

'But Oliver. Oliver Grey?'

'Yes, it's like the first time someone tells a child that the man in the Santa Claus suit isn't Santa Claus.'

Amanda stood up and walked restlessly around the room, looking out the window, touching a book and setting it down, cradling a paperweight and putting it back. Then she said, 'You'll need to know how it ended. It was when Aunt Lucille caught him coming out of my room. I think she must have been watching before that night because when he opened my door to leave, I saw her standing right there under the hall light, waiting. Then I heard voices from their room, which was near mine. They had a terrible quarrel, and I heard her crying. I lay there frightened to death, wondering what was going to happen next, even whether I was going to be punished. And I hated him so, I hoped she would kill him.

'In the morning she called me to her. Her eyes were red, and she said it was from her allergy. She put her arm around me and asked me whether I would like to go away to boarding school. "Lots of girls go," she said, "I think you'd like it, wouldn't you? Maybe out in California near your mother's cousins."

'Neither one of us, you see, was able to put the truth out into the light of day. You have to remember that this was in the sixties. People didn't yet admit that such things happened. She was a submissive woman; even though I was only thirteen years old by then, I saw that she was. All the time she had her arm around me, we didn't look at each other. And she went on talking about how she loved me and she knew I would be all right because the school she was thinking of was small and friendly. I would even be allowed to take my dog.

'The night before I left, I brought all the bribes, the gold watch, the bracelet, and most of all, the silver carousel, and dumped them on the floor in his study. The only thing I took with me when I left was my toy poodle, Coco. I didn't want to leave Dan, he was such a little boy, but I could only think of how I wanted to get away from Oliver Grey. So, a few days later, I left. I remember Dan with eyes all round and tearful and astonished. "You're going away, Amanda?" he asked. I don't remember what I told him.'

Still – Oliver Grey! And if this is true – if – then he has done this to our Tina. Feeling faint, she grasped the arms of the chair; then, rallying, she denied the thought. This whole story was preposterous. Oliver Grey?

'I didn't mind so much leaving Dan, since he was having a good time living with two other boys, even though they were older. Aunt Lucille was there.' Amanda broke off for a moment as if to prepare for what was next. 'She was not there long. I want you to know that she was a particularly careful driver. I remember her saying to me one day as she slowed the car down, "This is a dreadful spot for an accident, this sharp curve and then the culvert. A car can skid right into the river. It's a disgrace that it hasn't been fixed." Yes, I remember that well.'

'So you really believe she killed herself.'

'Either that, or she was so distraught that she didn't see where she was going. But I rather believe she did it on purpose, that he had destroyed her reason. She couldn't bear to look at her husband ever again. I'm sure I wouldn't have.'

Sally opened her mouth to speak, but no sound came out.

'I see that you still don't quite believe me. I can't blame you. Oliver Grey, the benefactor. Bizarre, isn't it.'

Then Sally found voice. 'Why did you never tell anyone? All these years, there must have been people you could talk to. Now you come here, and all of a sudden you tell me.'

'I didn't intend to tell you. It was the sight of the carousel that struck me. I can see it still, that shining, fabulous toy, as it stood on a table in the library, reflected in the mirror. Venetian glass, the mirror was, with a delicate fluted border. I see it clearly. He had exquisite taste, that monster.'

'And if it weren't for seeing the carousel just now? You're saying you would never have told anybody?'

'No, I said I never *had* told. In the beginning, when I was at the school, I was still too shocked and ashamed. You couldn't have dragged the story out of me. Later, I tried a few times to talk with professionals who I thought would be able to show me how to be trusting and lovable again. But when I got there, I couldn't speak the words. Then I had worries about Dan and the other boys, too. I didn't want them to suffer the public disgrace.' Amanda smiled. 'Maybe, too, I have a trace of the damn Grey pride.'

The room seemed suddenly too full to contain any more. The walls closed in, the air was thick and sultry with threat. If all this is true, Sally thought, then what else must be true? That he has done this to Tina . . . to my baby?

Amanda spoke into the silence. 'I haven't seen him since I left here. I didn't go to your wedding reception because I couldn't bear to look at him. I'm going to see him now, though. I can't get my rights from the young men, but I'm going to get them from the old one, I promise you.'

Sally forced herself back to the moment, back from the horror that she still could not let herself believe.

'Your rights? The buyout, you mean.'

'Yes, every dollar and cent of it. He'll pay.'

'He has nothing to do with it. He leaves it all to Ian and Clive and Dan. He won't even give his opinion.'

'Of course he won't. He's afraid of me. That's the only thing that's given me any satisfaction, the thought that he's lived in fear of me every day of his life.'

'But that's blackmail.'

'You may call it that.'

'And the rest of the family, the young men, as you call them. What do you think you will do to them?'

'I can't help it.'

So she will bring us all down to have her revenge on him, Sally thought. And she thought of Dan's labor, his pride and satisfaction in running the grand old company.

Yet, can you blame her – if it is true?

'I shiver to think of walking into that house again. That bedroom. That dining room with Lucille's portrait. That big linen closet where I used to sit and hide behind the long tablecloths hung on a rod. I was scared, too scared to make a sound.'

Something happened to Sally. A picture flared: *Last summer under the piano, with the window curtains drawn over her, hiding, dumb . . .*

'I've never had a loving relationship with a man, even a man I love. I still have nightmares.'

Nightmares. The cry from across the hall: *Mommy! Mommy!*

Amanda returned to the window and looked out. 'The snow's coming fast. I'd better start back to the hotel.'

'I guess you'd better,' said Sally, making no move to stop her.

'I've spoiled your day. I'm truly sorry, Sally. It wasn't a pretty story, was it?'

'No, not pretty.'

They were at the top of the stairs looking down when they heard the carousel. Tina must have come back.

River so blue, da da, da da.

Amanda stopped with her hand on the banister. 'Perhaps I shouldn't say this,' she began.

'Say it,' Sally cried sharply. 'Say it. Whatever it is.'

'All right. Did you say Oliver gave that thing to you?'

Sally thought she was falling, and gripped the banister. 'I don't recall what I said. It was a present for Tina, from Hawthorne. We thought it was from Clive. He adores her.

He gave her a pony,' she said, faltering and scarcely able to speak.

'A silver carousel, a museum piece. A queer gift for a child.'

'She – loved it. She said she wanted it.'

Amanda gave her a long look. 'I advise you to see about it, Sally. Yes, you had better.'

As soon as the front door closed, Sally ran back upstairs. 'Control yourself. Don't panic,' she said aloud. And slowing her steps to normal, she went into the room where the carousel tinkled and glittered.

'Time for a bath.'

She spoke cheerfully, lightly. It was important to keep everything normal when you wanted to get at the truth, not press, not hasten, not frighten.

'No,' said Tina. 'No bath.'

'Ah, but it's so cold out, and a hot bath will be cozy.'

'No, I said.'

You don't bribe children. That's no way to bring them up. Nevertheless, Sally coaxed, 'There's a new box of candy in Daddy's office, and you may have two pieces if you'll come nicely and take your bath.'

The candy box was produced, Tina took her two pieces and allowed her mother to undress her. The mother's hands shook as she took off the fancy pink panties, another of Happy's presents, put Tina into the tub, soaked and sponged her. The mother's eyes looked sharply over her child's body, searching for signs. But many things can be done without leaving a mark . . .

Rage and disgust rose to choke Sally's throat. If anyone had dared to touch this vulnerable baby! *Oliver Grey, if you've done anything, I swear I'll kill you* . . . But it was preposterous. Amanda Grey had to be crazy. But if she was not?

'Did you ask anybody to give you the carousel, Tina?' she began.

'I wanted it. Are you going to take it away from me?'

'No, of course not. I was only wondering who said you might have it.'

'Uncle Oliver. He'll take it back, too,' Tina said fearfully.

'Why would he take it back?'

'I don't know. But he would.'

'Would what?'

'Take it back, I said!' Tina cried impatiently.

She must go very slowly. Her words, her motions, must be very calm. Lifting Tina out of the tub, she wrapped her in a bath towel and sat down on a stool to brush her hair.

'You know, what I think about you? I think you keep secrets,' she said pleasantly.

'No, I don't.'

'Oh, I think you do. I think sometimes when people do things you don't like, you don't tell me.'

Alarm passed like a shadow across Tina's eyes, which were quickly lowered to the floor.

'You know nobody loves you more than Daddy and I do. Nobody.'

There was no answer.

Sally put down the hairbrush. Rocking and hugging, she repeated, 'Don't you, darling? And you can tell us anything. We'll never be angry, no matter what. If anybody is ever mean to you – '

'Nobody is.'

'Ah well, that's good. But sometimes you're upset, and that makes me think maybe somebody's hurt your feelings. I wish you would tell me instead of being sad all by yourself.'

There was still no response. Yet Sally went on, with a feeling that she had touched some sore, hidden spot.

'I remember the day one of the children accidentally stepped on your hand at school. You didn't say a word when you came home even though there was a big scratch on your hand.'

She felt, as the silence continued, that she was walking into deeper and deeper waters. 'And then,' she said, being very casual, 'there was the day the carousel came. You began to cry and wouldn't tell me why. That's funny, I thought. Such a beautiful present, and Tina's crying. But maybe you didn't really like it. Maybe that was the reason.'

Tina slid from her lap and screamed, 'I like it, I like it! You're going to take it away. He said you would if – '

'He? Who said so?'

'Uncle Oliver. If I told, he said you'd take it away.'

'Told what, Tina?'

'You know, what Uncle Oliver does.'

Sally shook her head. 'No. Tell me.'

'Takes your panties off and touches you. And if I tell, he'll say I'm a bad girl, I do bad things, and you'll punish me.'

Don't overreact. Don't let her know she has just put a knife in your heart.

'It's a secret, and now I've told!'

Sally swept her up and clasped her, whispering, 'No, no, no. It's all right. You don't do bad things, my Tina. He did bad things.' And in spite of her resolve to be unemotional, she wept.

'Why are you crying, Mommy?'

'Because I love you so . . . You're our good girl. You're the best girl in the world.'

Oh, Amanda. Forgive me for doubting you.

'You mustn't think about that anymore, because no one will ever touch you like that again. You mustn't let them. You know that, don't you? You've heard that many times from Daddy and Nanny and me.'

Stop it, she told herself. You're overreacting. Just say it quietly and then try to wipe it out of her memory – if you can. If you ever can.

'You must never let anyone take off your clothes or touch you ever again, my Tina. Now, let's go and have supper.'

The weather was bad. This fine, dry snow was the kind that lasted. It was a good thirty-five miles still to go to Red

Hill, northward and upward on a narrow, twisting road. A great storm was predicted for tomorrow. But tomorrow was hours away.

She had cleared her mind. There were no thoughts in it. There was only a bloody, red rage. She had no idea what she was going to say when she got there. She had only to concentrate on getting there.

The snow that had begun so lazily, so quietly, was now being driven by a risen wind that whirled against the windshield. On spruce and hemlock it lay in great white bouquets, and the black road was white with it.

The circling winds picked up speed, and the clacking windshield wipers were barely able to keep up with the pouring snow. Although it was still early in the evening, barely seven o'clock, only an occasional car was out, moving cautiously toward shelter and home. It was foolhardy to be traveling away from one's home on such a night, and Sally knew it, but she pressed on. Her sturdy four-wheel drive could make it, had to make it.

And she sat hunched forward as if, on horseback, she were urging the animal to hasten with all its strength toward some rescue, some good.

She watched; five minutes passed, then ten minutes. The minutes crept. She watched the speedometer: thirty-five, forty-five, fifty. The car slid recklessly across the road. Recovering, she slowed down. The car crept.

Houses were few, becoming fewer and fewer and farther apart. This was the forest; those who lived in this area were either solitary types in weathered shacks or city people whose sumptuous hunting and camping lodges were hidden away at the end of gated driveways. Rarely in winter, except for a few days at a time over some vacation or holiday, were these gates open.

Between their stone pillars Red Hill's tall gates were open now. She turned in. Passing Clive's new cottage, she had kind thoughts. *A sad young man*, Amanda had said. She was glad she had told Amanda some good things about him and sorry that she herself had ever had such evil suspicions about him. In some way, she thought, in my own mind, I must make it up to him.

A thick powder dusted her shearling jacket as she walked the short distance between the car and the front door. When she rang the bell, she still had no idea what she was going to say.

To her surprise, the door was opened by Oliver himself. A gentleman in a velvet smoking jacket doesn't answer his own front door! His eyebrows rose in surprise.

'Sally! You came alone? What is it? Is everything all right with Dan?'

'Yes, he'll be home tomorrow.'

'You scared me. You'd said you'd come out with Dan, so I wasn't expecting you. And in this weather! Well, come in to the fire. I've a good one going. Just right, just right for a night like this.'

She followed him up a few steps into the great central room. Deerheads hung over the rough stone fireplace, while above the mantel at the other end of the room hung the painting of this very house that had been last year's birthday present from the family. Indian blankets were flung across sofas and chairs. A long sawbuck table was strewn with metal objects, statuettes, old pistols and brass loving cups, mementos of past tennis matches and gymkhanas.

'I've been polishing all this stuff,' he explained. 'I enjoy doing it myself. It's a nice occupation on a lonesome evening, don't you think?'

She didn't answer, but stood there looking at him. Not seeming to notice, he went on polishing and talking.

'There's nobody here but the caretaker. The cook's coming up tomorrow with the dessert. She doesn't like the oven here for pastry baking. I don't know why, but then I don't know anything about cake baking. Do sit down,' he said, for she was still standing with coat, hat, and gloves on.

'Take off your things and tell me what the trouble is, if any.'

'I won't be long,' she said.

He put the polishing cloth down. 'What's the matter, Sally? What is it?'

She was staring at him, at silvery hair, a ruddy tan from the ski resort near Chamonix, a gleam of white collar against black velvet, a slightly quizzical tilt of the noble head. Brains. Charm.

'What on earth is the matter, Sally?'

'I saw Amanda this afternoon.' She had not planned to begin with Amanda, had not actually planned anything.

The eyebrows went up again. 'Amanda? Here in town?'

'She came to my house looking for Dan. Her lawyers will be here on Monday.'

'Ah, that business again.' Oliver shook his head. 'I wish you young people would settle your differences. This has been going on far too long. But I don't want to be involved, Sally. You know that. It's not my company anymore – '

She interrupted. 'We've heard all that before.'

No one ever interrupted Oliver, or spoke so rudely to him, and he looked his astonishment. When she did not flinch, he continued, 'And how is Amanda?'

'How do you expect her to be after what you did to her?'

'I did? I don't understand you.'

'You understand me, Oliver.' Her entire body was burning, her head swam as with a fever, and she took a deep breath. 'You're a devil, Oliver, a savage, a criminal. You're filth.'

He asked calmly, 'Are you sure you're feeling all right, Sally?'

'Meaning, "Am I sane?" Yes, I'm quite, quite sane, Oliver. Whether I'm in good health, though, is another matter after what you did to Tina.' She began to cry, and with a heavy glove, wiped her eyes. 'I wish you were dead. In your grave and forgotten.'

'Well now, Sally, that's quite a statement. What's this all about?'

'Don't play games with me! You molested my baby! Took off her clothes, put your hands on her and God knows what – your dirty hands on her!' Her voice was shrill and piercing. 'No games, Oliver. A doctor told us what was wrong with Tina, and we didn't believe it, but now I've heard in that baby's own words – oh my God!'

Oliver nodded. His eyes spoke tolerance, wisdom, sympathy. 'She's seen too much television, Sally. That's all it is. These lurid things make a deeper impression on a child's mind than we realize. I'm surprised that you let her watch them.'

'We don't allow it, and she doesn't watch it, do you hear me? She showed me what you did. In her innocence, her ignorance, she showed me. But she knew it was wrong. "I'm a bad girl," she said because you told her she was, and – and you gave her that damned carousel so she would keep quiet. "It's a secret," she said. And if she told, you'd take back the carousel.' Now Sally's voice died in exhaustion. 'You bastard. You disgusting old man.'

'This is the most preposterous thing I have ever heard in all my life, and I've heard a great deal.'

In his dignity, a dignity that could be formidable and was so now, he stood with one hand in his velvet pocket. His air of imperturbable superiority was maddening.

'You'll be hearing a lot more when Amanda tackles you. You abused her, too. She told me what you used to do to her.'

'Oh, so it's Amanda now. She's only a little bit crazy. Just a trifle. Always has been.'

'There's nothing crazy about Amanda, though if she were crazy, it would be no wonder. But you know she isn't, and that's why you have no opinions about the business. Oh, how nobly you remove yourself to "let the young people take over",' Sally mocked, 'when the fact is, you don't dare offend Amanda, don't dare come near her. All these years you've lived in terror of her.'

A small, lopsided smile played across the man's mouth, as with nonchalance he jingled coins or keys in his pocket. He means, she thought, to show me how unconcerned, even how amused was Oliver, and how weak, how powerless was Sally.

'It's too bad you can't see how ridiculous you are,' he said.

'You think so? You'll find out how ridiculous Amanda is, too. You, creeping into her room at night . . . You gave her presents, you gave her the same carousel. Until your wife found out and sent her away to safety. And afterwards killed herself. Lucille killed herself, didn't she, Oliver?'

On his cheeks the muscles tightened, and on his lips, the smile died.

'She went out that day when the fog was thick and drove her car off a road that she had traveled all her life, drove it into the river. Because of you, Oliver.'

There was a pause, an eerie silence. When Oliver broke it, his stance had changed. And she knew that her last words had struck to the heart.

'I don't know what you want, Sally, other than to make these cruel accusations. I really don't,' he said.

'I want to let the world know what you are. I want to expose the great benefactor, the scholar, the gentleman, for the phony, sick, fake mess that he is. That's what I want.'

'You can't really think that anybody would believe your lies.' And with hard, stern eyes, he tried to stare her down.

Through a cloud of tears, she looked up at him. There he stood among his treasured possessions, saved all these years by them, by his reputation and his good works, while within this cocoon, unspeakable crimes had been committed . . .

She didn't recognize herself. The screaming voice, the very words, were not hers. 'You'll see! The smell of you will rise to high heaven.'

'I doubt it.'

'Wait till Amanda talks, and I – '

'Go ahead. You think I'm afraid of you? I'll deny everything, and that will be the end of it. Go ahead.'

'Your disgrace,' she began.

'. . . will boomerang upon you.'

'Not when Tina's doctor hears me out.'

'Nonsense. Everyone knows you can coach a little child to say anything.'

'What motive would the doctor have? She doesn't know you from Adam. What reason would I have? There's nothing I ever wanted from you. I thought – I admired you, but tonight when Tina – ' For a moment the room went reeling. 'My baby. Oh my baby!' she cried, hiding her face in her hands.

Suddenly she felt that she had gone as far as, mentally and physically, she was able to go. And she looked up at him, saying quietly now, 'More illustrious people than you have been found out, Oliver. Some of them have had the decency to confess and be sorry.'

'Quite right. Most laudable behavior, provided you have anything to confess.'

'You'll feel better if you do. You can make it easier for yourself.'

He did not answer.

'You claim to be a religious man.'

'I am one.'

'Then let me ask you: Will you take an oath that you never did anything to my Tina that you shouldn't have done?'

'I don't need to take any oaths. My word as an honorable man has been enough wherever I go.'

'Honorable men take oaths in court.'

He did not reply. She saw the blood rising into his cheeks, and knew that he was in terror. There was sweat on his forehead, and his knees buckled.

'Swear to the God you worship every week. You never miss a Sunday. Swear that you never touched my baby in a sexual way. I'll get the Bible out of the library. Swear.'

'No.'

They were confronting each other, Oliver against the wall with his hands flattened on it, as though to support him, and Sally behind the littered table.

'You refuse,' she said.

'I refuse.'

He was trying to get hold of himself. She actually saw the process going on in the man, this man so reasonable, kindly, and correct, whose mask had dropped, had been stripped away. Slowly he drew himself up to his natural height, and raising his head, defied her.

'What more do you want, Sally? I'm getting quite tired of this.'

'I told you. I want to reveal you as you are, and I'm going to do it.'

'You try and you'll regret it.'

'I don't think so, Oliver.'

'You do that and I'll accuse Dan of molesting his own daughter.'

She was stunned; it was a moment before her brain received the full impact of what he had said. Then the enormity of this consummate evil drove her completely mad. And yet, in spite of it, she had enough control to keep from flying at his throat. Instead, her hands moved, seizing whatever they touched on the table, to destroy whatever was precious to him. She would have pulled the walls of his house down if she could. Her strength, like his, filled her veins and surged back. Blindly, in the seconds it took before he could cross the room to prevent her, she ripped the pages from an antique leather book and smashed to the floor a silver statuette and a silver presentation bowl with his name engraved on it, and a silver-handled revolver . . .

It went off. The crash almost broke her eardrums. She heard

Oliver cry out; she saw him stagger back and slump against the wall . . . She fled.

The first thing she was conscious of was the road. Somehow she had gotten out of the house, although she did not remember how. Then she thought she remembered banging the front door shut behind her. She must have started the engine because here she was, guiding the car with utmost caution into the flying snow. She was already past the bend where the road forked toward Red Hill before she was able to come awake.

I've killed a man. I've committed murder. Oh God.

Under the sheepskin jacket she was sweating. There were pulses all over her body, things beating and quivering. And she knew she must quiet down to think.

Her brain began to work. Like a little dynamo, fueled by panic, it began to click. The caretaker's wing was at the rear of the house with no view of the driveway. So far, only two or three cars had passed on the road; in the dark and in this tumult of snow and wind, it was impossible for them to have seen her license plate. People didn't ride around memorizing license plates, anyway. Then suddenly she realized that she had never removed her gloves while in the house, and a tremendous relief washed over her.

The car slid, tracing a figure S on the treacherous road. All she needed was to slide into a drift and be stuck; how then to explain what she was doing out here at night?

She gripped the wheel. God, don't let this car slide, she prayed. God, get me home, please. My babies are there.

It was so cold that the snow seemed to freeze on the windshield almost as soon as it struck. The snow danced in front of the headlights so that she could see barely a few yards ahead. The snow was an enemy. During the few minutes she had spent in that cursed house, the storm had tripled its power, no longer a storm but a full-blown blizzard.

Something touched her thigh as she moved in the seat. She

had actually run out of the house with the revolver still in her hand. And it was loaded.

Now panic gripped her again. It crawled up her back as it does when, in the deserted darkness, you feel someone coming behind you. With enormous effort, she kept herself from stopping the car to see whether anyone might be crouched on the floor in the rear. Every few seconds she searched the road through the rearview mirror.

Then she cried out to herself: 'You're driving. You're heading toward home, you fool, with the revolver in the car!'

It was not far from the river. So came the logical common instinct to dispose of it there. The slope from the road was steep, the slope down which that poor woman had raced into the water. It would be impossible to climb down and climb back in these mounting drifts. She could slow the car, lean over and throw it out the window. But if it should miss and lie there on the road or bury itself in the snow, only to be discovered when the snow was gone? No. She would have to stop the car with the risk of not regaining traction enough to start it again, get out and stand on the bridge to drop the thing safely into the river. There was always the risk that some lone driver out on this night would see her there and would of course remember the woman parked on the bridge in the midst of a blizzard. But she would have to try.

No one came. So far, so good, she thought. You have been lucky. Lucky! If you thought you had troubles before tonight, think again.

Her mind was unusually wide-awake. In a case like this, the authorities would question everyone, family, friends, and employees. You will be asked where you were this evening. Nanny will say you told her you were going to the movies. Therefore you must go to the movies.

But perhaps she should go to the police now, right now, and tell them about the accident? After all, she was Sally Grey, a decent person who had never even had a ticket for speeding. They would surely understand it was an accident, wouldn't they? *Or would they?*

If only Dan were home! Imagine walking into that police station all alone, crying. Tears were already lumped in her throat. She would be stammering into those grim faces. No, not tonight. It was impossible.

Lights were still bright in the small suburban center, and cars were still parked in the lot next to the theater. The drugstore was open. She parked the car and took her place near a group of people who were the first to leave the theater, and lingered a moment on the sidewalk with a deliberate air of uncertainty.

'Sally Grey! Can you believe what's happened in just two and a half hours? We'd never have gone out if we'd had any idea it would be like this.'

And the two Smiths, Eric and Lauren, stood in dismay, looking at the snow.

'I'm wondering how we'll ever get home,' Sally said.

'We'll follow you,' offered Eric. 'We'll stay right behind you so if you get stuck, we'll be there to help.'

Sally laughed. 'And what if you get stuck? I won't be much help, I'm afraid.' Then thinking further, she asked, 'May I ask you to wait two seconds while I run into the drugstore for my cold medicine? I feel as if I'm coming down with something.'

The druggist would make another witness to her presence in the village. 'Great picture, wasn't it?' he remarked as he made change. 'That woman, I never miss her pictures.'

'Wonderful. I loved it,' Sally agreed, making a mental note to read the movie reviews.

The cars plowed their way home. The snow was already banked high against the house and Sally struggled her way from the garage to the front door through drifts up to her thighs. For a moment, she stood surveying the landscape, a pure dazzle of unmarked white, with the snow still coming down. There will be no car tracks left anywhere, she thought.

She closed the door and then, with all her adrenaline by now consumed, went upstairs and collapsed on the bed.

Hours later she got up and went into her children's rooms. The tears that flooded her eyes at the sight of them in their innocent sleep were hot enough to scorch. Even the memory of what that evil man had done to Tina was faint compared with dread of what the future might bring to these little girls. And to Dan. And her mind went over everything that had occurred that night, seeking and analyzing every step: no fingerprints, the gun at the bottom of a turbulent river, the Smiths, the druggist, everything.

She seemed secure. And yet, you never knew. There might still be something, some tiny clue that had eluded her. You read about such things all the time.

On the return to her bed, she passed the sitting room where the children played. For no reason that she could explain, she went in and turned on a lamp. There on the table stood the carousel, glittering in its beautiful, absurd extravagance. Again for no reason at all, she reached out and touched it. Turning a trifle, it played the last few notes of 'The Blue Danube' waltz, and then she recoiled in horror, as if she had touched a snake, as if she had touched the evil that was Oliver Grey.

He was dead, and he deserved to die, although she had not wanted to be the cause of his death, or of anyone's. But so it had happened.

CHAPTER
—— 16 ——

She had slept a deep, exhausted sleep for two hours and on opening her eyes, had sprung from bed to look out the window. It had stopped snowing. The driveway was clear with no signs that an automobile had ever been near it. She hurried to shower and dress, taking special care so as to appear perfectly normal before Nanny, and thinking 'Trust no one!', she waited for the telephone to ring.

It rang at seven. The agitated, almost incomprehensible voice, was Happy's.

'Sally! I don't know how to begin, it's so awful, it's a nightmare, Father's been shot!'

'Shot! Is it bad?'

'He's dead! We got here last night and found him.' She began to cry.

'My God,' Sally said. 'How did it happen? Does anyone know?'

'Let me get a drink of water. Let me sit down. Ian is inside now with a doctor, waiting for the people to take the body. And the police, of course. We've been up all night – oh, it's unbelievable.'

'My God,' Sally said again. 'There's nothing that much to rob in that house, unless they thought he was carrying cash.'

'They don't think it was robbers. He had seven hundred dollars in his wallet, there was his watch and nothing was touched.'

'Then who can it be? I can't imagine that Oliver had any enemies.'

'Lord only knows. Some maniac, we think. Ian and I had a dinner date but we canceled it on account of the weather. As it was, we had a dreadful time struggling up here through the storm. We walked in just as the caretaker was laying Father on the sofa. He said he was taking a nap after supper when he thought he heard a sound like a gunshot, although his wife said it was nonsense, it was only the cold cracking a tree limb, but he got up anyway. Then we called the police. It took almost two hours for them to reach us. Even the front steps here were buried.' Happy was out of breath.

Sally had to say something, and yet be careful to say as little as possible. 'Everything is buried here, too. I should get out there to be with you! Later, after they clear the roads, I will.'

'No, don't come. There's nothing for you to do here. We'll stay until the detectives are finished – they're going over the whole house – and then we're leaving for home. This is a nightmare. And we were planning such a beautiful few days here, especially for Clive's sake.'

'How is he taking it? Of all people – so especially close to Father.'

'Badly. He fell apart, Roxanne said. But she's taking good care of him. She's a princess, a real princess. They'll come over as soon as a path can be shoveled for them. He's insisting.'

'I wish Dan were here,' Sally said.

'He's due in today, isn't he?'

'Tonight. But I don't see how. The airport can't possibly be cleared that fast.'

'This is hardly a homecoming welcome for him! Oh, Ian wants me. I'll talk to you later. Wait, I just have to tell you, there'll be detectives who'll want to question all of us, Ian says. It's ridiculous, questioning us, but I guess they have to do it. So don't be too upset.'

'I'll try not to be, but it's all beyond words.'

Indeed, she could not afford to be upset, just 'normally' upset. Now, what would be normal? To call Amanda. And so she put in a call to the hotel.

Amanda had already heard the news over the local radio station.

'Well,' she said, 'what a fortuitous death! Or I should say "murder". And when I came all the way to see him! Who did it?'

'They have no idea.'

'Was it a break-in, a robbery?'

'I don't think so. Nothing was taken.'

'He had no enemies, I suppose. Not Oliver Grey, oh no. Unless you can think of any.'

Sally said briefly, 'No, I can't.'

If it was Amanda's intent to draw her out, she was making a mistake. *Trust no one*. And Amanda was the only human being who, because of yesterday's revelation, could have the remotest reason to connect her with Oliver's death.

'I was so disturbed by what you told me yesterday about yourself and Lucille and everything that I had to get out of the house. In all that weather I went to the movies.'

'I suppose the funeral will be a big event.'

'I guess so.'

'I don't suppose you were too fond of him.'

'What makes you say that? As a matter of fact, until I heard yesterday what he had done to you, I had enormous regard for him. I was even fond of him.'

'Well, you live and learn, don't you. I wish I knew about the funeral so I could send a wreath.'

'I take it that you don't plan to go.'

'No. I'm flying out of here as soon as the planes move again.'

'What about the business you want to discuss?'

'It wouldn't be seemly to talk about money. I'll fly home and be back in a couple of weeks when the dust has settled. Anyway, I love to fly.'

There was something too snappy and flip in this inter-change. The woman was – she was brittle. Still, it must be quite a blow to be cheated out of the revenge you're so entitled to take.

'You'll be safe in sending a wreath to Oliver's church,' Sally said. 'I really don't see why you need to do it, though.'

Amanda laughed. 'I'm a Grey and we were raised by the book of etiquette. By the way, there'll be detectives, you know. Don't let them make you nervous.'

'I have nothing to be nervous about,' Sally said.

Indeed, two of them were in the house already, in the kitchen with Nanny. Apparently they had arrived while Sally was on the telephone with Clive, who, in the enormity of shock and grief, had been put to bed. From the top of the back stairs she was able to hear them and, given her circumstances, felt no guilt about eavesdropping.

'This visitor came from California, you said?'

'I said I thought so. I don't pay attention. It's none of my business,' Nanny said indignantly. 'If you want to know about this family's affairs, you'll have to ask them yourself.'

So they really were going over everyone with a fine-tooth comb. Well, she was as ready as she would ever be. And she came down by the front stairs to meet the men in the living room.

'Detective Murray,' said one, a neat, balding man who reminded her of her dentist.

'Detective Huber,' said the second, who was younger and looked like her hairdresser.

She had expected them to look – well, different, perhaps formidable, perhaps tough. But that was absurd.

'Do sit down,' she said pleasantly.

The young one began, 'We don't like to intrude on a day like this, Mrs. Grey. You're a family member, but – routine questions, you understand.'

'I understand.' And she wondered whether they were

always as courteous to people not like the Greys. Perhaps they were.

'Your husband is the nephew of the deceased?'

She nodded.

'I'm told he's out of town.'

'He's flying home today.'

'When did you last hear from him?'

'Yesterday. He telephoned from Scotland yesterday morning.'

'Using this number?'

'Why, yes.'

The balding man, Murray, made notes. They would check the telephone company to see whether he really was in Scotland.

'Are you certain that he did not take an earlier plane, that possibly because of storm warnings he decided to come back a day early?'

'I'm quite certain.'

'Can you give me the airline and the flight number?'

'Of course. I have it here in the desk.'

'Your husband and Oliver Grey were close, would you say, on good terms?'

'They were like father and son. A good father and son.'

'He will be shocked when he gets this news.'

'We all are. It's horrible.'

'Your husband has a sister in California, I understand. Your maid mentioned her just now. Nobody else in the family made mention of her being here.'

'They didn't know she was. She came unexpectedly.'

'Oh, you hadn't expected her either?'

Probe. Dig. She shouldn't have used the word 'unexpected'.

'It was a surprise, then.'

'Yes. A surprise.'

'Is she in the habit of making surprise visits from California?'

'In the habit? No.'

Murray raised his head from his notes. 'Often, does she do it often?'

'No.' The less said, the better.

'Well, how often? When was the last time she came to your house?'

'She had never been here before.'

'Oh?'

She hated the way he said, 'Oh,' with disbelief in the rising lilt.

'So she generally stayed at Hawthorne whenever she came?'

She would like to spare Amanda the grilling that was bound to come out of all this, but a saving lie would not really save because either Ian or Clive would state the facts.

'No,' Sally said, 'she's never been in Scythia at all, not since she was thirteen years old.'

'Peculiar, wouldn't you say? After all these years to surprise you at your front door?'

'I really don't know.'

'She must have had some reason. Didn't she give you any?'

'She wanted to see the children. She brought Christmas presents.'

'That's peculiar, too.' Huber's narrowed eyes seemed to be challenging Sally. 'Never comes in all these years, and all of a sudden decides to travel across the country with Christmas presents. No other reason given. Don't you find it so, Mrs. Grey?'

'I don't know. You'll have to ask her.'

'Your maid said Miss Grey was staying in town.'

'Yes, at the King Hotel.'

'Thank you. Now, after she left you – do you recall what time that was?'

'About five o'clock. My children's suppertime, maybe a little later.'

'So, you gave supper to the children. And then what did you do?'

'Gave them baths. Then I went to the movies.'

'Pretty bad weather to go out in, wasn't it?'

'Not that bad when I left the house. Anyway, I'm used to it.'

'And it's not so far to the shopping center, if that's where you went.'

'Yes, I saw *Judy's Daughter*.'

'Did you like it? What do you think of the ending?'

Thank God she had read that review! 'It was a real shocker. I never expected him to come back from the war.'

'It was a long picture, after eleven o'clock when it lets out.'

Thank God once more she had noted the time. 'Ten-thirty. At least that's what it said on the clock in the drugstore.'

They would, of course, check her story at the drugstore; they would check with Amanda, to find out when she had returned the rented car, and surely they would ask her about her conversation with Sally Grey. Amanda was clearly no fool, but neither were these detectives, so she could only hope that no accidental word of Amanda's would plant a seed in their fertile minds.

When they had gone, she was left with a well-remembered dread from her school and college years: Had she passed the finals?

She had a need for solitude. A frightened animal crawls into its hole, she thought. The dog hides in the closet when it thunders. And she went into the kitchen to tell Nanny that she was feeling sick with a cold.

'I'm going to shut my door and lie down,' she said. 'Will you keep the girls away for a while?'

'You just take care of yourself, Mrs. Grey. You look peaked, and no wonder. What a terrible thing! Some crazy up there in the mountains must have broken into the house. An awful lot of crazies are running around loose these days.' And Nanny shook her head, deploring the state of the world.

From the bedroom window Sally looked out upon the white expanse. There was no life in sight, not even a rabbit's track. Here and there a draft of wind lifted a flurry of snow and sent it skimming across the frozen surface of the earth. An intense melancholy filled the afternoon. She drew the curtains to darken the room and lay down.

In a few hours Dan would be home, and she tried to imagine how she would tell him what had happened. Often in reading the papers or watching television, she had put herself in the place of someone caught in one of the century's disasters, wondering how, for instance, you broke the news that the house had been bombed and the children were dead. Now she herself was to be the bearer of unbelievable news: *I killed Uncle Oliver*.

Oliver, he of the old patrician style. Now with her eyes closed, she saw his face – the distinguished old one and the new one, that of the furious, cornered, and, in the end, defiant man. Because of her work with the camera, she had considered herself to be a clever judge of faces, believing that they really were a revelation of character. She had read them well, and had photographed them accordingly: the daring astronaut, twin spirit to a reckless gambler; or the aging beauty, fearful of advancing time. But she hadn't read Oliver. Whatever message his face had conveyed might as well have been written in Sanskrit.

And then came the dour face of Dr. Lisle, whose disapproving schoolmistress manner had been so offensive to her. Now she could understand: The doctor had only been trying to convey a desperate message and had been frustrated by Sally's stubborn rejection of it. I owe her an apology, she thought now, and I will give it to her.

After a while she was awakened from a troubled doze by the sound of snowplows grinding up the hill. They were a sign of life and therefore welcome. But they were also a sign that

life was resuming its normal routine, from which there could
be no escape. Funerals, questions, and more police – all these
would be the aftermath of the storm.

Sally's natural impulse was to run into Dan's arms and there
find some kind of comfort. Instead it became at once clear
that, to the contrary, he was the one in need of comfort from
her, if there could be any.

He mourned. He raged at the world. 'Why do we allow
these beasts to prowl the earth, to cut short a life like this?
That man of all men, who gave so much and still had so much
to give. Why, why?' He flexed his fingers. 'If I could get my
hands on the one who did it, just get my hands around his
throat I'd – I'd make him suffer, I'd make him pay for every
second that Oliver suffered.' And he dropped his head into
his hands.

'He didn't suffer,' she said, with her throat so tight that she
was scarcely able to get the words out.

'You can't know that.'

'Bullets – I thought a bullet was quick.'

'Don't, Sally. I know you mean well, but please don't.'

She sat there looking at her husband, trying to imagine
herself in his place. The man had been a father to him . . .
And the longer she sat, the more impossible it became for
her to tell him the truth. Then the loneliness overwhelmed
her, there in the warm familiar room, a coldness, as if she
were lost, left behind by the last human being alive in some
region of the poles.

After a while he raised his head and, having recovered
himself, began to reason.

'If it was not a robbery, and apparently it was not,
Ian says, it must have been the work of some chance
vagrant, some mental case. I suppose the authorities will
start snooping into the company's business, after all that
stuff in the papers about a family dispute. But that's only
to be expected.'

She must tell him now about Amanda. The visit would be revealed by tomorrow anyway. So she began.

'I'm piling one thing on top of another, I know, but this is it: Amanda was here yesterday.'

'Amanda! What the devil did she want?'

Take it step by step, she thought, and taking the first step, replied, 'She wanted to meet with Oliver.'

'To pester him about the business! She's impossible, she knows he doesn't – didn't – want to be involved in it, she had no right. Could she have gone out there after you saw her? My God, Sally, the police should know this.'

'You can't suspect Amanda?'

'Is it possible? Could she have gone off the deep end? She's been so troubled. Poor Amanda – God, I hope not.'

'Dan, she did not go up to Red Hill and shoot Oliver Grey. Don't, please don't, even hint it to anyone. You'll make a fool of yourself.'

His conjecture had made it even more impossible for her to take the next step. After the funeral, after the normal period of cooling off, she would tell him gradually, first about Oliver's abuse of Amanda, and then, after some further cooling, would come all the rest. It would take courage, perhaps even more courage, to carry this weight and this fear alone – and then she would turn herself in.

Then came three wretched days. The police were everywhere, swarming not only through Red Hill, but through Hawthorne and the homes of Ian, Clive, and Dan as well. Family, servants, and deliverymen were minutely examined and it was apparent that neighbors were also being questioned. Plainclothes detectives were a tenacious lot, asking the same things over and over, about locks and keys and guns, about the handyman and the consortium deal. 'And everything,' Dan said, 'except what we all eat for breakfast.'

At the same time, they gave no hint of what they themselves might be thinking.

'That's to see whether they can trip anybody up,' Ian said.

And even though it was Christmas week, and one would think they had other more joyous things to do, the curious public came.

'Trial by fire,' grumbled Dan. 'It's hard to believe that so many people will actually get in their cars and drive all the way to Red Hill just to stand outside the gates and stare. What on earth are they expecting to see?'

Nevertheless, they were there, and at Hawthorne too, and at the houses of Ian, Clive, and Dan, observing the children in Dan's yard, watching the car that brought Clive back home from Red Hill and the delivery vans at Ian's.

'Morbid curiosity,' Dan grumbled again, in the face of reporters, flashbulbs, and questions about the rumored family feud. 'At least, though, the editorials have been splendid. At least the city appreciates the things he did for it.'

The funeral home was besieged with visitors and flowers, among the latter a most magnificent wreath of roses and orchids marked simply, *From Amanda Grey*.

'Mighty queer,' said Ian, who by then knew that she had come to town and departed.

'Very odd,' said Happy, who had never met Amanda Grey.

Clive made no comment. He had acknowledged no one's presence or condolences. It was as if he were hearing nothing and seeing nothing except the coffin, as if he were memorizing every grain and whorl in its polished surface. Bent over on the settee with Roxanne's arm about him, he seemed, as he clung to her forgetful of all else in his overwhelming grief, no larger than a child. She was the comforting, protective, pitying mother.

He had gone downhill overnight.

On the day of the funeral, the church, too, was besieged. Admission was by card only, so these were not curiosity seekers but friends, and as many of those who worked at Grey's Foods as could be squeezed in. The service was long, with several eulogies given by sincere people who kept repeating each other. The scent of the heaped altar flowers was crushing, and Sally grew faint. It crossed her mind that she might perhaps lose that mind; it was said that everyone had a breaking point and she wondered what hers might be. She was feeling much too close to it.

At Clive's house, after the battering arctic wind in the cemetery, the relatives gathered around the coffee urn. At doctor's orders Clive had been given a brandy and now, slightly recovered from the morning's ordeal, he half sat and half lay in his big chair, observing them. For all his life, except for the last few months, he reflected, he had been only an observer. He had learned to amuse himself with speculations about other people's motives, the reasons they flirted or flattered or gave subtle insults. So now again, he was an observer.

From his chair he had an oblique view of Ian, who was lingering near the front door as if he were afraid to set foot inside the house. Obviously, Roxanne had given him a full report of that terrible night.

Roxanne herself hovered about him with pillows, medicine, and food. She had not been able to find enough to do for him during these last three days. No doubt she was not only appalled at what had happened but dreaded what might still happen. Certainly, he thought with some bitterness, she must be thinking about his will and how he would change it! Well, let her wait and find out in time that he hadn't changed it. He would let her have the money. She had broken his faith in human beings, she had broken *him*, but also she had given him the greatest joy he had ever known. So let her have it.

Odd, isn't it, how events overlap and supersede one another? The loss of his father had quite wiped out his futile rage over her and Ian's betrayal; now only exhaustion and bitterness were left.

And he looked over at Happy, who had also been

betrayed but did not know it. Busy as always, she was serving sandwiches. He wondered what would become of her, poor woman, when those two made their final plans.

And I am dying, he said to himself; for all the doctors' encouragement, I know better.

That leaves only Sally and Dan, good souls both, who have nothing at all to worry about.

Shortly before the end of the year, Sally returned to the office of Dr. Katie Lisle. Nothing had changed, not the doctor's plain face nor the desolate view of the warehouse through the window behind her.

'I guess you're surprised to see me again,' she began.

'Not necessarily. People come and go.'

'I mean,' Sally said nervously, 'when I left last time I seem to remember that I – I'm sorry, I think I was rather brusque.'

The doctor waited.

'What you told me, you said, was so shocking, that I guess I was stunned and I couldn't believe it and so maybe I was even feeling a little angry at you. I mean, that sounds ridiculous, doesn't it, but I was so sure you were wrong.'

A fire engine went by and was followed by another. The clamor and shriek of them filled the little room so that Sally had to pause. While this pause lasted, the two women had nothing to do but look at each other.

To this dispassionate intelligence, thought Sally, I think I could speak, if I dared speak to anyone, which of course I do not. Only an hour before, she had overheard a group in the supermarket discussing the murder. *Positively brutal, a fine old man like him.* And she had felt a sinking of her vital parts, heart, lungs, everything, simply dropping out of her onto the floor.

'You were saying,' the doctor reminded her, 'that you were sure I was wrong.'

'Yes, but I have come back because you were right.' And,

her eyes filling, she opened her purse to scramble for a handkerchief, but found none.

'Here's a tissue,' said Katie Lisle, 'and take your time.'

The unexpected gentleness only produced more tears and embarrassed apologies.

'I'm wasting your time,' she murmured.

'We have two hours. I rather suspected when you called that you might need another hour.'

'Thank you.' How she had misread this woman! 'I'll be okay, I can tell you what happened . . .'

And so she recounted the story of Tina and the carousel. Of Amanda's experience, she said nothing; it need be no part of Tina's. Of Oliver also, she said nothing, referring to him only as 'he'.

'But since I am to work with Tina, I shall naturally need to have a name, Mrs. Grey.'

If this doctor were part of the city's old establishment, Sally thought, it would be out of the question to give her the name; her own linkage to Oliver's death would then be immediate. Even as it was, the newest newcomer in town had read the newspapers! But there was no way out.

She said very low, 'He was my husband's uncle, Oliver Grey.'

The doctor made no comment. After her fashion she waited once more for Sally.

So now she had done it, had left her footprint, her marker. Katie Lisle might do with it what she wished. And even if she were to do nothing, Sally knew, there were always others, someone encountered by chance on the road who suddenly, years after the fact, remembers something. Or there were innocent words dropped accidentally, perhaps even by herself . . . She would never be safe, never free.

'Yes, the man who was – who died last week. An unbelievable coincidence. The one had nothing to do with the other,' she added quickly, and a second later was aware that the remark had been completely stupid, so very stupid.

'I didn't think it had,' said Dr. Lisle.

'No, of course not.'

Worse and worse. I am a wreck, Sally thought.

'Doctor, why has Tina never said anything to me when she told you so readily?'

'Number one, she didn't tell me readily. When some of it came out accidentally through her play, I took the clue and went on from there. Number two, as to why she didn't tell you, I would say it was because she feared you would punish her.'

'But we're not punishing parents. We're quite the opposite.'

'Tina is a very bright child. You had told her not to let anyone touch her and she – at least in her mind – had disobeyed. Besides, you yourself said she had been threatened if ever she told, and cajoled with the silver carousel. It's not so simple, Mrs. Grey.'

Yes, it's simple, Sally thought, despairing. It's a long, straight, dark tunnel with no light at the end. That's what it is.

'Have you asked Tina whether she will come back to me?'

'She will come. If you were a man I'm almost sure she would not, but when I asked her whether she would go to play games with the lady, she agreed. Doctor, Dr. Lisle, tell me, will she ever get over this? Do people ever – ' Her voice broke.

'They don't forget, but they can be taught how to live with it and, when they are old enough, to understand it.'

'You haven't said anything about forgiveness, I notice.'

'Now we get into the realm of the spiritual,' Katie Lisle said, smiling, 'and I'm not a preacher. I can only try to heal.'

'Do you really think Tina can grow up and be well and happy and like – like other people?'

The doctor smiled again. 'Yes,' she said, 'yes, I do.'

Little Tina! I have done everything I can for you.

On the way home, Sally passed the route to the cemetery

where Oliver Grey reposed in a granite mausoleum. She raised her fist.

'I didn't mean to do it, but I did it and you deserved it, Oliver Grey.'

For the last few nights she had dreamed and for the last few days, in random moments, had seen before her eyes a tall, gray fortress-prison on a hill. Like the image on a computer screen, it blinked on and blinked away. And she knew, in the depths of her being she knew, that this was her future come to show itself to her.

So it was time to tell everything to Dan. She would start with Amanda's tale and proceed from there to Tina's and her own.

'I saw Dr. Lisle today,' she began. 'You remember, we agreed on the first of the year.'

'We did. It's okay.' And he studied her, frowning a little. 'Poor Sal! You're done in. Things have piled up too high, the worry over Tina, and now Oliver. I wish I could just take you away to lie on a beach and do nothing.'

'Take me out for a walk in the snow now. I need to talk to you.'

The snow was firm underfoot and the stars bright overhead. With no other walkers out and no other traffic, the night was so still and pure that it seemed an act of vandalism to speak what she had to speak. Nevertheless, it had to be done. So she opened her lips and began, 'When Amanda came to live at Hawthorne . . .'

Dan heard her without interruption to the end.

'And after she left, Lucille was killed. Amanda believes she killed herself.'

'That's it?' asked Dan.

'That's it.'

'Well, shall I tell you what I think? I think she's gone clean off her rocker. She was always eccentric. Ever since I was old enough to be any judge, I thought so. Eccentric. Unstable.'

'But don't you see, this was the reason why?'

He came to a halt facing Sally. 'No, absolutely not. This is simply another cooked-up, recovered-memory affair. I'm not saying they're all cooked up, I know better than that.' Angrily, he kicked at the snowbank on the side of the road. 'We discussed this kind of thing before, when Tina first saw that woman. But this one is very definitely cooked up and I'm sure I know why.'

She wished he wouldn't call Dr. Lisle 'that woman', but there were more important issues to deal with right now, so she let it pass, saying only, 'Dan, this wasn't cooked up. I was there. If you could have seen Amanda's face, and how she cried! She was broken apart.'

'Well, I'm broken apart too, when I think of Oliver. A man only in his sixties, with so many more good years and so much good he could have done! I'm not wasting my sympathy on my sister. This story is absolutely crazy, Sally, and I'm amazed that you fell for it.'

Taking hold of his lapel, she looked into his eyes. The light was so clear that she could read his righteous indignation in them.

'Listen to me,' she insisted, 'believe me, Dan, she was telling the truth. There are things you simply *know*, and I know this.'

'Sweet Sally, you're a softy,' he said, relenting. 'You always were.'

'You've never said that about me before. You've always said I was a clever businesswoman.'

'Yes, but you're soft all the same. A marshmallow. That's what's lovable about you. But you can't allow yourself to be hoodwinked by a gush of tears, Sally. Amanda is just mad as a hornet because we won't sell her share of the stock, and she wanted to make trouble for Oliver. Damn!' He kicked again at the snowbank. 'Well, let her be patient a little longer, because as soon as the forest is sold, she'll get her money.'

'I wish you'd believe me, Dan.'

Sally knew she sounded piteous, but the computer was flashing the iron-gray fortress-prison on the screen before her eyes, and she had lost her strength to combat him.

'Is it possible,' he said angrily, 'that Amanda could have gone out to Red Hill after she left you?' Then, seeing the horror on her face, he corrected himself. 'No, I forgot I asked you before and it's as crazy as Amanda's story. Let's go in. It's freezing out here.'

So quickly had he dismissed her! Still, she supposed, you couldn't blame him. What if somebody were to tell her that her own father – it would be unthinkable.

Sometime soon, though, she would have to try again; she would have to relate the other part, by far the worst part, of the story. But not now. She ached for sleep, a few hours of forgetfulness. If only the fortress-prison did not loom again in her dreams . . .

CHAPTER
—— 17 ——

February 1991

Amanda jumped off the cable car on the peak of Nob Hill. The soothing air of spring touched her face and she was not yet ready to go indoors. In a small park where children were still playing, she sat down; an extraordinary sense of lightness came to her as she watched them.

The day at the agency had been especially long and even more filled with desperate interviews than was usual. There had been one in particular, a runaway, sixteen years old, a delicate girl, sensitive and secretive. She had seen this girl twice before and been unable to pry much information from her. But something today had lit a lamp in her own mind and before she knew it, words had come tumbling from her mouth.

'I was molested,' she confessed. 'My uncle did it to me when I was younger than you. I was ashamed to let anyone know, and that was my big mistake.'

The girl had looked at her with such eyes – the startled eyes of some poor caught animal – and burst into tears. And after a while, with Amanda's arm around her shoulders, she had begun at last to talk.

It might not have been professional, and very likely was not, she thought now, but it had worked. The girl had agreed to see a doctor and go to live in the home, shelter or halfway house or whatever you wanted to call it, that Amanda supported.

Thinking about all this, she was swept again by that extraordinary sense of lightness. She sat until it was almost dark, thinking about many things, and was still thinking, over her solitary supper, about that odd sensation of lightness.

'Sheba,' she said to the cat, who had curled itself over her ankle, 'it is because a secret is a very heavy thing and that I've carried mine for too many years. So I had to get rid of it. But do not think that lightness means automatic happiness, whatever happiness means, for that matter. No, it does not. It only frees the mind to work more intelligently.'

When she had eaten, she went to sit by the window where the view spread widely over the bay to the bridge and the far, far East. When the cat sprang up beside her, turning up to her its heart-shaped little face and its wise green eyes, she spoke to it again.

'How that man lived with *his* secrets, I shall never fathom. I hope he sweated in agony through every sleepless night. But most probably he did not. It's funny, it took me all these years to come to a resolution: that I would go there and face him, accuse him and make him pay. Of course, as Sally said, it would have been blackmail, and that is a very ugly thing. So his death spared me from doing that ugly thing, or shall I say "cheated me"? At any rate, it's over.

'And here's another funny thing: I do not want the money anymore. It isn't worth the struggle. I have enough, more than enough. As Todd once said – I wonder what's become of him? It's been almost a year since he was here, sitting in that chair. "You're getting your fair share," he told me, and he was right. The lawyer thought I was a fool yesterday when I phoned him to say that I was dropping the case against Grey's Foods. "They're loaded," he said. "They're bound to give you something if only for nuisance value." Nuisance value! No, I don't want to be anyone's nuisance. I think too much of myself for that. "But we can take over the business," he said. "I've already got people with plenty of cash, Amanda." No, the case is closed.

'And I feel good about it, Sheba. I never really wanted to hurt Dan, or any person who hadn't ever hurt me. Especially now, because something tells me that Dan is in terrible trouble.'

She stood and went to the telephone, picked it up and put it down, uncertain what to do. The message to Dan about the company stock was simple; indeed, it would be a pleasure to feel again how reasonable, how magnanimous she really wanted to be. There was something else, though, which had been troubling her for over a month now, ever since, on that day of tumult, she had left Scythia.

I do believe Sally did it, she said to herself for the hundredth time. Remember how carefully she let me know that she had gone to the movies that night? She was so nervous that she could barely speak. Unless I am an utter fool . . .

There was too much coincidence for it to be coincidence. That man's death, her own story, which Sally had heard with such visible horror, the carousel, Tina's sick behavior, and at the last moment on the stairs, the horror again on Sally's face as if, in that very instant, the truth had struck her down . . . It all fitted.

They don't miss a thing, those detectives. They even gave me a hard time simply because I hadn't returned the rented car until the morning after I was at Dan's house. They will surely find out what happened. They may lie low for months but they will come up with the proof.

My God, poor girl, poor children, my poor brother!

This time she took up the telephone and dialed. It was evening in the East and Dan would probably be at home. When someone answered, who she guessed was the nanny, she asked to speak to him. After a short delay, it was Sally who came to the telephone and offered to take the message.

'Well, it's something about the business and you said you never have anything to do with it,' Amanda said.

'That's so, but I can take a message.' Sally hesitated. 'The fact is, Amanda, that Dan doesn't want to talk to you. He's

269

very angry, angry and hurt. I told him about Oliver and he doesn't believe it.'

'But you do?'

'Yes, yes I do.' Again she hesitated. 'Dan loved Oliver so much, you see. He feels such gratitude, such respect, and he's infuriated that you can say such things about him.'

With all the gentleness, there was fire in Sally. She wasn't afraid of an unpleasant truth. She could have covered up by saying that Dan had guests or wasn't feeling well, but she had not. She had been direct. Amanda liked that. And then, in the instant, she thought, it is this very quality that makes me all the more sure that she took things into her own hands that night.

'I understand,' she said, meaning it. 'Then please tell Dan, and he can tell the others, that I withdraw the lawsuit I was planning, that I am satisfied with the financial arrangements we have always had, and that for my part they can do what they will with the forest.'

Sally was astonished. 'But your project, your work with needy girls! The acreage you want to buy, and all your plans!'

'Dan told me once in an argument that my plans were grandiose, and they were. I can be just as helpful, perhaps more so, on a much smaller scale.'

Dan had also accused her of wanting to be admired and he hadn't been far wrong there, either.

'I didn't really need all that money. I only wanted to torture Oliver.'

'I understand very well,' Sally said in a voice so low that Amanda was not sure she had heard, and asked her to repeat it.

When she had done so, Amanda asked, 'Are you sure you're all right?'

At once the answering voice became brisk with the intonation of surprise. 'Of course. Why shouldn't I be?'

And Amanda knew that her innocent-seeming question

had gone too far. Sally was on guard. Nevertheless, she had to press further.

'And how is Tina?' she asked.

'Oh, fine. I'm sorry you saw her just when she was in an ornery mood. But as you said, we all have them now and then.'

'That's for sure.'

'I'll give Dan your wonderful message. It'll be very welcome, especially now with everything that's happened, and Clive so ill. I know you'll hear from Dan once he starts feeling like himself again. He'll be very, very grateful.'

So, politely, the conversation closed. Amanda had learned nothing. Still, she couldn't very well have expected Sally to burst out with *I killed Oliver Grey*, could she?

One Saturday, on a brilliant afternoon, she sat alone with a book. The day was too fine to be spent indoors, but a mood had come over her, not of melancholy exactly, but tinged with it, a feeling of loose ends, that something significant had been left undone.

She had no intention of pursuing any man, least of all Todd, and that simply because, paradoxical as it might seem, she had really loved him. For all she knew, he could be married by now. But somehow it mattered to her that he should have a good opinion of her. It was shameful to think that in the future, if ever by chance he should be reminded of her by someone's mention of her name, he would recall their last few hours, which had certainly not been among the best hours of her life. She wanted him to know that her lawsuit against the family firm had been dropped, exactly as he had advised. And so she sat down and wrote him a simple letter, merely half a dozen lines, in which she told him so.

Two days later the answer came by telephone. When she heard his voice, that rich, actor's voice about which she had once teased him, her own almost failed. But she had not lost her pride.

'I didn't want to intrude on you,' she began.

'You're not intruding at all! That was a very beautiful letter. I want to thank you for it.'

'Well, it was just something that needed to be said.'

'Well, it was a very beautiful letter.'

Here they were, connected across the city by a complex mesh of wires and unable, apparently, to disconnect with grace. Having said this much, there seemed to be nothing more to say.

In bumbling haste she came up with a dull question. 'Everything going well with you, I hope?'

'Oh yes, work as usual. And I took a trip to Mexico with my brother and his family last month. That's about all.'

Then he was not married, and probably didn't have a serious commitment either, or he wouldn't have gone on vacation with relatives. Then she felt a sudden flush of embarrassment: What could she be thinking of? A year had gone by. It was long over, dead and buried.

'What about you? Has anything interesting been happening?' Todd asked.

Interesting. Rage. Crisis. Murder.

'Yes, rather. But it's a long story, too long and boring for the telephone.'

'I don't bore easily. What if I were to come over tonight to hear it?' And before she was able to get her reply out, he added, 'I don't know how you feel about seeing me again, so if you don't – '

'No, no, come over. I'll be glad.'

Amanda was never one to agonize over what to wear. 'Take me as I am,' she would have answered anyone who brought up the subject. This evening however was different, and it was almost time for the doorbell to ring before she had gone over all her sweaters and skirts of various colors (too schoolgirlish), a velvet housecoat (too seductive and in the circumstances, all wrong), a smart black silk shift (too formal), and a pink woolen shift (no, it's candy-box pink). Then the doorbell did

272

ring. And there he stood, bearing a little pot of pink tulips in one hand.

'They were selling these on the corner,' he said. 'Something told me you might be wearing pink.'

'Angelicas, my favorite.' A lovely pink, they matched her dress exactly.

In the living room, facing the famous view, they sat down. They were so stiff and awkward, it was almost funny. Or else you might say, it was sad that this had happened to two people who had once been so close – but not close enough.

Todd opened the conversation, 'Sheba looks fit and sleek, I see.' For the cat had come in, and wound herself around his ankles.

'Oh yes, the best of care. All the vitamins.'

For a moment again, there was nothing to say. Or perhaps, Amanda thought, too much to say.

'You had a long story, too long for the telephone.'

A year ago, she reflected, she would have almost died rather than disclose such ugly shame to Todd, to him of all people. That thought flashed, and then, taking a long breath, she began courageously, quite simply now. 'After my parents died, when I went to live at Hawthorne . . .'

He did not stir. She was aware that his eyes never left her face, although her own eyes were fixed beyond his head on the bay and the bridge.

'That's what it was all about, you see,' she said when she had finished the story. 'I wanted to ruin him, to cut up his beloved forest, take a piece of his company and throw everything into turmoil. Everything.'

Todd had been listening with great concern. Now he said gravely, 'I wish you had told me sooner. It would have explained many things.' He reached over and held her hands. 'Don't you think you need some help? Need to talk to somebody? It's not so simple that you can do it alone, I think.'

'I believe I can. If I need help, I'll get it. But it's incredible how, the moment I told Sally, I felt that the monkey had fallen off my back. I hadn't been free since it happened to me and then all at once, I was. I didn't feel *wonderful*, but I felt free.'

'You deserve to feel wonderful, Amanda.'

The lowering sun had laid a broad band of silvered gold over the mirror on the opposite wall. And glancing there, she saw a tableau: woman seated, and man leaning toward woman in a posture that might be one of interest, or solicitude, or could it be of desire? And she thought, now that I am ready to *belong* to a man, to belong in the best way, the only good way without inhibition or fear, I hope so much that it may be desire.

'I have to make a confession,' he said abruptly. 'You've been on my mind almost constantly these last few months. I can't tell you how many times I've gone to the telephone, put my hand out to call your number, and then withdrawn it. I wanted so much to be in touch, to *touch* you again. But something held me back. I was afraid.'

'Afraid of what?' she asked.

'That I would only be asking to be hurt again. That last time was so final. I didn't think you'd want me.'

'But it was the same for me! Even when I wrote that note a few days ago, and the minute after I put it in the mailbox, I thought I shouldn't have sent it.'

'But why?'

The only way now, she knew, was total honesty. 'I thought,' she said, 'you had surely found someone less complicated, easier to be with than I was.'

He shook his head. 'No. There were plenty of people, and there was no one.'

Their eyes made contact, his the remembered ocean blue, so astonishingly soft in the angular face.

'You'll find I'm different,' she said.

'Not too different, please.'

'Only in one way.' She stood up. 'I'm going to say something I wouldn't have been able to say before now.'

'Darling Amanda, say it quickly.'

'I would like to make love to you. If you want me. If you don't, please tell me right out and I shall never bother you again.'

He did not answer, but putting his arms around her, led her into the bedroom and laid her down, kissing her throat, her mouth, and her eyes; then he leaned over her, took the phone off the hook and possessed her.

CHAPTER
—— 18 ——

February 1991

Ever since his father's funeral Clive's mind had been turned toward death. That was nothing to wonder at, Roxanne thought; the murder of Oliver, with all the rest of his suffering, could squeeze the strength out of a stronger man than Clive.

'What the hell difference does it make whether I live or die?' he demanded. 'I'm not going to leave anything behind. Lovely house – a shell. Lovely pregnant woman – not mine, neither the woman nor the child.'

What consolation could she give? It was unspeakably tragic, all of it. Sad too, she thought, that a person had to be sick before receiving so much attention: Happy had made a Japanese bonsai garden in a jade-green dish; even Amanda telephoned from California, and Sally, all unknowing, had given him a photograph of her, Roxanne. She had made her look angelic in three-quarter profile, with head bent over a tight bouquet of rosebuds tied to ribbon streamers, and had placed it in its silver frame on the table where Clive, from his recliner, could not help but see it every time he looked up.

'You don't want to keep this here, do you?' Roxanne asked him.

'Leave it. I like looking at the frame.'

His tongue, which had once spoken only the softest words to her, now cut like a knife. And she understood that he was trying to make her feel what it was to be cast aside, thrown away, without hope.

One day she said timidly, 'Ian would like to see you.'

'Oh, so you're in touch with him?'

'On the telephone only. He wants to talk to you.'

'I can't imagine what about.'

'About what's happened.'

'There is nothing more to say about it. And tell him not to try coming here, because I'll have him thrown out. Do you understand?'

'Yes. You said that night – you said you were going to throw me out, and you haven't done it. So do you want me to go?'

'Suit yourself.'

'You need care, you need to be built up, I can cook for you,' she said, aware that her tone was humble, although she had not meant it to be.

He gave her a derisive look. 'It's not so hard to hire a cook, you know.'

She hung her head. It was a new experience to feel so humbled.

'What's the matter?' he asked. 'Is Ian through with you?'

'Yes, he's finished.'

'I don't believe it. Has he told you so?'

'No, but I can tell. A woman can tell a lot of things.'

'Oh yes, a woman can tell a hell of a lot of things. What are you crying for?' he taunted as she wiped a tear with the back of her hand. 'You may stay. It won't be for long. You'll all be at the cemetery again before summer.'

Since that awful night and through the days that followed she had scarcely cried; no doubt she had been too shocked and terrified to cry. But lately, tears were always hovering just behind her eyes. He stood watching her wipe them away.

'I'm not crying. Why should you? Maybe I'll do some good with my death. My body, what's left of the wreck, is going to science. Maybe some clever brain will find a clue in some piece of Clive Grey. "Aha!" it will say, "here I am, the answer to the riddle of cancer, and it's about time you found me."'

'Ah, don't!'

She burst into weeping and ran out, up the stairs and into the room where she now slept alone. It was cold; she was cold. The chill seeped into her bones, and she took a thick sweater from the closet. *Hand knit*, read the label, and *Made in France*. One of Clive's presents. But wasn't everything Clive's gift? And now she turned hot with shame. It was all so ugly. Ugly.

At the window she stood looking out at the snow-covered garden, the place where the rose bed lay, and wondered where they would be when it next came into bloom. Perhaps it was true that he would be dead by then, his wretched, pitiful life over. Really, really he didn't deserve such an end. And I, she thought, and I didn't mean things to turn out this way. I don't know what I could have been thinking of, or whether I was thinking at all, but only feeling, wanting . . .

From the stair landing the tall clock chimed the half hour. She remembered the day they had bought it, remembered Clive's delight; 'a gem', he had called it. Every Sunday morning he wound it and every Sunday morning explained again how one must be careful not to overwind it. He was such a good soul! If only she could have loved him in the way he wanted! He loved me so, she thought. I was for him what Ian was for me . . .

Through the fog of tears she stood gazing into the dark afternoon. Presently she heard Clive coming up the stairs and into the room, but she did not turn until he touched her shoulder.

'I shouldn't have spoken like that just now,' he said gently. 'I'm terribly sorry. Terribly ashamed.'

'That's all right. I understand.'

'The trouble is all these thoughts. I try to drive them away, and mostly I'm able to, but every few days they're back again. I ask myself whether you and Ian can possibly have known each other before we were married. He behaved so strangely that day I brought you to meet Father. Then I tell myself that's so far-fetched it's ridiculous.'

She said nothing. What good would the truth do him now?

'If only I could wipe out of my head the picture of you two in bed!' Closing his eyes, Clive shook his head as if he were actually trying to dispel the picture. Then, opening them, he said ruefully, 'But this sort of thing won't help either of us. I know that.'

'It's all right. I understand,' she repeated.

'Yes, I guess you do. You've been very kind to me since – since everything happened.'

'I've wanted to be. It's the way I feel.'

'Christ, life is hard.'

'You never know what's coming next, do you?'

'Are you worried about the future? You needn't be. You'll be all right,' he said. 'You really will.'

'Did you mean that about the cem – about dying?'

'No. People say things when they're angry.'

'I hope you didn't mean it, Clive. You're too young to die.'

'I guess Sam Jenks down our street feels that way, too,' Clive said. 'But then, he's only ninety-one.'

'I guess so.'

'Come on, smile. I don't want to see you sad. And I want you to stay here, Roxanne. This is your home. If you want to stay, that is.'

'Thank you. I do.'

'Then come downstairs. We can watch the news together. Take my hand.'

'One good thing he has going for him,' Dan said, 'is Roxanne, surprisingly enough.'

They were on their way that Sunday afternoon to visit Clive. During the past week, he had been at the office only once, and then for just half a day.

'Yes,' Dan continued, 'I wouldn't have thought by the looks of her in the beginning, that she'd turn out to be so domestic, so devoted. She's certainly trying hard to pull him through. And you know, in spite of everything, I'm willing to bet he'll make it. He certainly looks bad, but that's to be expected, with chemotherapy. It's Oliver who's really set him back. Damn! The police don't seem to be getting anywhere. They haven't even found the weapon yet.'

'What will they do if they find it?' asked Sally.

'That depends on where they find it, on where it was bought, whether licensed or not, all sorts of clues.'

She was thinking: When can I tell him, how can I? To put this weight upon him, to make him an accessory after the fact . . . I can't. Can't tell the doctor that I'm ill, that I don't sleep, that food doesn't want to go down and sometimes comes back up. I am ill . . .

The car drove past the mini-mall. People were shopping; their station wagons were filled with children and dogs. The sweetshop window was decorated with boxes of valentine chocolates, red hearts in white paper frills. She must remember to get two tiny chocolate hearts for the girls. Susannah was old enough now to hold out her arms and demand everything that Tina had.

She thought: What will happen to them if I am found out and sent to prison? And to Dan. And to my shattered parents.

'It baffles me,' Dan said, 'that Ian can be so hardheaded about that marriage. He simply ignores the woman. It's just not right. You'd think he was a duke whose brother had married out of the aristocracy. I never thought he had that kind of snob stuff in him.'

All, all unimportant, Sally was thinking. Even if by some chance they never found her out – and she didn't believe that for a moment, because they always did find out – she would have to live with this thing inside her, a thing as lethal as whatever had grown inside Clive. And she asked herself whether it was possible to harbor such a thing without cracking, without going crazy and blurting it all out in a public place, on the street or at the market.

Or what if she were to dream aloud, to talk in her sleep some night?

'You're so quiet,' Dan said. 'What is it?'

She was staring ahead through the windshield, but still she sensed that his head was turned toward her and she turned back to smile at him.

'No, I just haven't anything too much to say.'

He laughed, retorting, 'That's certainly not like you.' And added then, 'But I can read your mind. You're thinking, as usual, about Tina.'

'I'm thinking,' she remembered truthfully, 'that I see some signs of improvement.'

'Enumerate them for me.'

'Well, she hasn't had one of her no-talking spells for two weeks now. She hasn't been glued to that darn carousel as much. And you saw her on the floor this morning rolling the felt ball to the baby.'

'That was a whale of a tantrum she had yesterday, though.'

'We have to take it bit by bit, Dan.'

At the latest interview, Dr. Lisle had advised her not to bring up the painful subject with Tina. If the child should mention it, Sally was simply to say that the bad man had gone away, and she would never see him again. Sometimes Sally hoped that her own personal dilemma would be solved if Tina herself were to tell Dan what had happened. But Tina had not talked of it at all and maybe it was just as well, because if Dan were to learn about it from the child, he wouldn't believe it. Or so she thought. But it was all a guess.

Clive was lying back on his lounge chair in the den with a plaid afghan over his legs when Sally and Dan went in.

'Happy made it,' Roxanne explained. 'It's the Black Watch plaid. She's teaching me to knit and I've started one to put in the living room. It's lemon yellow, a plain stitch, nothing as hard as doing a plaid. You do feel cold when you don't exercise.'

She looked so patient, sitting here with her work on her lap. Sunshine flowed over her, while all around her the room sparkled like a blue jewel. And Sally recalled her first sight and first impression of her. The change was – it was astonishing.

Their chairs were drawn in a circle about the patient. Dan led the talk toward neutral subjects, as far as possible from cancer or Oliver or anything that would be distressful.

Nevertheless, at one point he saw fit to mention the pleasant news about Amanda's withdrawal of the lawsuit. He had never been able to hold his anger for very long, and to Sally's relief had had a civilized conversation with his sister, in which with a whole heart, he had thanked her.

'Of course, I can never forgive her unspeakable accusations against Oliver,' he had told Sally, 'because "unspeakable" is the only fit word for them. But she's done a very decent thing now, and so I'm willing to say she had a mental aberration about Oliver and let it go at that.'

'What is her stand with regard to the forest sale?' Clive wanted to know.

'No stand. She doesn't care what we do.'

'And you, Dan?'

'I've told you. Let Ian do what he thinks best. I'll go along. One thing the business doesn't need is another battle.'

Clive sat up in the chair. 'I want you to do something for me, Dan,' he said emphatically. 'I want you to vote against the sale.'

Heaven help us, Sally said to herself, hearing Dan's deep sigh. Here we go again, just when we were all through with it.

Dan said quietly, 'I don't advise it, Clive. When I gave Ian the go-ahead, I meant it. This issue has torn the firm apart and it's not healthy.'

'If you go my way, we can outvote him. Now with Amanda willing to go with the majority, Ian won't fight us in court.'

'Maybe and maybe not. It's not only the firm, though, but the family that can be torn apart.'

'You don't want to see a bunch of investors, foreigners at that, bringing in their bulldozers,' Clive argued.

'Very true, but I don't like to go back on my word. Ian and I weren't even on speaking terms for weeks, you know that. Actually, it was your father's death that brought us together and back to normal. So I don't want to do it, Clive. I really don't.'

Now Clive pleaded, 'I've never asked anything of you before, have I, Dan?'

'No.'

Nor has Dan ever asked anything of you, thought Sally, protecting Dan.

'Well, then, since you agree with me in principle, why must you humor Ian? It's time my brother learned he can't have everything in sight, can't grab anything that happens to please him but belongs to somebody else. It's time.' And as if this effort to convince had been too much, Clive fell back in the chair. Still he was not finished. 'Greed!' he cried. 'Greed.' And he waved his arms as if he were making appeal to the heavens. 'What is it all about?'

'Twenty-eight million dollars, that's what it's all about,' Dan said dryly.

'May he rot in hell with his twenty-eight million dollars!'

This outburst silenced them all. Roxanne, who had been knitting, put the work down, and, unnoticed, the ball of yellow wool fell to the floor where the pug puppy seized it. Embarrassed and puzzled by Clive's atypical behavior, Sally studied a painting of two colts on the opposite wall.

Dan said mildly, 'I'm curious about your interest in preservation. It was always my impression that a few square miles of wilderness more or less didn't matter much to you. In fact, I've heard you say so many times.'

'That's true, but this is not for me. It's for Father's sake.'

Once more Clive heaved himself upright, trembling in the chair. His eyes behind his glasses were bright with tears as he repeated, 'For Father's sake. This was his love. All my life and for most of yours, Dan, that love of his was as much a part of him as his arms and legs. We used to go walking there and he'd point out every bird and tree. I was never much interested, but I knew what it meant to him. "Hold on to this," he'd say. "Keep it intact for the generations. Promise me that when you're a man you will remember what I'm saying."' Two tears slipped down Clive's cheeks. 'Please, Dan, do this for me. I want to think that if in some way Father still has consciousness somewhere, he'll see that I remember. And even if he hasn't – '

Dan started to say, 'It's very difficult' – and was interrupted.

'He was a father to you, too, Dan.'

'I know that, Clive.'

Sally's heart began the hammering that was becoming all too familiar and all too frightening. And yet, right now might not a heart attack be the best solution for her?

'Please, Dan, for our father's sake.'

The man was piteous. It was quite clear to her that, knowing her husband as she did, he would give in. His great sigh was visible again when finally he gave his answer.

'Okay, Clive, I'll talk to Ian. I can't promise what will come of it, but I'll do my best. Who knows,' Dan said, affecting cheer, 'maybe I'll be lucky and he'll even come to agree with you.'

'So you're back to square one,' Sally said that night. 'Clive shouldn't have asked that of you. It's been an awful year and you've had enough.'

'The European group is due here next month, too. The whole thing's finalized, financing and all. Ian will have a fair-sized fit when I walk in with my change of mind.'

'Don't do it, then.'

'Sally, I have to. You heard Clive. He's got right on his side. This is the least we – I – can do out of respect for Oliver's memory.'

My God, she thought. My God. All my life now is an act.

285

Pretend health, pretend good humor and energy, pretend even joy in the act of love. For all I can see while I lie in Dan's arms is that man's face with the words coming out of his mouth, taking shape in the darkness before me: *You do that, and I'll accuse Dan of molesting . . . his own daughter . . .*

'Here are your copies of the stuff that arrived this morning from Sweden,' Ian said, coming into Dan's office. 'Better look them over and see whether there's anything you want to change or just think about before we meet.'

Dan had not been looking forward to this moment, but it had to be gotten through, so he said starkly, 'Ian, I'm going to change the whole thing. The fact is, I've changed my mind.'

'You what?'

'I've decided I can't go along with the deal. I'm back to my original position. I don't want to sell.'

Ian slapped the papers onto the desk, scattering pencils and paper clips. 'God damn it,' he shouted, 'you stood right here and said to me, "Do whatever you want. I leave it to you." Didn't you? Didn't you, Dan?'

'I did, and I don't like to go back on my word. This isn't easy for me, Ian. But the way Clive put it – I can't help myself. When he spoke about your father and what Grey's Woods have meant to him, well, he convinced me. Besides, it was pathetic seeing him there like that.'

'Of course it was pathetic,' Ian said impatiently, 'I've seen him. He's dying. He'll be dead before the deal can be consummated.'

'I don't agree. Where there's life, there's hope, and that's not a cliché.'

'There you go, the invincible optimist. Step out of fairyland into the real world. You're talking about a death that's as visible as the nose on your face, and you're also talking about twenty-eight million dollars.'

'I don't need them, nor do you. Each of us is doing

pretty well. I wish I could make you see that and drop the whole idea.'

Ian groaned. 'Here we go again. Listen, I'm losing patience. Suppose you cut out this nonsense and get down to business. I want your word once more that you won't throw any monkey wrench into that meeting next month.'

'I can't give my word. It's a matter of principle and I should have stuck with my word. My mistake was made when I betrayed it. I don't know any other way to make clear to you that my mind's made up.'

The two men glared at each other, Dan in his desk chair and Ian standing. Presently, Ian went to the window and stood in a thoughtful pose, caressing his chin.

'Suppose,' he said slowly, still with his back to Dan, 'suppose I could tell you something that will force you to change your mind?'

Was this exchange to go on all day? Already wearied of it, Dan said shortly, 'Nobody forces me, Ian. You've lived alongside me long enough and well enough to know that.'

'All right, I didn't mean "force" exactly. What I meant was, I've done something for you, so maybe you'll want to do something for me in exchange.'

'And just what is it,' demanded Dan, 'that you've done for me?'

'It's this way. Suppose,' Ian said slowly, 'suppose I were to tell you that it's your wife who killed my father.'

'What did you say?'

'I said it was Sally who murdered Oliver.'

The window that Dan faced was a brilliant blue, all blazing sky, deep cobalt. The brilliance was killing his eyes.

Ian's voice was neither sharp nor angry; it was merely flat, as if to say *It is going to rain*. 'I said Sally shot Oliver. I passed her car on the road that night just before I turned off to Red Hill.'

Dan sprang up. His fists were clenched to batter, to maim, to destroy. He went berserk. Ian grasped his wrists before the fists made contact with his face, and they wrestled. Equal in size and strength, they struggled their way around the room, swaying and panting. A chair crashed; they tripped on the telephone wire and fell heavily against furniture, smashing Ian's knee and bloodying Dan's cheek. Grunting and tearing at each other, they thrashed about on the floor.

Suddenly Dan lost his strength. He got up and collapsed into the desk chair. Between gasps he spoke.

'You're foul. I always knew you loved money too much, and women. No, I never spoke of it. It was no business of mine. But that you could be as foul as this, that you could tell a filthy lie like this, I could never have expected.'

Ian was short of breath. He took a drink of water from the carafe, straightened his tie, and said, quietly now,

'Go home and ask her. She will tell you. Sally does not lie, I think, and certainly not to you.'

Dan's hands were covering his face. The gasps had become dry sobs. 'I never thought . . . Are you such an evil man that you would concoct a story like this? I never thought . . . we were like brothers . . . better than some brothers.'

Ian laid a hand on Dan's shoulder and now he, too, was close to sobbing.

'But listen to me: Would I concoct a story like this to hurt you? You of all people, Dan? There are only three houses on that road. None of them owns a Jeep like hers, and anyway I saw her face and that sheepskin hat she wears. I had my brights on in all that storm and I saw her. So help me God, I did. But you needn't worry, needn't fear; no one will ever know. No one has known in all these weeks. Two months it's been. Go home and ask her. She'll tell you the truth.'

My Sally! My wife! Dan thought. As if *he* has to tell me she won't lie to me! Sally, an open book with everything writ clear!

He pulled himself out of the chair. 'I'm going home,' he said, taking his coat from the hook. At the door he turned around to Ian. 'I wish I never had to see you again.'

* * *

He closed the bedroom door and locked it against any interruption. Sally was reading on the sofa.

'What's that on your face?' she cried.

'Dried blood. My cousin Ian and I had a little altercation, fancy word for a damn big blowup.'

'You came to blows? Whatever for?'

'Well, I'll tell you. I guess I have to tell you.' He was still shaking. 'He dared to say – he *dared* – that you killed Oliver.'

So here it was, just neatly taken out of her hands. Well, hadn't she been telling herself that somebody, something, somehow always turns up? She felt slightly faint. Yet she was able to speak calmly.

'What makes him think so?'

'He says he recognized your car, and you, on the road leaving Red Hill.'

She had never expected to be found out by anyone literally that close to home. As Happy would say: You never know, do you. She laid her head back and closed her eyes.

'Oh, Dan, it's true.'

There was a long, long silence. When she opened her eyes, he was standing there, still with his overcoat on, just looking at her out of eyes, a face, that you see on television when, in Bosnia or some other godforsaken place on this bloodied globe, you see a father or a mother holding a dead child. And then suddenly he fell on his knees and put his arms around her, burying his face in her lap.

'Oh my God, oh my darling.'

Presently, she began to talk. It seemed to her that her own voice was coming from far away.

'On the day that Amanda came,' she began, 'and told me the things that you have not been willing to believe, but will now have to believe – '

Then it seemed to her that she had been talking for hours before she reached the end: 'If you had been here with

289

Amanda, there would have been no doubt in your mind. Believe me, Dan. And if you had heard Tina, and seen, above all, seen, what she showed me.'

For an instant, when he raised his head, she did not recognize him; in three minutes – or was it five, or was it a century? – he had grown old. His eyes were seeing not Sally, his wife, or anything in the room; they were staring into some unfathomable black hole where all belief, all trust, all faith had vanished. Ah, she knew!

'It's true, Dan, undeniably true. Tina told me herself. I didn't suggest or hint or plant ideas in any way. I only listened to her words and saw her gestures. They were unmistakable. Her account and Amanda's were identical, even though one had been twelve years old and the other was five.'

'Five!' Dan got up. He walked to the chest of drawers, on which stood a wedding photograph, a group of twenty people or more, ushers and bridesmaids, cousins and siblings – although not Amanda – surrounding the bride and groom with Sally's parents next to her and Uncle Oliver next to him. They always joked about their royal wedding party.

'All it lacks is the balcony at Buckingham Palace,' they said, laughing at themselves and liking it, nevertheless.

'How is it possible?' Dan cried now. 'How is it possible?' And Sally knew he must be examining Oliver's fine face. When he turned around, he was weeping. 'Five years old.'

'Yes,' she repeated, 'the same story, the silver carousel – who wouldn't, especially what child, wouldn't be fascinated? A bribe for silence, a threat of punishment. That's how it was.'

'And he, he couldn't deny it?'

'He tried, but he knew he'd been driven to the wall. So he made his last attempt to back me down. He was going to blame you.'

'To say that I – hurt Tina?'

'Yes, that was when I started smashing things. I threw the

guns, pistol, revolver – I don't know what it was. He'd been polishing all the metal things. It was loaded.'

She couldn't bear the way he looked. Never before had she seen his tears. She ran to him and put her arms around him thinking only, What is to become of him and our babies when they take me away? Because now that Ian knows, they will. If not tomorrow, then next week or next month, but they will.

And with his tears on her cheeks, she murmured, 'Dr. Lisle says Tina will be all right. Just keep her going there. It's the right place. And I'm sure Happy will help you with the children. And my mother will come for a while.'

He let her go. Horrified, he demanded, 'What are you saying? You're not going anywhere! What are you talking about?'

'Darling, you know what will happen to me. For God's sake, I've killed a man!'

'Nothing is going to happen to you. I swear to you I will not let it.'

'It won't be up to you. If Ian knows, soon others will.'

'Ian won't tell. It's already been two months. If he had wanted to, he would have done it by now.'

She didn't believe it, and doubted whether Dan believed it either. The gray fortress-prison on the hill was looming nearer.

'You've kept this since before Christmas . . . why did you . . . I don't know how you lived with it . . . you're made of iron.'

'What are you doing?' she asked, while he was unbuttoning her sweater.

'Undressing you. Putting you to bed. Look at you, your ribs are showing. You're cold, you're sick and you never told me, never asked for help.' He bustled about the room, fetching a quilted bed jacket, drawing the curtains, turning down the bed. 'I'm going to bring up something to eat. Just rest.'

'I'm not hungry. Honestly, I can't eat.'

'You have to eat. I'll open a can of soup. Soup and a

sandwich, a cup of tea. You're freezing. It's nerves. I'll tell Nanny to put them to bed and leave you alone.'

He was frantic.

Late that night, lying awake, he protested, 'You are not going to admit anything. I won't let you.'

'You know I'll have to. It will come to that. I will be better off if I make a clean, voluntary confession before I am forced to.'

'No!'

'Dan, please. It doesn't help me for you to get so excited.'

'Okay, I'll say it calmly. Let me appeal to you for Tina's sake. We both agree that it will be hard for her to be labeled a victim. She'll be growing up here, and why should every kid in school find out what happened to her? If he – I can't say the name – were alive, it would be different. We'd bring him to public justice and let everything else be damned. The most I can do right now is go down to the cemetery and curse him.' Dan groaned. 'And the best we can do for Tina is to keep this quiet. We've agreed.'

'I wouldn't have to say anything about her or Oliver. I would simply say that I went to talk to him about Amanda, to make peace between them, and the pistol went off accidentally – '

Dan groaned again. 'In weather like that, in the dark and alone, you found it absolutely necessary to drive all those miles to talk about making peace with Amanda. It couldn't possibly have waited till daylight, at least? And you expect anybody in his right mind to believe a cock-and-bull story like that?'

'They can believe it or not. I can't go on living this way. The weight is too heavy. It seems to me that wherever I go people are pointing at me, "That woman killed a man," they're thinking. It's like wearing a brand, a scarlet letter.'

He stroked her forehead. 'It's your conscience, your sturdy, healthy conscience. Ask it what you'll do to Tina and Susannah if you confess.'

Too tired to speak any further, she whispered, 'No

more. We can talk tomorrow. I think maybe I can sleep a little.'

'All right, but promise me you will keep this between us two only, that you'll do nothing without me.'

'I promise.'

'Because if you don't promise, I won't leave the house. I won't go to work, I'll not let you out of my sight.'

'I promise,' she said again. 'Now let me sleep.'

Dan said, 'I struck you, Ian, and I've come to say I'm sorry, because you were right. It was Sally.'

His collar was too tight, he was choking, and ripping it open, he flung his tie on the floor.

Ian got up from his chair and retrieved it. Then he went to a cabinet, poured brandy into a glass, and gave it to Dan.

'Here, take this, you need it. You're dead white.'

'I haven't slept. She did, for the first time in weeks. I don't know why I didn't notice how she was suffering. I love her so.' And Dan turned away to hide his tears.

'Sit down. Take it easy.'

'She's going to turn herself in. She wants to. I won't let her, but she will anyway. Her conscience, she says. But it was an accident!'

'Take it easy, take another swallow. Then tell me what this is all about.'

'Anyone can have an accident. Isn't that so, isn't it?'

'I ask you again, what is this all about?'

'She went there to talk business. To make peace between Oliver and Amanda. He was cleaning guns – pistols – and when she touched it, it went off.'

'That's not the truth,' Ian said.

'It is the truth, it is.'

'No. But I can't force you to tell it if you refuse.'

The muscles in Dan's cheeks were working; he felt as if every muscle in his body was jumping. Only his brain was paralyzed. And the two men, who yesterday had been grappling with each other, sat motionless, staring at each other.

'Sally is not mentally ill, so she had a reason,' Ian said. 'What is it?'

'I can't tell you.' Had they not agreed to shield Tina, to tell no one what their child had suffered? And a picture flared: little Tina, black braids, red ribbons, ruffled panties under her skirt, being fouled, fouled –

'I wish I could raise him from the dead and pull him apart,' he shouted in an agony of hatred. 'With these hands, these two hands.'

Ian leaned forward across his desk, as if he were ready to leap over it. 'Since it's my father whom you're talking about, I have a right to know. Tell me now.'

So Dan told him. He was usually a fluent speaker, impatient of inaccuracies and hesitations, but this was different and he barely stumbled through what had to be said. He had, as he spoke, an odd sensation that these walls were incredulous, accustomed as they were to simple talk of weights, freights, and tariffs, of cereal and coffee.

When he finished, there was a long silence, during which Ian cleared his throat once and Dan, careful not to look up at the other man's face, looked down to the floor and the black polished tips of Ian's shoes. The other man, the son. It would not have been at all surprising if Ian had risen in fury from his chair and shouted his outraged denial. In fact, Dan half expected him to.

Instead, he said only, 'I am at a loss.'

At that, Dan raised his head. 'I am too,' he replied.

There was another silence. Then Ian got up and went back to the liquor cabinet.

'I never drink in the morning. Actually, I don't really drink at all, but I need it.'

Dan watched him, thinking that this quiet was unreal. And he said abruptly, 'You don't challenge me! You just accept. Or am I wrong about accepting?'

'I want to say I don't believe you. I want to say it's insane, that you're insane, or that Amanda is. I know I've said a hundred times when I was disgusted with her, that she's crazy, but of course I know she isn't. And Sally is certainly no hysteric.' He wiped his forehead.

Dan said gently, 'Sally says Oliver didn't exactly deny anything. I guess he was cornered, what with Amanda and Tina giving the same account.'

'Yes, it's laid out pretty clearly, isn't it? And I'm a quick study.'

That was true. Ian's mind was like the proverbial steel trap, that quick to grasp, that sharp.

'Yes, the child, Amanda, the doctor, even the damned carousel.' He went over and laid a hand on Dan's shoulder. 'I'm trying to take it all in. It's sort of too big to fit inside your head, isn't it? Of course, it's not the same for me as for you with a little girl, but still – '

He walked away again and stopped in the center of the room, with his back to Dan. His shoulders shook, and Dan knew that he was crying. Proud, he thought, Ian is prouder than I am. And that thought in some way filled him with pity.

Then he heard Ian talking, perhaps only to himself. 'A sickness, a crippling sickness, even priests . . . they must hate themselves . . . such disgust . . .' Then he whirled about. 'Nobody must know! Let his name be clean. For all the good he did, let him at least have a clean name. I know you can't care about that, though why should you?'

'No, I can hardly care about his name. Tell me, why did you keep it a secret when all the time you knew that Sally was the one?'

'Because he asked me to.'

'He – asked?'

'Yes, he was dying when we found him, shot in the chest, bleeding from the mouth. He knew me. I bent over him and he said – he could barely talk, but he was quite distinct –

"Nobody, no fault, no blame. You hear?" He even repeated "You hear?" And I said, "Yes, I promise. Nobody's fault. I hear you." And then he died.'

'Jesus,' Dan said. 'You're sure you heard it right?'

'I'm hardly apt to forget that scene.'

'Did Happy hear it?'

'No, she was in the hall telephoning for help.'

'So you kept the promise,' Dan said. 'But then yesterday you broke it. Why?'

Ian looked him straight in the eye. 'Frankly, I was furious that you went back on your word about the sale. It flashed through my mind that if I were to tell you about Sally, you would pay me back by doing what I want, that you would appreciate my having kept quiet during all the investigation.'

'Yes,' Dan said, with a bitter smile, 'quid pro quo.'

'Just about.'

'Well, but if I were unwilling to pay you back, you would have told.'

'Not at all. Never. I swear I would not. What good would it do to send Sally to prison, or even to risk a prison sentence? Wrecking your children wouldn't bring Father back.' He mused. 'Even if it hadn't been an accident.'

'It was an accident, Ian.'

'All right, I believe you. I also know that plenty of people would say he deserved it, accident or not.'

To that Dan gave no answer. Deserved it! My baby girl! And again came that image: black braids, red ribbons, chubby legs in white socks. Once more his eyes filled; he hadn't had wet eyes since the day of his parents' funeral.

'What's the use?' cried Ian, throwing up his hands. 'It's over. The harm can't be undone. He's buried, along with the good he did and the harm he did. We can't bring him back; if I could, I would beg him to tell me why. For God's sake, why? But there's no answer . . . I suppose you've taken Tina someplace to repair the damage.'

'Yes, and we'd appreciate it if you kept that strictly to yourself. We don't want Tina to become a public victim.'

'You don't have to tell me, Dan. Do you think I would hurt your kid? Well, we grew up together. I've got my ways, but I've got my limits, too.'

It was overwhelming. Mind and body, accustomed to a predictable routine, an orderly environment, all the ingredients of respectability and responsibility, needed more than the last twenty-four hours to comprehend that a bomb had been dropped upon the Greys of Hawthorne.

And Dan looked around the room where three generations of those Greys had done their work. His glance stopped at a vase of daffodils on Ian's desk; they were a reminder that the days had been growing longer and that the grim sky outside would again turn blue. Spring. But for us, he asked himself, what spring?

'She wants to give herself up,' he said abruptly.

'She can't do that. There's no sense in it.'

'She says she can't live with herself.'

'Let me talk to her.'

'I don't think so.'

'Dan – '

'Yes?'

'It's suddenly become so unimportant, but – we have to give those people an answer.'

'About the sale.' His mind had been so far from the woods and the sale that he had to jerk it back into focus. And he made a neutral palms-up gesture saying, 'It doesn't matter to me, except that I promised Clive.'

'An academic problem. He won't be here much longer, poor guy, as I've already said.'

'I don't know about that, but if it's so, that sort of gives you the answer, doesn't it?'

'Okay. Then we'll wait. They're not coming for another month, anyway.'

'Do you still want the money that badly?' Dan asked curiously.

'Twenty-eight million, brother. Half goes to the IRS, then divide the other half among us and – '

Funny how a man can be so large-minded as Ian had shown himself to be just now and still be so greedy! It must be some gene, like having a gift for music or an allergy to shrimp.

He finished Ian's sentence: 'And you would still have a fortune, more than you need.'

'I hate to say this, Dan, but if Sally does anything foolish, you'll need every cent of that and more for lawyers.'

Dan struggled to swallow the thing, the lump in his throat that was simply stuck there, growing larger.

'I can't work today,' he said. 'I have to get back. I have to be with her.'

'Sure, sure. Go ahead.'

He put out his hand, which Ian took, pressing hard, and then he went home.

CHAPTER
—— 19 ——

In the silent house Sally went from room to room, with the heavy, patient Newfoundland padding behind her. She ought to have taken the children to the neighbor's birthday party herself, but the energy just hadn't been there, so Nanny had taken them instead. The energy was never there anymore.

At every mirror she stopped, in the unfounded hope that the next one would show a less devastating image. It was not a question of vanity; that sort of thing belonged now to another phase of her life, a phase to which she could never return. It was a question of terror.

This was how she would look in prison, or worse. She had already lost twenty pounds since that night in December, and would no doubt lose more. A study in gray and black, she thought now: gray skin and black hair, the hair that, standing out on either side of her cheeks like a pair of fans, had once reminded Dan of an ancient Egyptian portrait.

She remembered every detail of that day, from the first glancing encounter in the shop with the silver carousel, to the café where they had sat drinking cup after cup of coffee until it was almost dark. She remembered the slow walk together under the burgeoning trees, the famous view from the terrace outside the Jeu de Paume to the Arc de Triomphe, a tiny boy and a tiny dog sitting together in a stroller, and the old woman selling violets out of a wicker basket. She remembered everything.

Well wrapped in a thick tweed skirt and a twin set of

299

sweaters, she was still shivering; the wind that swept the bare trees, so that they swayed to it as if begging mercy, had crept through every crack of wood and fissure of brick into the house itself. Or perhaps, she thought, it is only because I am so thin that I am so cold.

In the kitchen it seemed to be warmer. And putting the kettle on to boil, she sat down to wait for a tall mug of tea. Kitchens were homelike; their very walls drew themselves around you. It seemed as if no harm could reach a person, here in the heart of the house with the kettle singing, the bananas heaped in the old blue bowl, and the dog so comfortably asleep under the table.

At home, her parents' home, they had kept cats. The white one, appropriately called Blanche, had owned her perch on the window ledge where she liked to groom herself in the sun, licking each pink paw in turn. Then there had been Cordelia, after Blanche, and Emma and Mathilda. Saturday mornings in that house meant pancakes and bacon; in a jug at the center of the round table there was always a handful of something green, in summer whatever was in bloom and in winter a sprig of holly or pine.

All these things are part of you, these they can never take away. They can lock you up for as long as they want in the gray fortress-prison, but these things will stay with you, these childhood houses and people, your first independent proud success, your love for Dan and the days when your children were born.

The hot tea warmed her hands, which clasped the mug, but the chill still ran in her veins. It was the chill of dread. And, she told herself in total honesty, it is not merely the dread of what will be done to me – although it is that, too – but mainly it is an awful grief because of the children and Dan, and because of my parents, who as yet have a pristine image of my happiness. If it were my suffering alone, it would be bearable, and even though I am not especially brave, I would bear it, just as Clive bears the cancer that sooner or later will kill him.

Hearing the sound of a car in the driveway, she knew it would be Dan; he had left work early to call for Nanny and the girls at the party. She was making a mess of his workdays; if it were possible, she knew, he would give up work altogether to stay at home and watch her. That morning he had absolutely forbidden her to go out today, and she wondered whether it was because she looked so ill or whether in some uncanny fashion, he had sensed the change in her, her final resolve to speak out.

When she glanced up at the clock she noted the date on the calendar hanging below it. It was a memorable date, the day on which Dr. Lisle had told her that Tina had been molested and also the birthday of the monster who had done it. Beyond the red silk curtains, there had been a strong March wind like the one that was howling now. And somebody had remarked upon the carousel, the duplicate of the one that had brought Dan and her together. It all came back to her.

But the day, thank God, was memorable now for a better reason: Tina had at last been making some real, positive improvements. There was still far to go, that was true, yet the direction was clear and unmistakable.

The family now burst into the kitchen. Right away Nanny gave the thumbs-up sign, meaning that Tina had done well at the party. The girls put their loot bags, filled with miniature Hershey bars, plastic dolls, rubber balls, and sundries, on the table, while Sally unbuttoned their Sunday coats.

Tina had an announcement. 'I told Jennifer my sister is better than hers.'

'What makes you say that?' asked Sally.

'Because. My sister's bigger and knows more words. Her sister's dumb.'

'Dumb,' said Susannah. 'Dumb, dumb, dumb.'

Tina laughed. 'You see!'

Tina's laugh! It was worth gold. Gold and diamonds and pearls. Tina's long-lost gurgle of a laugh, with her cheeks puffed and her mischievous eyes gleaming.

And Sally gathered the two girls in her arms, hugging, rocking, and laughing with them.

Dan, watching, had a look on his face that broke her heart.

Almost every night it seemed, no matter how they tried to fill the space of time with something else, they returned to the same subject.

'It's Amanda's endurance that I can't get over,' Sally said. 'To live with that all these years! And no one had sense enough to see her suffering and try to find the cause.'

'But as you said, she never wanted to reveal it.'

'Yes, the Greys' pride, she told me.'

'Pride,' Dan said bitterly. 'It turned her into an angry woman.'

'She had plenty to be angry about . . . And you remember nothing?'

'Just phrases here and there, servants' whispers, long after she had left. They called her a 'difficult girl'. I didn't think much about it. I didn't even have much more than a quick impression of the day she left. It was all so sudden. Nobody had ever said she wasn't going to stay on at Hawthorne with me. I remember, I can still see her standing in the front hall with suitcases and a little poodle in a carrier. I was trying not to cry – Uncle Oliver said boys don't cry – but of course I did cry awfully. It was hard. First the plane crash, Dad and Mom disappearing, not even any bodies left, and now Amanda going away. It was hard. Yes.' Dan nodded. 'But then, as children do, I got over it. I got happy. I had a good life at Hawthorne.'

'Didn't you think it was strange that she didn't come home at all?'

'Well, there were those nice relatives in California, and I went there to visit every summer. Amanda didn't want to come home and Uncle Oliver said that was okay, that she shouldn't be forced to do anything against her will.'

For Sally, there was a kind of comfort in thinking about

Amanda. She had somehow survived; at least she hadn't foundered. Therefore, with the love and the care that Tina was being given, she ought to do very much better, ought to do more than merely survive.

'I wish I had known Amanda,' Sally said. 'She's a valiant woman, and a loving one too, I suspect. Think of how she withdrew her claim to the stock and apologized for having made it in the first place.'

Dan agreed. 'Let's invite her for a long stay as soon as spring warms up. I'd like that. In fact, let's phone her now and ask her.'

Sally put up her arm. 'No, wait. We don't know what will be happening this next month or two.'

'If you're back on that theme, Sally, I don't want to hear it.'

'Dan, you have to hear it.' Her voice sank very low. 'I can't go on like this much longer. In fact, not any longer.'

They were in their bedroom. She was lying back on the little sofa at the foot of the bed, and now he came to sit at her feet.

'Listen to me,' he said earnestly, 'and tell me the truth. You're worried because Ian knows. Isn't that it?'

'No, I trust Ian. He wouldn't hurt the children or me. It's not on account of him at all. It's on account of me.'

'Sally! It was an accident!' he cried. And he reproached her. 'You're torturing yourself needlessly. Can't you put it in a compartment and lock it away in your head?'

'You wouldn't say that if you were a lawyer.'

'Then I'm glad I'm not.'

'But we all live under the law.'

'Please don't lecture me.'

'I'm not. Maybe I sound pious or something, but there is such a thing as conscience and mine nags me day and night. Day and night, Dan.'

'He deserved to die.'

'I know, but not at my hands.'

'Your hands.' He bent down and kissed them, murmuring, 'Sally, you'll kill me and the little girls. I beg you, don't do this terrible thing to us. And what good will it do anyway for you to go through a trial and be judged, and God forbid, be sent to prison? What will it prove?'

'Only that we can't let the vigilantes run things.'

'For God's sake, you weren't a vigilante! It was an accident!'

'We're going in circles, Dan, and I am so tired.'

He stood and looked down to where she lay. 'Yes,' he said, 'you look like hell. I'm going to take you and the girls with Nanny to some warm place where you can lie in the sun, rest and put some weight on.'

'You've said that more than once, poor darling. But the sun can't take this trouble away. I have to tell, Dan, just as Amanda eventually had to.'

'That was entirely different.'

'Not really. It's just that things swell up inside you until there's no room for them, and then they burst out.'

'We've had this talk so many times before and we never get anywhere. Will you let Ian talk to you? After all, it was – he was – Ian's father. Maybe you'll listen to him.'

'Please darling, as you said, we've had this talk so many times. It's no use. I'm going to turn myself in on Monday.'

He clapped his hand to his forehead. 'My God, I think I'm mad.' He walked away, turned about to look at her, walked away again, and came back. 'Not Monday. You've got to see a lawyer first. That's common sense and I demand it. I happen to know that Larson's coming home from a vacation on Wednesday. We'll see him then. Do you promise you'll wait till then?'

She did not want to cry. Through sheer effort she kept the tears from starting. 'Yes, but I'm not going there to have him try to talk me out of it.'

'Don't I wish,' Dan said grimly.

Of course no lawyer of any repute would talk her out of it.

She knew that. But he would guide her, and then the fates, such as they were, would do the rest.

Since early morning, Clive had been at the hospital and now the afternoon was coming to a close. In a little anteroom next to his doctor's office, a private waiting room for privileged patients, he supposed, he sat flipping through magazines. The pain in his back was so severe that, in spite of all his shifting of positions, it was almost unbearable. So he stood up and that was just as bad. The pain had been spreading into his thighs, growing in small increments, day after day for – how many days? Ten? Eleven? He had lost count. The pain was blinding him.

Someone said, 'Dr. Day will see you now.'

He went in. The doctor was studying a little pile of papers. When he looked up, his expression was readable. Doctors' expressions always were; there was the cheerful glint in the eye that said 'Everything's negative,' and then there was the expression, slightly puzzled, that said 'I have bad news and I'm trying to figure out how best to break it.'

'Well,' Clive said, 'it's no good, is it?'

'There's always – ' the doctor began, but Clive interrupted.

'Forgive me for being impolite today. It's a bad day and my father's birthday and I know I'm dying, so please say it quickly. I'm ready for it.'

The doctor made the gesture with upturned palms and lifted shoulders that expresses inevitable failure.

'I'm so sorry, Clive. Damn, it's the hardest thing . . . Okay, here it is. The X ray, bone scans, MRI, all the stuff shows that it's spread. It's everywhere, bone, kidneys, liver, all over.'

'I see.'

'We tried. Damn, you seemed to be making such good progress after we took out your lung. Real progress all winter. Now this comes along.' Again, he made the gesture. 'Like wildfire, a forest fire that you can't put out.'

Clive held his head up. 'How long?'

He hadn't till now been conscious of a clock in the room. Suddenly, it was very loud. Tick. Tick.

'Anytime,' the doctor said.

Clive struggled out of the chair and found a few words. 'Thank you for everything. You did everything that could be done.'

'Where're you going, Clive?'

'Home. Where else? I want to be home.'

'I meant, how are you getting there?'

'My wife is driving. She's been here all day waiting in the lobby.'

The other man seemed to be striving for something to say and do. He got up and held the door open, shook Clive's hand, and shook his own head, saying, 'Waiting all day, that's a patient wife, do you want me to go down and talk to her, perhaps I can – '

'No, no. It isn't necessary, but thank you all the same.'

Then Clive hurried into his overcoat and in all his pain, ran down the stairs.

After he had briefly told Roxanne what he had learned, after he had heard the customary indrawn breath and the expected response, *Oh, but doctors have been wrong, my aunt was told nine years ago that she only had six months*, he asked for quiet.

'You mean well, but that's all nonsense and you know it is,' he said quietly.

'When – when did he say it would – '

'Anytime.'

He knew she was hoping it wouldn't happen now in the car or some other place right in front of her. He could hardly find fault with her for that. He would feel the same natural dread if he were in her place.

All he wanted right now was to get home and take something for the pain. Yet, there was also a part of him that wanted to

306

prolong the ride; it might very well be his last. *Never*. It was an extraordinary word when you had to apply it to yourself. And he looked avidly out at the sky, heavy with wintery clouds, at the wind, so fierce that you could imagine you actually saw it battering the trees, and at a dead deer lying on the side of the road; in a winter such as this one had been, there were many such deaths. But in May, in sixty days from now, would come the good time, new leaves and then myriad chirpings of returning birds; then the mare, scenting the spring, would break into a canter.

'I know you don't feel like talking, but I thought if there's anything you especially want to eat, I can stop at the store. It will only take a second.'

She reached over to press his hand, and held it. When he glanced at her in response, he saw the glint of her tears.

'Thank you, let's just get home.' He was moved beyond words. She was so very, very kind to him; never in all his life had he felt so cared for, so guarded, so cherished. Noiselessly, she moved about the house, gave him food and drink; took books down from the shelves for him and replaced them, put music on the player and replaced the discs; when he needed nothing, she went quietly up to the room that she now occupied, and let him alone.

Once she had asked him whether he wanted to hear the full story about her and Ian, but he had not wanted to. He had no wish to make more vivid the mental images that were so graphic, too searing and too humiliating. They were no longer important anyway. Yes, he thought wistfully, one's own imminent death does most 'wonderfully concentrate the mind'.

When they reached home, the house was dark except for the kitchen light that had been left on for the benefit of Angel, who now came rushing to be picked up.

'Go sit on your chair in the den,' Roxanne directed. 'It'll be easier on your back than sitting at the table. I'll bring dinner on a tray.'

She was taking charge, which was what people naturally seemed to do in the presence of imminent death. He found himself, as he obeyed, analyzing her probable emotions, and concluded that they were a mingling of natural fear and true compassion. And he could see her, on the night after his funeral, standing alone in this large house, probably holding the little pug to her chest, and remembering the day she moved in when it all belonged to her.

When she had set the tray down and turned to go back to the kitchen where she ate alone, he asked her to bring her food in and join him.

'It's time we spoke,' he said.

She answered eagerly, 'I've been wanting to ever since that night. I want to. I really need to tell you everything.'

'I don't want to hear everything. I don't want the details.'

'All right, no details. Let me just say it was rotten, what happened. But *you* should understand how when somebody falls for somebody it just – '

He stopped her. *You should understand*. She had put emphasis on the 'you'. But to speak of 'falling for' when it had been so – so glorious, a total transformation of self, a new life, a new *persona*! What did she know of that? She had never been inside his, Clive's, skin. It wasn't in her to know!

And yet perhaps it was. Perhaps it was a case of not having the vocabulary to express herself.

At any rate, there were practical things to be taken care of.

'That's not what I meant,' he said. 'I meant – what do you plan to do after I die?'

'I'm going away. I certainly can't stay here.'

'Who's going? You and Ian?'

'No! That's all over. You must believe me.'

'I see. What about the child?'

'I don't know. We haven't talked about it.'

Her head was bent, her profile outlined in the lamplight. Pure Greek, he thought, a classic head.

And he said abruptly, 'You will take no money from him. I am leaving enough for you. As far as the world knows, the child is mine. Don't punish it before it is even born by attaching a scandal to its name, and don't hurt Happy.'

'Oh, no, I would never do that. She's been a friend to me. She's the kind of woman – she's old-fashioned, not like me. What I mean is, in her position, if that happened to me, I would take the bastard for all he's worth, all I could get, and kick him out. But she – it would break her up if she knew, and what good would it do me? I said that once to Michelle. We were talking about Ian and me – '

'Don't tell me. As long as I know you will keep your word, that's enough.'

'I will keep it. I'm thinking, I'll go to Florida and be with Michelle. That is, if – '

'If there's money for her to stay on in school? There will be. Why should I punish Michelle either? She's a nice kid. As long as she's doing well, let her stay there and make a life for herself.'

Roxanne was crying. 'I don't know, I don't know what to think! You're so good! I never knew there could be people like you. I wish I could help you, do something for you. I'd go to China, Africa, anywhere – '

'You can do this. Go to the telephone, call Dan and Sally, then call Happy and Ian.'

'Ian?'

'Yes, yes, Ian. I want them all here at ten o'clock tomorrow morning. It's very important. They must come, all of them. And after that, call my lawyer, Timothy Larson, and tell him I need him here, too. The number's in my book.'

The medicine had begun to take effect, so that the pain merely nagged and could be borne. He looked around the room, at the muted reds and blues in old rugs, at his books, the horse paintings and the photograph of his mare, who perhaps would not even recognize him anymore. He hoped she would find a good home, for she and all his possessions would surely

309

be dispersed. Or maybe they might keep the mare until Tina grew old enough to ride her.

'Mr. Larson's away and will be back Wednesday,' Roxanne reported.

'Then tell them to send a partner. I don't care who it is.'

When she returned, he saw that she was very uneasy, and he said gently, 'You look so scared, poor girl. But there's no need for you to worry, I promise you.'

'If you say so. But I wish I understood what it's all about.'

'You will,' he said.

They were all sitting in a semicircle facing Clive. There was a certain drama in the situation, with him presiding, totally in charge, while all of them had to wait for him. The only persons there who did not seem distressed were Happy and Mr. Jardiner, the lawyer.

Ian kept playing with his little gold penknife; he was sitting close to Happy, while Roxanne was at the opposite end of the semicircle. Maybe it was true, then, that they were finished? She had said so, and he wanted so much to believe her. It did seem that way, though, for they were being very careful not to look at each other. Appearances, however, were deceiving. Indeed.

Sally and Dan both looked worn and haggard, as if they had not slept for weeks. He wondered what might be the trouble. They were two people who didn't deserve trouble, though that was not the way the world worked. Indeed.

'I asked you to come, Mr. Jardiner, because I want a responsible witness to what I am going to say.'

Mr. Jardiner, who was very young, probably just out of law school, nodded with appropriate gravity.

'There are two more people coming. In fact, I see the car now. Will you open the door please, Roxanne?'

Two men with the stride and posture of authority entered and took their seats. Clive made the introductions.

'Detectives Murray and Huber from homicide, Mr. Jardiner, my lawyer. The rest of us have met before.'

It seemed as if the entire semicircle had leaned forward, about to topple or at least to reach for their toes. It was very nearly enjoyable to watch the play as, like a puppet master, he pulled the strings.

Huber began, 'Do you have a clue?'

'No, I have the solution,' Clive said.

Alarm traveled from one to the other, all the eyes widened, Ian stopped fidgeting with the penknife, and Dan grasped Sally's hand.

'As the family members know, I am a sick man. My remaining lifetime can be counted in days. In this condition, a person has some very serious thoughts.' He paused. Let them wait. He would tell it in his own fashion. 'It came to me that at some time in the future, even years from now, some poor vagrant who breaks into a house may be seized as a suspect in the murder of my father. It's possible. That sort of thing has happened.' He looked toward the detectives. 'Isn't that true?'

Huber acknowledged the possibility. 'But not likely,' he added.

'Even so, I've asked you here to set a record straight. I am the person who shot Oliver Grey to death. I and only I.'

There was a long, anguished collective gasp. Happy gave a sharp cry, Ian stood up and sat down again, and Dan started to say something, but was prevented by Detective Huber, who held his hand up in a stop signal.

'Yes,' Clive resumed, 'I was crazy, mad, hysterical, whatever you want to call it. I had intended to kill my brother. Things had happened . . . yes, things. It doesn't matter.' He paused, gave a kind of gasp, and continued in a voice so exhausted that the others strained to hear.

'I took the gun. I can't really say what I was thinking or whether I even was thinking. I went out into the snow. I remember I fell on the back path going up the hill. I took off my shoes so as to leave no tracks in the house and went in at the back door. I knew that Father went to bed early and that Ian was there for the night. Of course he was late, he hadn't gotten there yet, but I didn't know that. I was crazy, mad, do you understand? It was almost dark in the hall and I mistook my father for Ian. Yes. My father. I was crazy, do you understand?' Clive looked from one to the other, across the stunned semicircle. 'The gun was a thirty-eight-caliber revolver. It's here now. Roxanne, take the officers upstairs. On the top shelf of my closet there is a green book, *Principia Mathematica*. It's hollow. The gun is inside.'

Except for Mr. Jardiner, who had begun to take rapid notes on a little memo pad, it was as if all in the room were dazed. No sound broke the thick silence while the three were upstairs. When they returned, the semicircle straightened its collective back to peer at the open book with the gun inside it.

Murray spoke. 'So you planned to kill your brother. Why?'

How to answer? Because all my life he got everything he wanted. Everything.

'Why?' Murray repeated.

'I prefer not to say, except that Ian has committed no crime. In that respect, he is an innocent man.'

This was enough. They had no need to know more.

'It would be advisable to answer, if you can,' Mr. Jardiner said quietly.

'I can, but I don't choose to. You have the gun and voluntary confession.'

The detectives were not so easily put off. 'It would help you in your defense if you would give some reason for this hatred you speak of.'

'I don't want any defense. I'll be dead before you can even convene a grand jury.' Then Clive read their thoughts. 'And it won't be suicide,' he said.

The room, the house, the vast morning outdoors, nothing was large enough to contain the emotional typhoon that swept him. And searching from one numb face to the other, his eyes glancing from Ian to Roxanne, he said, 'If there is anyone in the room who knows why, he *knows*, that's all, and no one else needs to.' His glance returned to Ian. 'I'm glad now that I didn't hurt you, Ian. You have a long life ahead. So, I've said it and I can go in peace, more or less.'

Huber inquired, 'Had you intended to use the weapon again? Most times the alleged killer disposes of it.'

Clive had to smile at the 'alleged'. 'I would have if I could have found a way, but I have been unable to drive myself and be alone. It's just as well. Now you can match the weapon with the wound and neatly sew up your case.'

On the instant, the echo came to his ears, into his very heart: *Wound*. Red, torn, wet, a gaping horror. And suddenly he cried out, as if there were no one there to hear, or as if it made no difference who heard, 'My good father! The only human being who loves – who really loved me since my mother died. He, who never harmed a soul on this earth, only did good all the days of his life. My God, my God.' And he rocked back and forth, weeping.

Then suddenly he rose from the chair, as the cutting pain came back, mounting higher than ever before, digging and rending, trying to break him in two. He stood up and took a step, as if he would run away from agony. Then he stumbled and fell.

When the ambulance took Clive away, Roxanne rode with him.

'There's room for one. His wife may go,' said the attendant.

'His doctor said the bone gave way,' Ian reported as he put down the telephone. 'It just broke apart. He wasn't surprised.'

Mr. Jardiner, while doing his best to maintain judicial calm, was as stunned as everyone else. Yet he thought to observe, 'Without question, the poor man's mind broke apart, too.'

313

Spoken like a lawyer preparing for his defense, Ian thought. And he quickly agreed. 'Yes, I've been seeing something coming for quite a while, although since I'm not a doctor, not qualified to diagnose, I didn't talk about it. But he's been in a frenzy, I can only call it that, over the sale of the woodlands. Quite abusive, unreasonable, really not quite – well, quite sane. He has to be forgiven.'

Mr. Jardiner made more notes. Happy, tearful and trembling, clung to Ian's arm, and Dan, frowning in an effort to recollect, tried to imagine a frenzied and abusive Clive. *Clive?*

And then again, in a flood came the realization that Sally had been freed . . . quite obviously, the report she had heard had been the sound of a blank. No one would have live ammunition in those fancy, silver-plated collector's items . . . They were all standing in the hall, near the door at which Clive had been carried away, but Sally had climbed a few steps up the stairs and sat there now alone. It was the aftershock, he knew, thinking, Now I will really take you away, we'll have a whole week to ourselves. Tina is doing so well, she can be left with Nanny, a whole week for you and me, for you to recover, oh my dear, my darling.

Detective Huber, who had been taking his turn at the telephone, rejoined the group.

'The boss got the devil of a shock. First, he didn't even believe me. Jeez! Never heard anything like it in my life. He'll be putting two guys there outside the poor bas – the poor man's room. Jeez! Never anything like it in my life.'

Murray said, 'Of course we knew it was an inside job, an employee, an employee who was mad about something, or possibly the family.' He flushed and, as if in apology to the family before him, explained, 'Can happen in the best, you know. So we knew. The house was full of valuables and nothing was taken. There was even cash on the table, seven one-hundred-dollar bills. Yeah, the bullet came from a thirty-eight, from this baby right here,' he said with the green book under his arm.

'Yup, as they say, if you wait long enough, murder will out.'

'Not always,' Murray reminded him, 'but most of the time.'

If only we could have known all this three months ago, Dan thought.

Happy was seeing the body on the floor in the hall, the body that could have been Ian's, her husband's, her love, her only love.

At least, Ian thought, Clive will die believing that Father was the man we always knew he was, while for me – I will live knowing otherwise.

Poor Clive. Did I not always believe there was something wrong with him? Sally said to herself.

'I think,' said Huber, as the two prepared to leave, 'you folks owe yourselves a good stiff drink.'

'Or two,' Murray added.

Mr. Jardiner tucked his notebook in his pocket, put on his overcoat, and gave parting advice.

'There will be reporters, of course. They'll be descending on you all like a swarm of hornets. Tell them nothing. Have someone else open the door and say that the family is not available. They may call our office if they wish, and, of course, they will wish. The facts are simple: It's been a matter of public knowledge that the family members have been in disagreement over the proposed new community in the forestlands. Clive Grey's cancer had spread to his brain and in the course of this ordinary business disagreement, he lost control. He was not responsible. That's it. As for you all, what is there to say? It's a terrible, terrible thing! I hardly know how to tell them at the office. I understand' – this with a nod to Ian and Dan – 'that you are third-generation clients of our firm. Mr. Larson will be devastated when he hears this.'

'Devastated,' Happy said when the front door closed. 'I guess the word will do, because really there is no adequate word.' Her eyes were red and she blew her nose. 'How are we ever going to get over it?'

The four stood waiting together in the hall, marooned, Sally thought, like people cast away, deciding what to do first, whether to put up a white flag for rescue, forage for food, or build a shelter. The house, after what had just occurred within its walls, was as ominous as that desert island.

'Poor Roxanne,' she said. 'Not married a year yet.'

'Imagine,' Happy said. 'Police guards outside his door. I had no idea his mind had gone like that. You never told me, Ian, and it's odd that I never noticed it. Did you ever notice anything, Sally?'

'Not like that, exactly, although he was always a bit odd, I thought.'

'Ridiculous.' Dan was indignant. 'There was never anything wrong with Clive until this cancer spread. Nothing. I'm going down to the hospital. What about you, Ian?'

'Of course. You all don't have to, unless you want to.'

Happy, needing to be busy, said she would stay and tidy the kitchen. 'Their breakfast dishes are still on the table. I think I'll take the dog back to our house, Ian. Roxanne will probably be gone all day and he'll mess up, with nobody here to let him out.'

Sally understood that need to occupy one's hands, to move about and make work, even when there was no work. 'I'll stay and help,' she offered.

Ian released a heavy sigh. 'A criminal trial. That will kill him, if the cancer doesn't.'

'By the looks of him, the cancer won't take very long about it,' Dan said gravely. And he tried to imagine himself, but could not, having a brother who had wanted to murder him.

When the women went into the kitchen, Ian said very low, 'Dan, I wanted to get a minute alone with Sally. I should get on my knees before her.'

'No need for that. You saw what you saw, and you reached a logical conclusion.'

'I put her and you through hell. Tell her how sorry I am, will you. Tell her I'll never forgive myself.'

'Ian, it's okay. It happened, that's all. The whole thing's a horror and absolutely no fault of yours.'

'You don't mean that.'

'What do you mean?'

Ian walked away into the living room. Dan watched him go to the end, stand before the fireplace with his head bowed, go to the window, drum with his fingers on the glass, and return to the hall with an expression of utter despair on his face, a despair so striking that Dan grasped his shoulder and gently shook him.

'Come on,' he said. 'This business has been enough to knock down ten men at once. I want you to go home and rest. I'll go to the hospital and let you know what's happening. Come on.'

'I want to talk to you. My head will split if I don't talk to somebody, and you're the one, the only one.'

What could it be? What new confession, what betrayal, might yet be forthcoming?

'Put your coat on, Dan. We'll talk outside.'

In the angle between the house and the garage, they stood out of the wind and Dan waited while Ian kicked at a patch of melting snow on the driveway. He understood that, whatever it was Ian wanted to disclose, he was having a hard time beginning or maybe was having second thoughts about disclosure.

So he said kindly, 'If you've changed your mind, say so.'

'No.' Ian now looked him firmly in the eye. 'No. This has to be said. It's damn hard, but here it is. What this is all about, you see, is that Roxanne and I – ' Here he kicked again at the chunk of snow. 'She and I, you see, we knew each other before Clive married her. I had no idea, I was as shocked as any of you the day he brought her to the house as his – his *bride*. No, I was a thousand times more so, couldn't believe what I was seeing. We had sort of broken up, sort of, but not exactly, and she did that to spite me.'

317

Dan felt his mouth drop open. 'And Clive never knew?'

'He never knew anything until the night he shot Father. Didn't know that we had started up again – not much, just a couple of times – and that the baby – you know she's pregnant, don't you? – isn't his. It's mine.'

'God almighty,' Dan said.

'We started almost three years ago. I met her – well, it's not important. Things happen. You have only to look at her and see how it happened. You can fill in the rest, or maybe you can't. I suppose you and Sally – but then I don't really know about you two either. Things are not what they seem.' Ian grimaced. 'That's cliché number one.'

The last thing Dan ever wanted to do was to sit in judgment; it wasn't his way. And yet, in the face of this revelation, he was unable to resist a little self-defense. And he answered quietly, 'Sally is everything to me. Everything.'

'You may not believe it, but Happy is to me, too. That's what we fought about. She wanted me to leave Happy. Christ! I'd cut my arm off first.'

'What if Happy finds out?'

'She won't. Roxanne doesn't want to hurt her because she likes Happy. Happy's been good to her. It's a funny thing, but there's a very decent streak in Roxanne, too. I think she surprises herself with it. So we don't know ourselves either, do we? Cliché number two.' Now that he had begun to speak, Ian seemed unable to stop. 'It's no excuse, but sometimes I think if I hadn't – if Father hadn't rushed me into marriage before I'd had a few more years of experience, I wouldn't have done so much chasing. Again, no excuse. My God, if anything could be a lesson, this is it. Jesus! I blew Clive's mind! My brother's mind! I've got to tell him before he dies, got to . . .' His eyes brimmed and the tears ran over. 'But I can't say, can't tell *him* of all people how it really was between her and me. I'd never had anyone like her. I knew I should end it, yet I wanted it to last forever. And then you know what, Dan? It died. These things always do. You never think they will, but they do. Suddenly something happens and they die. Dan, you're the only other person who'll ever know about Roxanne and me. That should tell you what I think of you. I trust you with this the way you trust me with what happened to your Tina. How is she?'

'Better. She's doing much better.'

'That's good. Thank God. That's another thing that haunts me. When Clive said that about Father's never having harmed a soul, I felt the shame and horror all up and down my back. I thought of Tina and Amanda. I know, I read about these people, but it doesn't register. I don't understand. I don't recognize my own father. God! It's one thing to fool with women, but to do what he did . . .' Ian groaned.

Dan said quickly, 'You're not responsible. It has nothing to do with you.'

'Dan, I've been hard to get along with. Restless and guilty and too stupid to be thankful for what I've got. You may not believe it, it's queer, but you know, these blows seem to have knocked the loose parts of my head into some shape. I feel – I'm not putting it very well, but I feel different. I *am* different. You'll see.'

The March wind came swooping around the corner of the house. Small broken branches went skittering down the drive. Ian drew up his coat collar and shivered. Suddenly his teeth began to chatter.

'You're freezing,' Dan said. 'Get in my car.'

'No, it's my nerves. I'll be all right, I'll pull myself together.'

'Let Happy take you home. We're going, too. We've all had too much this morning, and we're not through yet.'

On the third morning the nurse, who had for a short while left his room, returned to find Clive dead of a massive internal hemorrhage.

A few minutes later Roxanne arrived; a few minutes after her, came Ian. It was the wife's privilege to enter the room first

319

alone, which she did, emerging quickly to let the brother have his turn. He was to remember, and knew as he stood there that he always would remember, that small body, all yellow skin and bones, and that small hand already growing cold. He was to regret, and knew that too, that his brother had never been conscious enough for any last dialogue between them.

When the doctors had left and the burly guards had been removed from the hall, Roxanne and Ian went downstairs and out to the parking lot.

'I suppose,' she said, 'you're wondering what I'm going to do. Well, I'll tell you. I'm going away. You won't have to worry about my hanging around. I never want to see this place again. I feel like dirt here.'

'I don't feel exactly clean either,' he said.

'There's no comparison between us. At least you never lied to me.'

'Not to you, but to everybody else.'

'So you'll make up for it now.'

'It's too late to make up for it to him, if I ever could have.'

'Your trouble with him began a long time ago in kindergarten. If you weren't so damn attractive to people, he'd have been a different person. His body played a lousy trick on him.'

And yours was a gift from the gods, Ian thought. But she had lost her power over him. He knew that surely, as they stood with only inches between them. Her rich hair glinted in the light, her heart-shaped face was nestled in a silk scarf printed with violets, and he could smell her perfume. But no throb of any kind responded.

His glance moved to her abdomen and, quick as always, catching the glance, she said, 'Not to worry. I am his widow and so of course it's his. He wanted it that way. He was a good man – and he was crazed when he tried to kill you.'

'Yes, I know.'

'He's left money for me and my sister, too. I'm going to

sell the house and go to live in Florida. Keep Michelle away from the fights and the drunken grandpa. You'll be glad to know we're never coming back.'

He could certainly not deny being glad about that. Yet, mixed with the inner turmoil of guilt and blame was a feeling of compassion, and he said, 'I'm glad he's left you provided for. It's not as much as I promised you if we had sold the woods but – '

'You're not going through with the sale?'

'No. I've called it off.'

'All of that money?' she asked curiously.

'I've lost interest. I've come to think that it's crazy to want that much. It's like stuffing yourself with six sirloin steaks or six pies while one is plenty.'

'Haven't you changed, though!'

'Yes,' he said, 'I have, but it took a damn lot to do it.'

'Want to hear something funny? I've changed too. I really loved you, you know, and now it's all gone. Just like that,' and she snapped her fingers. 'And believe it or not, I'm going to miss Clive.'

'I know.' That was all he could think of to say.

'We won't be seeing each other except in a crowd at the funeral or someplace,' Roxanne said. 'So I'll say it now and shake your hand. Good luck, kid. It was nice knowing you.'

On the beach, in the sun, they lay looking out at the lazy waves. All morning Sally had been engrossed in a book, the first she had been able to read since last December. She was functioning again. Now, having put it aside, she mused.

'I still can't understand how Clive could have set out to kill his own brother. He really had to have been insane.'

'Not necessarily,' Dan said.

'Then what?'

'Oh . . . nothing.'

'You're hiding something. You have a secretive look.'

'Uh-uh.'

'That morning at Clive's house, you and Ian were talking a long time out by the garage. What was it about?'

'Business.'

'Dan Grey, I do not believe you. You're keeping secrets.'

'If there is a secret, Sally, don't ask me to tell it because I never will. Never.'

That she knew, so she asked no more, but lying back on the towel, let the sunlight warm her bones. And suddenly Dan spoke into the stillness.

'Can you believe that morning, that scene? It's like a title for a book: *The Day Our World Turned Inside Out*.'

'I wonder whether Dr. Lisle ever thought I was the person who murdered Oliver. And I've always had a hunch Amanda thought so.'

'Well, now they both know you didn't.'

'But why did Oliver slump against the wall when he hadn't been shot?'

'I think because he was terrified. He knew he was caught. Oh, Sally, think of it, we were going to see Larson on Wednesday so you could give yourself up! How you suffered, how brave you were! If anything ever happened to you – '

'Darling, nothing will.'

He sat up. 'Let's go back to the room. We came here to celebrate.'

She laughed. 'It's only two in the afternoon!'

'I don't give a hoot what time it is. Come on, I'll race you in.'

CHAPTER

—— 20 ——

The great house had come back to life. At the entrance, on a high stone gatepost, there hung a sign on which in elegant brass lettering was written: THE HAWTHORNE ECOLOGICAL MUSEUM AND STUDY CENTER. On this mild Sunday afternoon in late September, the dedication ceremony was taking place in the auditorium that had been created where the Greys had once had their dinners, read their books, and entertained their guests. A crowd had filled all the chairs, and standees overflowed into the hall. Speaker after speaker, experts from the universities, community leaders, and finally the mayor, praised with eloquence the preservation of the earth, the education of the young, and the vision of Oliver Grey.

'Tirelessly he gave of himself. We have all been the beneficiaries of that vision and his great heart. Among his many gifts, this building, along with the grand forests that his family has now so generously given to the state in perpetuity, to be kept forever wild, is his most enduring monument.'

Above the mayor hung a posthumous portrait of Oliver Grey. Sally remarked how accurate it was, catching as it did an expression that in some way had managed to be at the same time austere and benign. How extraordinary everything was today! And when she met Dan's smile over the heads of Susannah and Tina, who were sitting between them, she smiled back. They had come a long way.

After the speeches, the crowd dispersed through the building to see the classrooms and the exhibit halls with their

323

displays of wildlife, vegetation, and rocks. On the expanded terrace, where the caterer's crew served refreshments, the Greys were expected to hold court for an hour or so.

Happy, a sun-streaked blonde in rosy health, was exceptionally pretty today and Sally told her so. 'Pink becomes you,' she added.

'Last of the summer dresses, last that I can barely fit into, anyway.'

Happy was pregnant and full of rejoicing because she was carrying a boy. 'Yes, after all these years. How I longed for one! And Ian is so excited I don't recognize him.'

He was indeed a changed man. The swagger was gone, and in its place had come a subtle moderation, as if he had overnight grown into maturity.

They were surrounded by well-wishers, sincere friends, celebrity hunters, and the merely curious; it would take years before the great Grey murder would cease to be a thrill. So they stood patiently, shaking hands and making the pleasant small talk that people expect of each other on such occasions.

'Do you remember me?' a woman said. 'Joan Lennon, three houses down from Clive and Roxanne. We were good friends in the short time we knew them. Such a tragedy!'

Yes, they remembered her.

'I just came back from Florida, my mother lives down there, and I thought you might like to hear that I ran into Roxanne.'

At that, they were both interested. It had seemed unpardonable to Sally and Happy that Roxanne never wrote or even let anyone know where she was, although neither Ian nor Dan had been at all concerned.

'She asked to be remembered to you. She looks absolutely wonderful. Well, she always did, didn't she? She has a beautiful apartment with her sister, a lovely girl. Roxanne keeps an eye on her. And she has a man, a good-looking older man who seems quite crazy about her. I heard he's going to marry her. I'm glad for Roxanne. She had such a bad time, poor girl, and then losing the baby right afterward. It was awful. Somebody said it was an abortion, not a miscarriage, but of course I suppose you know much more about it than I do.'

'No,' Sally said, 'we don't.'

'No? Well, it is a woman's private business after all, isn't it?'

'I do wonder why we never hear from her,' remarked Happy when the woman left them.

'I always had a vague feeling that there was something unfortunate in her life that she didn't want us to know about,' Sally said. 'Something ugly that she was ashamed of.'

Uncomfortable with such conjectures, Happy merely shrugged. Like Dan, she was cheerfully inclined to think the best of everyone and everything.

'Ah, Amanda and Todd!' she exclaimed. And as they approached, 'You're late. We thought you might have changed your minds.'

'I wouldn't have missed this for anything,' Amanda said. 'This gloomy pile turned into something so lively! It was worth the trip. Besides, I wanted Todd to see you all. You hardly got in more than a hello and good-bye at that little wedding of ours.'

They seemed well matched; Sally had decided that, the first time she saw them together. Eyes told you so much, and she liked the way Todd's twinkled behind his glasses. He's got more humor than Amanda, she thought, and Amanda's so earnest, so energetic; they'll balance each other.

'Where are the girls?' Amanda inquired.

'Nanny's taken them down to the duck pond with stale bread.'

'You're keeping Nanny on?'

'I have to. I'm back at work, doing that book of animal photos. It's a huge job. And you?'

'I'm enlarging the home. Todd got hold of a great architect

325

and we're putting on an addition that will make room for twenty more girls.'

It was good to be talking about lives that were moving, producing. So they spoke together, until Todd and Happy drifted toward another group. Then the two who were left almost at once returned to the theme of that December afternoon three years before.

Amanda wanted to know what had been done with Hawthorne's furnishings.

'Everything was auctioned in New York. The sale was fabulous. People scrambled for the stuff. All the money goes to the foundation, paying for teachers and lectures and maintenance.'

Amanda looked out over the lawns and gardens, then up at the stone walls where ivy rose to the second story.

'That window, second from the corner, that was my room,' she said.

A shiver went through Sally and she did not comment.

'Whatever happened to the carousel?' Amanda asked.

'Sold with the rest of the stuff. I believe it brought more than seventy-five thousand dollars.'

Amanda said hesitantly, 'I have to confess that once I thought perhaps you – you knew something about – ' She stopped.

The two women looked at each other for a moment, Amanda with the startled, embarrassed expression of someone aware that perhaps she had said too much. Sally, comprehending, finished the sentence for her.

'You thought, at first, that it was I who shot Oliver.'

'I meant – ' and here Amanda stammered a bit, 'if you had a reason . . . no, this is absurd. Please forget I said it.'

Sally smiled. 'It's okay, I've forgotten.'

The man was dead and there was no need for anyone, not even Happy, who was so dear, to know what had happened to Tina. Except of course that Amanda really *knew*.

Often, she reminded herself, how frail the thread is on

which one's fate is hung. If Clive hadn't lost his mind and taken a gun in hand, then she, Sally Grey, would very probably not be standing in this place today. Tina would not have been discharged by Dr. Lisle, and the second-grade teacher would not have stopped her on the street the other day to tell her what a successful, delightful little girl Tina was. If, in that Paris antique shop, Dan had not been looking at the carousel . . .

If and more ifs, back to infinity. But today is now; the idea is always to look forward.

And she looked out ahead, to where her girls in their white dresses were coming back across the lawn. Tina was holding the little one by the hand. They were laughing. Beyond them rose auburn hills and forest and endless trees in their autumn splendor.

BELVA PLAIN

DAYBREAK

Things haven't turned out too badly for Laura Rice.

Husband Bud is handsome and reliable. He may crack the odd racist joke, but he is a devoted and kind husband and father.

Elder son Tom is intelligent and athletic. He's picked up some funny ideas from his new college friends, but he'd do anything for his frail kid brother, Timmy.

One day, out of the blue, Laura is visited by a local lawyer with some devastating news. He represents a family from the other end of town who are mourning the death of their son. Only he wasn't really their son. For in one of those million-to-one accidents that you just read about in the papers, they've discovered that he was swapped in the hospital at birth.

HODDER AND STOUGHTON PAPERBACKS

BELVA PLAIN

TREASURES

A child. That was all Laura wanted. A child, and for the family to stay together.

Travel. To get away from the small Ohio town to the wide open spaces of Texas. That was Connie's urgent dream.

While for Eddy, New York beckoned. Wall Street, wealth and influence.

The day of Peg Osbourne's funeral was to mark a turning point. The lives of all her three children were about to alter dramatically. But dreams can turn sour and ambitions mislead. And tragedy, heartache and disgrace are in store before the family becomes one again and each discovers life's true treasures.

HODDER AND STOUGHTON PAPERBACKS